THE CALIBAN

Colleran's palm was moist around the butt of the clasher. Each beat of his heart was an explosion filling his chest.

"I think we got it, sir," Fanjoy said, smiling through his thick beard.

"Perhaps we won't need your weapon after all," Vaillancourt said with much relief.

Suddenly a fist, utterly alien, the size of a primitive wheelbarrow burst up through the floor, curling back three-inch-thick metal plating. And along with it came most of the creature itself. Up it came with a yowling cry of outrage and fury, scattering the security personnel aside in a single, angry swipe. The special anaesthetic gas made of itself an aura around the beast, drifting like so much impotent oceanside fog.

The beast wrenched itself around in a sudden twist of its mighty frame and Colleran got a horrifying look at it. It had an armored skull with two large eyes set widely apart. The thing might have once prowled Mesozoic seas back on the Lost Earth—or on some other planet of the Mandala worlds—but Colleran didn't think it likely.

The remaining laser rifle was rendered useless by the sweeping arm of the creature. So was the woman who had carried it.

Then the eyes of the horror fixed themselves upon Colleran. They shone with intelligence and a kind of peculiar alien deliberation which startled him merely because he hadn't expected it. *This* was no lizard.

ON THE RIM OF THE MANDALA

Paul Cook

BANTAM BOOKS
TORONTO • NEW YORK • LONDON • SYDNEY • AUCKLAND

ON THE RIM OF THE MANDALA

A Bantam Spectra Book / June 1987

Epigraph excerpt from "Voyage in the Blue" in SELF-PORTRAIT IN A CONVEX MIRROR, by John Ashbery. Copyright © 1972 by John Ashbery. Originally published in THE NEW YORKER. Reprinted by permission of Viking Penguin, Inc.

ISBN 0-553-26582-2

Published simultaneously in the United States and Canada

Bantam Books are published by Bantam Books, Inc. Its trademark, consisting of the words "Bantam Books" and the portrayal of a rooster, is Registered in U.S. Patent and Trademark Office and in other countries. Marca Registrada. Bantam Books, Inc., 666 Fifth Avenue, New York, New York 10103.

PRINTED IN THE UNITED STATES OF AMERICA

O   0 9 8 7 6 5 4 3 2 1

—This is for Ron Fanning,
caliban-fighter *extraordinaire*

And so, into our darkness life seeps . . .
    —John Ashbery

As Lou Colleran, Three Spoke Regulator for the Mandala Authority, sat alone at his windowside table on board the *Judy Holliday*, he felt the buoyancy of his spirit lift along with the floating resort hotel. Through the thick windows next to his table, he could see the gentle aqua-colored curve of Okeanos gradually descend beneath him.

Colleran felt the connectedness of the way things worked in the Mandala. As he sat at his table waiting for Heidi, his lovely, to return, he thought—perhaps for the first time in his four hundred and thirteen years—that life in the Spokes of the great Mandala wasn't so bad.

Okeanos, a world entirely covered by water, was one of the few inhabitable planets of the eight Spokes of the Mandala that genuinely brought him peace, and he wanted to relish every remaining moment of it that he could. His birthday-sabbatical was nearly over, and he knew that it would be quite some time before he'd be able to return.

Some of the other tourists felt that same desire, and they gathered at the viewing rail to gaze down at the blue-and-white skies of the planet below and the stars now coming into view in the rapt black of orbital space above. They had all spent a sinfully luxurious month fishing and sailing the placid equatorial waters of Okeanos, and it was as if they could not pull themselves away from its beauty.

It was behind this momentary joy that Colleran suddenly felt a dark sense of impending loss—the loss of peace, the loss of beauty.

And it was in that period of spiritual abeyance, there at the windowside table, that Colleran saw Beatrice for the first time in many, many months.

She appeared to him as she always had, in the whisper of her ghostly form, moving among the tables and other passengers as if she belonged there, though only Colleran could see her.

Colleran blinked and tried to focus on her, but Beatrice, his personal hallucination, was—as ever—elusive. He had thought that his vacation would eradicate any impulse of his brain to evoke her, but for whatever reason that was not to be.

And he swore, for the first time, that she was now making direct eye contact with him. She was smiling, phantasmagorically, at him from across the crowded lounge.

He turned away, trying not to look upset, but a few of the vacationeers nearby caught his unease. Since he had begun envisioning Beatrice eighty years ago—a direct by-product of the immortality processes that had allowed him his long life as a Regulator—the visions had been getting incrementally worse. It bothered him enormously. And the one thing he could not afford at the moment was to be recognized as one of the Authority's immortals.

As it was, he resembled any other person who'd just spent three weeks in the sun. His golden tan was deep and bronze-rich; it contrasted remarkably with his almost white-blonde hair. Only his immortality made him any different from the rest of the men in the lounge. He was tall and wiry, and resembled a thirty-eight-year-old man of Lost Earth ancestry. His blue eyes sparked with intelligence, but often with a glint of suspicion, which to him always gave away the fact that he was, by profession, a police officer. A Regulator.

And no one much liked police officers, let alone Regulators. And even fewer people liked the specialness of those who were entitled to become immortals.

He shivered. The reflection of the lounge behind him in the concavity of the window by his table did not show any sign of Beatrice. But he knew that she was still there in a way: Beatrice was a Lei, a Latent Encephalic Image, a full-blown hallucination that older immortals experienced, though no one knew why. They were similar to epileptic seizures, but more of a visual character than a physical one. Beatrice, despite her ethereal beauty, was nonetheless disconcerting.

"Damn it," Colleran whispered to himself. "Go away. Please. I'm on vacation."

Colleran sipped at his peppermint tea and tried not to look too frazzled by the experience. He even managed a slight chuckle. The irony of a Lei experience was that it often brought a slight wave of joy, a rush of transcendental bliss that was also unexplainable. Even in the year 2497 A.D., he mused, there were still mysteries.

He glanced at his watch, then braved a look into the lounge itself. Beatrice had slipped away into invisibility, having only appeared for the time it took his heart to beat once or twice. But that had been enough. He knew that something was wrong. Beatrice appeared at those times when his deeper intuitive senses were being blocked, and the fact that Heidi was taking longer than usual to freshen up in the suites reserved for lovelies suggested to him that something was amiss somewhere on the laputa.

He turned to face the window and the vision of the curve of Okeanos beyond. The *Judy Holliday* seemed to be slowing in its ascent to docking orbit above the water world. Laputas rose like graceful balloons on gravity engines that, as often as not, could rarely be felt—just as Colleran could not feel them now. Perhaps that's what provoked the Lei experience.

One of the laputa's younger officers, dressed in the trademark trim whites of the Okeanos Reach, stepped into the lounge and made every attempt to look nonplussed and casual. But Colleran knew otherwise. Even without Beatrice, he could sense it.

"Mr. Colleran," the young officer said, walking directly to his table. He was just a boy, perhaps seventeen years old, seventeen *real* years. He wasn't a good actor.

"Yes," Colleran returned, keeping his voice low. A few vacationeers had taken notice of the junior officer's appearance. The boy's face was a study in barely hidden terror.

"Captain Vaillancourt would like to speak to you, if he could, sir."

The boy appeared to know that Colleran was a Regulator, despite his casual apparel. If Vaillancourt had told him, then it was serious business indeed.

Colleran again checked his watch. He said to the boy, "Tell the captain that I'll be up in a few minutes. I want to let my lovely know where I am. She's—"

The young officer glanced nervously about the lounge. "Sir, the captain needs your services," he said in a low and nervous whisper.

Colleran said nothing, and he could still feel Beatrice nearby, ready to manifest herself in the back reaches of his brain.

"Sir," the officer said quickly. "We have need of your clasher. The captain has informed us that you brought it with you and we need it. *Now*."

Colleran's heart began to speed up. "Why? What's going on?" Several of the wealthier tourists over by the well-stocked bar had begun to observe their conversation. Perhaps they too had noticed the halting of the anti-gravs beneath them.

Suddenly, as if they were all riding the swell of an ocean wave, the *Judy Holliday* seemed to heave ever so slightly.

But it was not so slight a motion that no one in the lounge noticed. A woman standing by a grand piano gasped, and someone dropped a glass, which splintered noisily.

The young officer's eyes widened and his face seemed to grow as white as his uniform. "That's why, sir. Can we go now, *please?*"

Colleran forgot about Heidi and rose away from the window-side table. He could feel it now: Beneath his feet the anti-gravs had ceased and the locks had been set in place. The laputa was being held in suspension two hundred miles above equatorial Okeanos, neither rising nor falling.

Out in the corridor the young officer dropped all of his staged authority, becoming a frightened seventeen-year-old. He began jogging toward the bank of elevators, speaking as he went.

"Captain Vaillancourt says that there is something alive down in number four hold, sir, just above the vehicle-servicing bays."

Colleran's gut tightened. Three weeks of boating and fishing the waters of Okeanos with Heidi by his side were instantly erased from his mind. He was suddenly back on the job.

"What are you talking about?" he asked as the elevator arrived with an audible hiss.

"It's killed three people," the boy said as they stepped inside. The corridor they had just vacated now filled with *Judy Holliday* support personnel, who seemed to be hastening to their emergency stations although no alarms were yet sounding.

Colleran's mind scrambled to recall the layout of the *Judy Holliday*. The various holds of the laputa were on the penultimate level of the floating, airborne resort, and number four hold was for the "fish" that the vacationeers, such as himself, had caught and were keeping in storage.

"You mean one of the fish has gotten loose?" he asked.

The elevator headed upward to the passenger suites, more specifically, to the suite that held an Authority clasher. *His* clasher.

"It's not a fish, sir," the boy said. "At least we don't think so. There's a bunch of creatures down on Okeanos, but nothing like this."

The boy still retained the glow of adolescence about his face, but the worry he exhibited was definitely of an adult nature.

The elevator let them out on the passenger level three storeys above the lounge. Here, everything seemed calm, quiet. The young officer spoke, almost as if to himself, to reassure himself that everything was going to be all right. He said, "The captain's locked the engines and sending out a mayday. We're just high enough for a cruiser to reach us."

"That sounds bad," Colleran said.

The look in the boy's eyes said it was.

There were two security guards flanking Colleran's suite door when they rounded the corner, although the door was not open. Colleran's aid was being requested, not forcefully enlisted.

He made his way through to the bedroom, noticing as he went that Heidi was not there. The lovely quarters were on the level below them, but on this trip she had spent all of her time with him in his suite. Even though lovelies were often thought of as commodities for a special kind of use, Colleran found himself worrying about her. At least in the lovely quarters she'd be safe.

The security guards stood mute with an eye out for passersby who might be alarmed at their presence on the deck. He could feel them tense up, and he could easily imagine their fear of a Regulator's authority, especially if that Regulator was authorized to carry—and use—a Langstrom clasher.

Colleran had brought only his Authority badge and his clasher, sealed tightly by the grip of his live-leather holster where no one could get at it unless they had managed to duplicate his very own skin-tint frequencies. He slipped the badge onto the belt of his khaki trousers, feeling awkward without the ominous black-and-silver Regulator's tunic he usually wore. He'd left that back on his homeworld of Karuna, light years away, toward the Hub of the Mandala. Still, it was the clasher that counted. The living seal of the holster popped open at his touch and he checked to see if its charge was at optimum. It was.

Suddenly, the lights dimmed.

"What's that?" Colleran asked, spinning around. The holster clamped itself dutifully to his belt beside the dangling hinge of his badge.

Then the *Judy Holliday* shook violently, enough to knock everyone off balance. Alarms began bleating, followed by the sound of many feet running.

"We'd better move," one of the guards said as they all tried to regain their footing.

As they plunged out into the corridor, red emergency lights guided their way through the sudden semi-darkness.

The boy in officer's clothing said, "The captain thinks that it was trying to make its way through the bulkheads, like it was headed for the gravity stabilizers."

"What?" Colleran asked, stunned. "That's impossible!"

Breathing hard, the boy summoned the elevator, now on emergency power. He said, "Whatever it is, it's put one stabilizer out of action and the captain thinks it's trying for all four of them."

The elevator car arrived and Colleran stepped in along with the young man. The other two guards remained, now that frantic passengers were rushing to their suites to salvage their belongings and head for the lifeboats.

"This is my first year," the boy said, slumping against the side of the elevator as they descended past the other suites, the lounge deck, on down to the vehicle bay and storage holds. The boy's name badge said *Ashton*. He looked very pale indeed.

The laputa shook once again, but the elevator did not stop its downward journey.

"Are you sure that whatever it is didn't come from Okeanos?" Colleran asked, tucking in his shirt, getting ready.

The boy looked up at him. "I've fished the waters of Okeanos all of my life. There's nothing like this creature down there. I'm dead sure of it." He swallowed hard with an imprisoned look on his face.

A muffled *thump!* crumpled right through the ship as the elevator reached the next-to-last level of the floating space resort. To Colleran, it sounded distantly as if something was using part of the ship's walls, the bulkheads themselves, as a punching bag. The doors slid open, letting them out, as another *thump!* slammed the *Judy Holliday*.

"That's it," Officer Ashton said, stepping into the hallway. "Jesus Christ, it's big!"

Here, under crimson emergency lights, men and women were running about. It looked to Colleran like a war zone.

Captain Julian Vaillancourt stood a slender six-foot-five, two inches taller than Colleran himself, and he wore a white mustache that curled up at either end anachronistically, centuries out of style. His hair was also shock-white. At sixty-one real years of age, Vaillancourt clearly had the bearing of a captain.

But at the moment he seemed rather harried. He was happy to see Colleran and shook his hand enthusiastically.

"I'm sorry to call on you like this, Mr. Colleran, but we're in a rather desperate situation," the captain said above the stammering alarms.

Several of the *Holliday*'s crew backed off as Vaillancourt escorted Colleran to the scene of the trouble. Colleran noticed how Vaillancourt's crew gave him a wide berth, their eyes fixating on the clasher and the Authority badge. He'd seen that reaction before.

They walked to a part of the resort hotel that the regular paying passengers rarely got to see. This was where the men and women who ran the *Judy Holliday* had to work. It was all high ceilings, ducts and pipes, and odd boxes and crates piled along the walls.

At the end of the hallway a number of men and women stood waiting with various kinds of weapons, some pistols, some laser rifles of limited capacity. All of it was standard issue for security personnel of any Okeanos Reach laputa.

"Just what are we up against?" Colleran asked as they came to the end of the hallway.

Vaillancourt seemed bent by the weight of the moment. He said, "It's big and it's not like anything I've ever encountered. Here or anywhere else for that matter."

"You've seen it?"

Captain Vaillancourt gave him an honest look, his white hair feathering out of place. "I got a glimpse of it as it was breaking through a bulkhead down below."

Everyone was silent around them. Someone had shut the alarms off, although the red emergency lights still twirled madly above them.

The captain continued as if with great difficulty. He said, "It apparently broke out of storage where some of your fish are." A pounding—or perhaps a *grinding* sound—resonated up through the floor of the entire corridor. Here, there were no plush carpets of exotic textures and walls pleasantly decorated. These were the workings, the innards, of the *Judy Holliday* laid bare.

Everyone backed against the surrounding walls of the corridor and looked downward, as if picturing the beast below them on the lower level. Colleran did the same.

Young Ashton blurted out, "It's gotta be *real* smart. It knew how to take out the stabilizer without electrocuting itself, and then it found the elevator. Okeanae can't do that. No fish is *that* clever."

"So how big is it?" Colleran asked the captain.

But Officer Ashton was nearly hysterical with nervous tension. "Bigger than the elevator shaft, that's for sure. It couldn't fit and so it started punching its way up through the ship."

"Thank you, Officer Ashton," the captain said tersely. He turned to Colleran. "It's underneath us right now. We've managed to seal off all of the levels and interconnecting passages, but I don't think that's going to stop it. It's exceedingly powerful."

The captain then made a furtive, anxious glance at the live-leather holster and the Langstrom clasher within. He said, "We've taken a couple of shots at it, but it's tough. I took the liberty of checking the manifest to see if you'd brought along your clasher. I think that's probably the only thing that will stop it."

Colleran nodded, understanding completely. There'd be no reason for a luxury hotel to have anything more powerful than a security laser rifle or two. *But then*, he thought, *that all depends on what you're up against* . . .

A woman of Lost Earth Eurasian descent came up to the gathering of personnel, lugging the ugly tube of a small bazooka and a waistband of teargas shells.

Vaillancourt shrugged. "It's the best we could do. Riot control. The Okeanos people require we keep them."

"Might work," Colleran said, listening to the commotion below them.

"Probably won't," the Eurasian woman said, hefting the weapon. "But it'll confuse it."

The scraping and knocking about on the level below were quite pronounced. A violent, frustrated cry shivered up the walls and echoed throughout the curved halls of the *Judy Holliday*.

"What the hell is it?" young Ashton gasped.

"What's it look like, Captain?" Colleran turned to the tall man against the wall. "Just what kind of beast are we talking about?"

Washed in the blood-glare of the corridor lights above, Colleran could almost feel the terror that lurked around them. Vaillancourt's voice was a strained whisper. "There's a very large fish on Okeanos called a *chaluk*."

Colleran knew very little about Okeanos, but he did know that *chaluks* were similar to Lost Earth's ancient plesiosaurs. Long-necked, passive animals, they swam throughout the southern climes of the water world, far from where Colleran and Heidi had done their fishing.

"It looks like a *chaluk*?"

Somehow he just couldn't picture it.

"No," Vaillancourt said in a deep whisper. "It's as *big* as a *chaluk* and seems to have a long body with at least six legs. I caught sight of it after it killed my third officer."

The small woman across the hall with the bazooka cocked it and looked up, nodding. She was ready.

Suddenly, all was still beneath them. The whole floating resort seemed caught like an insect in a trap of orange amber, going nowhere at all. Colleran could barely feel the gravity locks keeping them at their current altitude.

"What's it doing?" one of the men asked in the hallway.

"Shhh!" the woman hissed.

Then, without warning, the creature below them started attacking one of the walls of the corridor underneath. Each punch, each impact sounded like thunder.

"Everybody over here!" Colleran shouted to the security personnel. They scrambled over, trying to keep their balance.

Colleran had his clasher out and ready. A flick of his thumb and the deadly gun was armed. Oddly, he thought of Heidi just then through the agency of a fleeting image—quite like a Lei experience—of her sunbathing, thoroughly exposed to the sun above them, as they languished aboard their skiff. He wondered suddenly if she was safe, if the lifeboats were being made ready in case the worst happened.

But like the creature down below, lovelies weren't considered to be human. However, lovelies did not go around killing people and crippling ships two hundred miles into space.

"All I need is some idea where it is," he told the captain. He was center stage; all eyes were on him now.

Young Officer Ashton swallowed audibly, staring at the Langstrom clasher. "I've never seen a . . . clasher. It'll work through metal?"

Colleran said nothing, assenting through his silence.

"Jesus," the boy said, completely awestruck.

Down beneath them, it sounded as if metal walls were being torn like paper. Colleran could not even imagine what kind of creature it was, simply because in his four-hundred years of experience, there was nothing on the known worlds linked to the mysterious Hub sixteen light-years away that could in any way resemble what had to be on the floor below them. Even mammals back on the now Lost Earth were not as powerful or as ferocious.

Colleran began to be affected by the fear that the security guards were feeling. He gripped his clasher and held to the far wall, watching the floor.

The Eurasian woman knelt down, one hand holding the bazooka upright. She felt the rough texture of the floor and then pointed. "Captain, if we punch a hole in the floor here, I think I can lob a shell down. Maybe I can put it to sleep."

Colleran asked, "You've got an anesthetic?"

She nodded grimly, pulling out a blue-tipped rocket about six inches long.

Colleran faced the captain. "I think we should try it. I want to know what it is and how it got on board. The clasher—" He held the Langstrom Reach's best product out before them. "My gun would just disappear it."

This the captain had to think about. "I don't know," he said. More rumbling and rustling transpired beneath them. More metal cried out.

Another officer then said, "Sir, I think it's going between the sectioning bulkheads." He gave them a truly astonished look. "I don't get it. I think it might be heading for one of the outside ring-shafts."

Ashton cried out, frightened. "If it does that, it can climb all the way to the top! All the way to the command center!"

"I know where it can go!" Vaillancourt snapped. Sweat pearl-dropped the tall captain's forehead. But he had come to a decision. "Fanjoy!" he shouted to a hefty man at the far end of the hall. Fanjoy lumbered like a bear, due mostly to the compact laser torch strapped to his back. It was not a weapon; it was a tool. The beefy man looked as if he knew how to use it.

Vaillancourt pointed to the floor. "Cut a hole and do it fast. It's not going to sit and pick its toes while we put it to sleep."

"Right, Captain," Fanjoy said. He spread his feet and aimed.

The torch needled green light in a surgical cut that sliced out a dinner plate-sized hole in the floor. The metal gave way to a booted stomp on Fanjoy's behalf and the diminutive Eurasian crewwoman poked her bazooka into the hole. She pulled the trigger and a *choom!* sound coughed around them.

Another man came up to Colleran and the captain and tossed them gas masks, shouting, "Take these!" as another crewwoman wrestled a flat piece of metal above the hole in the floor to keep the sleep-gas down below. She jumped back as soon as it was secure.

The thrashing beneath them momentarily became more frantic, the crashing louder. Then it ceased. No goblins of anesthetic ghosted up to their level as they watched. The plate on the floor seemed to hold all the gas beneath them.

Colleran's palm was moist around the butt of the clasher as he watched. Each beat of his heart was an explosion filling his chest.

And for a moment he thought he felt Beatrice nearby, the blonde strands of her hair lifted by the slight winds that stirred the hold. . . .

"I think we got it, sir. Goddamn, I think we got it," Fanjoy said, smiling through his thick beard.

Colleran forced the vision of Beatrice away from his beleaguered thoughts, his heart calming.

Vaillancourt stood away from the wall, breathing a little bit easier. "Perhaps we won't need your weapon after all," he said with much relief.

Suddenly, he was thrown back against Colleran as a fist, utterly alien, the size of a primitive wheelbarrow burst up through the floor, curling back three-inch-thick metal plating as if they were made of sheet aluminum.

And not only did the fist come up, but along with it came most of the creature itself.

Up it came with a yowling cry of outrage and fury, tearing back an enormous section of the floor, scattering the security personnel aside in a single, angry swipe. The special anesthetic gas made an aura of itself around the beast, drifting like so much impotent oceanside fog.

2

In that moment of fierce and unexpected panic, as the creature exploded upward through the floor, Colleran's mind did what it had always done in moments like these: it went elsewhere.

Instinctively, Colleran threw himself out of the beast's range as his mind succumbed to a fleeting shifting of reality. It happened in the time it took to blink his eyes. He shifted to a vision of the place where Beatrice dwelled. She was not there, but the same feeling of transcendent joy was. And he could—for the breath of a moment—see the golden peaks of that land and the endlessly green meadows that led up to them.

But it was only for a moment. Not quite a Lei experience, but perhaps the residue or aftershock trace of one. He was back to the terror in the laputa's storage bay in a second.

"Christ!" yelled crewman Fanjoy who was rammed violently against the opposite wall. His laser torch smashed and splintered loudly beneath his bulk.

Assorted handguns—Lost Earth pistols of antique manufacture worn mostly for show—began barking through the sleep-gas cloud at the struggling monstrosity that had reared into view.

But the lead slugs hardly damaged the beast, making unpleasant slapping sounds as they sang off its bruised-red skin as if it were a kind of armor.

Both Captain Vaillancourt and young Ashton pinwheeled over against him near the wall. Two other crewmembers, having lost their protective masks, were suddenly snoring on the floor.

The beast wrenched itself around in a sudden twist of its mighty frame and Colleran got a horrifying look at it, obscured only slightly by the gas and dancing emergency lights still flashing in the corridor.

It had an armored skull with two large eyes set wide apart. It might have been a lizard of enormous proportions, but its eyes bore an insensitive intelligence that spoke of its true hostility. A wide mouth was clamped shut, but an occasional snarl could be heard from deep within its throat. The thing might have once prowled Mesozoic seas back on the Lost Earth—or on some other planet of the Mandala worlds—but Colleran didn't think it likely.

Colleran rolled out into the center of the beseiged hallway and rose up on one knee, taking aim with his clasher. The bullets were doing no good whatsoever, and the remaining laser rifle had been rendered useless by a sweeping arm of the creature. So had the woman who had carried it.

"*Get out of the way!*" Colleran shouted through the amplified mouthpiece of his mask. Crew personnel scurried to get beyond the clasher's deadly range.

Then the eyes of the horror fixed themselves upon him. They shone with intelligence and a kind of peculiar alien deliberation, which startled him merely because he hadn't expected it. *This* was no lizard.

The Eurasian woman with the stumpy bazooka rose up behind the beast and blasted a tear gas shell against the creature's mountainous shoulders, cascading a blinding white gas everywhere around it.

The creature, however, seemed unaffected. Its eyes lodged themselves on Colleran's clasher, then suddenly it was gone, back down through the hole before Colleran could fire.

"Get the crew out of here!" he shouted to Vaillancourt, who was helping a gagging Officer Ashton to his feet. The boy had momentarily lost his gas mask in the fall.

"What is it?" Vaillancourt shouted to Colleran, now that they had all gotten a clear glimpse of it.

Colleran looked up and down the hall, considering his options. "I'll be goddamned if I know," he told the elderly captain.

The thing was smart. Damn smart.

They listened as the creature crashed back to the level beneath them and scuttled out of sight, away from the wide hole it had made and the guns that might be appearing there.

In fact, crewman Fanjoy had abandoned the wreckage of his laser pack and hustled over to the hole in the floor with a pistol. He emptied it in a series of concussions that pommeled them there in the corridor.

Colleran grabbed the captain's arm as they hustled back down the corridor. "The *Parvardigar* is five light-years away and it can spindle here in about twenty hours, if you call for them now. If I can't clash that thing, we're going to need all the help we can get."

"I understand," the captain said, nodding his head awkwardly behind his mask. He stepped over to the corridor's com-unit and punched it, barking orders to the command center far above them in the domed, hovering resort.

As he did, Colleran could now hear a different kind of alarm resounding throughout the hotel. It was a shipwide alert to abandon the floating resort. Crewmembers, meanwhile, were taking quick turns firing down into the rip in the floor and jumping back out of sight. They seemed more desperate than efficient.

He and Vaillancourt began running for the elevators. He whipped off his mask when they'd gotten out of the effective zone of the anesthetic.

"What's the worst it can do?" Colleran asked. "The very worst."

Vaillancourt, waiting for the elevator, drew a shaking hand across his moist forehead. He was terrified.

"I . . . I don't know," he confessed haltingly. "No, wait. Yes. The gravity engines are locked. If it got to those and broke the lock or disrupted the power to the locks, we'd fall back to Okeanos. This high, we'd burn up."

Colleran looked back down the hall. Young Ashton was losing his lunch in the hallway; the tear gas had gotten to him.

"What about what Ashton said," Colleran began as the elevator arrived. "About it reaching the control center above us?"

Vaillancourt's blue eyes were pools of worry. He was out of his league now. He was a ship's captain and a hotel manager, not a military commander. He had the lives of two hundred paying passengers to think about rather than a troop of skilled soldiers who could take care of themselves.

"If it gets outside," he stammered, "and assuming it could survive without an environment suit, then, yes, there'd be nothing to stop it from climbing all the way."

"And that's unacceptable," Colleran concluded. He knew he was going to have to clash it. He only hoped that some of the conflict had been caught on videotape. The Authority was definitely going to be interested in this entity.

Vaillancourt held the elevator door open, but as he did, the Eurasian crewwoman came running up to them. She had thrown away her protective mask.

"Captain," she began, gasping for air. "It's stopped moving. We may have injured it below."

Aside from the abandon-ship alarm filtering down from the corridors above them, they could hear little else.

"No," Colleran said after a heart's beat. He recalled the intelligence in those alien eyes as well as the thickness of its bubbled crimson skin. "I don't think so."

Down the hall, through the dissipating gas, crewman Fanjoy shouted to them. "Captain! It's going outside! It's headed for the number four ring-shaft!" The burly maintenance engineer pointed dramatically at the far wall, in the direction of the number four ring-shaft.

A savage rending could now be heard coming up from the opening in the floor. The creature was out of reach of any of their weapons and trying to burst its way into space.

Vaillancourt shouted to his entire crew. "Everybody abandon this level! Fanjoy, seal this level off! If it breaches the hull, then we'll lose all atmospherics!"

"Sir!" shouted Fanjoy.

"To the bridge," Vaillancourt said firmly to Colleran.

"Right," he said, stepping in.

The doors snickered shut and Vaillancourt punched the button straight for the command center. He said, "Our lifeboats are in the ring-shafts. That thing will take them out one by one if it gets as high as the passenger decks."

Colleran swallowed hard. Passenger decks were above the lovely deck. Vaillancourt made it sound as if the lovelies were expendable. And in a way they were. The cloned lovelies could be manufactured at any time, and the insurance companies would absorb the liability losses of the catastrophe. *If* that happened. By now, Heidi would've gotten to her lifeboat. Lovelies often accepted their object status, but they were still living organisms and enjoyed their lives much like everyone else. However, the *Judy Holliday* would give rescue priority to the human passengers, the rich and famous human passengers, and let the lovelies fend for themselves.

The elevator rose to the chorus of a commotion far below them.

The captain gritted his teeth. "I hope Fanjoy was fast enough clearing that level."

"Why?"

"The creature just broke through the hull. That was it we just heard."

Colleran visualized the shape of the laputa in his mind. The *Judy Holliday* was an enclosed hemispherical platform, a dome one hundred feet high and three hundred feet wide. Straddling it were vertical ring-shafts, which ran from the bottom to the top of the resort and contained, theoretically, all the lifeboats the resort would need. However, the ring-shafts were themselves only wide enough to accommodate the lifeboats. If the creature was outside and still alive, it would have a difficult time climbing the rings.

Or so he hoped.

The bridge at the very top of the *Judy Holliday* under normal circumstances resembled the helm of a luxury yacht. There were even hanging plants dangling from the ceiling in glazed ceramic pots, and two floor-to-ceiling columnar aquariums, full of Okeanos' smaller finned denizens, stood at either end of the helm station. It was a place of comfort and ease.

But the crew, when he and Vaillancourt arrived, was rushing about in uncontrollable panic, as red console lights and bleeping alarms commanded their frenzied attention.

They were met by a bearded, meticulous looking man in his thirties. He gave Colleran a brief, if disdainful, look, not really knowing or caring who he was. Until he spied the Langstrom clasher. Then he suddenly cared.

"Where is it?" Vaillancourt said, walking around the man with the goatee. "Are we able to see it, Mr. Boyd?"

Boyd was erect with submission to Vaillancourt's authority. "Sir, the creature's outside. It's incredible, but it looks like it can survive there."

There were several other crewmen and women on the helm, monitoring the ship's various functions, and as Colleran made his way to the consoles with Vaillancourt, he noticed their sideways glances of disdain and resentment. No one liked the Authority being in their business; fewer still like immortals. Privilege was one thing, extended life another.

Colleran's first goal was to check on Heidi. His heart pounded for her. She was just a lovely, but they had shared much during the last three weeks.

A row of video camera-units brought several different views of the ring-shafts to them, and as they appeared, the entire crew tensed as the creature was brought into focus.

Colleran bent in close. The outer ring-shaft cameras were used mostly for repair and maintenance monitoring, even when it was down on the surface. Here, it showed the monstrosity slowly struggling up the wide ring of the shaft on the outside of the curved hull of the *Judy Holliday*. Behind the creature, and far below, was the azure blue sky of Okeanos and the blue-green of the oceans unblemished by any island or continent whatsoever.

"It's alive out there," one of the crewwomen uttered. "I don't believe it. . . ."

Colleran faced Captain Vaillancourt. "Start beaming this to the *Parvardigar*." Colleran's clasher was almost burning in his hand, ready for use. "This'll be all that we have of it after I'm through."

Vaillancourt glanced over to a communications officer, who, in turn, was already sending out the video to be spindled to the *Parvardigar* light-years away.

The com-officer announced: "There's a com-spindle leaving high orbit in ten minutes. It'll spindle toward the Hub and meet the *Parvardigar* within one hour. That's as soon as it's going to get there with this tape."

Vaillancourt moved around to another screen, loosening his tight, trim collar. He said, "But if we don't stop this thing, whatever it is, it'll reach the lifeboats in ring-shaft four—" He checked the console timer briefly. "In about seven minutes."

Another camera, this one farther up the ring-shaft, gave them a better view of the thing's progress in the light of the G7 sun high in the blackness of space. Colleran had *definitely* never seen a beast such as the one gripping the outer edges of the hovering laputa. It was easily thirty feet long, snakelike, with four torso arms attached to a sturdy upper body. It could have been a large insect, but it seemed more reptilian. Its eyes, from what Colleran could tell, were now shielded from the harsh realities of space and ultraviolet radiation exposure.

Colleran felt a slight shimmer up his spine and could barely perceive Beatrice lurking in the shadows of his darkest thoughts. His heart pounded excitedly. He bent over and whispered, "My God. It looks like it's built for climbing in outer space."

Everyone on the helm had heard. Sure enough, seen in just that light, the creature's four arms seemed to hoist itself gracefully from one ring casing to the next, its tail secreting a mucoid substance from its segmented underbelly, which allowed it to stick to the metal surface of the inner shaft.

"I'm sick," a younger member of the command crew announced, turning away, gagging.

Then another woman nearby spoke out. "Captain, lifeboats eight, nine, and ten are away, sir."

But as Colleran could see, lifeboats eight, nine, and ten were those belonging to the passengers of the upper suites. The rich and famous passengers with whom he and Heidi had not chosen to associate.

The creature, right beneath the fleeing capsules, approached a different string of lifeboats, the one attached to the level of the lovelies.

Heidi! Colleran thought suddenly. They weren't away yet. For whatever reason, lifeboats four, five, and six hadn't been cast off.

The creature, bracing itself as it made its ponderous way up the side of the hovering dome of a hotel, seemed in its insensate way to know what the lifeboats harbored. Colleran watched as the beast flexed, looked upward through the rings, and reached out to hoist itself closer to its prey.

"Get those boats away from there!" Colleran shouted, turning toward the elevator. He had to make sure that Heidi was safe. Damn those rich people!

"Captain!" Officer Boyd shouted above his screen. "It's warping the shaft! The boats won't be able to shunt!"

Colleran jumped into the waiting elevator. An awful wrenching could be felt resonating throughout the entire hotel. It seemed to travel like a scream up the curved outer hull of the *Judy Holliday*. Bolts popped and rivets lost their grip as the creature incredibly mauled the ring-shaft.

Colleran, sweating against the elevator's interior wall, felt suddenly guilty and slightly ashamed for letting himself relax too much these last three weeks. Now it was time to pay for his laxity. He'd been away from this sort of action for far too long, even though as an Authority Regulator, he'd found himself in all sorts of Mandala squabbles and gunplay. Now he was out of shape, at least spiritually. Four-hundred and thirteen years was a long time for a man to stay alert.

This, he conceded, was out of the ordinary.

The Langstrom clasher in his hand hummed with power, and Colleran knew that once he got within range of the creature the gun would solve all of their problems. With other rescue vessels from the Okeanos Reach already on their way, the lifeboats would be fished out of orbit within hours. Then they'd be able to decide what had happened and, more importantly, how the creature had gotten on board.

But first things first.

He lurched out into the hallway of the lovely suite and stumbled. Debris was littered throughout the corridor and not a soul was to be seen. Except for Beatrice.

Inexplicably, the Lei manifested herself as Colleran ran down the hallway toward the emergency lifeboat bays. He tripped as the sudden rush of *shin jong*, or the joy of emptiness, filled him from the experience.

"Not now," he said to her—to himself—as he ran, trying to ignore the euphoria her presence evoked. He dove right through her ghostly image, blinking her out of existence but nonetheless feeling the love he'd always felt during a *shin jong* encounter. *Shin jong* or Lei, it was the same affection he'd come to feel for Heidi even though she was an artificial person. You didn't make love to a lovely for three weeks and not feel *something*.

It only made him more desperate to make certain that she had gotten away with the other Okeanos lovelies.

Her quarters at the end of the hallway were abandoned, but much of her wardrobe lay scattered about, as if she'd been interrupted at something.

Then the whole laputa shook, throwing him against the door, only this time the wrenching was fiercer, and much closer.

More bolts popped and the lights dimmed. The ring-shaft was giving way!

Colleran punched the com-switch. "Captain! I'm down on level seven. What was that?"

Vaillancourt's voice was abrupt, almost shrill. "It just tore out the entire bottom of the ring-shaft, Mr. Colleran. Two boats are headed straight down, out of control. Clash it *now*!"

Which two boats? *Which two boats!*

He had a vision of the lozenge-shaped lifeboats tumbling end over end, helplessly, burning in their long fall in the peaceful skies of Okeanos.

Colleran ran to the emergency lifeboat exit. They'd been locked shut behind the evacuees and Colleran knew that the creature was just beyond the wall, climbing the ring-shaft.

Another wrenching shook the ship, and the sound of the thing was much louder now. It was close, *very* close.

He braced himself and aimed his clasher. He pulled the trigger and could nearly feel the Langstrom clasher at work although it emitted no sound or colorfully luminous ray.

The Langstrom Reach only manufactured guns. They were the best. Clashers, issued exclusively to Authority Regulators and other vital officers, operated on a simple principle. They were true disintegrators, straight from long-ago pulp adventure novels. They sent out beams of energy that "clashed" with the strong forces holding molecules together. They simply pulled apart in a rather nondramatic, but rapid, process that left nothing but dissolute gasses behind. The handguns were useful only on organic beings. The larger clashers could take out denser molecular structures—such as metals—and were often the pride of ships such as the *Parvardigar*.

Colleran had used his clasher more than once in his long, long life as a Regulator. It was a fact he wasn't particularly proud of.

"I got it, Captain," he said, standing next to the open com-unit on the wall. He slid the gun into the waiting live-leather holster, which clamped itself shut hungrily.

Nothing could be heard beyond the exit doors.

But then Second Officer Boyd appeared on the com-unit. "The hell you got it, Regulator. It's two levels up. It's headed for the main passenger suites. You'd better do something!"

How could he have missed? *How?*

Panic rose up in him like a river suddenly swelling above its levees. He ran down the hallway, now feeling Beatrice nearby. He had the strangest sensation that the plush carpet of the hallway was turning into a field of soft, green grass. . . .

His clasher had never failed him before. Unless he had actually missed. But with a clasher, that didn't seem likely.

The main passenger level, which contained his own suite, was its own disaster area. Just like those below it, there was a wild, hurricane-strewn scene of clothing and carrying cases abandoned everywhere. Doors to the private suites gaped open, furniture lay overturned.

Everyone, however, had fled, and that meant that they were presently in their lifeboats. Or so he hoped.

Colleran hit the com-unit in the hallway. "Are the boats at this level away? I can't shoot through the wall unless I know that there aren't any people nearby."

"The boats there are gone," Second Officer Boyd's voice grated. "The others have fallen. Do it!"

Colleran felt the lurch of another lifeboat leaping away from the *Judy Holliday*, but that one was far above him.

And again Beatrice was with him, only this time the Lei appeared as only mist, a glowing evanescence that lingered at the fringe of his consciousness.

Jesus, he thought. *Am I going crazy or what?*

The creature was directly beyond the exit bay. The carpet itself was a trail of discarded jewelry boxes and silk dresses left behind in someone's desperate plight. Fishing tackle and nylon lines had been ungraciously deposited right where an ensign had no doubt ordered. Colleran understood. The passengers would have wanted to take every precious little thing they had with them.

They'd be lucky to escape with their skin attached. They could retrieve their jewels later, but not their lives.

Captain Vaillancourt's voice thundered from a nearby com-unit speaker. "It's directly in line with the exit bay, Mr. Colleran!"

Colleran lifted his gun at the gray steel wall, and presumably at the grotesquery beyond it. He pulled the trigger.

Silence.

Red emergency lights swirled around him, almost like the capes of bullfighters from Lost Earth long ago. He waited. No bulls attacked; no crowds cheered. Beatrice had vanished in a wall of silence at the exit bay.

"You got it!" came Vaillancourt's announcement.

The crowds were cheering after all. Colleran could hear their voices in the background on the bridge.

He leaned against the corridor wall, flooded in the crimson wash of lights. Everywhere about his feet were jewels of one kind or another. There must have been some very well-to-do vacationeers on board this last month or so. He didn't care. Jewels meant little to him.

He turned and headed for the elevator when the overhead emergency lights ceased their fevered flashing. It was over.

Then Vaillancourt's voice shouted, "Colleran! Get out! Get out! *It's coming through!*"

"What?" he called out, facing the far end of the hall. "That's impossible!"

A terrifically deafening cry of bursting alloyed metal came from the exit bay as *something* forged its way through.

Vaillancourt shouted again. "It separated itself from the lower half of its body! You only got its tail! The other half is—"

Coming through.

A fist powered its way through the wall with more strength than Colleran believed possible. And it did so quite suddenly.

Colleran fired his clasher, but the charge was too low. And a fraction too late. There was nothing on the other side but outer space, and the whole corridor instantly depressurized as the creature tore a hole big enough for it to climb through.

Colleran fell to the floor, being sucked along, as the temperature dropped to well below zero, heading toward absolute.

The creature was still alive, staring at him malevolently as the outrushing air screamed all around it.

Gasping for oxygen, Colleran tumbled over and grabbed the edge of an open suite door. One boot was snatched right off his foot, and his Langstrom clasher bounded helplessly toward the opening, completely useless now.

And those things were followed by all else abandoned in the corridor: pillows, clothing, suitcases, paintings from the walls, even broken lighting fixtures. Colleran felt as if he'd suddenly found himself hanging above a very deep well and everything around him was being drawn down.

He wrestled to get inside the suite before it was too late. An icy snowfall began condensing around him, accompanied by the tap dancing of someone's forgotten jewels being swirled along. Whole gemstones raced by Colleran from the door of the open suite, but he hardly noticed. He didn't have the *time* to notice. The rend in the hull was getting wider, and the creature was coming inside.

But then something happened to the beast. Either it was being blinded by the flotsam sucked toward it, or the loss of its lower half from the clasher's beam had deprived it of part of its vital functions. In any case, Colleran caught a final glimpse of the creature in its death throes as he fought to seal the suite door. The creature's long, mottled arm swept the carpet as if grasping for the jewels themselves, ripping out a long shag in its desperation.

Tornado winds wailed and the creature answered with a scream of its own.

Colleran began to get dizzy, fighting the suite door. Seconds left . . . just seconds.

The suite door clomped shut and overhead he heard the whine of the atmospherics trying to pump emergency air into the sealed-off room. Outside, in the hall, though, it was a nightmare.

He slid down the wall in a faint. He thought briefly of all those stupid jewels. How useless they were in the face of death.

And he thought about Heidi.

He blacked out to a vision of his Lei walking toward him over the streets of heaven, set with cobblestones made of the same walnut-sized jewels that seemed so much in abundance, here, in this place that was clearly *not* heaven.

3

The place where Lou Colleran found himself did not seem to be a dream, although, like a dream, it possessed its own kind of pleasant unreality.

Meru. Only his long years of being an immortal and having his occasional Latent Encephalic Image encounters enabled him to recognize where he was. There was no sun in the sky, as usual. Light seemed to diffuse itself from every object on the plains, on the clusters of acacia or stunted pin oaks, even on the snowcapped peak of Mount Meru, the center of the universe. Or at least this universe, real or unreal. It was as if the sky were a living being radiating down its pure warmth of love on the fields of what the Tibetans of Lost Earth might have called their own towering Mount Meru. The center.

Colleran breathed deeply. Pine scents wafted on the wind.

Columbine sprays bunched in huge families in the meadows stretching out before him.

It's all so real, he thought. Vivid dreaming was r ever experienced with this kind of facility. But then, what was the world if not the form of the perceiver's intentional reality? Only location mattered.

He looked down at his hands, an old Castaneda technique that let him know that he was . . . elsewhere. He noticed that he was now garbed in the black-and-silver tunic of his Regulator's uniform, though the Langstrom clasher was missing along with the living holster that herded it.

It was always this way, he remembered. He had always felt as if he belonged in his Regulator's outfit and that he belonged here, but it was always without his weapon. In this place there never was need for a weapon.

He breathed slowly, savoring the purity of the landscape. Flowers were the main decoration, gathered in families of purples and yellows and cochineal reds. The cerulean sky overhead watched over him and the ruins of the plains seemed to beckon.

Ruins, he mused. Ancient, idyllic, they seemed as if they had always been there *as ruins*. Yet they held a patina of newness, appearing only for him to be experienced in just this way.

That's the way heaven would be, Colleran reflected as he walked slowly through the gentle grasses of the plain. Meru, that Lost Earth place of Tibetan Buddhist nirvanic repose, had been rumored to have such tranquil properties, nothing out of place, not even those who dwelled there. Not even himself.

But what did he know about these things?

What he did know was that out in the field ahead of him, calf-deep in the grasses, was Beatrice urging him further into this placid dream. The ruins behind her, a congregation of albescent pillars of crumbling marble and fractured domes, seemed to require their presence, as if there was still a need, even in this perfect place, for men and women to give it a human dimension.

However, even as he inhaled what seemed to him to be real air, he knew that—for the time being—he did not belong. He looked at his gloved hands once more and realized it to be true. *Not yet. Heaven is for those who earn it.*

And looking up, Beatrice was gone the way of the wind over the sere ocean swells of meadow grass. . . .

* * *

"Good," came a kind but firm voice. "He's coming around. He's going to pull through."

Colleran awoke to a hospital or infirmary bed in the ordinary world with several concerned individuals hovering over him. He suppressed an urge to fall back into the transcendent joy of the Lei experience, allowing the endorphins in his brain to readjust themselves as he loomed toward full consciousness.

"I told you he'd make it," a familiar voice prattled nearby. "He's too tough to die. Either that, or he's blessed."

Only the speaker laughed, but Colleran recognized the voice and opened his eyes.

"Goddamn, Brodie," he whispered, his throat dry. "I didn't think there was a garbage scow due til Tuesday."

Kit Brodie, a One Spoke Regulator and his closest friend, stood next to the bed in all of his Authority regalia, which meant tunic, badge, and Langstrom clasher in a living holster keyed to Brodie's own vibrations. The nurses and lone doctor, however, seemed unimpressed by Brodie's enormous presence. Brodie stood a mere six-foot-three, but he was about a mile wide at the shoulders. The medical personnel next to him looked like midgets in an oldtime circus.

Colleran propped himself up rather feebly on his pillow, leaning back on his elbows. "Where am I? This isn't the *Judy Holliday*."

"The *Parvardigar*," Brodie said proudly. "We got here just in time, by the looks of things. We hear you've been wrestling alligators."

"Something like that," Colleran said, pushing back a strand of blonde hair. He discovered a knob just above his forehead. "Ouch," he mumbled, gingerly touching it.

The doctor, whose badge on her tunic said *Jenda*, approached him. She was all business and concern. Her efficient fingers carefully examined his head. She said, "You got that falling to the floor right after you pressure-sealed the cabin. We have it all on video."

Brodie crossed his massive arms and stared down reproachfully as two nurses began helping Colleran into a better position.

"You're lucky to be with us, Lou," Brodie said. He was still a rookie, as far as Colleran was concerned, two hundred years younger than he.

"Ouch," he said again, still fiddling with the bump on his head. "So where's the *Holliday*?"

"Vaillancourt lifted it to high orbit when the *Parvardigar* arrived." Brodie, who was normally outgoing and convivial, deepened in his concern. "It's bad business all the way around, Lou. We've seen nothing like it."

"What do you mean?"

"They lost fifteen crew members, all told, along with twenty-one paying passengers. Three lifeboats went down into the atmosphere and one other fell into low orbit where no one could reach it. Evidently they didn't know what to do, how to pilot it, and they suffocated by the time they made an orbital pass for us to retrieve them."

"Jesus," Colleran said, sinking further into his pillow. Then he looked up at the huge Brodie. "Kit, I had a lovely with me, a good one this time. It was a Heidi Beryl."

Brodie was brutally quick, telling it the only way it could be told. "She went down into the atmosphere on lifeboat number five. Sorry, Lou. Vaillancourt and his crew did what they could to see that everyone got safely away. But—"

"But lovelies are lovelies."

Colleran swung his aching legs out of the bed and planted his feet on the floor. He felt weak but serviceable. The bump on his head was the principle cause of his discomfort. All else worked. He must have gotten into the suite just in time to prevent oxygen-deprivation to his brain. He did notice that his skin was red from the cold induced by the sudden depressurization in the corridor, a minor form of frostbite.

But still there was a hurt deep within him. Heidi hadn't made it. She'd finished her days as a meteoric flash in the sky above the serene seas of Okeanos. And no one had probably noticed.

Dr. Jenda helped him to his feet as Kit Brodie watched.

The doctor said, "Go easy for a while. You didn't suffer a concussion, but there might be a hairline fracture that our scans missed. It happens."

Colleran glanced into Dr. Jenda's eyes. They were sky-blue and possessed that peculiar distracted quality that newly inducted immortals get when the Kotlicky-Powell gene-splice takes hold. Her skin was smooth, but in her light brown hair were traces or filaments of gray. She couldn't have been more than thirty-seven subjective years of age, but she would keep the strands of gray with her for as long as she lived. And if she continued to work as part of the medical contingent on board the *Parvardigar*, battle cruiser for the Mandala Authority, the chances were good that she would live for quite some time.

Dr. Jenda, however, had passed him a disapproving look when she'd overheard his confession that he'd been with a lovely. *She'd learn*, he said to himself quietly. Falling in love with ordinary mortals was the bane of those pressed into Authority service, who quickly outlive the common run of humanity. Dr. Patrice Jenda had yet to experience that particular kind of loneliness that would compel her to seek a lovely, male or female. She was still proud, still holding to the old ways. And as they all knew, the word *whore* no longer existed with any kind of cognitive referent in the languages of the worlds of the eight Spokes connected to the distant Hub. Still, she was young, on the cusp of her new life as an immortal.

"Okay," Colleran began slowly but firmly. "The big question. What happened to it?"

The nurses and even Dr. Jenda turned their gaze on the two Regulators.

"What we've captured on tape," Brodie began, his arms still crossed, his dark eyes growing darker with the telling, "isn't too clear. There was a great deal of outgoing atmospherics that clouded the creature, but evidently when you clashed its lower half, you got the part that counted. It was probably dying when it attacked you."

"What happened after that?"

"It stopped struggling about the time you locked yourself in the suite. It dropped back outside in the rush of air from the corridor, then fell away from the laputa. At first it looked as if it was going to get tangled in the ring-shaft girders it uprooted, but it just went into a tumble, sliding away. Our guess is that it'll burn up on re-entry about this time tomorrow."

"We can't get at it?"

"No."

"Damn," Colleran said with disgust. He wanted more than just a few fogged images on videotape.

Brodie checked his watch. "Better put some clothes on, that is, if you can walk. The boss is here and she wants to take us on a tour of the *Judy Holliday*. The tour no one gets to see but us."

"Sagar is here?" Colleran asked, truly surprised.

Brodie grinned, and that often meant trouble. "She was on

vacation, too. In Spoke Beta, where she didn't think she'd have to babysit us. Guess she was wrong."

"I guess. She's been wrong before."

"Not in my lifetime."

That grin again. "What do you know, you're just a kid," Colleran countered.

"Right, pops." Brodie stood aside as the nurses filed out. "Ready when you are."

Colleran wondered if he'd ever be ready. He had a bad feeling about all of this.

Colleran, as it turned out, had been unconscious for nearly ten hours. In that span of time Captain Vaillancourt had limped the *Judy Holliday* into a higher orbit above Okeanos. There, various rescue ships assisted in the transfer of personnel and passengers to the waiting jitneys, which in turn wisked the wealthy vacationeers back to their homes, which were scattered throughout the stars of the Spoke.

The *Parvardigar*, one of seven Authority "preservers," had arrived some time after Vaillancourt—with the Okeanos Reach's blessing—had begun the rescue and transfer operations. The laputa itself was now in a stable orbit, three hundred miles above the equator, and the crisis management team of the *Parvardigar*, which was not inconsiderable, had already begun its investigations into the incident.

Colleran, now in his Regulator's tunic, strode alongside the hefty Kit Brodie as they stepped from the elevator into the lower storage hold of the *Judy Holliday*, part of the "tour" Brodie had promised him.

The entire floating resort had been cordoned off to all but Okeanos personnel and the Regulators from the *Parvardigar*, which loomed in orbit above the *Judy Holliday* like a small, swift planetoid. From the helm above down to this, the first level, the place had the feel of a ghost town, and along with it was the presence of death. Colleran could feel it; he could almost smell it. And it was nothing like the fragrances of the fields surrounding Mount Meru, whose memory he could evoke with startling clarity.

"There she is," Brodie indicated with a nod as they rounded a corner on their inspection of the lower hold of the laputa.

The "she" in question stood as a lone female among a pack of white-suited Okeanos inspectors, which included Captain Vaillancourt and a grim Officer Ashton, who seemed intimidated by the gathering of so many serious grown-ups. Colleran, however, focused his attention on Administrator Brianne Sagar. She was the center of authority in the warehouselike hold. She ran the *Parvardigar* and was a living symbol for everything the Mandala Authority stood for and could do. Everyone deferred to her.

Admin Sagar, also in her Authority black-and-si'ver tunic, waved the two Regulators over. Sagar was much younger than Colleran, only slightly older than the youthful Kit Brodie. Her true age had been halted at thirty-four years, yet Colleran understood that she was at least two-hundred-fifty-five, a figure she would neither confirm nor deny. Colleran himself was one of the longest-lived immortals in the Authority, but he had chosen long ago to stay away from Mandala politics and out of the Authority's immensely intricate bureaucracy. Brianne Sagar, however, had a flair for it, and she carried herself quite well in the midst of so much power.

She stood only five-feet-one and her short black hair had been bobbed in such a way as to resemble a helmet. She would have looked quite like a youngster had it not been for her rather ample bosom. Her manner, however, was rarely sexual or enticing. She was the business-end of the Authority and she did her job well.

"Glad to see you're alive," Admin Sagar said to Colleran as he and Brodie walked up to the gathering.

"Thanks for the concern," he said dryly, trying to inject a shred of humor into the situation. Sagar's tight-lipped acknowledgment squelched that.

The tall captain, though, did smile at Colleran, glad that he was present. Young Ashton also seemed relieved.

Sagar said, "Thought you'd like to see where our mysterious beast came from."

The entire hold had been sectioned off with long ribbons of yellow police tape. A young man who Colleran had never seen before followed them with a portable video unit balanced on his shoulder. The tech spoke into a pin-mike in even tones, describing the investigation's every step.

The expansive hold was the breadbasket of the *Judy Holliday* and at every turn Colleran could see boxes and crates neatly stacked in rows or pushed up against the bulkheads. The laputas of the Okeanos Reach—the only ones allowed on Okeanos itself—were capable of sustaining their crews and passengers for stints of up to forty days. Laputas simply ferried, if rather slowly, their vacationeers from orbital space down to the floating surface ports in the tropical waters of Okeanos where they would wait for two to three weeks before returning back to orbit. Everything required for the comfort of the passengers and the welfare of the crew was contained in this large, cavernous space.

The place was a disaster.

Debris had been strewn about with such ferocity that it startled Colleran. Having glimpsed the monster, he could easily imagine it at work down here, venting its frustration on the stored goods it probably knew the humans above would eventually need.

Brodie and Colleran flanked the diminutive Admin as she escorted them under a long curl of police tape into a specific area. Unshielded lights overhead glared down rudely as the Okeanos crew followed.

"It was hatched over here," the Admin stated flatly.

"Hatched?" Colleran glanced sideways at Brodie, and by the expression on his face it was evident that this was the first the younger immortal had heard of it as well. Life was full of surprises.

The elderly captain cleared his throat, then said, "It's right over here, Mr. Colleran. I found it while you were recovering. Apparently it had been in storage for quite some time."

What Vaillancourt indicated with an almost elegant gesture was a big, torn-open crate that seemed rather undistinguished from a good dozen others just like it nearby. All of them were neatly stacked and bolted into place along one wall of this section of the hold.

"And the thing was hatched?" he asked.

A sickly smell, of rotting amniotic fluids, seemed to hover in the lifeless air of the unventilated hold. The captain, in long strides, took them up to the crate, knowing now that it was safe to approach it. The box was about ten feet by twelve and was perhaps eight feet deep.

Hatched is about right, Colleran suddenly realized. A creature of the magnitude he had fought would have to have gotten on board, balled up and stowed away until the time was just right.

But hatched?

Vaillancourt said to Colleran, "We brought the Authority in on this because you Regulators deal exclusively in commercial traffic among the worlds of the Spokes." The crate, completely torn open at one end, gaped at them in the shadows of the hold as if it were an aperture to hell itself. The young tech with the video unit attached to his shoulder stepped around to get Colleran into the shot. Vaillancourt, tweeking the ends of his stylish mustache, continued. He said, "We've checked and rechecked our shipping records, and this particular crate just doesn't exist."

Colleran walked closer to it as Brodie crossed his arms like some kind of guardian. Colleran commented, "Yet it got here. Someone off-loaded it from a freighter and someone else tucked it in here."

"Oh, we know who bolted it down. We've got a whole crew that oversees those matters." Vaillancourt waved his arm around, encompassing the entire hold. "This is their job, all of these crates. It was just another supply shipment to them."

The Admin came up to Colleran. "Look over here at this, Lou. Ever see anything like it?"

Colleran kneeled down by the edge of the crate where it had been splintered outward by something on the inside. Sagar cracked back an arm's length piece of wood, the nails that held it in place complaining loudly.

What Colleran saw genuinely amazed him.

Inside the crate were the brittle remains—still stained by embryonic juices—of the "shell" that had harbored the creature during its gestation.

Colleran tugged out a large, smooth piece about the size of a washbasin. It had an off-white tincture to it with mottles or speckles of a brownish hue, like cancers, on the outside. On the inner surface of the shell, a thin film still adhered, and still smelled.

It was like nothing he'd ever seen—or smelled—before.

Colleran stood up with the sample and pondered the other crates still piled high and bolted in place along the wall.

The Admin stood as well. She informed him, "We've checked them all, including their bills of lading. This is the only one." She took the hunk of shell from Colleran. "At least we've got an organic sample of the creature. With a little bit of effort, we'll be able to analyze its chromosomal makeup, see what kind of creature it was."

"To say nothing of how it got here," Brodie interjected.

"Or who sent it," Colleran added. "Unless it got here all by itself."

Everyone stared at him as if he'd just said a dirty word. But dirty words no longer existed. This was something entirely different. For if they could not determine the kind of creature it was, they were left with a rather unthinkable alternative.

And that was a new kind of lifeform that might be competing with the Reaches of the Mandala.

4

The window in Admin Sagar's office on board the huge *Parvardigar* was an illusion. Like so much lately in his life, Colleran was coming to understand that behind, or beneath, the surface of things existed the truth. Just like this window with its spacious view of Okeanos far below.

The window was, in fact, a large, real-time display screen patched into the office from an outside videoscanner. Admin Sagar's suite was deep inside the *Parvardigar*, where she could be in closest proximity to the mainframe computers, the labs, and the communications complex. The *Parvardigar*, rarely using its destructive facilities as a battleship or "preserver," mostly acted as a roving administrative complex for the Authority among the scattered worlds of the Spokes. The window, though, was a pleasant touch; it tended to remind one of what all the machinery was for: to preserve the peace and tranquility of places such as Okeanos and the corporations, or Reaches, which ran them.

Colleran stood alone before the window and watched the *Judy Holliday* slowly, almost imperceptibly, sink down its gravity well to the surface docks for further repairs. There was only so much that the captain could do in high orbit. Work on the ring-shafts could be conducted only on Okeanos itself.

It would be some time before Vaillancourt would welcome on board a new flock of well-to-do vacationeers—assuming the

Okeanos people could weather the gossip that would spread as fast as it could leak throughout the Alpha Spoke. Actual news would be scarce since Brianne Sagar had posted a security black-out around the incident until they could learn more about the beast.

The computers in the Admin's office were busy trying to figure out what they could, and Colleran could hear in the outer hallways of the *Parvardigar* the rattle and clatter of Authority personnel at their work. With a communications black-out surrounding the attack, they might have the time to determine who had sent the creature and why.

Colleran perused a report on Brianne's desk as he sipped that morning's third cup of coffee. The report was merely a rundown of the major phyla that flourished in the waters of Okeanos. Like a great many Earth-normal worlds of the eight Spokes of the Mandala, most were quite primitive, with very few highly evolved species, particularly nothing of the sort that had so devastated the *Judy Holliday*.

Colleran took all this personally. After all, the aberration had tried to kill him, and it *had* killed Heidi. Murder is always quite personal.

However, he was also a Regulator, a kind of border patrol agent, and as part of the Authority it was his duty to make sure that what traveled the spaceways did so within the confines of the law.

And Colleran knew that shipping a creature such as the one he'd fought with wasn't any different from shipping a small-scale nuclear device. Someone wanted the *Judy Holliday*, and/or its captain and crew, dead. That a Regulator had been on board enjoying the company of a lovely and taking a vacation had been incidental. And rather fortunate. Nothing like this had ever transpired in the Authority's history before.

Kit Brodie walked into the Admin's office clutching a sheaf of freshly printed papers. Colleran glanced up from the taxonomic report. Brodie, in his somber black-and-silver, resembled a god carved from obsidian stepping out of the night sky just looking for trouble. And he was smiling.

"Morning," Brodie chirped, walking over to Sagar's large desk. He tossed the papers down by the small CRT screens.

"Coffee's over there," Colleran said, pointing. "Brianne ordered a gallon of it. I think we're going to be here for a while."

"Great. I'm for it."

Colleran brooded. "Your enthusiasm is less than commend-able."

Brodie poured himself a large mug of coffee, using Brianne Sagar's personal cup, as it turned out. He gleefully ignored Colleran's dour remark. "You old guys really get grumpy when you turn four hundred."

There was some truth to the remark and Colleran couldn't think of a suitably witty riposte.

Brodie, however, continued. "I think we've got something to go on." He indicated the report he had just deposited on the boss's desk. "That's a prelim study based on what our biolab people have come up with. They ran a basic spectroscopic and genetic scan on the substances inside of the eggshell and on the shell itself. Some space jockey even went outside and scraped a sample of slime from the outer hull of the *Judy Holliday*. It was all we had to go on, but it seems to have been enough." He slurped his coffee noisily, triumphantly.

The report on the albumin from the inside of the shell was broken down into trace elements, enzyme structures, bonding compounds, even the amount of alkaloids in the shell. The conclusion was quite remarkable, considering what the shell had contained. It was an ordinary eggshell, nothing special. Nothing innately alien.

"But it is one of a kind," Brodie added as Colleran considered the conclusions of the report.

"That's impossible," Colleran stated. "There are no one-of-a-kinds in this universe."

Brodie grinned, quite proud of his part in this investigation. "Except the universe itself."

"You know what I mean."

"I know exactly what you mean. But in this case, the facts say you're wrong." Brodie pointed a finger at the report in Colleran's hands. "Look closer. You see what the shell's made from?"

As the report stated, although the shell served a normal shell's function, it wasn't organically based. It was mostly silica interlaced with inorganic polymers. An inner layer of alkaloid substances allowed the organic contents within the albumic sac to gestate naturally, even though the shell itself was composed almost entirely of plastic.

"It's plastic," Brodie said. "And nothing that I know of lays plastic eggs."

"Does Brianne know this yet?"

"Everyone knows," Brodie said. "I've been looking for you for about an hour."

Colleran sat back in the Admin's chair, watching the steam from his coffee wave a small banner of mist. He recalled the visage of the creature.

"Plastic. I don't believe it," he said to Brodie as the window behind him glowed with its view of Okeanos below.

Colleran mused. "No creature that we know of evolves from silicon, and certainly not from any kind of inorganic polymer base."

"Not unless you're one of a kind," Brodie challenged with a smile.

"That thing I saw wasn't made out of plastic."

"Nobody says it was. It was just hatched in a plastic shell." He came over to the desk, moving like a mobile hill. "Just think of this, Lou. Imagine the chicken that laid that egg."

Colleran returned to the report, peeling back its pages.

Brodie gestured with the mug in his hand. "We then ran a chromosome profile of the albumin and some of the fluids we found. There's nothing in our files comparable to them. They're not plastic, but they're also not like anything we know of living in this Spoke. Or any other Spoke, for that matter."

Colleran had to admit it: the creature seemed definitely one of a kind, unique to his four-hundred year experience. "This is just impossible," he concluded.

Brodie slid down into a moldform chair, which adjusted itself to the junior Regulator's girth. "Well, maybe yes and maybe no. There are eight Spokes to the Mandala, three of them more or less colonized, the others uncolonized but explored."

"Except for Theta Spoke," Colleran reminded him. "Nothing seems to live there." Colleran had an older brother who was one of the Authority's chief Mandala scholars and was currently exploring the Theta Spoke where—for reasons known only to the original Makers of the Hub, which linked the eight Spokes—there was no life or habitable planets.

"Right," Brodie conceded. "In any case, it still could have come from one of the Spokes. I mean, it *had* to come from somewhere. Maybe it came from the Hub itself."

Colleran had considered that possibility already, and it scared him. "I know," he said solemnly. "The Makers."

"That's what they're saying downstairs. It's all over the *Parvardigar*. We might be up against the Makers."

Colleran sat forward in Brianne Sagar's throne of a chair and made a temple of his fingers. The Makers, whoever they were, were responsible for the way they all lived their lives, giving them their rather unusual form of faster-than-light travel, the so-called spindling process. It was a technology that still baffled the humans who had spread themselves throughout the worlds linked to the Hub, and if the Makers were now coming out of their shell, so to speak, Colleran knew that they all might be in a great deal of trouble.

The Mandala, as it was now called, was something of an oddity unparalleled in the history of both physics and astronomy. It had been the discovery of the Hub—the very center of the eight Spokes of the Mandala—in the winter of 2079 A.D. that had changed all of their lives on the earth, an earth now lost.

In February of that year, a radio astronomer named Rolf Andreesen, who had been part of a team of scientists on the moon's far side, began picking up very unusual signals coming from a source in the constellation Cygnus the Swan, some fifty-two light-years away. The "beam" itself contained signals that were clearly of intelligent origin, but when people on earth determined the full content and nature of the incredible energy coming from the Hub, as it was later termed, everything changed.

Andreesen's discovery was that the earth and the entire solar system had just begun passing through a vast beam of undefinable energy emanating from a single source. This beam would become the Alpha Spoke, just one of eight Spokes coming from the Hub. The Hub was utterly invisible and the energy itself—along with the signals—could be detected only when the Spoke was entered. The Hub, which was first called Object Andreesen, sent out the signals in a single cone, beamed directionally. The Hub may have been drifting through the galaxy for eons, sending out its signals, sending out its peculiar "spindling" power, but it had only been around the year 2079 that humankind had been able to receive them.

The earth, as they later determined, had been "between" the cones of energy called Alpha Spoke and Beta Spoke. According to the studies now completed, the earth had drifted through the influence of the Beta Spoke during the last Ice Age, when there was no one on the planet capable of picking up the transmissions from the Hub. Then it drifted out into the spaces between the beams of energy where it wouldn't have done the earth much good anyway.

However, the signals that Andreesen and his team picked up, which announced the presence of the Object, was what counted most. The signals, once broken down mathematically and interpreted, turned out to be instructions for a special kind of engine that could harness the subspacial energies that the Hub was transmitting. No one knew how the Hub generated its special power, but the consensus was that it was artificial and not stellar.

At that time in history, the earth was being swallowed up in a spate of ceaseless wars, ecological breakdowns, and basic bureaucratic lethargies that had begun crippling the planet. Only those colonies in space seemed to cohere, almost by dint of their extreme enviromental requirements. The discovery of a new kind of spaceflight changed all of that. The Andreesen engines were built—later called "spindles"—and the great migrations had begun.

Only there was a catch. The Andreesen engines drew their power from the faraway Hub and the ships could only travel within the cone of energy coming from the Hub. The ships would draw the mysterious energies into the Andreesen engines and "spindle" in toward the Hub, then shoot right out again at FTL, or faster-than-light, speeds to wherever their captains had programmed them to go, either in the same Spoke or in any of the other seven Spokes spaced equidistantly around the Hub.

The eight Spokes were a maximum of sixty light-years long, with a sixteen light-year radius at the farthest end from the Hub. Closer in toward the Hub, the spaces were much narrower, and the Hub itself—Object Andreesen—seemed to be about the size of a modest black hole without the dangerous event horizon to destroy anything that came near.

But despite the limited field of movement within the Spokes, there were many, many stars in each Spoke, and many of those star-suns, especially in the Alpha, Beta, and Gamma Spokes, had at least one human-habitable planet. It was in the empty areas between the Spokes where the most danger lay. Colleran's own father and uncle had been among the early Spoke explorers, and they had made the tragic mistake of attempting to fly from one Spoke to another by going in a perpendicular path from the Alpha Spoke to the Beta Spoke, using only a ship powered by a spindle engine. They were never heard of again, for spindling did not work there—only in the range of the Spokes.

So the object that Rolf Andreesen had discovered became the Hub to a vast array of eight radiating Spokes, like a great Mandala drifting through space. No one knew, despite years and years of analysis, just who had made the Mandala or why, and the debate still continued. But humankind made the most of the opportunity to spread itself where it could to mine, harvest, and manufacture the goods it needed for its expanding civilization. Yet, always in the background of their thinking lurked the presence of the Makers of the Hub. Colleran's own brother, Daryl, another immortal in the service of the Authority, had spent nearly all his life studying the habitable planets in the Spokes, trying to find something, anything, that might suggest a previous planet-bound civilization. But the stars that drifted in and out of the Spokes as the Hub slowly rotated with the rotation of the galaxy all seemed to be accidents of their passage.

And that was the tragedy of the Andreesen discovery.

In the year 2355 A.D., as Andreesen himself had calculated, the solar system moved out of the influence of Alpha Spoke, taking with it what civilization remained there. It left the men and women in the Spokes with a mantle of guilt, knowing that only the poorest of peoples had to remain behind, and of them, billions were still left on the earth. The Lost Earth. Radio and television signals were still picked up, and the news there was not good. The greenhouse effect had kicked in, and two small-scale nuclear wars had done away with much of China and the Mideast. And what made matters worse was the fact that, according to their calculations, the path of the sun's journey through the galaxy would never again bring it within range of a Spoke. Relativistic flight was still possible, but the costs were prohibitive and what few expeditions that had gotten away would still take decades to arrive in the Alpha Spoke. Those who remained on the Lost Earth were all alone in a very real sense.

Colleran stared intently at the report in his hands, feeling the full implication of what the creature might mean for them all if, indeed, it turned out to be one of the ancient Makers. Although why the Makers would take the considerable trouble to hide one of its representatives in the hold of an ordinary luxury resort on Okeanos, a world midway through Spoke Alpha, perplexed him. There were hundreds of other targets, especially the home world of the Authority, which was only one light-day from the Hub itself. The Authority was the place to strike.

"I don't get it," he muttered. "I just don't get it."

At that juncture, the Admin breezed into the room and Kit Brodie practically snapped to attention. Brianne Sagar's sharp hazel eyes caught sight of the mug in Brodie's hands and Colleran saw the huge mountain of a man become a molehill, a nervous one at that.

"I take it Kit's briefed you," Sagar said to Colleran as he yielded the chair. She had brought with her another cluster of papers, and she tossed these upon the desktop along with the others.

"Yes," Colleran confirmed. "Nothing seems to add up, though. At least I can't make any sense of it."

"Nobody can," she said sternly. "But we're going to give it our best try."

Brianne's small hands deftly leafed through the new reports on her desk. One of them she gave to Colleran, the other she slid across the desk to Brodie, who jumped up and retrieved it.

"We've traced some of Vaillancourt's records to the Abou-Farhaats. They were the merchants who brought some of the crates to the *Judy Holliday* the last time it was serviced in orbit." She considered Colleran evenly. "That was about the time you arrived there for your vacation-sabbatical."

Brodie swallowed hard as he went over the report in his large hands. "So you think the thing was incubating all that time?"

"Looks like it," she said. "We need to do further work on the shell and the organics left inside of it. But, yes, it was waiting for just the right time to get free."

Brodie turned a page. His black eyebrows went up with surprise. "So, what's this?"

"Orders," Sagar said, leaning back in her chair, drumming her fingers on the armrest. "There's a storage facility on Asarhaddon Four that might be a possible source for the creature. A small Abou-Farhaat freighter downloaded a shipment there and picked it up again just weeks before it went on to Okeanos."

Colleran looked at the Admin. It didn't quite sound right to him. "Wait a second. The Reach of the Abou-Farhaats has been doing business for at least a hundred years. Maybe longer. What do they have against the Okeanos Reach all of a sudden? I mean, we're talking about *business* here."

Brianne Sagar looked like a small child in her father's big chair. She said, "That's what Kit's going to look into. There's a spindle waiting in the topside bay. It's all set to go."

Brodie set down the mug. "Right," he said, suddenly tight-lipped and serious—not at all his usual gregarious self. "I'm on it."

Colleran had turned the page to his own stamped orders. Attached to them was a com-spindle communication. A distress signal. All communications in the Spokes went by way of com-drones, which took their recorded messages down into the well of the Hub and on out again. It was much faster than direct-beam radio transmissions, at least over the long haul.

The Admin said, "That just arrived. If we're fast enough, we can probably do something about it."

Colleran felt the tingle of an oncoming Lei experience as he scanned the com-spindle message. *Dear, dear God*, he thought.

Sagar's voice was tense. "There's a small mining colony three light-years from here. The Cronin Reach operates it. They don't know what they've got, but it seems to be something like your beast."

Colleran stood away from the desk. The Admin gazed levelly at him. She said, "That's a Spokewide distress signal. I've ordered the *Parvardigar* to set sail, but you can get there hours before we can. Good-bye."

"Good-bye," Colleran said, and he was gone.

5

Colleran spindled away from the orbiting *Parvardigar* in a hauntingly desultory mood, not quite ready for any of this. Something sinister was gnawing away at him on the inside, and much of it had to do with his primary reason for seeking out a place such as Okeanos and a lovely such as Heidi. He was getting old, tired of the mysteries, wondering when his luck would change.

That human beings—and lovelies—had been killed rather horrendously by an unknown entity was one thing; that they might have perished at the hand of the Makers was another. He felt like a Lost Earth pagan perhaps stepping, for the first time, into the prismed halls of the Chartres cathedral during the late Middle Ages: the Makers made him feel woefully inadequate. A sword in that pagan's hand could do little to overcome the god who dwelled in a place like Chartres.

Even though he was now a Three Spoke Regulator, he knew that his office only meant that he had the privilege to cover more interesting territory; it did not give him any more confidence in understanding his place in that great Mandala. He knew that someday their blessed lives would have to change. However, being alone with his Heidi Beryl for three weeks allowed him to suppress, if temporarily, his discontent. The Heidi Beryls were true lovelies. They were sensitive, loving, and in their own right intelligent and companionable. Yet, he felt the clutch of some hidden obligation peel back the veil of truth. No matter how long people sought to ignore what was transpiring around them, sooner or later that reality would reach in and involve them. Colleran was now involved.

* * *

Colleran had never visited Surane Four, even though it was
located in the Alpha Spoke, his first and longest tour of duty. The
people who owned the mining rights to Surane Four, the Cronins,
operated on many worlds, although the fourth planet around
Surane was their only foothold in that particular system. The
Cronins, as his computer updated him, were a mid-level Reach
and dutifully paid their taxes and kept all of their commerce
licenses up-to-date. All of which entitled them to the full
protection and assistance of the Authority.

On Surane Four the Cronins mined only one mineral: titanium.
Vital to all industries flourishing throughout the worlds of the
inhabited Spokes, titanium gave the Cronins some influence in
Mandala politics. The Cronins were a relatively new Reach in the
Alpha Spoke, a mere two hundred years old, unlike most of the
Reaches with which he had some dealings. When the great
migrations occurred in the years after the Andreesen spindles were
devised, whole corporations began moving up and down the range
of the Spoke along with the human population. They became
Reaches. The Authority evolved at the same time to police the
spaceways and they were funded by the successes of the Reaches.
The Cronins, while modest in size, were industrious and devoted
to the mining of worlds that the other Reaches ignored.

As Colleran scanned the CRT, he noticed that the Cronins had
accumulated only a handful of minor violations, all of which had
been settled in court and litigated through all of the proper
Authority channels. Moreover, as he read on, none of them were
related to shipping violations that might have involved the Abou-
Farhaat Reach, which was itself the largest shipping corporation
in Spoke Alpha.

However, there would be time to trace the relationship of the
aggressive Abou-Farhaat family with the Cronins—if there was
one—once he found out what was behind the rather desperate
character of the com-drone message. The miners on Surane Four
were a hearty lot, and if they were up against anything remotely
similar to the beast he had fought, then there'd be trouble.

Surane used to be a red giant star sometime before it was swept
into the path of Spoke Alpha. It had gone nova, however, millions
of years earlier and blown away the inner three planets, shearing
off the atmosphere and topsoil of the fourth. What remained of
Surane Four was a rock of solid metals, titanium being the most
accessible and more marketable by the Cronins. The star, Surane,

was a wretched F2-type and was otherwise good for very little. Most people ignored it as they spindled up and down the spaces of the Spoke.

The distress signal had been only two hours old by the time Colleran had left the *Parvardigar* and spindled outward from Okeanos toward Surane. Another two hours in transit made Colleran wonder if he'd be able to do any good.

But when he soared into low orbit around the cobalt-blue rock of Surane Four, he ran into a full-spectrum radio broadcast of all sorts of messages, shouts for help, and angry accusations aimed at the Cronins responsible for allowing something like this to happen.

Colleran transmitted his Authority-register code and at the same time called out for landing instructions.

"Where can I land?" he hailed. "Where is it safe?"

The main mining facility seemed to be a spray of tiny crystals on the surface of Surane Four, but there also seemed to be fires coming from the location of the usual landing fields.

A harried male voice pierced the static over Colleran's radio. "We have a beacon to the main surface complex. Avoid the gantry! Avoid the gantry area and landing zone! Do you understand? Please acknowledge."

Colleran picked up the new directional guide beam. It was coming from the city miles beneath him in the darkside shadows of Surane Four. There indeed appeared to be a wide area of destruction just east of the complex, right where he would normally have set down.

"Acknowledge," Colleran returned. But as he dropped his spindle down toward the night side of Surane Four, he tried to imagine how the creature had destroyed the entire gantry lift area. He tried thinking of the chicken that hatched the egg. Maybe this was the work of the chicken. . . . .

The man in the silver fire-suit who met Colleran in the hangar of the main complex looked as if he'd never had a pleasant day in his life.

"There's just one of you?" he asked, looking past Colleran as though hoping to find more figures in the cockpit of the spindle.

"It's just me," Colleran said, bemused.

"Shit!" the man swore. He had dark smudges on his face and an even darker disposition underneath. "I thought you were bringing a preserver with you. We need an army for this, dammit!''

"The *Parvardigar* is a lot bigger than my spindle and a lot slower, but it's on the way. Don't worry."

Other personnel, also clad in their emergency fire-suits, had begun filing into the hangar. Their expectant faces were a kaleidoscope of fears and dark terrors. And all of them had their eyes on Colleran's live-leather holster and the clasher within.

The man facing Colleran pinched the bridge of his nose as he thought. "That's not going to be enough. We don't have that much time. We need a dozen Regulators with a dozen clashers."

"Why don't you let me be the judge of that?" Colleran said in even tones, trying to sound reassuring. "Why don't you tell me exactly what it is we're dealing with here. Your message wasn't too clear."

The mining exec looked around the hangar and gestured toward a far door, which led to the tunnels. He did not do a good job of hiding his disappointment.

The man said, "What we're dealing with is some kind of animal that's tearing up our operation, piece by piece. It's already trashed the gantry and lift facilities for our ore. We can't even get off the planet now—"

As they walked, the other men and women made way for them. The executive mining operator was gangly and taller than a miner probably ought to have been, but he did—to Colleran's mind— seem quite capable of running the facilities here.

Quitting the hangar, they found themselves in a sloping area that boasted several trams and tube cars, which no doubt took the Cronin engineers down where the ore snaked its way through the planet. Here, however, scores of individuals had gathered, some with hastily packed bags, others in their mining gear, waiting to escape the calamity below them.

All of them awakened from their fright when they saw the silver-suited man enter with Colleran. Their busy chattering ceased the moment they raced for one of the tunnel carts.

A woman, perhaps in her forties and stained with smears of smoke on her face, came up to the exec officer clutching a bundle of belongings to her chest.

"Mr. Lounsbury, they say it's on level three now. My husband is down on four!" Her eyes were pockets of desperation, and her glances shot back and forth between Lounsbury in the fire-suit and Colleran in his black-and-silver.

Lounsbury gently pushed the woman aside. "The Authority is on its way, Mrs. Ransom. Mister—" He turned to Colleran and passed the baton on to him.

"Colleran," he said quickly, awkwardly. "Don't worry, Ma'am. I'll do what I can."

And, strangely, the woman's reaction to his presence had been like that of Lounsbury's. Her eyes widened with incredulity, and she suddenly laughed. "What? *You?* Just you? Are you crazy? There's something loose in the tunnels and it's killed at least twenty people!" No longer did she appear as a helpless, frantic wife of some miner down below. This woman was like the rest of them: capable and intelligent, and she clearly knew the situation. She was merely scared witless.

Lounsbury turned to Colleran. "Maybe now you see why we need an army for this."

As they climbed into a tunnel cart, the woman persisted. "You've got to do something, and you've got to do it *now!*"

"We will," Colleran informed her, watching all the other personnel in the illuminated hallway, who were in turn watching him. "Trust me," he concluded.

The harried woman backed off and all emotion seemed to drain from her face. Her voice was heavy. "Right. Sure. I guess you can afford to live a little longer than us. What's a few lives to you?"

"That's enough, Mrs. Ransom," Lounsbury said, engaging the tunnel cart. "You'd better get back with the others. We'll keep you posted on our progress."

As the cart pulled away, leaving the panicked topside personnel behind, Colleran had to struggle to control his emotions. He could feel the woman's plight, as if death mattered only to those who could die soon. Who cared about the grunts who had to work for a living? Grunts were like lovelies: mortal and expendable. He'd gotten that reaction many, many times before in his long life. And it always hurt.

As the tunnel cart raced down the long slope ahead of them into the bowels of Surane Four, Colleran had begun smelling smoke, but it was not from the fires of the smelting procedures.

Lounsbury kept his eyes ahead of him. Far out in front of them were other tunnel carts coming their way, bringing with them other fleeing personnel. Some of the men were even walking on the sidewalks that flanked the wide tunnel avenue.

The exec officer said, "I don't know what it is, but it's definitely alive. It's about three times the size of a man and humanoid in shape."

"You've seen it?"

"Damn right I've seen it. When it started taking out the gantry, our monitors picked it up immediately. Killed five of our best people like it was a goddamn machine. It just pulled them apart."

Colleran's gut twinged. That didn't sound like the same kind of creature as the one that attacked the *Judy Holliday*.

We might need the Parvardigar *after all*, he suddenly believed. Perhaps the man was right in his assessment.

"But it's highly intelligent. It knew exactly how to cripple us," Lounsbury reported. He looked aside to Colleran. "It's as if a bunch of guerillas with pulse-guns had been slotted down from orbit. It went right for our lift jitneys and managed to blow up the whole landing field. It got two freighters on the ground and then started heading down below."

"Sounds like it knows what it's doing, all right," Colleran said. His right hand cradled the living leather of his holster, which seemed eager to fly apart and give him the clasher.

Lounsbury's dark eyes fell sharply on the Regulator. "You know what it is? You've seen it before?" Anger seemed to braid the spaces between the engineer's words.

"Something like this happened on Okeanos a few days ago," Colleran confessed.

"Okeanos," the man cursed, now staring out ahead into the tunnel where it ended. "Never heard of it."

The tunnel cart came to a halt at a juncture that was a vast assembly of buildings resembling a small underground village. Men and women were racing about, some with fire-extinguishing equipment, others with torches and laser drills. Alarms were braying from the mouth of one tunnel in particular.

However, most of the personnel were in the process of clearing the area. They were miners, not soldiers. And here the air was thick with soot, smoke, and fumes, most of which was part of their normal lives as miners. Colleran almost choked, wondering how they could stand it.

This was the command center for an entire system of tunnels

and shafts underneath. Miners in dirty gear and glowing helmets stepped aside on the causeway as the tunnel cart halted and Colleran climbed out. Again, he received the same distasteful stares.

Colleran was truly surprised when a man stepped out to greet them who definitely did not belong there. He was tall, almost effeminate in his mannerisms. He wore a tunic of royal purple with gold epaulets and a stickpin at his collar which held a modest jewel.

"Jack!" the dandified individual called out to Lounsbury. "God, I'm glad you're here. We're tracking that thing right now. It's halfway here. It's cut off all the tunnels between us and the gantries. There's only one way for it to go, and that's us."

Lounsbury made a slight face at the man; he evidently did not like him, but just as evidently he had to put up with him.

Still, the fancy man persisted. "I hate this place. You didn't say it'd be like this!"

"You chose to come here, Johnson. Don't blame me for your bad decisions."

Johnson looked as if Lounsbury had punched him in the face. To Colleran's way of thinking, Johnson had the air of an aristocrat who was suddenly down among the *lumpen* proletariat, for whatever reason, and not liking it much.

Johnson, a handsome man, was clearly not used to Lounsbury's type. "You listen to me, Jack. I do the best I can down here—"

Colleran stepped between them as the other miners watched. "Not now!" he shouted. "You two can settle this later."

Johnson jutted his chin out proudly, the bejeweled stickpin glittering as if it were alive.

The assembled miners, who had been gabbling among themselves, began whispering, pointing in awe at the Langstrom clasher at Colleran's side. They backed away reverentially.

"Help's on its way," Lounsbury told Johnson in a voice that also embraced the gathering of miners. "But right now, I'm turning all of this over to the Regulator here."

The wiry Johnson sneered. "What can he do?"

"A lot more than you think I can," Colleran said. He continued, taking up the momentum of the moment. "But what I need right now is a schematic diagram of your tunnel system, preferably up in 3-D, with some kind of visual feed to the shaft where the thing is right now. Can you do that?"

The control station behind them with its beveled windows held several engineers who were waiting and watching. Lounsbury pointed to the station. "Johnson can help you with the schematics. I'll get the rest of the men—"

But Johnson was not one to be given orders, especially by someone qualified to give them such as Lounsbury. "Don't tell me what to do, Jack. You don't run things down here!"

Lounsbury steamed. "Well, then, forget it! Just get the hell out of here! Save your own ass! I'll finish the job for you, since you can't get your hands all dirty—"

"Hey!" Johnson shouted, grabbing Lounsbury's silver sleeve. "This isn't my fault, you know! It's not like it's after *me*!"

"Who the hell'd want you?" Lounsbury blasted back. "Let go of my arm, you piece of shit!" He jerked away violently.

Johnson's right fist came up and cracked a sharp blow on Lounsbury's exposed chin, and the engineer fell back into the crowd of cowed miners.

"You son-of-a-bitch!" Johnson said lividly, his fists clenched. "I don't get paid enough to take this kind of crap from you!"

With that, Colleran swung the handsome Mr. Johnson of the golden epaulets and stickpin around and kicked him in the balls, putting an end to the tussle right away.

Every one of the miners gasped as Johnson fell to the grimy floor, bowing down with pain.

Colleran ordered the miners to escort Johnson to one of the tunnel carts and take it to the surface complex to await further instructions. This they gladly did.

Colleran lifted Lounsbury onto his feet. A nasty bruise, like a squashed plum, had sprouted on the engineer's jaw.

He seemed embarrassed. "We've been under a lot of stress lately," he said, as if confessing some dark sin.

"I'll do what I can," Colleran told him.

The tunnel cart with Johnson and the other miners hissed its way back up the sloping tunnel. Lounsbury watched it go. "That guy's a real ass. I don't even know why the Cronins hired him." He rubbed his jaw.

"He's someone else's problem now," Colleran said. "Let's see what we can do about *our* problem."

6

Lounsbury entered the control station with Colleran right behind him. Three entire walls of the room were ablaze with computer boards, their emergency lights singling out one dysfunction after another.

Lounsbury punched up a hologram profile of the mining complex as Colleran hovered behind him. The other technicians watched as the holo revealed the operation in a skeletal profile of reds, greens, and yellows, each representing a tunnel, shaft, or main station complex such as the one they were in at the moment.

From space it had been impossible to determine the extent of the Cronin mining operation. Here, Colleran could see just how efficiently they had established themselves. The shafts, glowing in yellow, had tunneled quite deeply beneath the surface of Surane Four.

Lounsbury pointed into the hologram at the uppermost reaches of the colony to a place just between the landing gantries and the surfaceside main complex where Colleran had set his spindle.

A female tech nearby murmured, "Like a blood clot in a vein."

The creature showed up as a black, somehow evil-looking dot in the schematic floating before them, and "the clot" moved like a stroke waiting to happen along one yellow line that was a tunnel nearby.

Lounsbury said breathlessly, "It's coming right this way."

Colleran pointed to an area in the holo nearest the creature. "Why are those lines flashing?"

Another female tech—Colleran could actually smell her fear— came up to them at the board. She said, "Those are conveyor tunnels that go directly from the smelters to the gantries, where the tugs lift them away. The creature's shut them down and the coolants aren't working right. All ventilation's gone in those tunnels."

She looked up at Colleran, an ordinary woman made twenty years older by her work in the mines. She concluded, "There were people in those conveyor tunnels. They're dead now."

"All right, Mercy," Lounsbury said in a careful voice. "Thank you."

"I want to see it," Colleran told him. "Bring me a visual if you can."

A television screen image came through a field of interference. Then it appeared. Colleran crossed his arms and pondered what he saw as everyone else crowded around.

It was nothing at all like the barbarism that had torn through the *Judy Holliday*. It stood quite tall and was more-or-less humanoid, but its pitch-black skin made it difficult to see it clearly in the smoke-filled corridor as it ran. However, on its face—if, indeed, it could be said to have one—glowed a single red eye quite like an infrared scanner.

It's a perfect night-fighter, Colleran suddenly realized, feeling a tremblor of fear quake through him briefly. *This one's faster and more agile than the reptile that attacked the* Judy Holliday.

Jack Lounsbury quickly threw several switches on the console control board, and Colleran watched on the screen as a gigantic steel door clanged shut, blocking the beast's passage on that level.

"That won't hold it, Mr. Lounsbury," Mercy said behind him. "It's finding its way around all the passage seals."

Colleran nodded in agreement. "But that might work to our advantage. As long as it can be detoured, we might be able to stop it before it gets to this area."

"I sure as hell hope so," Lounsbury said. "But it hasn't worked so far."

Colleran touched his live-leather holster and at his urging, the holster coughed up his clasher.

Just then, Mercy said, "There it goes! It's found a way around the seal!"

She had been watching the hologram, and the black blip had begun heading down to another level by means of a vertical shaft that had itself been closed off from above.

Lounsbury's brows knitted. "I don't get it. It can't be that stupid."

"Why?" Colleran asked. "Where does that tunnel go?"

"That one goes down for about three miles. It's part of the ventilation grid. It can only go down, not up."

The blip on the holo—now where their video eyes could not pick it up—began to inch its way down the tunnel.

"It can see in the dark," Colleran affirmed. "It's not having the slightest problem moving."

The creature stopped and began moving horizontally again.

Then Lounsbury announced, "It's on the level below us. If we hurry, we can head it off there."

Colleran, however, was studying a larger chamber on the holo, which was just below them in the complex. "What's that place?"

Lounsbury frowned. "That's our fusion generator." And as soon as he said it, they all knew.

"Oh, sweet Jesus," Mercy said.

"Let's move," Colleran snapped, spinning around. He and Lounsbury were out of the control room before anyone else could react. Mercy sagged into Lounsbury's vacated chair.

Their tunnel cart now held another six men, each armed with the only weapons available to them: laser drills and power packs. They shuttled eastward toward the direction of the ruined gantries, powering down a long, glass-fused tunnel that was otherwise devoid of people. The creature would be coming at them from the opposite direction just one level below.

The cart stopped at a small crossroads juncture in the silvery tunnel, and the men scrambled out. A giant flat wall was before them: a steel door had been sealed, closing off that level. Guards stood there waiting. They were surprised to see a Regulator with their boss.

"This way, Mr. Colleran," Lounsbury said as the guards let them pass. A large service elevator was their destination.

They thundered in, crowding for space, and Lounsbury punched in for the level below. "This'll take us to the fusion facilities quickest. I should've thought of this right away. That thing has a plan in mind."

Colleran held his clasher tightly, feeling slightly claustrophobic in the elevator with the troop of grim miners. He said, "If it can shut down the mining facility by crippling the generator, it can kill everyone off at its leisure."

"Right," Lounsbury said. "Except for one thing."

"What's that?"

"With the generator down, we'd all suffocate, freeze, or burn anyway—depending on where we were in the facility. It knows what it's after."

The knuckles of all the miners went white around the grips of their laser drills.

A crowd of men and women were waiting for the elevator when it arrived at the station below. A woman in her fifties, whose eyes were big pools of seductive blue, stood before the others. She was rather hefty herself and seemed capable of ordering anyone around, including the beefiest miner.

However what startled Colleran was that the woman also wore a modest piece of jewelry just like the arrogant Mr. Johnson he had seen above. It was entirely out of place, Colleran thought, surrounded by so much griminess. *What strange people these are!*

Yet, the woman did not seem unduly alarmed.

"Where is it?" she asked Lounsbury as they stepped from the cage of the elevator.

"I thought you were tracking it!" Lounsbury bolted with genuine surprise. "Lila, you're supposed to—"

Colleran raced around them and out into the corridor. He stared eastward down the long silvery tunnel. It hadn't been blocked off yet.

He spun around and shouted, the fusion station's operation center glowing brightly behind them. "I want this place sealed off! Now!" he called.

Just like the aristocratic Mr. Johnson, the large woman here obviously did not like taking orders. At least not from him.

She turned to Lounsbury. "I want to be appraised of the situation first. He's got no authority—"

Lounsbury nearly exploded. "He *is* the Authority, you fool! Do as he says!"

"*I* run this place," she insisted. "Not you, not him. And I want to know what's going on."

Suddenly a sound filled the silvery corridor that seemed to come out of Satan's worst nightmare. Utterly unhuman, it cascaded around them, shaking the plastic windows of the fusion station, even causing one miner to drop his laser drill and stagger backward.

Lila blanched and put a manicured hand over her brooch as if to protect the ornament from the danger beyond.

"That's what's going on," Colleran shouted as everyone scattered back toward the station, away from the intersection of the fused corridors.

Colleran squinted down the silver tunnel where the lights had been shut off. He saw something move there. A glowing crimson orb danced for a brief spell as the creature sought its best avenue of approach.

Colleran leveled his clasher, but hesitated.

The woman rushed up to Colleran. "Well, shoot it! What are you waiting for?"

"It's too far away," he said. "And it's being careful. It knows that something's up."

The gemstone on her breast seemed to call attention to itself, a sign of rank or privilege. He felt suddenly contemptible of her, considering what lurked at the opposite end of the dark, smooth tunnel.

His holster swallowed his gun and he grabbed Lounsbury. "Give me lights in that section—" And quickly he pointed down the maw of the corridor, which seemingly could not contain the creature's continued raging.

Lila's ash-blonde curls bobbed as she looked from Colleran to Lounsbury, utterly perplexed.

"What's he doing?" she demanded. "Let's get this over with!"

Colleran ignored her and turned to the phalanx of miners with their ponderous laser packs. "You men seal the door shut when I'm inside. If you still hear noise in seven minutes, then you're on your own." They looked to one another, equally as confused as the fusion station boss. Colleran finished. "If I can't clash that thing, it'll come right through this door. It's after the fusion plant, nothing else. It might go around the door once it's sealed, but it'll probably try straight through first. So watch it."

The laser drills weren't weapons, but for short-range combat, they would do. Colleran knew, however, that if the creature got within thirty feet of those men, it would be too fast for them. He was going to have to clash it.

But first, he wanted to see it up close.

The miners, collectively, nodded and backed away as the large steel barrier began lowering on Lounsbury's command. The woman, Lila, however protested, acting as if she'd suddenly found herself surrounded by cowards.

"You're so brave, Mr. Regulator," she snapped.

Lounsbury jerked her back away from the descending door. "What is your problem? He's doing the best he can!"

"Hey!" she shouted at Lounsbury fiercely, "I told you to close down tunnels five and seven an hour ago. That would have done it!"

Colleran shook his head and stepped in front of the shield door within seconds of its closing. These *were* strange people.

The corridor lights became fully luminescent, extending down an eternally glowing silver tunnel. Colleran saw it. The creature crouched in a defensive position, a dark stain on a tapestry of shimmering silver. Its one red eye narrowed with hostility, watching.

Colleran ran directly at the beast. Enough was enough. These might be strange people, he told himself, but they were people nonetheless. Lila, whoever she was, was a troubled soul and would have to work out her own problems. Meanwhile there were a few things *he* could do.

The creature, sixty yards distant, suddenly dodged sideways, off into a side corridor Colleran hadn't seen on the schematic. It did so with a roar, crashing into some machinery that clattered madly in its wake. It was blocked off.

Colleran slowed to a careful walk, his heart hammering frantically in his chest. He was now within the range where the clasher would work most effectively, and he definitely wanted a direct line of fire for this one.

Then the lights flickered. And went out.

"*Oh, Christ!*" he blurted, rolling down on the floor in a judo tumble, off to the far side of the tunnel.

"Lounsbury!" he shouted out, hoping for either a video or audio feed still functioning somewhere above him. "*Lounsbury!*"

The creature still smashed its insensate way in the corridor just around the bend in the tunnel, and Colleran could suddenly hear the sizzle and sparkle of freed electricity. The creature had managed to find the tunnel's electrical conduits and had evidently yanked them out of the walls, flooding the place with darkness.

But no crimson slit opened itself to Colleran above the floor in the sudden darkness anywhere near him. No nightmare stalked him.

The creature, instead, had found a way around the corridor and had no apparent intent of facing any Regulator. Perhaps the challenge wasn't great enough. He should have known. It was after something much more valuable and challenging.

Colleran jumped to his feet, clasher out, but he was still blind. He ran slowly toward the bend in the corridor, following what sounds he could make out. He *had* to.

Then quite suddenly, everything was quiet.

The creature had ceased its mindless rampage. Or was it just reconsidering? Perhaps it was waiting for the humans to make the next move. After all, Colleran reasoned, that would be the smart thing.

A spectral show of eerie lights came, sporadic bursts of yellows and reds from the snapped electrical leads in the corridor around the bend to his right. Smoke stung his nostrils with an acrid caress.

Seconds later the entire corridor shook with a gut-deep rumbling. And with it came the creature's strained voice, but this time sounding muffled or distant.

Colleran stumbled through the darkness toward the tear in the walls where the wires had been severed. Coughing and slugging his way through the smoke, he staggered into what appeared to be some kind of minor maintenance station, most of which was on fire. Several electrical cables, very much alive and dangerous, snaked around the floor where the creature had tossed them.

However, the creature was not in that corridor.

Instead, it had found another corridor and had gone into it, a corridor, Colleran suddenly realized with horror, that would take it to the fusion-generating plant.

Now Colleran heard the screams. Human screams, and female at that.

He ran out into the corridor, through a hole in a bracing wall the creature had made in its flight, and found himself back where he had started from: the fusion plant. But he suddenly froze.

The creature lay dead, apparently, skewered from the greenish lances of close-range laser drill bursts. Indeed, one miner still snarled away at the creature's head, but Lounsbury had already begun shutting down his power pack. It was over.

However, the humans had sustained one loss. The creature's hands were tightly wound around the upper torso of Lila, whose legs still spasmed in their death throes. The creature had made no attempt to get to the fusion plant, choosing to die right where it had stumbled upon the plant supervisor.

Two miners were down on their knees vomiting and Colleran felt the urge to join them. However, he managed to hold back.

Something deep within him told him to get used to occasions such as these.

7

"Are you all right?"

The voice of Brianne Sagar appeared almost out of nowehere in the cordoned-off hallway just beyond the fusion plant.

"I think so," Colleran said distractedly. "Sure."

The tiny woman strode authoritatively into the center of the corridor where the lanced hulk of the creature lay. It was now beginning to stink from its own decay, having lain where it had been killed for over twenty hours.

The tincture of death, though, had made Colleran woozy, and for a brief instant as he pondered the creature, waiting for the Admin to arrive, he had to fight back his natural inclination to evoke Beatrice. The stress of the last day and night had suppressed the urge of his brain to counteract it all by summoning a Lei experience. And that was something he truly did not need at the moment.

The mining colony of Surane Four had re-established its daily routines in most of the untouched sectors by the time the *Parvardigar*, using its big Andreesen engines, spindled into orbit above the barren planet. With the further assistance of Jack Lounsbury and his team, Colleran had blocked off the corridor where the creature lay. But despite the forced ventilation in the tunnel, the stench of death was everywhere.

The woman who had perished so unpleasantly in the creature's last desperate stand had been removed long ago. Colleran had done his best to blot out his memory of her; he'd seen much in his long life. Still, her feet kicking in their last motions stayed with him. It must have been a terrifying death.

Large lights on high poles were set in place around the dead beast as several Authority and Cronin Reach supervisors examined it. Elsewhere in the colony, engineers were busy rebuilding the gantries and lift platforms so that those miners who wanted to leave could. There was no shortage of departers, and Colleran made note of the fact that Johnson of the purple tunic and bejeweled stickpin was first in line. Colleran wished him good riddance.

An elevator arrived at the corridor and a young man in a white pathologist's tunic stepped out. He had a face mask bunched under his chin and he toted a bag bursting with instruments. Several assistants were with him. The pathologist was bearded, exuberant, and almost grotesquely happy over what he was being given the opportunity to do.

"Dr. Hathaway's been briefed on these attacks," Brianne Sagar told Colleran as the young medical examiner came around them.

"You must be Lou Colleran." The youth shook Colleran's gloved hand. "Hathaway. James Hathaway. I hear you've got a degree in exobiology, too."

Colleran nodded modestly and managed an embarrassed smile. "One of seven. Most of them useless, I'm afraid."

Hathaway's eyes were already on the creature even as he spoke. "I know how it is. Every new habitable planet discovered rewrites all the textbooks." He looked up at the lanky Colleran. "How old are you?"

"Four-hundred and some."

"I'm only one-thirty myself." He grinned at the black bulk of the dead beast before them. "God, I love this." He stepped over the cordon and went at the creature as if it were a playground and he was a child with all sorts of wonderful things to dig up. He tied up his face mask, and he and his assistants began to work.

"Where'd you get him?" Colleran whispered aside to Brianne. She said, "Found him on our doorstep."

"Oh."

Jack Lounsbury, now wearing a clean supervisor's tunic, stood beside Colleran, watching the young pathologist go about his examination. Several video techs were taping the process at every angle, moving in and out carefully catching it all.

Lounsbury accepted the presence of so many Regulators much

easier than the other Cronin executives topside at the main complex. However, he was acting somewhat nervous and Colleran noticed this.

"What?" he asked. "What is it?"

Lounsbury shuffled, looked down at his boots, then squinted at the creature. "Might be my imagination."

Brianne Sagar, arms folded beneath her breasts, looked up at Lounsbury. "What do you mean?"

Lounsbury's dark eyes were like small creatures huddling with fear. "It's hard to say, exactly."

"Say it," Colleran urged. "It might help."

"At this stage, anything will help," the Admin commented.

Lounsbury looked behind him. Others of his crew were at the large windows at the fusion station, most of whom were watching the examination of the creature.

He said, "There've been rumors lately."

"What kind of rumors?" Colleran asked.

"Well, that the Cronins were in some kind of trouble. Not us here on Surane Four," he quickly added. "We rarely see any of the Cronin family, maybe once a year. But production had been stepped up and there was talk of an exchange of personnel."

Looking deep into Lounsbury's troubled eyes, Colleran allowed his intuition to take over. He saw instead . . . *fields of endless green grass . . . wind in trees for which he had no name. . . .*

Brianne Sagar's voice snapped the oncoming Lei experience. She said, "We've been going over the Cronin's records. They seem to be up to standard with only minor violations. They're not in any kind of trouble that we know of. Of course, there's always competition with the other Reaches in the Mandala. But that's none of our business."

Lounsbury shrugged. "I don't know what it was. We've gone through a lot of administrative changes. People we never heard of coming and going. It kind of stirred things up. But when *this* thing happened—" He pointed to the creature being picked over by the examination team. "When this happened, it made me think of the last Reach war."

Colleran and Sagar exchanged sudden, knowing looks.

Colleran pursed his lips and spoke slowly. "Well, yes. That had occurred to us, too. But the last Reach war was about seventy years ago. It had nothing to do with the Cronins and was fought in Beta Spoke."

"That was before my time," Lounsbury said without the slightest trace of resentment. Few mortals got along well with the immortals of the Authority. Lounsbury seemed more self-confident and centered as an individual than most. He went on. "But the rumors are that a Reach war is building up topside."

"What do you mean 'topside'—here?" the Admin asked.

"No, not here," Lounsbury said, but then he changed his mind. "On the other hand, they *did* attack us. Did a goddamn good job of it too."

Colleran gave Brianne a quick glance. Her hazel eyes were now a bright blue, which meant that she was *very* interested in this bit of discourse.

To her, Colleran said, "Are we sure the Cronins are clean?"

"Positive," she insisted. "They've even volunteered to fork over their entire financial database, employee shareholding information, pension funds investments—everything. They're hiding nothing from us. At least nothing that we'd be interested in."

Hell, Colleran reflected, *even I don't do that.* The ARS, the Authority Revenue Service, was everyone's nemesis. But this was serious if the Cronins were yielding up their private business holdings. It could mean one of two things: Either the Cronins had nothing to hide from the Authority, or they had a great deal to hide and needed the proximity of the Regulators with their preserver overhead to protect them. If a Reach war was brewing somewhere in Alpha Spoke, the Cronins would need some kind of defense. The *Parvardigar* would do the trick.

"But," Lounsbury meditated aloud, "where did *this* thing come from? I didn't think Reach wars were fought with commando units."

"Usually, they aren't," Brianne said. Drills were now buzzing as the medical examiner and his team started to penetrate the seemingly solid outer skin of the beast. Dr. Hathaway was singing to himself. The Admin continued in the midst of all the noise. "Reach wars are usually fought the way Lost Earth corporations went at each other. Unfair competition, unfriendly takeover bids, corporate espionage. Although sometimes they actually got right down to it and hired mercenaries to eliminate their rivals. But the last Reach war wasn't fought that way."

"Well," Lounsbury said, sounding frustrated, "this one seems to be fought with mercenaries, unless someone's jungle beast got shipped to the wrong place."

They watched in silence as Hathaway dug his arms deep into an undefinable area above the creature's chest.

Lounsbury turned to Colleran. "Didn't you say that something like this had attacked another place?"

Colleran nodded. "Right. Okeanos. A few days ago."

"Okeanos," Lounsbury mouthed, shaking his head. "What do they do there? Are they a mining operation, too?"

Colleran flushed with a tinge of embarrassment. He was the only one there in the chamber with a golden tan and sun-bleached hair. He said, "They're a vacation and resort Reach on a water world a few light-years from here, in toward the Hub."

"And they were attacked by one of these things?"

"Not quite one of these," the Admin jumped in. "We don't know what it was. It got away."

An automated medicart was being loaded with several sample tubes from the creature by an assistant when Dr. Hathaway, bespattered with clotted creature blood, spoke loudly down to them from his lofty perch. "Admin, I think you might be interested in this."

The three of them climbed over the barricades and stepped closer to where the stench was wretchedly distinct.

Hathaway spoke to his assistant, also spattered with slime and necrotic fluids. "Lynn, hand me a number three lockwrench."

"Right," the tech said. The wrench came up.

"What have you got?" Sagar asked.

The number three lockwrench went down into the skull of the creature and came up again in Hathaway's capable hands. At its tip was clutched something solid. Hathaway shook away some adhering brain matter. He pulled his mask down and for once looked serious. He held up the lockwrench.

"I wouldn't have expected this," he announced, pondering what the wrench held. To them, he said, "This animal's unlike anything I've ever seen, living or dead. But it is organic, totally. Except for this thing."

It seemed to be a glasslike accretion, perhaps a crystal about half an inch in diameter. It caught the bright lights around it in such a way as to glow ever so slightly.

Lynn, the masked tech, held out a stainless steel bowl into which Dr. Hathaway dropped the object with a noisy rattle. He then said, "The answer to your next question is 'I don't know.'

But I intend to find out when we get back on the *Parvardigar*. It doesn't belong in there, and I'm *real* curious as to what it is."

The tech put a cap over the specimen. Hathaway went back to work on the beast.

At that moment, from far behind them at the door to the fusion station, a station supervisor—a new one—appeared and called out for the Admin.

"Admin Sagar," she hailed. "There's a priority call coming down from topside for you. It's from the preserver. You want to take it?"

Sagar spun around and jogged to the entrance to the fusion facility. It sounded serious.

Colleran, meantime, took the specimen bowl and lifted the lid. The glass bead, still tainted by the fluids of the creature, seemed a very faint lavender color. Inside it were tiny streaks or flaws. It seemed like a dirty piece of drift-glass one might find in a tidepool. That it came from inside the huge creature repulsed him greatly. He gave the bowl back to the tech, who in turn placed it among the other samples.

Brianne Sagar was gone for only minutes, but when she returned to the barricades she wore a long look on her face and her eyes were filled with trouble. Or perhaps sorrow.

"What is it?" Colleran asked.

"Kit Brodie's been killed," she said.

8

As Colleran waited for his spindle engines to powerdown on the rain-puddled landing field on Asarhaddon Four, he pondered the glowing-green list of names on his computer screen: the Tally. Already, Kit Brodie's name had been added. In the time it had taken Colleran to spindle away from the airless rock of Surane

Four, the experts who kept track of such things had already
verified Brodie's death and punched it into the permanent record
of all known immortals who had died in the service of the
Authority. *The Tally*.

Although Brodie was a much younger immortal, he had been
one of the few real friends Colleran had. Friends tended to vanish
if one was an immortal and the friend wasn't. If time and death
didn't ruin the friendship, alienation did. Colleran rarely consulted
the Tally for it was the literal graveyard of both friends and family,
and now Brodie's name had been lodged there as if carved on a
marble tombstone in a lonely field of witchgrass and occasional
delphiniums. And though they had rarely consorted together
during their off-duty hours, it hurt nonetheless to know that he was
dead. It hurt just as much to see, several names before Brodie's,
the name of a great, great, great-granddaughter of his own, who
had recently perished in the Epsilon Spoke. Colleran switched it
off. His world was slowly emptying itself of the familiar.

Asarhaddon Four was an earth-normal planet quite close to the
mysterious Hub. Indeed, its blue skies and herds of cumulus
clouds could have been transported directly from the climes of the
Lost Earth. Here, creatures similar to birds coasted in the
oceanside air of the port city and tiny, insectlike things burrowed
in the grasses. It constantly gave Colleran the impression that the
Makers of the Mandala worlds had the Lost Earth in mind when
they located the Hub near the star now called Asarhaddon.

And like the Lost Earth civilizations before the great migration,
life here on Asarhaddon Four was a melange of nations with vast
corporate and mercantile interests. The planet was one of the first
in the Alpha Spoke to be enthusiastically colonized by the
migrating humans. Asarhaddon Four, as such, could claim a
planetary population of over two and a half billion. It was a busy
place.

No one Reach in particular governed Asarhaddon Four, but
most of the planet's commercial activity centered around the huge,
oceanside city of Anshar, which would have rivaled the nearly
mythical New York City for its power and influence. The
Authority's central headquarters for Asarhaddon Four was located
there, and Colleran had set down on their private landing field.

Colleran felt the smooth palm of ocean air drift across his face
as he walked away from his spindle. And for an instant he felt a

fleeting moment of peace—not a Lei experience, but a genuine space of tranquility. However, that vanished when he saw who was waiting for him beside an Authority aircar.

Executive Mtazi Hardt was the tallest woman he had ever known. Her folk hailed from a tribe of South Africans back on the Lost Earth called the Ndebeles. Her people had been "allowed" to spindle away in one of the last migratory jumps by the landed Afrikaners who were slowly coming back into power. They saw the migration as a convenient way of getting rid of undesirables. Mtazi Hardt's people were happy to go.

However, the tall and beautiful black woman was not happy at the moment. Her Exec badge scintillated brightly on her chest as she waited for him to cross the field to the car. Her black-and-silver against the sterile white of the aircar and the flat gray of the cement concourse made her stand out strongly. She seemed an exclamation to the seriousness of the situation.

Colleran handed the driver of the car his travel bags and looked up at the graceful Exec. She was the only person in the Authority he *had* to look up to.

"I take it that we've got a situation on our hands," he said to her.

Mtazi Hardt nodded, holding the door open for Colleran, who quickly climbed inside. "You could say that," she said calmly.

Colleran knew that few Execs actually drove out to meet incoming Regulators, even a Three Spoke Regulator, of which there were perhaps twenty—and that depended on when one consulted the Tally. Exec Hardt, though, was more concerned than anything else.

"We've closed the port down," she said tersely as the aircar lifted itself above the mirrors of puddles on the concourse. She continued, "And we've been running crosschecks on all incoming and outgoing shipments."

Colleran looked at her, surprised. "Just here in Anshar, or—"

"Everywhere around the planet. No one's getting on or off without Regulators bending a few noses."

The aircar threaded the spires and helixes of the towering buildings of the city.

She turned to him. She had known Brodie quite well. "You'll see why when we get to where Brodie was killed."

Colleran could sense the woman's keen authority just by feeling the timbre in her voice. He could also feel it in her age. According

to last count, there were few immortals in the service of the
Authority as old as he, but Mtazi Hardt came close. In her eyes
churned the knowledge of all she had witnessed, both as a
Regulator long ago, and more recently as an Executive on the
Authority Council. *This* is *serious*, Colleran realized, calling to
mind the names in luminous green on the Tally.

The city's sprawling grid spread out below them. Ground traffic
moved among the suburbs, monorails sped through their above-
ground tubes. Dozens of helicopters flitted like impatient insects
here and there. Colleran even saw a laputa hovering at the far
north of the city, another hotel belonging to another resort industry
Reach. It was an ordinary day in Anshar. Life as usual. Just ask
the lone water-skiier being pulled behind a foaming white vector
on the Stillion River, which meandered through Anshar. Colleran
almost envied him his freedom. Whoever he was.

"The *Parvardigar* is on its way," Colleran informed his boss of
bosses. "As soon as the pathology team gets the Surane Four
creature on board. Brianne estimates thirty hours at most."

Mtazi Hardt's dark eyes didn't seem pleased. "The Surane
caliban. I'll want to see it."

"The what?"

The aircar followed the twist of the Stillion River to where the
city itself had begun to thin out. The rectangles of an industrial
park, with its warehouses and factories, began to appear instead.

"That's what we're classifying them as. Calibans," she
reported. "Prospero's barely human servant from *The Tempest*.
Shakespeare."

He gritted his teeth. "I know. I've got a doctorate in English,
remember? Three-hundred and eight years out of date, but I still
recall my Shakespeare." He delved back into his enjambed
memory. He quoted, "'This thing of darkness I/Acknowledge
mine.' That sound about right?"

"Good," Exec Hardt said. "Maybe you can use your Shakespeare with your other six Ph.d.'s to help us figure out what we've
got. I hope they're a bit more practical."

"They are," he said. The name had more poetry to it than the
beasts actually deserved. For now, *caliban* would do.

Unless they wanted to call them the Suras, the gods of the
Wheel of Life—the Mandala. But that was unthinkable.

The aircar came in at rooftop level over a row of undistinguished warehouses. A laputa landing and lift field was a mile to

the east where materials were off-loaded and on-loaded. One warehouse, though, was surrounded by police cars from Anshar itself with several Authority aircars like black beetles squatting among them.

Colleran also noticed that there weren't any pesky newschoppers hovering about anywhere near the warehouse district. *This is bad*, Colleran suddenly realized. *A total news black-out and a planetwide records search. . . .*

A man wearing a shabby police tunic—and soaking wet up to his thighs from wading in water somewhere—came up to the aircar the instant it set down near the police barricades.

The Exec introduced Colleran to the man. "This is Lieutenant Farinas. It's his jurisdiction."

His clipped mustache belied the policeman's unkempt appearance. He seemed more concerned with the messy job at hand than with what he looked like to passersby. The wind ruffled his deep brown hair. He wasn't an immortal, but to Colleran he didn't seem to mind the presence of Regulators.

"I heard that the Regulator was a friend of yours, Mr. Colleran," Farinas said, shaking his hand. "I'm sorry."

Mtazi Hardt walked beside them as they headed directly for the wide, open door to one warehouse in particular. Colleran didn't miss the appearance of a police riot tank nearby nor the ten police guards with pulse guns.

"And I'm sorry about the mess, too," Farinas said as they stepped into the interior of the warehouse.

Inside, it was as if someone had brought home a friendly tornado to play with. Boxes and crates—none of which were bolted or secured to walls or floor as they were on the *Judy Holliday*—had been tossed everywhere, along with their varied contents. Fruits, machine parts, skeins of clothing and textiles, and huge spools of wiring were all thrown about, most of it a complete loss for their owners.

"What happened?" Colleran asked the police lieutenant.

Farinas sighed, rubbing a film of sweat from his creased forehead. "It's hard to say. There aren't any witnesses. But from what we can piece together, Regulator Brodie came here with a standard-issue search warrant and began specifically with this group over here."

Ahead of them, flanked by Regulators with their Langstrom clashers, was a row of irregular boxes, crates, and aluminum alloy

canisters. One big canister was tipped over and its shipping seal—
about four feet square—had been broken.

From the inside.

Mtazi Hardt crossed her long arms and surveyed the damage for
the second time that day. She said, "Two warehouse workers were
also killed by the . . . caliban . . . that evidently got Brodie."

Colleran sucked in his breath trying to imagine the caliban that
attacked his friend. "Who were the warehouse victims?"

Farinas said, "They were part of the day shift. A third worker
was busy clearing the search warrant with headquarters when it
happened."

Colleran then noticed the smell. It was the same as that from the
beast the miners had slain on Surane Four. Much of what he
smelled was coming from the open ends of the alloyed canister,
but some of it lay slimed on the floor.

Colleran looked inside the canister and his worst fears were
confirmed. It contained an egg, although an egg of an unusual
sort: it seemed to conform to much of the inside of the canister
itself. *Made to match*, he thought. *Someone's got access to some
very advanced technology. Unless, of course, we're dealing with
the Makers.*

He kept his thoughts, dark as they were, to himself. Every eye
in the place was on him. Gossip had already spread among the
other officers and Regulators; everyone now knew his role in this
affair.

"Who owns the warehouse itself?" he asked the soggy lieutenant.

"The land is owned by the county, but it's leased to a holding
company run by a group known locally as Riocello Associates."

"What's their link with the Abou-Farhaats?" Colleran queried.
"Or is there one?"

Mtazi Hardt said, "We're working on that now. But it looks as
if the Riocellos are in the clear. Their tax docket and licensing
records are completely legitimate. Accurate even. The Riocellos
own dozens of storage facilities and warehouses like this one, and
like a lot of corporations and Reaches, they deal with the Abou-
Farhaats constantly.

Colleran pondered the boxes and scattered crates, as well as the
other canisters along the wall. He could picture how Brodie would
have gone about his investigation. He'd have arrived with a

regulation search warrant, and the Riocellos, or a representative, would have said, *Sure, go ahead, take a look.* And the boistrous Brodie, along with two ordinary, but unsuspecting, warehouse workers, would begin examining the most recent cache of goods brought in by the Abou-Farhaats.

Then quite suddenly, as one particular canister was being taken apart, the *thing* within, feeling some kind of imminent threat, would have leapt out with all of its stored might. With Brodie eliminated—along with the use of a Langstrom clasher—the other two men would have had no chance. Even had they gotten hold of the clasher, their body frequencies would not have allowed it to work. The ensuing struggle would have then spread throughout this section of the large warehouse, knocking over and destroying what crates were in the way.

Colleran noticed that the interior of the mammoth storage facility was puddled with flat lakes of water. Most of the Anshar policemen were also soaking wet as well.

"Where'd the water come from?" he asked.

Lieutenant Farinas glanced down at his trousers and boots. The waterline had gone clear up to his crotch.

He said, "Before my men and I arrived, the other personnel here had to fight the . . . organism . . . the best way they could. There were only some fire extinguishers and water hoses."

"Organism," Colleran said, thoughtfully. "Why do you call it an organism?" There was a curiously warm feeling beginning to take form in the back of his brain.

The statuesque Hardt cleared her throat. "The caliban wasn't quite formed yet. It seems to have been mostly ameboid protoplasm with some kind of chitin or interior bone structure to give it form."

Lieutenant Farinas evidently had not been briefed by the Authority on the other caliban incursions. He proceeded as if the one that attacked Brodie had been the only one in existence.

Still, the lieutenant seemed more astonished by the ferocity of the creature's attack than anything else. He said, "The warehouse personnel, once they heard what was going on, tried fighting it with water, tried holding it off. When we got here, my men and myself, the organism had disappeared."

"Disappeared?" The tingling in his brain had suddenly become more pronounced. A Lei experience was approaching and he didn't know why. . . .

Lieutenant Farinas, whose mustache and manner indicated that he was probably under normal circumstances a very dapper man, tugged almost childlike at his soaked pants. "It found its way into a drain grid." He pointed off to the far end of the cavernous warehouse where a considerable amount of debris was jumbled and guards stood waiting. He continued, "It tore its way through and disappeared into a storm sewer underneath."

For a frightening, disconnected moment, Colleran thought that he was going to swoon. *The creature loose in the sewers!* He almost could feel the wind off the plains of Mount Meru at his back, the diaphanous gown of Beatrice fluttering nearby.

No, he said to himself, thinking instead of Brodie, thinking instead of Heidi. *Not now. There's time for that later.*

"Are you all right?" Exec Hardt asked him, taking notice that something might be wrong.

"I'm fine," he acknowledged. He rested his hand on the sealed flap of his living holster, feeling it tremble with transferred anxiety.

Farinas concluded. "But we were on to it by the time it got into the sewer, and we had the county close the sewage line." There were no windows in the place, but Farinas seemed to stare at a point beyond the warehouse. "If it would've gotten into the Stillion River, we would've had a problem. Anshar itself is only a half-hour float downstream and there's nothing in between to stop it, especially in its protoplasmic form. Christ," he said, shaking his head, "I'd sure like to know what the hell that thing was."

Colleran rubbed his brow. A small blue sun seemed to be tunneling into existence at the base of his skull.

"I want to see Brodie," he said.

An ambulance aircar waited silently, its engine purring as the attendants let Colleran into the back door. A dark, green body bag was unzipped for him to see.

Stagnant winds from the marshes beyond the warehouses mixed with the digestive juices still filming Brodie's body. Colleran turned away.

"My God," he gasped.

Digestive fluids were hard at work on Brodie's upper body. Only the special alloyed metal of his Regulator's badge seemed resistant to the harsh acids the creature had contained. But now the badge seemed pinned to bone rather than tunic. Brodie's face was gone.

"Go," Colleran said, backing away. The attendants hurried to close the door. They didn't much like the sight either.

A hawklike creature, indigenous to Asarhaddon Four, knifed the air above the warehouse district, crying out for its dinner. It had one of its many eyes on something scurrying for cover in the reeds near the Stillion.

Colleran turned on his heel back to where Lieutenant Farinas and the black Executive were waiting. This was his show, his move.

"I want to see it," he informed them.

The Exec barely nodded to the lieutenant. She said, "I'll wait here. Go ahead."

Colleran found himself grimly escorted to an open manhole just behind the warehouse where the asphalt ended and the marsh grasses began. Guards—both Authority and Anshar police—stood ready.

Approaching one of the guards, Farinas asked, "Is Bo still down there?"

"Yes, sir," the guard reported stiffly.

"Good," the lieutenant said, then proceeded down a waiting ladder.

The sewer tunnel clearly was not that old, evidence of the growth that the city of Anshar was still experiencing. The warehouse district was relatively new, and the brick lining of the inwardly curving walls of the sewer line had hardly had time to cultivate scum of any kind.

But Colleran didn't care. With his clasher out of its organic holster, he followed Lieutenant Farinas through ankle-deep waters down the capacious tunnel. Overhead, the police special tactic squad had strung emergency lights to guide their way.

They came to an intersection where a threesome of Anshar police met them. A skinny officer in protective armor, and thoroughly soaked, stood up. He wore goggles on his head.

"You're too late," the young officer reported.

"Sergeant Bo," the lieutenant began. "This is Regulator Colleran. He was a friend of the other—"

He didn't continue; Sergeant Bo knew.

Colleran walked around them, peering down the tunnel opposite from the one Sergeant Bo had indicated. "Where did you stop it?" he asked.

"Over this way," Bo said. "It's not far."

They slogged through the water, now getting knee-deep as the tunnel leaned downward toward the aquifer of the Stillion River.

Sergeant Bo pointed to a solid wall of reinforced metal, which had been dropped from above, blocking off the drainage tunnel.

He turned to Colleran; the muscles of his face seemed tight. "As soon as we knew where it was heading, we got the county's computers to trace the tunnel and seal it off. But when we got here, this is all we found."

Colleran watched as the unarmed Bo—either bravely or stupidly—bent over into the sludge and groped around in the foul water. He pulled up what seemed to be a partial skeleton. Colleran jerked back slightly as the sergeant held it up before him. It was now just an assembly of cartilage and bone splinters, the color of mother-of-pearl, almost pristine.

Already it was decomposing.

Bo said, "I think the water was acting on it even as it tried to get away."

The cartilage didn't even look like it belonged inside of anything, let alone a beast.

Bo dropped it back beneath the brownish soup. Colleran felt his heart drop with it as well. There was nothing here to account for Brodie's death.

Then the sergeant reached into a pocket on his armored vest. "However, we did find something of interest. At least, *I* think it's interesting."

He handed over a small, shiny object to Colleran's waiting hand. Tiny sparkles glistened off it, lavender with touches of carnelian.

"I can't figure what it is," Sergeant Bo said. "But then, that's not my job."

Colleran held it up to one of the emergency lights overhead. "I think I know," he muttered.

It was an awkwardly shaped crystal, a jewel.

"You found it where?" he asked the tactic squad officer.

Bo pointed to the sunken remains. "It was attached to the dissolving skeleton. I pulled it out before it got lost in the water."

Colleran felt Beatrice nearby and could almost smell the flowers of the plains where she lived—even in this dingy, disgusting place.

The jewel in his hand was exactly like the jewels he'd seen abandoned in the suites on board the *Judy Holliday*. It was the same color, the same size. Indeed, it could have been one of them.

9

Mtazi Hardt's mild perfume seemed to remind him of something. Something far off, indescribably distant. The elegant African woman's natural musk, mingled with the subtle perfume she wore, shifted the back reaches of his mind to . . . *sawtoothed mountains on the horizon, snowcapped . . . plains of purples and greens, grasses and flowers . . . and there in the midst of it all are the ruins. . . .*

He and the Exec stood behind a wall of thick, protective duraplast glass, watching several waldos dangle from the ceiling on the other side as a good dozen of the caliban canisters and crates were being examined. Colleran seemed to absorb Mtazi Hardt's unique aura and briefly allowed a Lei experience to seep through the hemispheres of his brain.

The Exec caught Colleran's mood with a cagey, sideways glance. "Are you all right, Lou?" she asked, worried.

Colleran, standing at the window, toyed with the artifact from the beast that killed Kit Brodie, unaware that he was doing so. He shook his head slightly, wiping away the vision of the ruins of Meru and the suggestion of Beatrice who had been nearby.

"I think so," he said weakly. "It's been a bad few days."

A bevy of service technicians were manipulating the long arms of the waldos, dragging fluoroscopes before the suspected caliban canisters. It had taken them four hours to move all of the canisters to this location, which was a special Authority analysis facility close to the Anshar spaceport.

Mtazi Hardt smiled at him in an almost motherly way. "Just how old are you, anyway?"

Colleran considered the question. "Why?"

The Exec shrugged, turning her attention back to the drama transpiring on the other side of the duraplast wall. She said, "They've got a drug now for us older folks. Its short name is metatryzine."

"What's its long name?"

"Something with fifty-eight letters and six numbers in it."

"What's the drug for?" Colleran tried to appear disinterested. But he knew it wasn't working.

"Metatryzine is a Lei suppressant," the Exec related. "They've been working on it for decades, now that some of us immortals are living longer than they thought possible."

Colleran felt suddenly chagrined that his Lei experiences showed themselves so obviously. "I didn't know they were that bad," he said in a low voice.

"Brianne has mentioned to me that you've been experiencing some unusual Lei episodes. At your age, or so they say, the visions are supposed to be quite intense. Metatryzine is relatively new and it seems to work."

Almost under his breath, he said, "I don't know if I want them suppressed, to tell you the truth."

Exec Hardt crossed her thin arms and smiled ruefully. "I know what you mean. I'm just beginning to get them. That's how I found out about the drug."

"How old are you?" he dared ask.

"You're not supposed to ask a lady her age," she whispered to him. Some of the techs had been watching.

Colleran understood. The Lei phenomenon occurred in those older men and women who'd undergone the Kotlicky-Powell gene-splice centuries ago. The gene-splicing technique amplified normal immune system macrophages, which in turn did two things. First, it allowed a more efficient regenerating of nerve and muscle cells, and second, it vastly increased the ability of white blood cells to curtail the spread of diseases. However, over the long, *long* term—three centuries was the median cut-off—for whatever reason, the memory-retention capacities of the neocortex in the brain began to shrink the vital linkages of the corpus callosum, which connects the right half of the brain with the left half. The Lei phenomena were somehow tied into endorphin levels and massive surges of intuitive responses to so many accumulated memories. Each immortal had his or her own unique Lei episodes, and while they were rarely spoken about, Colleran knew that they began occurring in the early to mid three hundreds.

"I'm three-forty-two," Mtazi Hardt said at last. "When you can, consult your Hopkins mode and ask him for a mild dosage to begin with and see how you get along with it."

"I'll give it some thought," he conceded.

Lieutenant Farinas walked in through a back door. For him, it was afterhours, but as far as he was concerned, he was still on duty. He'd gotten himself a clean tunic and dry boots.

The Exec and Colleran met him near a tech who was examining a large canister through the agency of a computer scanner. Farinas had some news for them.

He said, "We've got the storage manifest from the Riocello people and with them came some dates."

Colleran listened, but he also watched the scanner, which the tech—with the use of the waldo inside the room—had placed before the canister.

Farinas continued. "Even though these twelve crates came in together on the same shipment, they're all scheduled to be picked up on different dates." He pointed at the canister presently being scanned. "This one right here is the first on the list. The one that got your associate was fifth on the list."

"Where is this one supposed to go, then?" Colleran asked.

"We don't know," Farinas confessed. "I've faxed the list to your boss—" Farinas blushed, glancing up at the imposing Exec. "I mean to Admin Sagar on the *Parvardigar*. It's her decision now, I guess."

The Exec nodded. "That's right. The Admin'll make her decision accordingly and pass along recommendations to us on the Council."

Farinas sweated as if he'd just committed some kind of bureaucratic slipup. He went on quickly to hide his discomfort. "Anyway, we don't know where the shipment's bound, only that the register indicated rental space for just a few days."

"That isn't usual," Colleran said. "Goods remain in storage for great periods of time." He leaned against the clear wall of impenetrable plastic and tapped his gloved fingers on its smooth surface. He looked at the Exec. "I wonder, though, if maybe one of these guys here might have been meant for the Riocellos."

"Possibly," the Exec said thoughtfully. To Farinas, she said, "The Riocello Associates have any enemies?"

"What man or woman in business *doesn't* have enemies?" Farinas said with a touch of frustration in his voice. "There are only a small group of worlds that aren't in some way involved in our capitalistic system, and those worlds don't feed into the tax system of the Authority."

"The old Russians," Colleran muttered. "Maybe they're behind this."

He thought it unlikely, however. The Soviets had a massive space program when the Hub was first discovered, and they quickly spindled off into the starry reaches of the Alpha Spoke along with all the rest. However, over the years, the Marxist dream of a unified mankind collapsed when each world went its own way. What few true Communist worlds remained were part of an isolated Soviet Federation in the barely inhabited Eta Spoke, where the Authority left them alone. The several preservers in the Authority fleet made sure that Soviet expansionist dreams contained themselves to the Eta Spoke. *No*, Colleran mused. *Forget the Soviets. . . .*

"We're checking on the Riocellos, though," Farinas said. "But they're considered innocent so far. Victims like the rest."

The female tech manipulating the waldo beside them gasped when the canister came into full view in the screen.

"It's one of them, all right," Colleran said, staring into the scanner. The fluoroscopic image startled them all.

The canister was of a sturdy, lightweight aluminum alloy and it was still bound tightly together by its steel shipping bands. But as they saw on the scanning screen, inside of it was *something* in the midstages of evolution. A coil of alien flesh wrapped around a structure of bones that seemed destined to become a caliban, the likes of which he hadn't seen before. Intestines twisted in fluids pulsating pinkishly on the screen, and incipient legs seemed folded up, claws sheathed, beneath what looked to be the segments of a knifelike tail. The room full of techs paused over their waldo controls and were silent, almost reverentially so.

To Colleran, it was like being in the armory on board a preserver, faced with twelve deadly solar bombs ticking away.

Lieutenant Farinas slowly looked up at Mtazi. "So, you want to tell me what we're looking at?"

"That's what we're trying to find out," she answered in a reassuring voice, loud enough to be heard by the assembly of techs.

The female tech rotated the container through the use of her waldo arms and hands. They allowed the canister to afford them a different view of its contents through the scanner.

Again, the tech inhaled audibly. "What's *that?*"

Farinas bent over the screen to see just what it was she was indicating. "Where?" he asked.

But Colleran could see it. In fact, in his right hand he held one.

The beast growing within the silver canister apparently had an arrow-shaped skull. However, inside of it there seemed to hover, suspended in the gelatinous growth of its developing brain matter, an object that—theoretically—shouldn't have been there.

"It's another one of our jewels," Exec Hardt affirmed.

The crystal in the embryonic creature's skull seemed to be exactly the same size as the one in Colleran's hand, as if it had achieved all the growth it was going to while the rest of the animal's body continued to evolve. It had many of the same features—at least as far as Colleran could make out—as did the stone removed from the head of the slain beast in the dim tunnels of Surane Four.

"This beats anything I've ever seen," Farinas admitted.

Behind them, the door to the examination room wheezed open and Brianne Sagar walked in followed by three other Authority personnel. She acknowledged the techs and Lieutenant Farinas, but she spoke directly to Colleran and her superior, Exec Hardt.

"We need to talk," she said, glancing up at them both.

"Continue your scan," the Exec said to the techs, and she and Colleran removed themselves to an outer hallway where Brianne could brief them.

Admin Sagar had brought with her a small printout, and this she handed over to Colleran. "This is the passenger manifest from the *Judy Holliday*. There were some bogus names on it and it's taken this long to trace them down. But it might be the best lead we've got so far."

"What about the Abou-Farhaats?" the Exec asked as Colleran perused the manifest.

None of the lovelies, he noted, had been listed. Not even among the dead.

Brianne Sagar's eyes glinted challengingly and she actually smiled. She said, "The Abou-Farhaats have informed us that they want to see a court order. They say it's none of our business who flies their freighters, or where they get their cargos, or who they work for—as long as they pay their ARS taxes and don't break any flight rules."

"That's an interesting twist," the Exec said. "Did you tell them you can deliver all the court orders they want with the *Parvardigar?*"

Sagar, however, seemed blunted by the realities of Mandala protocol. "That didn't seem to bother them. So, by God, I'm working on getting the blasted court orders. If they don't willingly give us access to their records, then we can tear into them. We'll work it out in court later."

"Right," Colleran said bitterly. "And the last time we did that it took us twenty-seven years to straighten it out."

"We won, didn't we?" Brianne countered.

"This isn't a mere corporate dispute or case of industrial espionage," Colleran told them. "And I don't think we've got twenty-seven years."

"No," the Exec said, "but I can convene the Authority Council on this matter. We can shut down the Abou-Farhaats, at least until we know more about what we're dealing with."

"It might be too late for that," Colleran said, holding the printout for the Exec to see.

Brianne said, "Lou just happened to be on the *Judy Holliday* when there was a group divorce celebration going on. That's why some of the names were false. The women didn't want their husbands, or I should say their ex-husbands, to know where they were."

They were the rich and famous, mostly of the Alpha Spoke, but a few of the names bore residences in the neighboring Beta Spoke. And they had gone to Okeanos to *party*.

Sagar went on. "I don't think Mrs. Regina Wahlander and her crowd are going to keep silent about this. If we bind and gag the Abou-Farhaats, then we're going to have to track down all the *Judy Holliday* passengers and crew—"

"And the miners of Surane Four," Colleran interjected. "Don't forget them."

"Right," the small Admin said up to them. "We've got a lot of trouble as it is."

Mtazi Hardt handed the computer listing back to Colleran. "So who is Regina Wahlander?"

Colleran held the computer listing in one hand and the jewel from the creature that killed Kit Brodie in the other. He said, "She's the one who left her jewels behind in her suite on the *Judy Holliday*." Colleran held the stone for the two women to see. "Jewels that looked exactly like this one."

10

Regina Wahlander was as good a place to begin as any other, Colleran decided, when further investigation had revealed that much of the *Judy Holliday*'s spacious suites had been leased by Mrs. Wahlander and an entourage of several other aging debutantes. Colleran's own suite had been located in a different section of the palatial laputa, and, as such, he had never really paid any attention to the other passengers.

Colleran's interest at the time had primarily resided in several needed weeks of fishing and lounging around the waters of Okeanos and sharing as much of that time as possible with his lovely of choice, a Heidi Beryl. What Regina Wahlander had done down on Okeanos for all that time, he had no idea, although there was more than enough to do. The *nouveux riches* always could drum up something delicious to fill their precious leisure time. Regina Wahlander had the feel of a real leisure veteran to Colleran, with or without the excuse of a divorce.

However, as Colleran spindled in toward the narrow regions approaching the Hub, where Regina Wahlander's homeworld lay in its lazy orbit around the stable G7-type star, he realized that the rich were not likely to be quick to confide their intimacies to the

ordinary people who had to run the Mandala worlds for a living.
That meant him. The families who had established the earliest
Reaches understood the utility of the Authority, but they also
resented it. Colleran wasn't looking foward to this, especially if
the woman was experiencing any grief over the dissolution of her
marriage.

But whereas she was a major unknown factor, she was also a
major link. He'd have to convince her of that regardless of her
suspicions or her anger.

Oakstaadt was a short spindle from Asarhaddon Five in toward
the Hub, only three and a half light-years. Since some of Regina
Wahlander's entourage also resided on that forested world, he
would be able to query several other of her party if she turned out
to be of little help. He didn't relish that prospect, either.

Oakstaadt itself resembled Colleran's own homeworld with its
large, pleasant continents and planet-girdling oceans. He had been
to the main port city of Oakstaadt's largest continent many, many
times in his capacity as a Regulator, and once, a century ago, had
tussled with a chieftan of a black market syndicate who had
managed to stretch out his smarmy tentacles of influence into
nearby star systems. The chieftan's clashed molecules were now
drifting dust motes and his organization just an electronic cluster
of bytes in the Authority's computer archives.

It felt good to be back.

Colleran left his spindle in the Authority dock at the lone
spaceport on the continent called Grove, and took instead an
overland surface ferry. Much had changed since he had last
visited. The impossibly wealthy corporate heads of the various
Reaches who presently dwelled on Oakstaadt had abolished all
highways and roads outside the major cities. High tension wires,
even airplane traffic had disappeared. The continent of Grove had
been aptly named. An extensive region of forests and meadows,
Grove was the haven of country estates and little else.

Surface ferries were the only authorized mode of transportation,
and from the air five hundred feet up Colleran could feel the
wildness of much of the countryside, and the ensuing peace. With
his clasher at his side and his Authority badge burning brightly in
the afternoon sunlight through the windows of the ferry, he
suddenly felt like a viral intrusion into an otherwise healthy body.
He felt as if he didn't belong here.

The Wahlander estate was actually a small country town that appeared to service what looked—from the air—like a Lost Earth medieval or Renaissance manor home. Clearly the houses that flanked the Wahlander mansion were the homes of the servants.

But it *did* take Colleran's breath away. He had known some wealthy individuals in his time, but the sight of a home the size of a small city bedazzled him. The estate sat on the edge of a placid lake that extended well over the horizon. Lake Frederick was over a thousand square miles in size and surrounded completely by dense forest. The trees themselves were like the conifers of the Lost Earth, but these were of a much heavier greenish hue and much, *much* taller. This was more a place for fairy-tale princesses and princes with feathered caps instead of multibillion-dollar lawsuits and divorce decrees.

The ferry hissed down to a landing area, a verdant cove of coiffed and manicured grasses. Colleran stepped out, being careful to keep on the flagstones that led up to the mansion's entrance. He didn't want to befoul the lawn or cause the rows of phlox to wither with his passing.

Still, he paused, feeling the breeze lift off Lake Frederick as it ruffled his blonde hair. The wind through the leaves and branches of the leviathan trees seemed to sing to him.

"You!" a voice shrilled from the manor.

Colleran spun around, one hand on the live-leather holster, which had instantly schismed. *Easy, boy. Easy now . . .*

Standing on the wide, covered portal of the estate entrance, with no guards or servants in sight, was the majestic figure of a woman whom he presumed to be Regina Wahlander.

"Am I under arrest, or what?" she asked with a disarming smile. She stepped down from the marble steps of the porch onto the grass of the landing alcove. "My men flashed me that you were coming. Regulators mean trouble. At least, that's what they say."

Regina Wahlander stood a sturdy five-feet-eight inches tall and seemed to be one of those faintly annoying individuals born with more than her share of cheer. She was robust, fortyish—in real years—and she carried herself with an athletic grace. She had it all.

The woman wore khaki riding breeches and a modest white cotton blouse with a stickpin at her ruffled collar. Her boots, though, were clearly expensive and fresh, as if she had put them on for the first time that morning and would never again use them.

He was completely thrown off guard by the woman. Somehow, he'd expected an imposing matron, a dowager followed by a train of kowtowing, fearful servants and a horde of yapping, sniveling Lost Earth chihuahuas.

"Sorry," Colleran said, holstering his clasher. "It was just a reflex."

She did make a face when she saw the flap of the clasher holster seal itself shut like a tongue. "Is that one of those living holsters I've heard about?"

"I'm afraid so."

"Yuk," she said girlishly, carefully walking up to him. But as she got closer, a wave of recognition passed across her beautiful face. "Oh, *you* were the Regulator on the *Judy Holliday!* It *was* you." She seemed happy with the discovery, revealing perfectly white teeth in a smile, Colleran realized, that could sink ships.

The ruffles of her collar shivered in the soft winds from the lake. Her breasts and hips were a trifle larger than he had originally assessed, and he thanked his lucky stars that he'd never seen this woman until this moment.

"I was on vacation," Colleran told her as they walked toward the mansion. "No one knew about it except the captain." He chose not to mention the lovely.

"Bad for business, right?" Regina Wahlander said coquettishly, her blue eyes flirting.

"Something like that."

A servant or two had now begun appearing in the doorway and at the windows, and a stiff-spined butler waited just inside the large door to the mansion itself. He seemed to have more rank.

Colleran's heart clumped in his chest and his hands sweated. He suddenly realized that this woman was *divorced*. Someone had turned her loose, and here he was standing within striking distance. He swallowed hugely. This was the most attractive woman he'd seen in a *long* time.

And powerful. She fairly radiated such power. She strolled into the immense manor home like a queen through her castle, and her servants were there to contribute to this climate of royalty.

"You're lucky that you caught me when you did," Regina said matter-of-factly, utterly at ease with herself and her station. The manor house bustled with activity now. Servants pulled traveling cases, bundles of water skis, and there was an assortment of other equipment Colleran couldn't recognize. He was too busy gaping rudely at the treasures that filled the rooms she took him through.

He brought himself out of his trance. "Why? Why was I lucky?"

She sighed melodramatically and pouted, almost as a spoiled twelve-year-old girl might. "I didn't get enough vacation. We're going out on the lake for a few days. Your ferry wouldn't have been able to reach us. You'd have to use a motorboat, but then my guards would've blasted you out of the water."

Again, she sighed. Then smiled at him. Colleran felt like a puddle.

Through the lavishly decorated and furnished interior of the mansion, he could make out the women of her entourage in a rear area that led down to the boat docks on the lake. Their voices were cheerful, girlish and excited. As though they were all going to camp.

He also noticed through the windows that out on a large porch, sipping drinks and waiting for their masters, were an assortment of lovelies—male and female alike. They also seemed animated by the journey out onto the peaceful waters of the lake.

Colleran halted and felt a bolt of energy rush through him. A beautiful blonde lovely, wearing a haltertop and shorts and holding a drink in her hand, had turned and smiled at him.

It was a Heidi Beryl.

All the lovelies—by virtue of their unique cloning procedure—had eyes so widely spaced that they seemed ever so slightly elfin. Even the male lovelies nearby had the same quality. The Heidi Beryls were fashioned after a Lost Earth "escort" and model, and rumors of telepathy among the individual lovelies aside, this Heidi acknowledged him in such a way as to indicate familiarity.

But it wasn't exactly a happy wink. If the rumors of telepathy among the lovelies of specific models were true, than this one might recall the horrible last moments of his Heidi as she plunged into the skies of Okeanos.

She, however, turned away. She wore a tasteful wide-brimmed yellow hat and sunglasses, and clearly she belonged to someone on the yachting party. She walked away with another lovely, this one male and black. Colleran recognized a Walt Richardson lovely by his black dreadlocks curling down his back. He was fashioned

after a Lost Earth *reggae* singer, and Colleran guessed that he had
been brought along to provide live music.

Regina caught Colleran's interested stare as he watched the
gathering on the rear portico. Drinks went around and there was
much gaiety.

She smiled knowingly at him. "Oh, I forget." She indicated the
lovely. "You have some experience with lovelies. Is it Heidi
Beryls you like?"

Colleran couldn't hide his emotions. He said nothing, however.

But Regina knew the ways of the perfect hostess and diplomat;
it came with her natural sense of grace.

She said, "You've got good taste. They're nice people."

Colleran stared levelly at her.

"Oh, I know," she tossed off. "Most people think lovelies are
unhuman just because they serve special purposes so willingly.
My husband," and here her face went dour, losing its pleasant
character. She continued, "My *ex*-husband had a thing for
lovelies. That bastard."

A drink on a tray floated by in the hand of a blank-faced servant
and she plucked it as she would an apple from a tree.

"But he's history now. That's what this is all about. We're
celebrating. My friends and I all got divorced on the same day last
month. Same judge and everything. We're all going to have such
fun!" She was back to being happy. Colleran marveled at her
resilience.

Several of the servants were already passing some of the
visitors' luggage out to the rear, being careful of the plush
furniture and *objets d'art* in the main living area—which,
Colleran couldn't help but notice, was twice the size of his own
house back on his homeworld of Karuna. The lovelies were also
stepping down through the rear garden, moving to the ferry that
would take them out to the Wahlander yacht, which Colleran
could see on the waters of the blue lake.

He tried to follow the Heidi, but he lost track of her. He turned
back to the former Mrs. Wahlander, and as he did a ghost of
dizziness set in and he thought for a moment that he had visualized
Beatrice in the place of Regina Wahlander.

"Are you all right?" she asked, touching him on the arm.

Colleran shook the Lei experience away as quickly as it had
appeared. What was he here for? He tried to remember.

"Look," he began, covering his momentary lapse. "I won't

keep you from your party. I do need to ask you some questions, though. If you don't mind."

"Not at all," she smiled, linking her arm with his. "Why else would you be here? It'll give me something to talk about with the girls."

"I'd rather you kept this confidential."

"This sounds serious." She was flirting with him.

"It is."

"Follow me," she said, pulling him into a long carpeted hallway. "We can talk in private."

He found himself in a larger room, probably a sitting room of some kind, used for afterdinner get-togethers. The furnishings were intimate and a well-stocked bar lined one whole wall. Colleran recognized an ancient Lost Earth rug of Navajo design hanging on one wall and a painting by Rothko hanging on another.

"You like it?" Regina Wahlander asked, showing off her home.

"It's hard to say," he said in a barely audible voice.

The former Mrs. Wahlander didn't seem to mind. "It's all my husband's, or at least it was. When the settlement goes through in a few days, I'll get everything. His lawyers aren't contesting it."

He cleared his throat and got down to business. He unclasped the hinge of one pocket and withdrew the gemstone they had found in the sewer on Asarhaddon Four near the Stillion River.

"I was on your suite level just after Captain Vaillancourt ordered you and your friends to evacuate." She watched him intensely, perhaps too intensely. Life was a playground to her, and the men in her life were its various amusements. He went on. "I won't go into what I was doing there, exactly, but I found a lot of these things on the floor and in the corridor."

He gave her the odd jewel and surveyed her response to it as she held it to the light canting in from the window.

Captain Vaillancourt had recovered the jewels and other items and returned everything that he could to the passengers of the floating resort. However, he and his crew had managed to keep the passengers—with a couple of exceptions—from seeing any of the video playbacks considering that they had all been evacuated in the first place. Those few exceptions were presently being tracked down. The fax-blabbers of the Spoke media network had already made it known that something unusual had struck the *Judy Holliday*.

"Is it one of mine? I thought the Captain had returned everything." She handed it back.

"No," he related evenly. "But I wanted to ask you where you had gotten yours. And, if I could, I'd like to examine them a bit closer."

She folded her arms beneath her large breasts and tapped her foot impatiently—but she smiled nonetheless. "Are you after my jewels? I'm not a divorced woman yet, Mr. Colleran. However, I've never made it with a Regulator before—"

Colleran's embarrassment must have lit up the room. She laughed playfully. "Don't worry. I'm not going to let any man nail me for a while. You're safe. Follow me."

She drifted past him almost in the same way that Beatrice had moments ago. Women had always been a mystery to Colleran, as if they were some sort of secret frontier for which, in order to cross, one had to have a special kind of knowledge, a certain adaptability that would, all by itself, be enough to survive that particular journey. He'd wondered how he had managed to survive this long.

He followed her, lost in the wake of her perfume, to a spiral staircase, which, in turn, led to a private chamber adjacent to her bedroom. The wide window of the chamber faced the lake to the north and through it Colleran could see the sleek form of the Wahlander yacht, white and silver in the sun. Small ferries were already shuttling some of the guests out to it.

"They're not valuable, if that's what you're thinking," she told him as they entered the chamber.

"Oh?" He turned away from the window. The yacht on Lake Frederick was the size of his spindle, and no doubt cost as much. Wealth was omnipresent on the Wahlander estate.

"They're flawed. In case you haven't noticed. I keep them because my lawyers advise it." She pulled aside a painting on one wall and twirled a clockwork dial of a combination lock to a hidden wall safe.

She glanced at him over her shoulder and the curve of her smile sliced through his heart. He also had a hard time avoiding the angle of her breast as it suggested itself seductively through the cloth of her blouse.

"Don't look," she said.

She swung open the safe and pulled out a velvet-lined box. There were other boxes within the safe and bundles of papers were stacked there as well. Dollar signs fairly flew from the cache like so many butterflies.

She opened the case and showed him a neat row of extraordinarily beautiful stones. Each one was the same light purple color and was exactly like the one he held.

He picked up one of them at random and took it to the light of the window. It, too, seemed to possess the same, miniscule flaws within it, dark lines or etchings that no doubt were part of the crystalizing process that made them. He compared the two.

"Where did you get them?" he asked.

He had seen all sorts of contraband in his long life, from money to jewels to actual stolen goods. But he had never seen gems such as these. They seemed imbued with a kind of power and he could understand why someone might covet them.

But Regina Wahlander's eyes clouded with suspicion. "Why?"

Colleran, to ally her fears, put it back. "I need to know."

"Rex didn't hire you, did he?" She slammed the lid of the box loudly. "If that son-of-a-bitch—"

Colleran laughed at the performance. "No, that's not it at all. We can't be bought that easily. At least *I* can't."

Again, she had to think about this, and as she did, she returned the jewelry box to its haven in the wall. She closed the safe, twirled the dial, and slid the painting back in place.

"In divorce settlements, the wife gets the jewels," she informed him, holding her ground.

"I understand that," he told her. "But we need to find out what your jewels have in common with this one." He pinched his stone between his narrow fingers.

She walked over to him, and stood, he thought, rather closer to him than their short acquaintanceship seemed to recommend.

"Why?"

"I can't answer that. Do you know where your husband obtained the jewels?"

She pouted. "No. He had them before we met. He gave them to me along with the rest of my jewelry." She spun around suddenly. "Why? Are they stolen? What has Rex done?"

She seemed now both frightened and excited at the same time. Frightened, he thought, over the prospect of losing her jewels, regardless of their worth, and excited that her husband might be in some sort of trouble with the Authority.

"Mr. Wahlander's done nothing that we know of, although we

are busy tracking him down. You wouldn't happen to know where he is?"

Now she laughed, but there was no mirth in it. "Your guess is as good as mine. Even his lawyers can't find him. He ran off with his lovelies four years ago, the coward. I haven't seen nor heard from him since. That's why I'm having this party. It's taken two years just to plow my way through the divorce courts. I wanted to declare him dead, but his lawyers, who were running his estate at the time, insisted on the equivalent of a common-law divorce decree based on desertion. And I won, hands down."

She stood by a large, open window and brightened considerably when she glanced out at her friends, who reassured her with laughter and happy smiles.

Opening the window further, she yelled down, *"I'll be there in a minute! Don't leave without me!"*

Someone yelled back up, *"Bring the Regulator! He's a cutie!"*

She closed the window, latching it. "If you find him, tell me. Or tell my lawyers, Sammons, Golby, and Banales. Rex might be able to contest the settlement. Even so, I'll fight him all the way on this. I'm tired of paying the taxes from my daddy's account. Besides," she smiled flirtatiously. "Rex always was a creep."

Colleran took out a piece of paper. It was a special warrant with computer fiber strips lined within it so that it would signal the Authority when it arrived in the physical proximity of its intended designee.

Colleran made a slight adjustment on it, however. He removed the computer strip with the name of Regina Wahlander, leaving behind the strip with the name of Rex Wahlander. He delivered it to the manicured fingers of the beautiful woman before him.

"This is merely a supoena. We need to talk with your ex-husband. Give this to your lawyers or any party who might find him. We are already looking for him on our own."

She took the card and frowned. "Is it that bad?"

"We don't know yet. We just want to ask him some questions."

She waved the card slightly, considering it and what it meant. Then she set the subpoena aside on a shelf of a bookcase lined with freshly dusted Lost Earth volumes. Colleran was surprised that anyone who lived here read at all. The books were thin tomes of poetry. The title of one volume was *All Beautyfull and Foolish Souls* by someone named Harley Elliott. The book was hundreds of years old from the looks of it.

Foolish souls, Colleran thought, agreeing with the archaic sentiment of the book's title. Men and women never stopped picking at each other, never stopped blaming the other for the failures of a relationship. Perhaps that was why he had been with lovelies for the past sixty to eighty years. It was easier.

However, he didn't imagine that the poet Harley Elliott had that concept in mind.

He buttoned the pockets of his tunic, making sure that the lone caliban jewel was safe. "I'll leave you now, Mrs. Wahlander. Sorry if I've caused you any delay in your plans."

"Call me Regina," she said. "And I'm going back to my maiden name. Robbins. Regina Robbins. Sounds better, doesn't it?"

"It does," he confessed.

He walked over to the window to get a last look at the magnificent Wahlander yacht and at the party below.

His attention was suddenly taken with a rather unusual sight out in the garden, something he hadn't noticed before.

He unlatched the window to get a better view.

"Awful, isn't it?" Regina Wahlander said, standing close beside him. "I wanted to get rid of it, but my lawyers won't let me touch it. Rex loved it."

Out in one corner of the sculpted garden, amid the multi-colored flowers, stood a pedestal with the tall skeleton of a prehistoric resident of the planet.

Slung low, it had many legs, a long spine, and an even longer tail. Its head was bone white and its efficient jaw made room for dozens of razor-sharp teeth. The skull had sockets for four eyes.

Regina said, "It's one of the creatures that used to live on Oakstaadt a zillion years ago, before the Hub opened it up. Rex put it down there. *I* hate it." She sighed. "Which is probably why he put it there."

Colleran stared at it, sensing its familiarity, sensing also the gossamer drift of Beatrice at his back.

11

Colleran picked up something on Oakstaadt, deep within the wooded halls of the Wahlander mansion, that he had not expected. He *had* expected to come away with one of the jewels for analysis; locating them, however, would have to be enough for the moment.

What he had unexpectedly picked up was the sudden urge to go home.

The Wahlander manor estate was clearly home to Regina Wahlander and her hangers-on, and it impressed Colleran with his own desires for something familiar and reassuring. He'd been spindling around the Spoke for much too long.

The *Parvardigar* had moved into the space above the Authority homeworld of Karuna, which was only light-minutes from the Hub. Colleran lived out in the countryside, far from the Authority's main city complex on a large mid-latitude continent. However, when he took a jitney home, he found that his house—for whatever reasons of its own—had moved itself. It took him an hour to find it.

Colleran's demesne was a sprawling section of hilly terrain that was mostly grasslands with an isolated stand of Lost Earth pines and maples. He found his home near the river that coursed lazily through the hills. Downstream were other homes, most of them owned by Regulators who were presently out among the stars of the Spokes.

"They said you were dead," Colleran's house said when he approached it on foot, over the gravelly bed of the river's bank.

The house, an oblong affair, was a product of the Stella Reach, the same people who made the much larger laputas. This was a small-scale version, called a Mobile Urban Domain, or MUD. It possessed autonomic circuits bordering on full-fledged artificial intelligence and its gravity-lifts allowed it to be moved freely—or move itself freely—wherever its owner, or the house, wished.

"Why did you move?" he asked of it, slinging his duffle bag into the reeds of the shore. Behind him halfway into the stream itself, sunk to its knees, was the jitney, steam snarling from the cooling engine.

"I got lonely," MUD said as it floated in place several feet above the shore, quite close to the security of a clump of deciduous trees.

MUD had selected a compatible spot, better than the one Colleran had previously chosen on the other side of the hills, where the grasses were dry most of the year but there were fewer MUD units nearby. Colleran noticed, as he entered the living room, that MUD had turned the large window in the direction of another MUD unit, this one on a hill about half a mile away.

"Lovelies live there," MUD commented. "They are the Hofmeister Williams. The little one, Ruth, comes and plays by the stream, although the older sister, Mara, yells at her. I like them."

Renegade lovelies were rare, but they did exist. He took some comfort knowing that his closest neighbors did not belong to anybody but themselves. As he recalled, the Ruth Hofmeister Williams model would be about six years of age. Fortunately, there was little in this region of Karuna that might harm her if she played by the river. Unless, of course, it was a vindictive twelve-year-old sister model.

Colleran felt at home within the space of half an hour, once he had cleaned up and once MUD had begun recycling the air and charging the environmentals.

"We understand that there's a Reach war building," MUD said as Colleran sat down to fresh tea and lunch MUD had prepared.

"We don't know yet," Colleran said aloud. MUD's circuits had been designed with Colleran's own personality matrix, but he had never gotten fully comfortable with these comprehendible two-way conversations with his house.

However, as MUD reported the local news in the nearby city of New Cambridge, Colleran began to feel the true isolation of his life. He also felt the need for a lovely. Perhaps it was the light of the sunset approaching through the wide window, or the sound of the Hofmeister Williams children chasing each other about down

in the stream. Lovelies somehow filled his life in the way that
human women had ceased to, and he had carried with him from
Oakstaadt the strong impressions Regina Wahlander had made on
him. He knew, though, that he was not in her realm at all. The
physical attraction was there, certainly, but so was an enormous
price. And he was tired of paying such a price. After sixteen
marriages in a three-hundred-year-plus history of adult life, he had
gotten tired.

It was in that quiet moment, listening to the Hofmeister
Williams girls giggle and scream, that Beatrice drifted through his
living room. At first, he was merely numb to the Lei appearance,
then he sat bolt upright. She seemed so distinct to him that it
frightened him.

And not once did he lose track of knowing where he was. She
just floated on by like a breeze passing from one open window to
another.

"MUD," he called out, setting his tea down. "Summon the
Hopkins mode for me," he requested.

"You bet."

MUD uplinked to an available satellite, which downlinked to
the university in New Cambridge, which had the Hopkins mode
program in storage. Instantly, there appeared a hologram image in
the center of Colleran's living room, in full color and full
fleshtones, of his last great teacher. Professor Hopkins stood, as
he always did, with his hands in his pockets, wearing a light tan
shirt with an open collar, casual slacks, and tennis shoes.

Hopkins, in his lifetime, had been a very tall man. He had a
high forehead, Nordic features, reddish blonde hair, and was one
of the best teachers of the Humanities in his day. However, at the
time of the migrations into Alpha Spoke, he had chosen not to
apply for the Kotlicky-Powell gene-splice, even though his
contributions to humanity were many. As a Christian of the old
school, he had no wish to live forever, and opted instead for
submission to a personality scan into the university computer
systems of the Mandala worlds. The man had been dead for over
three hundred and twenty years, but his holo image persisted, his
lessons still valuable.

Colleran was only too glad that he had known the man when he
had been alive.

The Hopkins holo looked around the living room like a

stranger. "So, you've come back to roost," he said, smiling spectrally down at Colleran.

"*I* thought he got killed," MUD interjected.

Colleran ignored the self-interests of the house. "Professor, what do you think are the chances of a Spokewide Reach war breaking out?"

The professor's main field of study, when he had been alive, was the Humanities, with an emphasis on history and religion. Over time, the computer database at New Cambridge University had added to that.

Hopkins walked confidently through the living room, coming to a halt before the window. He showed no interest in the sunset.

He said, "The Authority is far too young—as an empire, if you want to see it as such—for it to collapse. But that doesn't mean that it can't be threatened. There's a lot of empty space in the unexplored Spokes."

Colleran leaned over, huddled in his bathrobe from his shower, wishing for human—or lovely—companionship. "So it's not likely that whoever has attacked the Okeanos Reach and the Cronins are part of something bigger than the Authority."

"That'd be a good guess," Hopkins said. "But remember that the Authority only regulates and charts Spoke traffic. It doesn't run things."

"I know."

Colleran got up and stood near a wall that held dozens of photographs of his progeny. His wives were missing, but the pictures of his children and their progeny were present. He hadn't seen some of them in over a hundred and fifty years, scattered as they were like dandelion spores on the winds blowing from the Hub. Only his brother Daryl was in touch with him, and that was on rare occasions. Daryl, the last he had heard, was off exploring the Theta Spoke, looking for the ruins—if there were any—of the Makers. To Daryl, it had become an obsession.

That made Colleran think of the Tally. As the Hopkins holo watched, Colleran spoke to MUD. "I'd like to see the Tally on the screen, MUD."

But Hopkins gave him a frown. "I'd advise against it, Lou."

A computer screen above the kitchen counter lit up and the ominous list appeared. Colleran poured more tea.

Even in this short lapse of time, more names of Authority immortals had been added to the Tally of the dead. Brodie's name was now eighth from the bottom. The Mandala was a large sprawl of worlds and people perished every day and every night.

"It happens," Hopkins said moodily. "People die. Even immortals. Even *I* died." He held out his hands dramatically and tried smiling for him. It didn't work.

"Is Daryl anywhere on the Tally, MUD? Someplace I've missed?"

"No."

However, that didn't make him feel any better. Death always won out in the end. Even when the Kotlicky-Powell process allowed for a theoretical lifespan of nine-hundred-plus years, anything could happen. Usually it did.

There had been those individuals who had chosen not to undergo the gene alteration, and mostly they had done so for religious reasons. The failure of the Millennium to manifest itself converted much of humanity to religions of the East. Reincarnation, however, had its downside. Being immortal, while allowing one to do good deeds, also gave one opportunities to accrue unwanted burdens of karma. Colleran had no answers for any of these perspectives; he only knew that he liked his job as a Regulator. He also knew, however, that the longer he lived, the more isolated and lonely he felt.

Perhaps that had been his reason for choosing to spend so much time with his lovelies. Year after year, the same model would always be available.

Colleran contemplated the image of the Hopkins standing before him. He asked, "Professor, you're linked with the Mandala network. Are there any new developments, official or unofficial, regarding the Makers of the Hub?" He was thinking of his brother just then. Daryl would be on top of any such discoveries.

The holo seemed to hover indecisively as it sped through its uplinked memory. Hopkins shook his head. "None that I'm aware of. Are you looking for anything in particular?"

"I filed a report suggesting that these so-called calibans might be the original Hub Makers, the Suras. Has anything like that appeared in recent journals?"

Again the holo image paused as the Authority mainframe in New Cambridge raced through its updated banks.

"No," Hopkins reported. "Nothing yet. If I find anything, I'll be sure to let you know."

"Do that. Find me wherever I am and let me know," Colleran told the image. "It's very important."

Hopkins smiled. "I'd imagine that it would be." The ethereal image wavered a bit, then changed the subject "So let's talk about something different."

"Like what?"

"Like your erratic Lei encounters."

"Oh, those," Colleran said, turning slightly away from his teacher, preferring to brood.

"I've been informed that Exec Hardt and your Admin have given me authorization to give you a prescription of metatryzine."

Colleran heard the dispenser in the kitchen rattle as two spansules appeared in the ceramic dish beneath it.

"They work fast, don't they?" Colleran said with a touch of sarcasm.

"What, the women or the spansules?"

"Take your pick," Colleran quipped. He looked up at the hovering image. "So how long has everyone known about metatryzine? I'm older than anyone I know, and I just heard about it."

"It's been around for a few years, mostly being tested on some immortals in Gamma Spoke. It's now been given clearance by the Food and Drug people for general consumption. After all, we wouldn't want you to cave in under all the stress and Go Off. Metatryzine will help."

Going Off was common to most long-lived immortals in the service of the Authority. For some, the weight of all those years was just too much to bear; for others it was often the loss of loved ones. Suicides were quite prevalent among the Regulator corps, and the Tally was full of the Gone Off.

"I'm not that bad off," Colleran reported.

"You've been seeing . . . what do you call her? Beatrice. You've been visualizing Beatrice, or so the records state."

Brianne's beady little eyes were everywhere. Had it really shown that badly? As he thought about it further, he must have been under some kind of surveillance for twenty years if the Lei experiences had been discovered to be so disruptive.

Colleran walked into the kitchen and picked up the two spansules of metatryzine from the white bowl. Outside the kitchen window and several feet below the floating MUD unit, he could see the strange Williams daughters playing. They were throwing rocks at his jitney.

"Hey," he called out at them. "Stop that!"

Ruth, the six-year-old lovelie, turned around and smiled up at him. Her older sister, Mara, stood farther up the bank. Both had that moon-eyed look so common to all lovelies.

"Hi!" little Ruth sang out. She was invincible. She did stop throwing rocks at the spaceship, however. Mara stood up and waved at him as well.

Even lovelies get lonely.

The image of Heidi came to his mind as he watched the two girls cavort happily in the sunset. He recalled how beautiful Heidi had become beneath the sun of Okeanos, how her breasts seemed like ripe bronze pears, how her hair had gone as white as his own in the sunlight.

As he stood holding the spansules, everything disappeared around him. Perhaps it had been the voices of the renegade lovelies, perhaps it had been the somber autumnal sunset beyond the kitchen window—but quite suddenly he had shifted into a profound Lei experience, his defenses entirely let go.

He found himself standing in the grasses of a meadow that was ringed by a leafy green forest, a forest unlike any he'd ever seen on any planet in the Spoke, a dream forest of smells and motions beyond comprehension.

And there Beatrice stood as well, beckoning him. Nothing was more real than this, he thought as his heart trembled with an ardor he once believed he had lost. Oh, the joy of it!

He started walking toward her, tyring to hold his happiness in check; too much of this and his heart just might burst.

Beatrice stepped into the dark corridor of the woods—and he found himself standing in his kitchen.

The sun had gone down, the little girls out by the shallow stream had gone home for supper, and the Hopkins mode had been called elsewhere for someone else's comfort.

MUD had drawn him out of his Lei experience with an urgent call. "I think you should see this, Lou. It's been flashing for a while now."

Disbelievingly, he turned slowly in the kitchen to the computer monitor screen. The spansules, dry and undissolved, were in his hand still.

The *Parvardigar*, high above the skies of Karuna, was sending down a priority message. It said: *Abou-Farhaat freighter responsible for Okeanos delivery located. Coordinates on board your spindle. Good luck. Don't die. Brianne.*

How long had he been gone? He started shaking his head and his hands got moist. He recalled the forest and the meadow, and he resurrected Beatrice's beautiful smile. He was in that world for only a few precious moments, but in this world hours had seemingly lapsed.

He drew a glass of water from the tap and swallowed the spansules of metatryzine.

12

Colleran's sleek spindle hung in the dark void of space like an ancient Japanese fishing buoy cast free and lost on northern Pacific tides, curling toward the Oregon coast of the Lost Earth. The metatryzine made Colleran's mind keen enough to follow the metaphor. He recalled the stories his maternal grandmother used to tell about finding the weathered glass orbs on the beaches near Newport, Oregon, when she was a child. The image somehow seemed appropriate: Colleran was going to float in space and ensnare an Abou-Farhaat.

They now had a plan.

Exec Hardt, back in her office tower in the city of Anshar on Asarhaddon Four, had their computers uncover any information concerning the Abou-Farhaat ships in the vicinity of Asarhaddon, especially if they were on their way toward the Hub, bound for another Spoke. Sure enough, a midsized freighter registered to the Abou-Farhaats under the name of *Scimitar* indicated a planetfall on Asarhaddon Four to unload cargo and, more importantly, to take on cargo.

The cargo it filed to take on was six of the previously stored crates and canisters, which were now known to harbor embryonic calibans. As Colleran emerged refreshed from his quick-sleep couch in his spindle, he thought that either the captain of the *Scimitar* was incredibly stupid or that the man was overly confident of his mission. Whatever the mission was.

However, Mtazi Hardt and her Council in Anshar decided on a different tack than merely detaining the *Scimitar*, arresting its captain, and pumping him full of blab drugs. On the suggestion of Admin Sagar, they decided instead to allow the captain to onload his cargo and follow him.

Through quickly installed monitoring units, the Regulator Council watched the young, hawk-nosed, walnut-skinned captain of the *Scimitar,* a twenty-eight-year-old relative of the Abou-Farhaats named Zir Mohammed, orchestrate the rather mundane task of transferring his cargo to a gravity-lift and escort his load up to the waiting *Scimitar*. The process was standard; no one batted an eye, especially the Riocello warehouse operators who assisted with the freight transfer.

Colleran studied the *Scimitar*'s manifest. The six crates were all bound for different Reaches in three adjacent Spokes. Those canisters the *Scimitar* did not pick up were under constant guard, wired for sound and movement, and a diligent Two Spoke Regulator was on duty all of the time. With her clasher.

Colleran's spindle hovered in the blankness of space only light-minutes from the Hub, along the projected flight path of the approaching *Scimitar*. They didn't know which canister would be delivered where, so Colleran was ordered to wait until they were certain which Spoke the captain of the *Scimitar* would choose.

Colleran's spindle registered the passage of an occasional incoming spacecraft, flashing out of the Hub full of spindling energies. But traffic seemed light. That would make pursuit a bit easier for him.

Colleran waited at his console until a com-officer on board the waiting *Parvardigar* in the Asarhaddon system called him. "Mr. Colleran," the woman's crisp voice hailed out.

"I'm here. What have you got?"

"Zir Mohammed Abou-Farhaat has filed the coordinates of his intended first destination. He's just spindled out of orbit."

"I copy," Colleran reported as the same coordinates spun themselves out across his computer screen. The *Scimitar*'s first stop was to be a planet around an ordinary M-type star in Spoke Beta, twenty-light years from the Hub.

"Perfect," Colleran said to himself as he prepared for the jump toward the Hub.

Brianne Sagar's voice came at him. "Lou, you'll sight him in seven minutes. Stay at least fifty-thousand miles behind. He'll think you're just traffic."

"Right. Where will you be?"

"Another fifty K. But we'll be farther behind you when we spindle out into the Beta Spoke. We don't want him or his people suspicious yet."

Colleran felt clearheaded and excited over the prospect of their first real lead in the case. It was probably the metatryzine at work as well.

A signal went off minutes later on his board as his spindle ship picked up the passage of the inbound Abou-Farhaat freighter. Around him was utter darkness with a peppered firmament of stars in the far distance. The freighter would be invisible at fifty-thousand miles, but his own spindle could follow it easily, especially since they both were now being drawn toward the Hub.

Colleran strapped himself in and called out one last time to the *Parvardigar* over their special coded frequency. "I'm on my way."

"We'll be a few hours away. Don't spook him."

The *Scimitar* was five times the size of Colleran's police spindle, and as such it required more time to "spindle in" toward the Hub, but not nearly as much time as it would take the *Parvardigar*. Colleran's spindle, however, had already absorbed the subspace energies it would need within its waiting Andreesen engines.

Colleran watched his console as the *Scimitar* took in the energy it would require for Hub passage. Then quite suddenly it spindled away, leaping into subspace.

Colleran braced himself. His own computers caught the jump and his spindle lurched off in pursuit, his Andreesens whining high.

Colleran stared out at the Hub from the narrow window of his spindle cockpit. In normal space the Hub was impossible to see. In subspace, it took on a discernable visual character, itself like an eight-sided cyanic jewel radiating its unfathomable power. Colle-

ran was pressed back into his cushioned seat as his spindle was
reeled in toward the Hub. He loved Hub passage. It ranked high in
his personal experience along with his Lei encounters. Nothing in
the physical universe could match it.

Colleran could now "see" the surrounding influence energies
of Alpha Spoke as his spindle followed the *Scimitar* in toward the
Hub. Here, the Spoke's influence was like that of a narrow cone of
light striking, at its most confined point, the massive side of the
Hub, which was just one side of eight. Colleran could feel the
energy take hold of every molecule of his body, every atom of the
ship as it drew it in.

The *Scimitar* was now visible to him as well. It appeared as an
inward-streaking arrowhead of greenish light heading right toward
the Hub's facet. Other ships were other arrowheads of green light,
some going in, others coming out of the Hub bound for their
sundry destinations.

As always, Hub travel exhilarated him, if only because the
energies were so profound and so peculiar—and because it always
seemed as if one's spindle ship was going to collide directly with
the Hub's Spoke facet. Colleran always wondered what the first
Spoke traveler—the man who managed to go from one Spoke to
another—had felt when it seemed inevitable that he would strike
the Hub itself. But that never happened. No one had ever struck
the Hub; no one had even set foot on it. In its own mysterious way,
it was unassailable. The Hub merely drew the Andreesen spindles
in and flung them back out. Its energies were antientropic, alien,
and unexplainable. But it made star travel possible and thrilling.

The *Scimitar* suddenly glowed a dull orange as it slowed in its
approach. It was almost consumed by the turquoise light coming
from the Hub, but Colleran kept on it as his own spindle began to
decelerate. Contact-moment, as it was termed, was only seconds
away.

An alarm chimed when contact-moment was reached, and
Colleran stared out at the indescribably huge "facet" of the Hub,
now only a mere one-hundred thousand miles away. His heart
always pounded at this particular instant, for it was here at the
contact-moment that one could sense the utter alienness of the
artifact. The facet that generated the Alpha Spoke seemed to be
nothing more than a blue plain stretching for thousands and
thousands of miles. Someone had built this, Colleran always
thought at this moment. Someone very, very powerful. . . .

Then quite suddenly, the entire facet rotated a full forty-five degrees—or that's what it looked like to Colleran as he and the *Scimitar* hit the contact. Actually, his own spindle had moved into the adjacent facet of the Beta Spoke, and now Colleran's ship was rocketing outward into that Spoke, following the *Scimitar's* projected path.

Colleran gripped his console as his spindle ship continued its flight and the Hub fell away behind them. The *Scimitar* was on its way to a place called Roe Three, twenty light-years away, and all he had to do now was follow.

Spokes Alpha and Beta—for no other reason than the luck of the draw—boasted the most habitable planets for humanity's expanded civilization. Roe, an ordinary M-type sun, had the good fortune to have two earth-normal planets, though one had a slightly warmer and the other a slightly cooler climate than Lost Earth. Roe Three, the slightly warmer world, was mostly tropical and rather densely populated.

Roe Three also meant a great deal to Colleran other than another station for his Regulator duties. Some time ago he had had a wife down there, and children and grandchildren. But that was quite some time ago, indeed. It bore other memories as well. However, those memories didn't deserve a caliban, despite their unpleasantness.

His spindle drew in closer toward the *Scimitar* as the freighter announced its approach to an orbital docking station around the planet of Roe Three. As part of the plan, the contingent of Regulators on board the docking station had been warned of the *Scimitar's* contents, but were advised to stay clear.

Colleran did notice, however, that all was not on the up-and-up with the *Scimitar*. As soon as it cleared itself with the docking station, it had begun tight-beaming a shielded signal down to someone on the planet.

Quickly, Colleran punched a decoding-descrambling mode into his computer and threw it over his audio pickup.

Zir Mohammed Abou-Farhaat sounded scared. "If you want what I'm carrying, you've got to come up and get it yourself! I've got a patrol spindle on my tail and I want to know why!" the young captain shouted. "Somebody down there better tell me what's going on. Now!"

"Rats," Colleran breathed. His spindle must have been picked up by the freighter's own radar. But that didn't matter. All that counted was that the Authority discovered who was to get the shipment of the first canister.

Colleran quickly signaled the Authority personnel on the docking station. "Are you tracing the transmission?"

"We're on it," came a com-officer's voice from the station nearby.

Seconds later Colleran's computer registered the point of origin planetside of the transmission with the *Scimitar*. It came from the corporate headquarters of the Bensonhurst Reach.

The Bensonhursts? Colleran sat back confused as the tight-beam traffic continued back and forth from the ground to the orbiting *Scimitar*. Their eavesdropping had gone unnoticed.

Colleran had dealt with the Bensonhursts frequently. They were an agricultural firm and shipped heavily between the Beta and Alpha Spokes. He struggled to make some kind of connection between them and the Okeanos Reach or the Cronin Reach, and came up blank.

Colleran signaled the docking station's com-officer. "Refuse docking privileges to the *Scimitar*."

"Acknowledge," the com-officer returned.

Colleran listened as the docking officer hailed the approaching *Scimitar*. Zir Abou-Farhaat became outraged.

"Are you serious? On what grounds?" the merchant shouted.

The com-officer in the docking station chuckled. "If there's an Authority spindle following you—and there is, by the way—then we don't want what you're carrying either. Permission to dock and unload is denied."

Communication from down below on the planet was instantly severed. The *Scimitar* was an item that nobody wanted.

"Well, what am I supposed to do with it?" yelled Zir Abou-Farhaat frantically, now over the standard frequency.

"Take it somewhere," the station officer said. "Or jettison it. However, the Authority is watching and we don't need an Authority investigation at the moment. Dump your contraband."

"I'm not carrying contraband!" Zir Abou-Farhaat retorted. "I'm just carrying a shipment for the Bensonhursts. I don't *know* what it is!"

Long, barrier poles eased out from the docking port, preventing any kind of hookup with the port facility and the incoming

Scimitar. Zir Abou-Farhaat did some backing off and slowing until he could assess the situation, but not without a few audible expletives that frizzed the ears of all who were listening.

Colleran, knowing that the *Scimitar* was now aware of his presence, switched over to the shipping frequency.

"Hello, *Scimitar,*" he announced. He then sent over his Authority badge number and standard boarding request into the *Scimitar's* computers.

"By the great god Allah!" ranted the captain of the jilted freighter. "I've done this a hundred times! Why now?"

"You tight-beamed a message to a specific person in the Bensonhursts," Colleran began. "To whom is the cargo bound?"

"It's none of your business," Zir Abou-Farhaat growled.

"Then that's why you're getting the Authority treatment at this particular time."

Abou-Farhaat's reply was incoherent.

Colleran brought his spindle in toward the *Scimitar,* matching velocities with it. He spoke again to the captain. "I'm coming over. You may consider yourself officially seized by the Mandala Authority. I refer you to your shipboard regulation file number 800-B38 and the following subsections on search-and-seizure proceedings."

Colleran paused, expecting a further volley in Arabic describing the ancestry of his parents, but nothing was forthcoming. He also anticipated the sudden departure from orbit of the *Scimitar,* since its Andreesens were still bursting with Hub energies. But that didn't happen either.

"Are you there, *Scimitar*?" Colleran threw out. "I repeat. Are you going to let me board, or am I going to have to cut my way in?" If he had to, he could cut the freighter in half.

The *Scimitar* merely drifted in its cloak of sudden silence, its docking lights blinking on and off like mindless eyes.

"Zir Abou-Farhaat," Colleran called out one last time. "Acknowledge or I'll come over immediately."

From the docking station another voice came over the frequency. "This is Commander LaFlame, Regulator. We're picking up a downgrading of the energy quotient in one of *Scimitar's* Andreesens. Do you know about this?"

"No," Colleran confessed, checking his own sensors. "I don't." The commander of the docking facility was correct, however.

Colleran fired back. "But he's not dumping his power. He's *losing* it."

"I don't see any damage from here—" the commander continued. A large viewing window with docking station personnel was at the center of the orbiting facility. They were following the drama visually.

Colleran, however, was unbuckling his seat belts.

The commander asked, "Do you know what kind of crew he's carrying? Could there be a mutiny over there?"

Colleran, never a man for false optimism, began removing his clasher and its holster from a side compartment.

"There's no mutiny going on over there," he reported to the commander. "But I've got a good idea what *is* going on."

He punched in an automatic docking program. The *Scimitar* was dead in space. And he knew why.

13

Colleran felt a sparkle of excitement sizzle up his spine as he turned his spindle in toward the drifting *Scimitar*. Automatically, he sent out an assistance signal to the other Regulators who were no doubt watching everything from the windows of the docking station. And, indeed, a swift Authority patrol spindle appeared in the distance on its silent approach.

"I'm tractoring you," Colleran announced to the quiet, unanswering helm of the *Scimitar*.

Although his own spindle ship was much smaller than the Abou-Farhaat freighter, its tractors were strong enough to enable the two ships to maneuver together. This action used a great deal of energy, but the situation called for drastic measures.

Suddenly, from the other side of the ship, a rescue pod popped out into space, spurned by gas jets already made weak by whatever had shut down the enormous freighter.

A voice shot in over the com. It was the docking station commander. "Mr. Colleran, the pod's in a planetfall descent mode. It's out of control."

Got you, you son-of-a-bitch, Colleran said to himself, grinning. "No problem," he shot back. *No problem whatsoever. . . .*

Colleran's spindle hove around and threw out a tight tractor beam, capturing the drifting rescue pod before it had moved too far away. Down below, Roe Three ponderously turned beneath them in all of its serene and utterly indifferent beauty.

"Zir Abou-Farhaat!" Colleran challenged over the rescue pod's only radio channel.

The voice returning over the emergency channel from the pod was extraordinarily calm. Zir Abou-Farhaat was clearly edging close to hysteria, trying to hold himself back.

"What's going on," the freighter captain demanded, pronouncing every syllable of every word. "I want to know what's going on. I want to know what's happening—"

"Suppose you tell us," Colleran fired back.

The bigger ship, its docking lights still functioning, seemed like a vessel of ghosts.

"Where is the rest of your crew?" Colleran asked.

Quickly, a profile diagram of the freighter's general class spun itself out on Colleran's console screen. The cargo hold was located halfway between the crew compartments and the massive Andreesen spindle engines.

Zir Abou-Farhaat said, his voice quaking, "They've been attacked and killed. At least, that's what I think."

Another sleek and raven-black Authority spindle rose up from the blue-green surface of Roe Three. Colleran would have rather seen the *Parvardigar* appear nearby, but for now the three patrol spindles would have to do. With five or six growing calibans on the *Scimitar,* they just might need clashers of the size that only preservers carried.

"You *think*? Don't you know?" No further rescue pods were leaping into space. Colleran barked, "You mean you left your crew behind?"

The computer profile indicated that the *Scimitar* normally staffed a crew of five. It could function with as few as three and could carry as many as ten.

"If they're alive, *Mister* Regulator, they know where their pods are and they know how to use them. I want to know in the name of all that is holy *what is going on!*" His demands were shrill and desperate.

To Colleran, the voice didn't sound like a conspirator in a fledgling Reach war. He suddenly felt that itch in the back of his mind return. *This*, he thought, *doesn't sound right*.

Was the metatryzine wearing off or were his instincts trying to tell him something?

In the sepulchral silence of space, with the vast steel crystal of the Roe Three docking facility above them and the lush tropical world below them, Colleran's attention was suddenly grabbed by a change in the *Scimitar*'s heading. It lurched.

"My ship!" cried Zir Abou-Farhaat from the confines of his captured pod. "*Look what it's doing to my ship!*"

The top section just above the Andreesens peeled back as if pulled by an invisible hand. An explosion pushed outward in a slow, silent effusion of furious energy.

The station commander, who was recording all of this for the inquiry they all knew would follow, shouted, "Spindle engine number two has been destroyed, Mr. Colleran. The ship's down."

"I copy," Colleran reported flatly.

"What's going on over there?" the commander continued. "Are there explosives on board? What was he carrying?"

"We're about to find out," Colleran told the commander.

"Good luck!" Zir Abou-Farhaat laughed in a voice that sounded high pitched and brittle. "But before you do anything, you'd better notify my family *and* the Authority!"

"Why do you think *I'm* here?" Colleran returned.

"I don't know why you're here, but something's destroyed my ship and I want to know what and why. I want everyone to know!"

"Be quiet," Colleran said. "I want your manifest. The one you flew by, not the one you filed back on Asarhaddon Four. Beam it over to me now."

"It's in the ship's computers. You think I'm stupid enough to print a fiche when that thing—"

"What thing?"

"I don't know what thing! But it's alive and it's got teeth—teeth that eat metal!"

"What's he talking about?" came the station commander's voice. The commander then spoke directly to the rescue pod.

"Listen, Zir. I've told you before, no transferring of nonindigenous lifeforms—"

"It was my *cargo*! I didn't have anything to do with it!" he shouted to them all. "It's sabotage, that's what it is! I'm going to sue! My family's going to sue! I'll see all of you in mother—"

Colleran switched him off.

"*Teeth?*" came someone else's voice from the docking station. "Did he say it eats metal?"

One of the Authority spindles had already moved in quite close to the disabled *Scimitar*. Its pilot called over to Colleran.

"Hello, Lou," she said. "Are you there? It looks like your spindle. It's me, Marji."

Colleran had been watching the injured *Scimitar*; now he focused all his attention on the Authority spindle nearby. He almost choked. "My god, Marji, what are you doing here?"

"I'm the boss, is what," Marji Ciani replied. "I'm an Admin now. I was surfaceside when I picked up this little embarrassment of yours coming over the channel."

"You're an Admin now?" Colleran was surprised more than he thought. "I guess you *are* the boss."

He had last seen Marji Ciani about seventy-five years ago when his last marriage—his sixteenth—had fallen prey to entropy and ennui. She herself had been a Two Spoke Regulator and they had met on Authority exercises on Roe Three. He had been promoted to his Three Spoke ranking and she had helped him make the transition back into his bachelorhood. They had lived together on an island there for about three years until circumstances compelled them to part. She was a much younger immortal and had become attached to someone permanently stationed on Roe Three—and he had started seeing Beatrice. It seemed natural that they should separate.

"Listen, Marji," Colleran began. His palms were now sweating. It had never occurred to him that Marji might still be here. "I can handle this." But quickly he switched over to their scrambled Authority frequency. "Have you been briefed on what the *Scimitar*'s carrying?"

Her voice was quite businesslike. "I've been informed that one of our Reaches might be in for some troublesome contraband that was being escorted into the system by you."

Colleran quickly told her—in no uncertain terms—just what it was they were up against. "I've fought these things. They're exceedingly dangerous."

However, Marji Ciani's black spindle was already making for the *Scimitar*'s docking port. Her radio silence told him that she was determined. He knew her as a strong person long ago and her current rank of Admin was proof of that. He could not deter her.

Black-suited and terrible in their armor and weapons, the Regulators met in the transfer hold of Ciani's larger spindle. Three other junior officers waited behind them, one brandishing a clasher rifle while the others carried pulse guns.

Colleran could only catch the barest glimpse of Marji's eyes behind the shielded faceplate of her helmet, but they were the same vivacious dark-brown eyes he remembered so well. They brought back pleasant memories, as did the sound of her voice, now that she was so close to him in the docking tunnel.

She pressed her gloved hand against his chest—a standard spacer greeting—just enough to be felt. "It's good to see you again, Lou."

Her words were warm and honest. But he also noticed the clasher pistol she carried in her other hand. "Circumstances could've been better," he said.

She merely nodded in agreement. She then glanced over Colleran's shoulder to the last member of their party: Zir Mohammed Abou-Farhaat.

Colleran had brought him in tow, officially under arrest, from the pod he had reeled in earlier. The arrogant Abou-Farhaat captain was the only civilian among them and the only one left unarmed. That was to keep the fear of God in him. Colleran had also ordered one of the junior officers to keep a pulse rifle aimed at him in case the Abou-Farhaat did anything remotely amusing.

Admin Ciani prodded the merchant captain's unshielded chest in a nonspacer greeting. "We're going in after your computer manifest and you're going to take us right to it."

Colleran liked the sound of her authority. She'd grown much in seventy-five years.

Abou-Farhaat stammered. "You don't know what you're getting yourself into, Administrator. I'm warning you—"

Still, the man was mortally fearful.

Colleran told him, "We will handle whatever it is that has crippled your ship. Your job is to deliver the manifest to the

Admin, personally. All of it, not just the convenient names and dates. *All* of it."

He thought he heard Abou-Farhaat swallow heavily. He then said to him. "You stay behind with them." He indicated the waiting team of junior Regulators. "When we say so, you go get the disk. And *no* funny business."

Zir Abou-Farhaat glared at him.

"Okay," Colleran announced. "Let's see what we've got in here." He turned and faced the docking tunnel, hauling himself across using the convenient handrungs. Marji Ciani followed right behind him.

When the main spindle engine had blown, most of the *Scimitar*'s electrical power had collapsed. Some battery-run emergency lights still persisted, but when Colleran entered the injured freighter, it was like entering a tomb.

Marji held out a motion sensor, which was itself attached to a bright beacon. There was still air within the ship, but the artificial gravity functions went with the power, so they were still weightless. Sound, however, would carry. Colleran would need all the assistance available to thwart the caliban.

Marji pulled up beside him, feet locking temporarily in rungs in the wall to hold her in place. "You said there were six canisters on board."

"Right."

"What if all six got loose?"

"That's a possibility," Colleran said, glancing down a dark, unearthly corridor, listening for movement.

"I only saw one of them," Zir Abou-Farhaat radioed to them.

"Quiet, you," one of the Regulators said back to him, a female with a pulse gun.

Suddenly, a shudder rippled throughout the ship and they all fell against the nearby corridor walls.

"That's it," Zir Abou-Farhaat said frantically.

Colleran found a small monitor screen inset in the wall and punched it to life. "Good. There's some emergency power still tied into the computers."

The small screen brightened up their end of the hallway as the caliban made disruptive sounds far out ahead of them. On the screen appeared a schematic of the ship.

"I know where it's at," Zir Abou-Farhaat said.

"I want to see the engines," Colleran told him.

On the screen the computer gave them a glowing red dot in the
skeletal green framework of the ship. It meant that there was a
"problem"—as the computer saw it—just aft of their position in
the ship, near the remaining Andreesens.

"Found it," Colleran said, pointing a gloved finger at the
screen. "And there's just one of them, too. The other canisters are
undisturbed. That's a relief." He turned around and faced Marji
Ciani. "It's safe to retrieve the data disk. I'll see what I can do
with the caliban."

Admin Ciani rotated slowly around with the slightest jet gusts
from her suit and addressed her ranking junior officer. "Tallarico,
you escort Mr. Abou-Farhaat to the pilot's station and retrieve the
manifest. Shoot him if he refuses."

"Yes, ma'am," Officer Tallarico said.

"You wouldn't dare," Abou-Farhaat protested.

"Sure she would," the Admin stated. "Move. *Now!*"

Officer Tallarico and the reluctant merchant captain went one
way, the rest of them went the other. Colleran, though, wished that
Marji had gone with Zir Abou-Farhaat. But he kept his unease
about the decision to himself.

Colleran had much experience with freighters such as the
Scimitar. There was evidence, as they proceeded, that the various
holds had been modified by the engineers of the Abou-Farhaat
Reach, but mostly the overall design of the *Scimitar* was
consistent with ships of its class. The computer schematic helped.
It pinpointed the source of the trouble.

However, the rumbling continued and it now sounded like a
kind of frustrated beastial growling. The creature had to be large
and strong in order to be felt the way it was; Colleran could feel it
thrashing about each time he placed a gloved hand on the walls.

"Lou—" Marji started.

"I know. Let's just be careful. It's close, very close."

Colleran held out his clasher, which was fully charged. Out
ahead of them was an intersecting corridor, and the sounds were
getting louder and louder as they approached.

"What if it turns some of its friends loose?" one of the officers
behind them asked.

"We'll take them one at a time," Colleran said. "Shoot and
don't ask questions."

They drifted into the intersecting corridor like divers in an undersea cave. Bits of debris filled the spaces of the corridor, shimmering like kettle fish in the lights of their helmets.

One of the junior officers saw something. "Sirs, take a look at this."

Colleran drifted over and stared into the hallway they had just passed. A large, nearly circular hole had been cut in the wall of a hold. It was at least six feet in diameter.

Colleran gently pulled the two remaining junior officers aside. They deferred to his authority. He could almost feel their hearts pounding excitedly, a symphony of fear.

The rim of the hole was cool and smooth. It looked as if something big had neatly cut its way through the wall of the hold as if it had been composed of simple plastic.

One of the officers reached out to examine the glass-smooth edge of the cut in the wall.

"Don't," Colleran admonished suddenly. "Look at it closer."

Vile wisps of silver-white gas, an acidic residue, could be seen dissolving ever so slightly in the glare of their helmet lights.

"It's eating its way through the ship," he told them. "Those are digestive juices, and if they could cut through these walls, you can bet they'll eat right through your armor."

The junior officer backed off and clutched his clasher rifle, looking around.

However, as Colleran glanced into the hold itself, he discovered that this was where the caliban canisters had been originally stored. The other five were sitting, seals unbroken, in the murky shadows. One, however, was completely demolished—from the inside out.

"It seems to be heading for the port engines," Colleran said, backing away from the breached hold.

They followed the trail of its movement through the corridor. To Colleran, it appeared to be some kind of giant earthworm, burrowing through the ship. Each caliban now seemed to be a different creature entirely, as if sent for different purposes each time. Commando specialists.

Over their earphones, Officer Tallarico suddenly signaled. "Admin Ciani."

"Right here, Linda," Marji said quickly, nervously. The creature had stopped moving, perhaps sensing that there were now adversaries on board.

"I've got the fiche. All of it."

Colleran stared into the Admin's smoky eyes as Marji acknowledged. "Take it and Mr. Abou-Farhaat back to our spindle and deliver the disk personally to Commander LaFlame. Don't stop for anything, understand?"

"Yes, ma'am."

She turned to Colleran. "We'll be seeing a lot of each other, once the lawsuits start rolling in."

"I imagine so," he said to her. However, he did feel very much relieved.

The rumbling began again, echoing down the corridors around them. A wall sounded as if it had given way and they could feel a slight movement of air in the passageways.

"Just what the hell is it doing?" he wondered out loud.

"Let's find it and put it out of its misery," the Admin said, moving forward.

"The engine room is right there," one of the Regulators behind them said when they came to the end of the cargo hold.

The corridor out ahead of them, facing the stern of the *Scimitar*, had two enormous holes on either side of the walls.

"Where did it go?" one of the officers asked.

"Shhh," the Admin whispered.

Colleran couldn't imagine how both of those transversing holes had been made when evidence of the creature's passage suggested that it had been moving toward the engines down the hallway in which they were presently located. It could have turned either to the left and bored toward the main engine of the freighter, or it could have turned to the right and struck out toward the port engine.

But how could it have gone both ways?

"Stay back, you two," the Admin said to her junior assistants.

She and Colleran drifted together down the dark hall, their lights aimed directly at the two gaping holes on either side of the corridor. Digestive juices waved tiny flags of malodorous gas along the seared edges of the holes.

"Be careful, Marji," Colleran breathed uneasily, listening to the thunder of his own heart.

The Admin moved cautiously toward the left-hand hole in the corridor wall as Colleran drifted toward the right-hand gap.

Then suddenly, as Marji peered into the darkness of the left-side hole, one of the guards behind her cried out, "What . . . watch it! *Watch it!*"

Colleran turned rapidly away from his side of the corridor to see the creature, whose mouth had been lining the hole itself—lurch out at the Admin. It had been lying in wait.

It clamped down on Admin Ciani with a motion so startlingly fast that Colleran had no time to react. Her scream exploded horribly over the radio link.

"Marji!" Colleran shouted.

The creature slammed its featureless head down onto the floor of the corridor, and Marji Ciani was swallowed whole. The screams persisted over the radio link, but with them came the vibrations from the floor of bones being crushed by teeth strong enough to shear through metal.

"*No, please, God, no!*" he cried out loud as the two junior officers backed off rapidly, raising their guns.

But Colleran knew what he had to do, for he could not bear the sound of the creature's continued mastication.

He clashed it—and along with it went Marji Ciani. The light that filled the corridor was brief, but in its own way it lingered in Colleran's mind for some time after that.

14

In the time it had taken the *Parvardigar* to bounce off the force field of the Hub and enter the Beta Spoke, where tragedy had struck the skies above Roe Three, Colleran had secured what was left of the helpless *Scimitar* and—with the help of Commander LaFlame—quarantined the whole planet. It was through his station that all traffic passed, and Colleran had to put a lid on the situation; he had to keep everything secret.

Not that it did any good. The Bensonhursts, by their very nature, were in constant contact with the other Reaches of Beta Spoke, and while Colleran and the engineers of the docking station struggled with the *Scimitar*, several com-drones had slipped into orbit, and subsequently out of orbit, with all sorts of tidbits for the faxblabbers. Colleran was too occupied to stop them. He could, however, stop anyone from leaving the planet and that would be useful in helping the Authority track down the intended victim of the caliban.

At the moment, Colleran had his hands full keeping Zir Abou-Farhaat from being throttled by several interested parties who had years of disgruntlement to settle. Commander Bruce LaFlame, a compact, warhorse of a man, had spent several long minutes slamming the young, frightened Abou-Farhaat against the wall of a briefing room on the docking station, until a representative from the Bensonhursts arrived. Then *he* went at Zir Abou-Farhaat for a while.

By the time Colleran had collected himself—and taken two more spansules of metatryzine to prevent the shock of losing Marji from overwhelming him with an unassailable grief—he had managed to pry Zir Abou-Farhaat away from the Bensonhurst rep. Asher Morgan may have been an executive, but his size and strength indicated that—like so many of the Bensonhursts themselves—he had been a farmer for years and years. He wasn't much for diplomacy, and one large hand of his was capable of pulping the skinny neck of the terrified merchant.

Brianne Sagar stalked into the room in her full black-and-silver regalia, knifing right through the gathering of angry men. She was angry herself and Colleran backed off, letting the metatryzine calm him. This was Brianne's show. This was particularly true if they were now in the midst of an unannounced Reach war. The Admin would suddenly become General, and the look she brought into the room with her indicated to Colleran that she was close to becoming such.

The Admin squared off with Zir Mohammed Abou-Farhaat, who was sitting, shrunken and defeated, in an isolated chair. "You, my good fellow, are in a whole hell of a lot of trouble."

"But I'm innocent!" the young man protested. His nose might have been broken and there was a slight encrustation of blood just above his neatly clipped mustache, though there was none on his captain's tunic. "I was only to transfer the cargo. You've got the manifest. It says so."

Colleran stood back and tried to determine the source of

Brianne's anger. Had she known Marji? *Likely*, he thought. Had she known that Marji and he had been lovers many years ago?

He thought about that prospect for about ten seconds. *Probably*, he concluded. In a peculiar way, they were family. Now one of them was dead. *Another* one.

Asher Morgan, wearing his ornate robes and cloaks and assorted frippery of his station, stood like a tree stump in the partial gravity of the docking facility. He belonged on a tractor, not on a space station. He also looked as if underneath his executive's robes he was wearing overalls and workboots. Nevertheless, he was angry. *Very* angry.

"Zir Abou-Farhaat," he began, controlling his rage. "You are not about to pin this conspiracy on us. We have no records that we were to receive any kind of shipment, from you or from anybody else." At the man's throat clung a jeweled clasp. It bobbed every time he spoke.

"I don't care," Zir Abou-Farhaat pleaded. "I have nothing to do with this! Nothing!"

Brianne Sagar pushed Asher Morgan aside scornfully. Commander LaFlame watched, waiting his turn, his arms crossed in front of his chest like two powerful pythons. "We've had nothing but trouble from you, Zir," LaFlame said.

"That's a lie! Not with me, you haven't!"

Brianne Sagar stopped the commander. "He's right. I've just gone over the *Scimitar*'s licensing records and shipment bills." She had brought a briefcase with her, and from it she drew a freshly minted report on everything they would ever need to know about Zir Abou-Farhaat and the *Scimitar*. "He's relatively clean," she said with leering emphasis on the word *relatively*.

She handed the file over to Colleran, who was momentarily lost in recollection of a MUD home he and Marji had leased on an island in the mid-latitudes on Roe Three. He loved that house. He loved Marji.

Brianne Sagar evidently was not aware that Colleran was deep in his idyll of lost love. She continued, directing her speech to both the commander of the docking station and the Bensonhurst Reach representative. "We've been tailing the *Scimitar* now for a while and what Mr. Abou-Farhaat says is true. He's not responsible for what he's carrying."

"Ha! So there!" Zir glowered from his mold-form chair.

Asher Morgan's fists were as tough as gnarled oakwood, ready to crack someone's skull. One skull in particular.

"But he seemed so goddamn eager to deliver it," he groused, his cape luffing lightly in the partial gravity.

"I'll deliver anything I'm paid to deliver," Zir said. "That's my job."

Colleran spoke for the first time. There was an electric tickle at the base of his skull that was slightly pleasant, and he had to do something to help him ignore it. He said, "How did the creature break loose of its shipping seals? It was sealed with duraplast strips and double-bonded, just like the others."

"Others?" Asher Morgan paled. "Are there others?"

Commander LaFlame grabbed Zir Abou-Farhaat by the throat and lifted him, even as the mold-form chair held the young merchant down.

"Ack!"

"Talk or your head comes off!"

The Admin rubbed her eyes.

Colleran tugged the commander's arm away. Zir Abou-Farhaat choked.

"The money," he gasped.

"What money?" Colleran asked, leaning over him.

"I wanted to see what was worth so much money to ship," he finally managed to get out.

Asher Morgan turned to the Admin. "What's he talking about?"

She held a confidential Authority report in her hands. "The Abou-Farhaats received ten-thousand transfer credits, cash up front, to deliver each canister."

Asher Morgan laughed unbelievingly. "That's absurd. That's ten times the amount anyone would pay. No one in their right mind would spend that kind of money for—"

"For a Reach war, they would," Colleran interjected. The words fell among them, deadly as a grenade.

The Bensonhurst executive's eyes grew as wide as plates. "A what? You can't be serious."

"Someone," Colleran began, "has gone to a lot of trouble and expense to send you, or someone you know, a little gift."

"I don't believe you," he protested.

"Welcome to the real world," Colleran said dryly.

The Admin considered the reports in her hand. To the captive captain, she said, "The faxblabbers have already been broadcasting rumors that something is going on among a few of the Reaches. All we can do is deny it or discredit anyone who insists that these attacks are genuine. But, in order for us to do that, we need to know who requested the canisters to be shipped and to whom, specifically, they were meant to be sent."

Zir Abou-Farhaat held his ground. "I can't tell you that. I don't know."

The Admin turned her attention on Asher Morgan. With so many armed personnel in the room, he was clearly uncomfortable. She said, "The name on the destination manifest is that of Robinson Valhern. The tight-beamed message sent up from your offices acknowledges that there is, indeed, a Robinson Valhern employed by your Reach. He was to receive the canister. Do you know who he is?"

The bureaucrat shrugged. "Not really. But all deliveries come through our main port facility. Valhern, whoever he is, would have had to register the receipt when it arrived and when he picked it up. Admin, we've got thousands of people working for us and tens of thousands running the farms and plantations. I can get Valhern for you, if you want, but this accusation isn't fair."

"I've lost a Regulator and an Administrator, both of whom were close personal friends," she said, holding back her fury. "Don't think that I won't turn over every rock on every planet to find out what's happening. Robinson Valhern is under one of those rocks. And that rock is on *your* planet."

Now Commander LaFlame reacted. He was not part of the Authority, but instead ran the docking facility on behalf of another space-transfer company. The money was better, the work less dangerous. But if the Authority plowed into the Bensonhursts with a full-scale investigation, his own company would suffer.

He turned to the short woman in black-and-silver before him. "So what's this about a Reach war?"

Clearly, Brianne was frustrated. "Nobody knows yet. But specific Reach establishments are being struck with these . . . things . . . and we don't know who is doing it or why."

Zir Abou-Farhaat, although he may have been culpable, was definitely scared. If there was a Reach war brewing, most trading and merchant Reaches would be affected first.

Asher Morgan was the most perplexed among them. He threw out his hands in a gesture of helplessness. "But who would attack us? There are dozens of Reaches like ours doing business. Why us?"

"Locate Robinson Valhern for us and we might find out," Colleran said. But if the faxblabbers had already blabbed, then Robinson Valhern had probably headed for—anywhere. Assuming he knew that the caliban was meant for him. Colleran was beginning to feel some of Brianne's anger over so many questions and so few answers.

The Admin glowered at them all, then sighed heavily. "What's actually happened here was an accident, despite the deaths of the *Scimitar*'s support crew and an Authority Administrator. The caliban was meant to be taken by Robinson Valhern to wherever Valhern works. That's my guess, anyway." She paced the room, thinking aloud. "We have to locate him and find out his part in this. Then the next thing we need to do is get us another freighter and have our young friend here continue on with his deliveries."

Zir Abou-Farhaat almost exploded from his mold-form chair. Asher Morgan didn't like the plan either.

"You're going to let him go?" The rep was indignant.

"Certainly," Brianne said, standing her ground. "He's innocent for the time being. You might take some comfort in knowing, however, that the Authority is obtaining court orders to examine the Abou-Farhaat account to see just who had paid for the deliveries. So far, all we have are numbers and dates of transactions. However, it *is* important to let Mr. Abou-Farhaat continue with his deliveries."

Zir Abou-Farhaat swallowed audibly as the Admin continued. "And if he can keep from fooling with them, we might be able to discover some kind of pattern among the deliveries."

"You can't—" began Zir Abou-Farhaat.

"You wouldn't do that," Asher Morgan stated. "That would be murder . . ."

"It's a Reach war," Commander LaFlame said. "That's what it looks like to me." He pointed an accusatory finger at Zir Abou-Farhaat. "And you started it!"

Colleran hated to think that Marji had perished in a Reach war. But if, indeed, Marji had perished in a Reach war skirmish, then so had Heidi. He felt the loneliness creep in on him like a night-fighter crawling through the dark woods that had suddenly surrounded his life. Even Kit Brodie was now a casualty.

"You can't make me carry those things!" Zir Abou-Farhaat squirmed.

"Can and will," Colleran said solemnly. "You're in this up to your testicles. I can pull your whole family's plug, just like that," he said, snapping his fingers.

"You can't do that!"

"Sure he can," Brianne Sagar said. "And if *he* doesn't, *I* just might."

Asher Morgan stood tall, trying to hoist himself above the squabbles of the Authority. "Well," he announced, "I can say flatly that the Bensonhursts are not part of this. We're just interested in doing business, not conducting a Reach war."

Commander LaFlame made it known that he didn't like the representative any more than he liked the Abou-Farhaat in their midst. He said, "Just you try to hide down there, Morgan. See how far you can run from a Reach war."

LaFlame had all the look of a Reach war veteran, and it wasn't a happy look.

Just at that point in the discussion, a female com-officer came into the conference room. She addressed Commander LaFlame first. "Sir, there's a message coming in from a drone for the Admin."

"Thank you, Bobbie," LaFlame said, cooling somewhat.

Sagar walked over to a console at the desk and opened a channel.

"Yes?" the Admin said. "I'm here. What have you got?"

"Another female voice, this time coming from the *Parvardigar* which intercepted the incoming com-drone's message, spoke out.

"We've got a tag on information about Regina Wahlander for Mr. Colleran."

Brianne looked up at him and Colleran stepped over to the console quickly. "This is Colleran. Go ahead."

"We're not exactly sure, Sir. But the Oakstaadt Authority is on it right now."

"On what?"

"Evidently, there's been some kind of fire fight at the Wahlander estate. A commando-terrorist unit of some sort has wiped the whole place out. We tagged it when it went over a local faxblabber channel. Thought you'd like to know."

Colleran felt as if Beatrice was lurking nearby; he started

shaking. Oddly, his first thought was of the Heidi Beryl that Regina Wahlander owned.

And of Regina Wahlander.

He looked at his boss. "Give me three days."

"You got it," she said.

15

You're running, Colleran chided himself, blank-faced and steel-jawed. *And you've been running for the past one-hundred years of your miserable life.*

His palms sweated so much that he had to remove his gloves, and as the surface ferry snipped at the frilly treetops of the Wahlander estate in its race to get there, he found himself fidgeting and more nervous than he had ever been. Two metatryzine spansules had almost dissolved in his hand before an auto-dispenser in the ferry could provide him with water to down them.

And now I'm running from Beatrice or whatever she is, he said to himself, watching the landscape flash beneath him.

His memories of his life with Marji Ciani had been as clear to him as if they'd happened yesterday. For three years they lived in paradise on Roe Three, and now she was dead. She had been the last true human he'd loved.

Now, humans and lovelies were under attack, and they all seemed to be people he had known personally.

But that was ridiculous. In a Reach war, if such was underway, everyone would be affected. Friends, lovelies, *everyone* . . .

The Wahlander estate was now a smoldering banner of dissipating smoke on the horizon as the ferry approached. There had been no further communication with the estate, but that had been due in part to an Authority black-out, which was meant to keep the faxblabbers away. He only hoped that the metatryzine would kick in fast enough. During the flight through the Hub, his Lei had been fighting to reach out to him, to pull him back to what lay beyond.

"Are you all right, sir?" a young female lieutenant at the pilot's controls asked. She was a junior grade Regulator but was authorized to wear a Langstrom clasher. She had met him at the port city and had already been at the scene of the attack.

"I'm fine," he reported. "Just keep flying."

She didn't respond and banked the ferry in toward the ruins, which had, by now, almost burned themselves out. Even much of the support city surrounding the Wahlander mansion had been devastated. *So sad*, Colleran thought. It was as if someone had gotten tired of all the beauty in the world and had begun eradicating it.

It brought to Colleran's mind something his mother had said long, long ago, how sadness was the last emotion, an old person's affliction. She had felt it when her husband—his father—and her brother-in-law had become lost near the outer fringes of the Alpha Spoke when they tried spindling beyond the energy barrier that comprised the Spoke. She had become saddened by the loss because at that time in her life everyone seemed to be leaving— leaving both her and the earth. *Going away*, Colleran thought unhappily. *Going off. Only death is the winner in the end*.

However, for all the sadness encroaching upon his mind, he also felt a burning anger, and along with it was the strong desire to rectify the situation. He wasn't entirely helpless. It had been the constant urgings of his Lei that had announced to him his true, inner feelings. He might be sad, but he was also angry.

But to accomplish what he needed in this world, he had to suppress Beatrice's world. He couldn't stand another alluring vision of that perfect place, even if it was only in his imagination. That would be unneeded torture.

What he had to do at the moment was investigate the Wahlander attack. He had already sent out a Mandala-wide arrest bulletin for Rex Wahlander, to protect him if anything. Someone else was already looking for Robinson Valhern back on Roe Three. The Authority wanted some answers, and they wanted them *now*.

As the ferry circled to find a suitable landing place, Colleran surveyed the damage from the air. He was stunned at the thorough job the commando team had done. A single flash-grenade might have accomplished as much, but the ruins had all the touches of someone who enjoyed what they were doing. A flash-grenade lacked the personal touch.

The ferry settled itself carefully on a scorched area of earth that was once the grassy front lawn of the estate. The tall, tall trees had been reduced to sticks with white-ash painted on their sides. Barren, ugly rock lay strewn everywhere. The mansion itself was a holocaustic nightmare.

The female pilot climbed out of the ferry and said a few words to the Regulator leading the investigation. She then returned to her duties among the rest of the team.

"Jay Heger," said the Regulator approaching. He shook Colleran's hand.

"I don't believe it," Colleran said, astonished at the view up close. "I was just here."

Heger was in charge of the investigation, but he also wore a military utility belt and a heavy duty clasher, one that would clash metals and denser plastics. His light brown hair was unkempt and smelled of smoke. His quick eyes were on the lookout for trouble. Colleran could feel Regulator Heger's tension.

In the ruins, Authority personnel were picking over the debris with all sorts of equipment. They had the look of soldiers about them.

"You don't have to say it," the weary Heger said, gesturing offhandedly at the wreckage of the Wahlander estate behind him. "It looks like they parachuted in from the sky with heavy artillery and just flattened the place."

Many of the timbers that composed the framework of the mansion were still burning. Part of the upper floors remained, but fire personnel were busy pulling them down. The place—once sorted through—would ultimately be razed.

Colleran and Regulator Heger walked toward the entrance of the bombed-out mansion. "What about Mrs. Wahlander? What happened to her?"

Heger rubbed at a smudged streak on his cheek. "You know, that's what baffles me about this." He pointed through the blackened stumps of the trees to the blue lake beyond. "She was out on her barge with her friends when this happened. Whoever it was, for as smart as they *had* to have been to pull this off, didn't even think that she might not have been at home. They just landed and started blowing the shit out of everything in sight."

For the first time Colleran could make out—just barely—the swanlike form of the "barge" Heger referred to. The yacht was anchored about a mile off shore. It seemed untouched, inviolate.

Heger reported the rest. "They struck in the middle of the night, first taking out the communications station on top of the mansion. Then they systematically went about killing everyone left behind. Along with it, they destroyed the place."

"They killed everyone?" The small town that flanked the Wahlander palace was also a pulverized moonscape. Ash and smoke still drifted in the wind.

"Right," Heger responded. "When it was all over, if our records are correct, a total of eighty-one men, women, and children were eliminated." Heger had crow's feet wrinkled at his eyes that might have gotten there from years of an easy disposition. Now, they seemed to indicate his true age as an immortal. He was old and had seen much, but nothing quite like this. "I swear, Lou, it's like a goddamn war."

"A Reach war," Colleran said unhesitatingly.

To this, Heger agreed.

They stepped around the mansion and climbed onto the marble steps of what once was the rear portico. Colleran observed, "They used everything but Langstroms."

"I know," Heger affirmed. "Lasers, pulse guns, explosives, the works. They did everything but salt the earth when they were done."

A good dozen Authority men and women were mulling over the ruins, taking readings, looking for clues that the assailants might have left behind.

Heger then said, "They knew the layout of the entire estate, evidently. They landed out back where there was the most open space for several craft. We think they then split up into teams, with some of them going into the homes of the servants next door."

Colleran stared at the ruins. They had even blasted the wonderful flower gardens out back. Anything that had life to it, they had removed.

"The way I figure it," Heger continued, "is that the only person who'd want to do this—and who would know how to go about it—is Mr. Wahlander. But we can't find him."

"We've got a Mandala-wide warrant out for him," Colleran said. "I thought of the same thing coming in."

Colleran stepped down into the garden and scanned the soot-layered mud and grass. He was looking for footprints—*large and unhuman footprints*—but there were none. There were, however, dozens of human prints.

Regulator Heger caught Colleran's cursory examination of the staging area in the ruined garden. "We estimate that there were at least eight assassins. Perhaps as many as ten. It all depends on what kind of assault craft they used."

Aloud, Colleran whispered, "Where would Rex Wahlander get assault craft? You don't just pick them off trees."

"But it fits," Heger nodded somberly. "It seems to have been a surgical strike, meant to catch Mrs. Wahlander at home."

"I don't understand any of this," Colleran told the other Regulator. "And it's just getting worse."

"Brianne informed me of some of your encounters lately. Do you think this is one of them?"

Colleran focused his attention on the yacht languishing on the waters of Lake Frederick. "I don't know. I'd say so, but whoever did *this* used weapons. And these look like human footprints to me," he said, waving a hand at the gouged-up garden.

Colleran, though, began thinking of something else as he stared out at the balmy waters of the lake and the yacht anchored there.

"What makes you think that Mrs. Wahlander was the target?" he asked Heger. "It might have been Rex Wahlander himself destroying his property. He could've hired someone to flatten the place so that the estate lawyers wouldn't turn everything over to his wife. She is on a divorce spree, and it's on all the faxblabber channels. It's been known to happen."

Colleran had been thinking of his last wife, a woman he thought of only as the Plunderer. She had left him long, long ago to pursue her "destiny," as she called it, leaving him devastated. What her destiny amounted to, he never did find out, though he had heard rumors that she suffered occasional psychotic episodes. It hurt nonetheless to be abandoned.

It hurt also to recall that after the Plunderer had left his life in desolate ruin, he had transferred to Roe Three and had met Marji Ciani.

It was as if, he suddenly realized, that two Reach wars were developing: one on the outside, affecting places like the Wahlander estate, and one on the inside, reminding him of all the wars of the heart.

Jay Heger said, "There's a reason that we think Mrs. Wahlander herself was the target." He called over a female tech who pulled down her filter mask.

"This is Becky Lehman. She's heading the investigation. Show him."

"Right," Becky said. "Watch your step. It's pretty nasty here," she told Colleran.

Lehman was covered entirely in a flabby yellow coverall suit made from protective plastic. Her assistants made way as they approached the winding stairway, which still stood, if a bit uneasily.

"As you can see, Regulator Colleran—"

"Call me Lou."

"I can't," she said. "They'll fire me."

"Forget that foolishness." He urged her on nevertheless.

She was all by-the-numbers anyway. Heger followed them with a wry smile on his face. Clearly, there was something between them, but the situation required an established etiquette.

The upper floors—what remained of them—were ready to collapse, and they had to be quite careful. Only the masterful construction of the base framework kept it from folding in entirely. He followed the female tech down the hallway, now open to the blue sky above, toward Mrs. Wahlander's bedroom and private adjoining chamber.

Lehman pointed at the bedroom and the area beneath it. "Magnesium dust bombs had been placed underneath her room and the corridors surrounding it. Since the attack occurred late in the night, they assumed she'd be asleep."

Colleran saw the ruins of the sculptures and the art treasures. Whole paintings, centuries old from Lost Earth, were now flaking into ashes. The wind, which easily made its way through the blackened gaps in the walls, lifted the ashes like black butterflies fluttering on the breeze.

They reached the remains of Mrs. Wahlander's boudoir. "This is it. Take a look."

The room was gone and Colleran could stare down to the floor below—and on into the cellar, which used to harbor expensive wines. It was now awash with shattered glass and about three feet of water from all the broken plumbing.

"Nobody survived this," the tech said in a low voice. "Not even the lovelies."

Colleran's heart skipped a couple of beats. "Lovelies? I thought she took them with her."

Lehman and Heger exchanged meaningful looks as she began drawing out a small box from her bulky technician's tunic. She opened it and inside were four dime-sized crystals of a slight amethyst color.

"Lovelies melt under very high temperatures. But these remained."

They were lovely brainstems—all that survived of the cloned lovelies, whoever they were. They were the matrix crystals that gave each lovely his or her unique personality and that wide-eyed, moon-faced expression. Colleran felt sick to his stomach.

As he held one of the matrix crystals in his hand, he could almost feel it burn with the life it contained, although that life was no longer attached to anything living. It was just a data chip, now dead.

He thought of Heidi burning up as she plummeted into the atmosphere above Okeanos. He thought of the lovelies who had perished here, in this place, safe from the vagaries of the real world of suffering and travail.

And he thought of running, but not *from* something this time. He knew what he must face.

He left his confederates and headed toward the decimated dock out behind the demolished estate.

16

"Of course that bastard's responsible!" the indefatigable Regina Wahlander declared as she held court rather tempestuously in her private suite aboard her yacht.

Colleran stood somewhat abashed, taking the full force of her fury, almost as if he were somehow responsible; after all, this was just the sort of thing Regulators were supposed to prevent.

The Wahlander yacht had already turned tail and was now—even as they conferred in the sumptuous quarters—headed back out into the lake, where it was safe. Colleran had almost submitted himself to a strip search when he came on board, but Regina called off her guards, who had each lost a loved one in the village surrounding the mansion. The party, which seemed permanently affixed to the yacht, however, never lost its momentum. Servants, maids, and cocktail waitresses—and the usual lovely—went hither and yon as the floating crap game, as Colleran thought of it, churned its way as far from the scene of the disaster as possible. Music from the lovely Walt Richardson and his MorningStar Band chimed their tinny tunes throughout the yacht. They never seemed to quit.

But no one inside the special suite seemed particularly happy. Not the guards, the redoubtable Mrs. Wahlander, not even Colleran himself.

Regina Wahlander still maintained an air of normalcy by dressing blithely for the occasion. She wore a light, floor-length gown of an ochre color, with a conch belt around her voluptuous waist that seemed to shine in its own light. Inlaid on each oval conch were jewels that reflected the sharpness of her anger as she plunged about her cabin.

"Four years that son-of-a-bitch's been gone, and now he has the balls to try something like this!"

Colleran stood back and watched the show. He couldn't gauge her quixotic moods and decided to let Regina Wahlander rule as she wished. Two large, shirtsleeved men with ordinary machine guns waited by the door, ready to annihilate anyone she wanted.

Colleran tried to calm her. "There are some things you might want to know. But there are some things I need to know first."

She found a gold cigarette case next to a settee and drew from it a short, hand-rolled *arillo*. Colleran didn't bat an eyelid. The narcotic effects of the *arillo* alkaloid would be useful in calming her. In his time, he had busted whole shipping concerns for trafficking as little as a pound of the illegal soporific. But right at the moment, he had bigger targets in mind.

She smoked furiously and he tried to stay out of her reach. It would take several minutes for the narcotic to work.

"Like what?" she finally responded, her eyes flaring. The two security guards did not move, deaf to whatever might pass between them.

"Like the possibility that you weren't the target of the attack," he said calmly.

She laughed, and it was hearty, lined with serrated edges of bitterness and hurt. "What? Are you kidding me? I'm taking him for everything he's worth and *then* some. That shithead's philandering days are over." She walked through the carpeted suite, the folds of her gown flowing majestically.

The folds of Regina Wahlander's dress reminded Colleran of something, but he couldn't place it just then.

She took a hefty drag on her *arillo*, dropping a large ash on the lush carpet. She exhaled mightily. "But now it's gone. It's gone. He's finally won. After all these years and something like this happens."

Colleran wasn't entirely sympathetic, although he was somewhat amused by the show of power. He cleared his throat and began. "Actually, you still have your five estates. Two of which are on different worlds. You are worth—on your own, without your husband's contribution—seven and a half million credits. You have interests in eight major corporations, three of which will become Reaches in five years, thus doubling your investment. Forgive me for saying so, but I don't think you've lost that much."

"*What?*" she exploded. "How do you know what I've lost! I've suffered!" She thumped herself on her chest, her bosom shaking just enough to attract his attention.

He looked back at her eyes. He then straightened, placing his hand on his live-leather holster and the clasher within. One of the guards saw it and got nervous. But it had its effect.

"Just the same, Mrs. Wahlander," he said slowly, "we think that it's just possible that whoever attacked your home was after your husband, not you."

She stared at him down the length of her *arillo* as she drew thoughtfully on the cigarette. Within seconds she would be malleable enough to deal with sensibly. Or so he hoped.

"I don't get it," she claimed. "Who'd want to kill Rex?"

A different guard came in and whispered something to one of the two already on duty, who nodded and left. Colleran could see by the wide spacing of the eyes and the slightly elfin look that this new replacement was a lovely. It was a Jack Fuller model, as mean as they made them.

"That's what I'm trying to determine, Mrs. Wahlander," he told her.

"Regina," she said, suddenly shifting. "Didn't I tell you once to call me Regina?"

Colleran didn't know what to say as she swept gracefully across the suite like a ballroom dancer, swaying to the forward drift of the ship's quiet engines. There was a grin on her face now.

She stubbed out the *arillo* in a gesture as old as time. *Uh, oh,* Colleran said to himself. He had to do something, to throw her off.

"Was your husband supposed to be on board the *Judy Holliday,* by any chance?" he asked suddenly. "Were the two of you staging some sort of rendezvous on Okeanos?"

The grin disappeared from her face and she pouted, stamping her tiny feet, which, given the shape of her shoes, resembled hooves. "I told you I haven't seen him in four years. He's either dead or in hiding. After today, I'd say he's better off dead."

Colleran walked slowly through the cabin suite, listening to the *reggae* music drift in through the paneled walls. The sea birds that followed the yacht seemed to sing on the pitch and yaw of the songs Richardson and his band played.

"That's what I can't understand," he conceded.

"What? A husband getting even with his wife? I thought you'd be old enough to know that," she said.

"Then whoever is doing this might be after both you and your husband." He glanced idly out the porthole, which gave him a peaceful view of the lake with no land in sight. "But then, who would destroy an entire villa estate and the people who run it?"

Regina Wahlander sat down heavily and brooded on her couch. Clearly, she was stoned now. "I lost everything," she moaned. "This boat's all I've got on Oakstaadt now."

She looked up at Colleran and in that moment became very human. "This was my *home*. This lake is where I really wanted to live. Forever." She choked back her tears when she realized that *forever* was a term understood differently between them.

"I can understand that, Regina," he told her.

The air in the cabin seemed sweet and light. He was beginning to be affected by the *arillo* residue hovering invisibly about.

Listening to the party on the dance floor above them on the

center deck, he turned to her. "What about your friends up there? Were they with you on Okeanos?"

She nodded. "Of course. It's a divorce spree. They're my support group and we're all going through this together."

He sat on the couch beside her. "Regina, we're going to have to cross-check your friends up there. Their husbands—"

"Or wives."

But Regina Wahlander seemed to comprehend the situation. She stood up from the couch, awesomely stoned. She said, "On the fax channels they're blabbing that there's an old-fashioned Reach war starting. There hasn't been one of those for years and years." She was almost like a little girl now, telling herself a story. "Is all that true?"

"It's a possibility," he told her. "It's starting to look that way."

She sidled up to him. He suddenly felt that familiar sizzle climb up his spine and tickle the base of his brain. He inhaled the slight acridity of her breath, smelling the *arillo* smoke. *Reggae* music behind them filled the air.

"Is that what's happening here?" she asked, finally.

"Maybe, maybe not," he vacillated.

"Why?"

"Because Reach wars aim their violence at specific points of strategic interest. Certain factories, docking facilities, even certain people."

"Okay, so they attacked me."

Colleran moved away from her as the guards watched. He said, "Not just you. They've attacked several people, none of whom have anything to do with you or your husband, from what we can tell."

The *arillo* smoke lingered. He could feel it now, working in his bloodstream. It would not, however, be enough to throw him. He changed the subject.

"What was your husband doing at the time he left you?" he asked as she watched him. Her eyes were big, pupils dilated. "What did he do for a living?" He almost asked: *Or did he do anything at all?*

"Why?" she returned, teetering slightly. "What's he done this time?"

"He hasn't done anything—at least anything that we know of," he said, trying to coddle her. "We do know that he had extensive investments throughout the Mandala, especially in Gamma Spoke and Beta Spoke. But that's all we know."

Thinking about her husband was not a happy occupation for Regina Wahlander these days, and it showed. She sighed. "He worked for a long time in the Meurer Reach. They're in Gamma Spoke. That's where we met. My family lives close in to the Hub in Gamma Spoke." She uttered the words as if they were part of some bedtime story she had once heard.

In an unexpected way, Colleran found himself liking her in this childish mode, even though the transformation had been brought about rather artificially. And illegally.

"But the Meurers went out of business. Collapsed about six or eight years ago, if I remember correctly."

"Six years," she said heavily. A light awakened behind her eyes as she recalled more than she wanted to. "We met when the Meurers were going strong. But when the collapse seemed inevitable, we moved here to Oakstaadt. My god, how he lied to me! He showered me with jewels and gold and he swore that it would never stop. Then the Meurers went out of business and he disappeared."

Colleran paused, then delicately asked: "Were there any children?"

The light in her eyes turned to hurt. "No. I was twenty-five then and he said we could wait. Instead, we had lovelies."

"The Hofmeister Williams?" He recalled the renegade girls who lived in the same valley into which his MUD had moved. Lovely children were quite popular among non-immortal couples.

"No," Regina said. She hugged herself, struggling with her emotions. "They were the Volners. Real cute kids, and always in trouble. But the people who leased them to us took them away after a while."

"Why?"

"Because Rex abused them, and they were always being left behind whenever we went anywhere. The little one, the Betsy Volner, kept getting lonely and cried a lot." She gave Colleran a fierce, proud stare. "That's why I treat my lovelies better. And my friends. I couldn't live without them."

Colleran understood. Inside his tunic was a small, carefully wrapped cloth. He slowly withdrew it and began unfolding it. "Those jewels you showed me in your bedroom. The ones in the safe."

"What about them?"

"You didn't bring them along with you, by any chance?"

"No," she said. "Why should I have?"

Colleran didn't answer but instead carefully drew out the lavender gem taken from the beast that had killed Kit Brodie. "Your jewels all look like this one, right?"

She gave it a cursory inspection. "Maybe," she said. She then unsnapped her conch belt and gave it to him. "These jewels are from Rex's collection. I had a silversmith make them into this belt."

The silver conch plates—ovals about an inch and a half long—had thumb-sized jewels set in their centers. Each one was a light purple color, each one flawed by the presence of small bubbles or streaks.

"They're all I took with me this time," she said mournfully. "If the house is gone, then so is the rest of my jewelry."

This close to her, breathing the light suggestion of *arillo* in the air, he could almost—*almost*—sense the fields and streams of Mount Meru nearby. This, however, was real, and the pleasures of Regina Wahlander were much more tangible.

He needed more metatryzine—or less Regina Wahlander.

"Your husband could really be after your jewels," he finally told her. He stood away from her.

Regina Wahlander, though, seemed too stoned to let the possibility register.

She managed a laugh when Colleran seemed so taken with the discovery. "Rex said that they're worthless. A long time ago."

"Maybe they aren't worthless," he told her, rattling the conch belt. "Maybe he wants them all back."

"Bad enough to kill hundreds of people?" She shook her head. "I can see him trying to get even with me, but those creatures the faxblabbers are talking about . . . Rex wouldn't know anything about them. Not Rex. He's too slick."

Colleran felt suddenly deflated. "Perhaps you're right. This operation is aimed at people scattered throughout the Mandala."

He examined the conch belt, turning it over, trying to see how it might have fit within the mystery. He felt slightly fuzzy, breathing the enclosed air of the cabin. He looked at Regina Wahlander and noticed for the first time how, without her belt, her gown had unfolded so that her breasts were exposed. There were more mysteries in heaven and on the planets than any man had the capacity to fathom.

The answer to one mystery, however, came quite unexpectedly.

Something struck the side of the yacht and the ship pitched to one side. Regina Wahlander fell off her couch, and the Jack Fuller lovely was thrown savagely away from the door, which splintered inward.

Screams came down from above as alarms went off and the ship was assaulted once more. It shook.

"My god!" Regina shouted. "*We're sinking!*"

17

Colleran found himself being tossed quite efficiently by the force of the impacts from outside. He rolled into an antique table, which was composed of carved glass and fragile wood, and it crashed around him.

The Jack Fuller lovely was on his feet helping Regina Wahlander to hers. Outside, through the commotion, Colleran could hear the *pocka-pocka-pocka!* of machine guns and the crackling sizzle of a laser rifle. All of Mrs. Wahlander's guests were screaming as if it were the end of the planet.

It may very well have been.

"Stay here!" Colleran shouted to Regina Wahlander as he climbed to his feet away from the ruined table.

"We're under attack," the Jack Fuller said.

Colleran tossed Regina the bejeweled conch belt with one hand and fought to remove what was left of the door with the other.

"Here," the Jack Fuller said. "Let me help."

"Watch her." Colleran looked at the lovely as they broke out into the covered passageway.

"Right," the Jack Fuller said. He knew his job.

Colleran ran out into the passageway and found himself in the midst of unleashed panic. Guests, most of whom were inebriated, clambered over one another as the ship lurched violently.

"Wait!" came a voice behind him, and he turned around to see Regina Wahlander trying to follow him. "Wait! Don't leave me here!" The Jack Fuller was caught in a stampede of desperate passengers trying to reach their cabins and their lifeboats.

Gunfire from above on the fore command deck could be heard distinctly, and several of Mrs. Wahlander's guards were escorting the less-inebriated guests to the nearest lifeboat station.

Colleran pushed some of the frantic passengers—and some of the lovelies—aside as he and Regina found a stairway leading up to the top decks. On the way up they ran into the captain, who was on his way down looking for his mistress.

"What's happening?" Mrs. Wahlander shouted above the din, all traces of the *arillo* high gone now.

The captain, however, reported directly to Colleran. He said, "It's a submersible of some kind. It's underneath us, but one of my men might have gotten it already."

Regina grabbed Colleran and spun him around. "It's Rex! I know it is! He's been waiting in the lake!"

Colleran nodded to the captain, and the three of them climbed the stairs to the upper deck and broad daylight.

There, the junior officers were trying to take aim at something deep down in the blue waters of the lake. Bullets zippered the choppy surface futilely.

On the lower deck, where the smaller lifeboats were being unwinched by the emergency crew, Regina Wahlander's guests were a frightened bunch who kept falling over one another, their gowns torn, their shoes of expensive magdalene leather cast aside like so many forgotten toys.

"Mrs. Wahlander!" someone cried out from below.

"Regina!"

She shouted down to them. "*Follow my men! Get in the lifeboats when they say!*" Then she turned and asked the captain, "What did we get hit with? Torpedoes?"

Colleran didn't think so, and the captain agreed.

"No. Something came up at us from the bottom. It rammed us on the starboard side."

Guards ran along the sides, trying to get a view of whatever was beneath them. Colleran, at the same time, poised his hand over his organic holster.

The yacht suddenly seemed to rise from the fore as they were struck once more from underneath. They fell back onto the captain and shattered glass splintered about them.

"We're going down!" one of the junior officers screamed as more guns tried getting at what was underneath them.

"Call the shore!" Colleran yelled back at the junior officer who was rushing about handing out lifejackets. "*Call the goddamn shore!*"

The fore end of the yacht was already nosing down into the cold waters of the lake. Colleran grabbed Regina and pulled her back out of the captain's way.

The Jack Fuller, cut over one eye, raced up the steps and shouted over to them. "Mrs. Wahlander! We've got your lifeboat!" Smoke billowed from somewhere behind him.

Colleran pushed her toward the guard and followed.

At that moment, he collided with the Heidi Beryl who was also in a panic. This was the first he'd seen of her since he had come aboard, and the shock of it registered—on both their faces.

"Heidi!"

"What are they doing to us?" she cried out in his arms. She was now just another lovely, just another passenger who feared for her life.

"Follow the crew," he told her. "Do exactly what they say!"

He could only pray that Mrs. Wahlander's crew would be a bit more generous in their aid to the lovelies on board than was Captain Vaillancourt's crew.

He pushed her toward the lifeboats, fighting his own sudden concern for the lovely. She was identical to his Heidi, only the skin tone was lighter. His feelings for her were startlingly similar.

An explosion from the aft end of the boat seemed to force it further into the water and the sloping floorboards made it difficult to walk. He pushed Regina Wahlander to the railing to see what was going on.

The yacht was now so far out on the waters of Lake Frederick that there was no sight of land anywhere. Nor were there any aircraft in the sky. However, from what Colleran could tell, there weren't any craft *on* the lake surface either. Much turbulence roiled directly underneath the yacht, but Colleran couldn't make out any sign of a small submarine.

But then, he knew it wasn't a boat that was attacking them.

He looked upward to the foredeck. Regina ran up to the stalwart captain and the two of them scanned to the port side.

"What is it?" Colleran shouted up to her.

"It's over here!" she turned and called down. A pair of guards were already taking aim with their machine guns.

Colleran fought his way to the port side just as the ship began to roll at a sickening angle. The smaller lifeboats being lowered on that side slammed into the fractured hull, spilling their contents into the bubbling water. Colleran saw the lovely Walt Richardson plunge into the lake, along with another lovely band member who was desperately trying to hold on to his expensive steel drum. The musician went down briefly, but came back up without his heavy Lost Earth instrument.

Then as Colleran braced himself against the rail, he saw it. He saw the horror that was attacking the beautiful yacht.

The caliban—the largest he had yet seen—came up from underneath the injured ship and took a bite out of it. A *big* bite.

This creature had an aquamarine color, all smooth and sleek, with dark ridges running along its back, ending with a large dorsal fin three times the size of a man. Its mouth was a doorway to hell itself, flanked by teeth the length of a man's forearm. Its widely spaced eyes were full of vengeful intelligence, seemingly bent on as much destruction as possible.

And it was incredibly powerful.

With a sideways lurch of its massive, muscular tail, it tore out a hole the size of a lifeboat in the hull of the yacht and shook it angrily before nosing out of sight in a welter of frothing water.

Colleran was thrown back against the wall of the foredeck, cracking his head against a pane of shattering glass.

But instead of reaching for his clasher—his holster anxious and ready—he touched the emergency com-signal at his belt, which fired a coded distress signal to the Authority personnel above in high orbit. That signal, in turn, would go out to a com-drone bound for the *Parvardigar*, and the same signal would be relayed to Regulator Heger and his alert crew back on shore. But whether they'd make it out here in time remained in doubt.

The creature came up again as bodies struggled and thrashed in the water around the sinking boat. The beast was born to do this, Colleran saw, engineered for exactly this kind of destructive might. It rammed its orca-like snout into the hull on the starboard side, knowing precisely where to strike.

The yacht rolled over.

Colleran fell into the shockingly cold waters of the lake as people—lovelies and humans alike—tumbled about him in a galaxy of glittering gowns and terrified shrieks.

As he treaded water, he felt the creature sound beneath him as it made another deep dive. He shed his boots and looked around for Regina Wahlander. Currents sucked at his feet as the caliban swirled silently underneath them.

On the capsized hull of the yacht, a few remaining guards and crewmen were trying at once to rescue the nearest passengers and take shots at the swiftly moving creature. The captain was gone.

"Regina!" Colleran cried above the screams and shouts of the guests. "*Regina!*"

A strawberry blonde head rose above the water nearby and choked out, "Lou! Help me! *Help!*"

Swimming as fast as he could, Colleran made for Regina Wahlander, who had been tossed farther out from the yacht than the others because she had been on the higher deck of the pilot's compartment. She was cut and bleeding. Others were nearby, trying to reach the few upright lifeboats.

Suddenly, Colleran felt a swell of currents beneath him, and he rose into the air.

A monstrous force of power, like a living mountain, rose from underneath and the creature breached the surface. Colleran found himself sliding down the smooth hillside of alien flesh as the beast pierced the surface next to him.

Instinctively, he yanked up his legs. It saved his life. The caliban had come up underneath him and tried to swallow him and the others nearby in one large gulp.

It *had* gotten the Jack Fuller lovely and several guests.

Colleran skidded down the wall of aquatic flesh, his hands automatically grabbing for support at the ridges along the beast's back. And for a brief moment, he was out of the water entirely as he slid down the creature's side. He then jumped out as far as he could from the creature as it crashed back into the lake, mouth frothing with the blood of humans and lovelies.

"Lou!" he heard someone shout.

Colleran swirled around in the sinking creature's wake and

caught sight of Regina. The creature had killed all those who had been between himself and Regina Wahlander.

But on the other side of him, nearer to the sinking yacht, was Heidi, who was also crying out.

From the currents flagging at his feet, Colleran suddenly knew that the creature was coming up again. Glancing at the guards on the capsized boat who had a better vantage point, he could see that they were in trouble. The guards pointed at them and shouted.

"Please!" the Heidi cried out as she floundered, gasping for air. "Please help me!"

"Lou!" Mrs. Wahlander screamed.

The water rose beneath him and he swam for Regina. Heidi cried out as the lake's surface came up around her. The creature's ugly snout lifted the waters surrounding her like a shroud.

Gunshots erupted from the guards, and the whole lake became a choir of singing lead, but it was too late for the lovely. The creature's mouth was a maelstrom of inrushing currents, and Heidi was sucked in past the rows of razor-like teeth.

He felt Regina Wahlander's arms wrap around his shoulders as the gigantic mouth continued on its mindless path toward them. Instantly, he reached for his clasher, but quite suddenly he discovered that the hinge flap of the holster was unyielding beneath the water.

The holster had drowned.

"No!" Colleran cried out.

He ripped the flap off, fighting it with both of his hands. Regina Wahlander's weight dragged him down. Darkness enfolded them as he saw the creature's jaws close about them. Regina screamed hysterically. Colleran yanked the clasher free.

Up for air, the cries of the lovely echoed in the beast's gullet and Regina Wahlander screamed one final time. He lifted the clasher straight up amid all the cries, human and lovely, all the beautyfull and foolish souls . . .

His clasher came up in the devil's darkness and he fired it right into the ribbed mouth, feeling its muzzle vibrate and glow.

The world exploded all around him.

18

The woman who sleeps peacefully next to him is breathing softly beneath the soft folds of a single silken sheet. He has awakened from a dream, a nightmare wherein he had found himself choking and coughing in the waters of an inland sea.

In that dream he had one woman in his arms and he was trying to rescue another as a monstrosity itself born of the most vile imagination opened its merciless mouth and tried to ingest them. And there had been a gun. Sitting on the bed he shakes his head. A gun? It made him tremble to think of it. Guns are for killing. And here in Meru there is never a need for such things—nor has there been for untold thousands of years.

Colleran quietly gets up, not wanting to wake his beautiful companion. He pulls tight the drawstring of his shorts. Earlier they had made love and he doesn't want to shatter the delicate balance of that memory.

Beatrice, though, sleeps on. He doesn't want her to be burdened by his persistent dreams of the Lower Worlds where all mundane human dramas occur. He doesn't want the beauty of her life in Meru disturbed by his occasional dream-journeys.

He considers her as he stands in the moon shadows. She is so beautiful to him that she makes him glow in his own light when he thinks of her. Every night they make love, and every time his heart merges with hers as the voice of her passion fills his ears when she whispers to him the secret language only lovers know. This is heaven. This is Meru. . . .

Colleran, still touched by the dream, steps out into the slight chill of the still-dark morning. Nothing stirs in the white city of the grassy plain. High above him is a crystal sphere—their nameless moon—its cratered face the face of an impassive, yet benevolent god. And surrounding that face are stars in a spray of constellations he cannot recognize. It is a perfect world made only slightly less so by the occasional bad dream.

Down the empty street he sees a figure move and thinks that it must be one of the Suras, one of the original inhabitants of the Meru plains. The nocturnal figure is tall, clad in a white tunic, and he walks slowly with the stateliness of a passing cloud.

The figure turns and sees Colleran and waves. Colleran waves back. It is the Hopkins and for a moment Colleran is confused. Out for a midnight walk, the robust Lost Earth professor is taking in the night air—or perhaps this is a different encounter altogether. Perhaps he is being deceived in a friendly way by one of the Sura down from Mount Meru to the north. Perhaps, as it is said, that none of us are whom we think we are, but are instead gods on the wheel of life: on the rim of the Mandala, where life is an illusion. We need only to break through.

The white-tunicked figure disappears around a corner in the chalk shadows of moonlight above. Even had that not been his ancient Lost Earth professor, it might have well been one of the Suras. Perhaps he needed to be reminded at just this moment of his life—particularly after such a violent dream—that all people could aspire for more. The Hopkins had made it seem so easy.

Colleran inhales the freshness of the late night air drifting in off the meadows surrounding the white city. In his dream of the Mandala, there was always some task left undone, always some yoke of unhappiness weighing him down.

He returns along the marble walkway, back to his villa of white stone. Beatrice is still asleep. As he enters, a shaft of moonlight slants in exposing the curves of her uplifted breasts. Her hair glows in a platinum light. Gently, he lifts the sheet to cover her. He has loved her, always.

But then there are the dreams. The dreams of Maya, that veil of illusion hiding the true reality of the heart. He bends over and kisses her lightly on the lips, feeling the soft feathering of her breath. It reminds him of other lips he has kissed, other breasts he has caressed in the night. . . .

The woman standing before him, wearing a white physician's tunic and a stern expression, was someone he had seen before. He tried to focus on her, but the wide conference screen behind her distracted him.

"Welcome back to the real world. Again," the doctor said.

"Dr. Jenda," he gasped with a glimmer of recognition. If the woman didn't take herself so seriously, he thought, she might be attractive.

He was in pain. A lot of pain. Tubes plugged into his wrists pumped glucose and metatryzine into him in equal order, and there were other tubes attached elsewhere that caused him more distress, if not a little embarrassment. He felt naked, exposed, and helpless.

However, he knew from the vibrations coming through the walls that he was now on the *Parvardigar*, and that meant that he was safe. That he was alive.

The doctor poured a small cup full of water and helped him take a few tentative sips. *Water. He'd been surrounded by water. It had tried to kill him. . . .*

Dr. Jenda spoke in even but sympathetic tones. "Usually I don't get many repeat performances. You seem to be after the record."

He tried to sit up, but he was all aches and pains, so he abandoned the idea.

Dr. Jenda coaxed the automatic bed up slightly so that he could sit more comfortably and see better. She nodded at the conference screen on the wall. "The Admin had me turn it on in case you woke up. It's an Authority council meeting happening upstairs and they wanted you to be in on it. But I didn't want to wake you. You're banged up pretty good."

A small, overhead camera—aimed right at him—blinked its red transmission light on, and Colleran knew that he was being watched. He was now part of the meeting.

"Hello," Brianne Sagar called out on the screen. She sat at a conference table with other Execs and Admins gathered around, and all of them were watching him.

He was hardly awake and not a little abashed. Their eyes seemed to stare directly down at him; he felt vulnerable, exposed.

Brianne Sagar, however, seemed slightly angry. He would have expected that she would be pleased that her best Regulator had survived the most brutal caliban attack yet. Even Mtazi Hardt at the table seemed upset.

Brianne folded her tiny hands and spoke directly to Colleran as the other Authority giants watched. She said, "We found traces of *arillo* alkaloid in your blood. Can you explain that?"

What the hell is this? An inquisition?

He sipped some more water and put the cup down slowly. "I wasn't aware that I was on trial. I've just discovered that I am alive. So you'll have to excuse me if I don't do cartwheels to answer your every question. Come back next Tuesday." He leaned back.

The Admin turned a livid crimson color and almost flew out of her chair. Mtazi Hardt reached out a long arm and held the small woman down.

"You're lucky to be alive, Lou," Mtazi Hardt said, her voice a fraction more civil.

He had a sudden impulse to rip away all the IV units and scramble up the elevators and trash the entire Authority conference. Dr. Patrice Jenda saw it coming and put a steadying hand on his shoulder as she stood by his side. It was a standoff.

"You tell me," he said churlishly. "I was there. What's this all about, anyway?"

Brianne Sagar was apparently in charge of the meeting and she sat forward. Reports were all over the table. She held one of them but did not consult it. She had all the grim statistics ingrained in her mind.

She said, "It's about the deaths of thirty-four people in Lake Frederick. That's what."

Mtazi Hardt's African features remained impassive as the Admin grilled him.

He drew a battered hand through his blonde hair, dragging an IV tube at his wrist. "I wasn't able to see the creature until it was right on top of me." He glared at them. "I did the best I could."

The Admin sat back. "You were stoned. It slowed your reaction time considerably and you've been in a classic Lei coma for two days. Two days, Lou!"

Dr. Jenda stood beside his bed like a guardian angel, his only ally of the moment. She said nothing as she watched.

"What happened to Regina Wahlander?" he asked under their scrutiny. Everything was coming at him so fast.

Brianne Sagar seemed suddenly relieved. She fussed with one of the files before her. Even Mtazi Hardt looked relieved. The Admin said, "She's alive. She was waterlogged and hysterical when Regulator Heger reached the scene just minutes later. Dr. Jenda will confirm this. Ask her."

Patrice Jenda nodded darkly. "That's correct. Mrs. Wahlander has been taken to a special care unit about thirty miles from her . . . home." Dr. Jenda was clearly uneasy with these caliban attacks; they were her first *real* experiences with Authority business. The casualties were starting to mount.

Colleran turned to the conference screen and the watchful telecamera above it. "There were lovelies on board. There was a Heidi Beryl—"

Sagar was resolute on the subject of lovelies. She folded her hands as if in benediction. "Several of the lovelies survived, along with the regular passengers and crew. The Heidi Beryl was not among them, I'm afraid."

Colleran began to unwrap the tape around his wrists. "Help me out of these things, doctor."

"You're not ready yet," Jenda said in a low voice.

"I can move and I can talk," Colleran snapped back. "And I'm not going to let those people railroad me—" He indicated the conference screen with a sideways nod of his head. "I'm not going to let them accuse me of incompetence while I'm lying down."

Brianne Sagar, her hand in a conciliatory gesture, said, "Slow down, Lou. Nobody's accusing you of incompetence. But if you smoked *arillo* joints, then we have to consider disciplinary actions."

"That's it," Colleran said, ripping off the tape of one IV and painfully removing it.

"Don't!" Dr. Jenda jumped at him. "Here, let me."

Colleran reached under the cover and started with the catheter. He snarled up to the camera. "Regina Wahlander had a whole box full of them and was smoking when I got there. Talk to her about it. I had to breathe the same goddamn air. It's called a contact high. You might have read about it—"

"Lou," Mtazi Hardt said. "Okay, you win. We just needed to know. We had suspected some *arillo* traffic down on Oakstaadt for a while now. We were just surprised . . ."

"So was I," he countered.

Colleran allowed the doctor to administer fresh bandages to his wrists where the IV's had been. He was steaming, angry over the Admin's sudden seriousness and angry over his inability to save the people he cared for. Heidi was dead once again. *He could hear her cry out as the cold lake water slid down the craw of the caliban*. . . .

Yet, he had chosen to rescue the human, Regina Wahlander.

She was evidently a drug user, a rich and spoiled woman, wealthier than ten thousand men or women taken altogether, a woman who used people like so many field artillery pieces.

He had to let Heidi die.

He hobbled to his feet, but Dr. Jenda saw that it was not quite time yet. She carefully assisted him into a sitting position on the edge of the bed. He was quite weak despite his anger.

The Admin, perhaps mitigated by Colleran's energetic defense, moved on to a different, less accusatory subject. She began, "Lou, just take it easy. We're all glad that you are alive. The entire incident is being handled by Jay Heger and his team, but I thought you'd like to know that we're upgrading the attacks to Reach war status."

"Swell," Colleran muttered as the final tubes were unplugged and the last of the small bandages set in place. "Now all we have to do is find out who is fighting who."

"'Whom,'" the doctor said softly.

"Whatever."

But now it was serious, for an investigation into a possible Reach war would mean a shifting of Authority resources, to say nothing of personnel and equipment. Dr. Jenda did not look too happy over the prospect of tending the thousands of men and women who would no doubt be hurt in a true Reach war. She was much too young an immortal to have experienced the last official Reach war over eighty years ago. She would have been barely an intern.

Hell, Colleran thought, *she's just a kid*.

Just like Kit Brodie was a kid. And he was dead.

Brianne then asked, "Lou, what did Mrs. Wahlander tell you about her husband?"

The eyes of the council were on him, the catheters and medical apparatus having been removed.

"So you think Rex Wahlander is in this," Colleran said, looking up.

Mtazi Hardt spoke out. "We've run a computer check of the canisters that Zir Abou-Farhaat had on board the *Scimitar*. Each one is destined for a different Reach. However, while you were still under—yesterday, in fact—the Abou-Farhaats received a call to transfer the other remaining canisters left behind in the warehouse outside of Anshar."

Colleran felt a rise of adrenalin in him at the mention of Zir Abou-Farhaat. "And?"

The Exec had her own report before her. She said, "The five remaining canisters were to go to other Reaches as well. But the last one is addressed directly to Rex Wahlander."

Colleran was not totally alert. "What? Where is he?" If Regina Wahlander's lawyers couldn't find him, then he was very well hidden.

Now they had a bead on him. Thanks to the devious Abou-Farhaats.

Exec Hardt commanded their attention completely. "If the manifest is accurate, the last canister is to be sent to the headquarters of the Klasa-Eisner Reach in the Gamma Spoke."

"He's working for the Klasa-Eisners? Mrs. Wahlander told me that he's been missing for four years."

Colleran cranked himself up away from the bed, quieter now and thinking. In the closet next to the wall screen he saw a fresh Regulator's tunic and a living holster to replace the one that had drowned. The clasher would be new as well, already geared to his palm's sensitivity. He began putting them on.

Colleran slid into his tunic trousers. Those around the conference table waited in silence.

Finally, he asked, "So what does this have to do with the Meurers?"

His words took them all by surprise. He strapped on the clasher, feeling much better now.

The Exec whispered something to Admin Sagar. Brianne looked up at him. "The Meurers? What do you mean, the old Meurer Reach?"

"Yes," he informed them, buttoning his tunic up to his tight collar. "Mrs. Wahlander said that her ex-husband had worked for the Meurers for quite some time before they went out of business, or collapsed. She met him during those last years."

The two women at the conference table spoke to each other in low whispers as the other council members looked on. This was a new twist for them, evidently. Colleran did notice, however, that the commander of the *Parvardigar* herself was present. Arlene Littel was a mid-range immortal and had been the *Parvardigar's* commander for sixty years or more. If she was along for this particular ride with the council, then the Authority genuinely expected something fairly nasty by way of hostilities. Normally the commander of a preserver such as the *Parvardigar* spindled to wherever its Admin wanted it to go. If there was another Reach war to be waged, then the chain-of-command would alter somewhat. Arlene Littel's eyes were heavy with concern for what they might be up against.

Brianne Sagar said, "We have no information in any of our investigations about a Meurer connection. They've been officially defunct and off the tax rolls for five or six years."

Colleran pulled up his boots. "At first I thought that Mrs. Wahlander's estate might have been attacked by her husband. But that doesn't seem likely to me now. Not if he's on the caliban attack list."

One of the council members was already typing a request for information about the Meurers into a console at the side of the council room.

Colleran continued. "If you look into the shallows of Lake Frederick, next to the Wahlander estate, you'll probably find a large caliban canister. Someone is after both of the Wahlanders, and it might be of some use to cross-check any records we can dredge up relating to caliban victims and their former places of employment."

"Such as in the Meurer Reach?" Brianne asked.

"It's possible."

"That will take a lot of computer time," the Exec said. However, she didn't make it sound as if that would be too difficult to arrange. If it would help.

Colleran stalked the hospital room rubbing some of the soreness out of his wrists and hands. He said to the Exec, "If you try certain individuals, you might narrow your leads considerably.

"Such as who?" Brianne Sagar asked.

"'Whom.'" Colleran corrected. "Try Robinson Valheren, for openers. He was due to receive the creature that killed—" Here, he paused. Under normal circumstances this would be a ripe occasion for a Lei incursion. However, all that arose in his heart was a rather cold memory of Marji Ciani. A glance at Patrice Jenda told him that he was probably doused with megadoses of metatryzine. All matters of the heart—including the captivating Lei experiences—were suppressed.

He said, "It was the creature that killed Marji Ciani that was meant for Robinson Valhern. Find him and grill him about the

Meurers. See what you come up with. Either that or sequester his files."

Mtazi Hardt had been watching him closely, as one of her ancestral Ndebeles might have long ago on the Lost Earth African veld. She said, "But how do you explain the attack on the *Judy Holliday?*"

Colleran's mind now simmered; it was the metatryzine. It had to be. He was well ahead of them. "Also you might want to find out where a woman named Lila on Surane Four worked before. Jack Lounsbury there will help you with her comp files." He thought of someone else. "There was also a man named Johnson working for the Cronins there as well. I'll bet everything that they're all tied into this."

Mtazi Hardt leaned forward and stared into the camera in the conference room as a secretary in the background furiously took notes. She said, "Lou, you didn't answer my question. Mrs. Wahlander, as far as we know, was the only person on the *Judy Holliday* who has any connection with this. And *she* didn't work for the Meurers."

"No," Colleran said, going over to a large set of drawers that held some of his belongings. From them he pulled out a tiny folded cloth. "But her husband did. And I think the caliban that attacked the *Judy Holliday* was after these things."

He held out the flawed purple, gemstone-like crystal, the one from the horror that ended the life of Kit Brodie. He stood before the conference telecamera and the screen.

He said, "I wasn't a Regulator long enough in the Gamma Spoke to have dealt with them, but what I do remember is that they excelled in bioengineering." He carefully examined the small crystal in his hand. "The Meurers fed most of the worlds and colonies in the Gamma Spoke with the meat from specially evolved cattle, chickens, and pigs."

He looked at them, feeling the adrenalin beginning to mix powerfully with the stabilizing chemistry of the metatryzine. "They raised very *large* cattle, chickens, and pigs. My guess is that the Meurers might still be in business."

He held the crystal right up to the telecamera's lens for all of them to see.

19

Zir Abou-Farhaat seemed to have an unusual biological predisposition to sweat more than the average human being. He was doing so now, and the sweat was mingled with the sour tinge of fear.

"You can't do this to me," he attested as the freighter's Andreesens wound down to a barely audible hum. Colleran had skillfully brought to port the borrowed freighter *Khadija* without Zir Abou-Farhaat's aid or consent, and the young man was not at all happy about it.

Colleran glanced out the window of the cockpit of the *Khadija* as the port maintenance personnel of the Klasa-Eisner Reach swung the docking gantry gates over to the newly arrived ship.

Colleran said, "Since you and your family are not providing us with the information we need regarding who's paying for these shipments, we're going to use *you* to get to the source."

"This is illegal," the young man protested from his chair.

"This is also war," Colleran told him. "Let's go."

The canisters and other crates from the destroyed *Scimitar* had been transfered to the new *Khadija* and allowed to spindle to the Klasa-Eisner Reach in the Beta Spoke. However, the Authority had opted not to inform the Klasa-Eisners what was coming in on board the *Khadija*. The Reach was far enough within the Beta Spoke—forty light-years from the Hub—that com-drones with faxblabbed messages had yet to reach it.

The *Khadija* vibrated with hold-lock contact as the gantry crew began to secure the transport ship. Zir Abou-Farhaat was now thoroughly outraged.

"You will make many enemies because of this," he growled.

"I can handle enemies," Colleran said as he lifted the merchant captain from his chair.

No one in the Abou-Farhaat Reach had come to the aid of Zir Abou-Farhaat. Their lawyers were informed of the detainment of their captain and of the wreck of the *Scimitar*, but they had decided not to do anything about it as they immediately proceeded to shut down computer access to tax records and shipping documents. Massive injunctions and court orders were flying, by way of com-drones, from the Abou-Farhaats to the Mandala Authority headquarters. Zir Abou-Farhaat was not aware of all this maneuvering on behalf of his family; he saw it only from the perspective of being a prisoner of war.

This, of course, meant that the Abou-Farhaats saw their captain, regardless of his relationship to the Abou-Farhaats themselves, as utterly expendable. It also meant to the Authority that the Abou-Farhaats "knew something" about this matter that they chose not to discuss. Clearly, they saw some profit to the shipment of the calibans, but just what kind of profit the Authority could not figure. Colleran was determined to find out on their behalf.

Sounds of the Klasa-Eisner longshoremen could be heard thumping through the lower regions of the *Khadija* as they opened doors, depressurized seals, and began moving things about.

There was only one *thing*, however, that Colleran wanted transferred, and Zir Abou-Farhaat's sweating was related to it.

"Let's get going," Colleran urged.

"I want a gun," Zir Abou-Farhaat demanded.

"No guns."

They made for the main elevator. "I saw the scan of the canister, you know. It's almost ready to come out. If it does, I want something to defend myself with. You owe that to me!"

"I owe you nothing but a well-aimed kick," Colleran said. "I can give it to you now or later. Which do you want?"

Zir Abou-Farhaat stepped into the confined elevator and gave Colleran a contemptuous glare. They sank to the main gantry in hateful silence.

They walked out of the upper lock onto the top gantry. Down below them on another level they could see longshoremen, overseen by an efficient woman, wrestle a large aluminum-alloy canister from the main hold. Fumes and steam rose up about them like wrathful spectres. It had rained the night before and the entire landing facility was muggy and thick.

The planet was called Lowen, and it circled a young star that the Klasa-Eisners had chosen to call their home system. They had achieved Reach status a hundred years earlier through various syndicated consulting operations, which in turn led to banking and commerce. Lately, the Klasa-Eisners had begun involving their interests in farming and agriculture with the intention of becoming the breadbasket for much of the Beta Spoke.

This was an interesting revelation to Colleran, once he had examined the Klasa-Eisner's financial records and their yearly shareholders' reports. If Rex Wahlander had worked at one time for the Meurers—who fed both the Gamma Spoke and the Beta Spoke worlds—then it only made sense that he would seek a position of influence in the Klasa-Eisners, who were just now moving into the areas of bioengineering and high-yield farming.

But *why* the man had to work at all baffled him. The property settlement in Regina Wahlander's divorce case valued his half well in excess of twelve million Mandala credits. However, since Rex Wahlander hadn't been seen in four years, most of it languished in banks or financial institutions, forcing Regina, year after year, to pay his share of the taxes on the interest and dividends he'd accumulated.

All of which led Colleran to think that if certain marriages were made in heaven, then certain divorces were made in hell.

"Never heard of Rex Wahlander," the port chief, a cigar-chewing hulk named Bull Barton, said. He held the manifest for the canister as it was being on-loaded onto a flatbed truck beyond the transfer area near the gantry. He went on. "I know it says here that it's to be delivered to a Rex Wahlander, but I'll be damned if I've ever heard of him. Maybe he's an exec in some other city. Who knows?"

He gave Colleran back the clipboard with the manifest attached to it. He grinned maliciously at Zir Abou-Farhaat who had been standing at a distance. "Didn't think we'd be seeing you for some time, Zir. You with him?" He indicated Colleran.

"He's under arrest," Colleran told him. He was watching the longshoremen carefully attach the canister to the flatbed.

"His natural state," Bull Barton said. "We wouldn't have allowed him here if it hadn't been for your clearance."

"Why's that?"

"Because he doesn't like paperwork," Bull Barton said. His cigar was dead in his mouth. "Do you, Zir?"

Zir Abou-Farhaat overflowed with hatred for the two men before him.

Bull Barton turned to Colleran. "The boy seems to want to fly in, unload, and fly out without taking the time to let us know that he's arrived. Won't even sign his name to even the smallest pieces of paper. Legal-type papers."

"Don't worry," Colleran informed the port chief. "He'll be filling out papers for some time to come."

"Glad to hear it."

A dark and sleek helicopter flew over them, circled the *Khadija* once, then sped off toward the city in the distance. It was an Authority chopper in camouflage green with the pod of a large Langstrom clasher hanging from beneath its stabilizer wing.

Bull Barton's bushy eyebrows knitted with deep concern. "I was going to ask you about all the security. What's going on?"

Colleran squinted into the morning's bright light, watching the chopper race for the city spires several miles away. He said, "Nothing much. We're just trying to track down some people."

The port chief shook his head, wiping his neck with a soiled hankerchief. "Must be someone important." He pointed to the manifest. "But as far as I'm concerned, you're clear to transfer the cargo. My men will drive and we've got a car waiting for you."

"That's fine," Colleran acknowledged.

Bull Barton took the manifest, signed it, and gave it to a waiting assistant. He nodded at the silent Zir Abou-Farhaat. "You taking him with you?"

Colleran shook his head. "No. He stays with you. Keep an eye on him. He's like grease when it comes to sliding out from underneath you. I'll pick him up when I return."

Bull Barton managed a grin. "We've got a place for him. Me and Zir go way back. Don't we, Zir?"

Zir Abou-Farhaat growled something in Lost Earth Arabic that neither Bull Barton nor Colleran understood, but probably had something to do with various barnyard animals their mothers must have had sexual relations with.

Bull Barton snapped his pudgy fingers, and two strapping longshoremen came over from a load of crates they had been stacking and stood beside the Abou-Farhaat.

"We'll watch him," Bull Barton said.

* * *

The city where the Klasa-Eisners had their headquarters lay to the north of the landing field. Beyond it were purple-shaded hills, and farther beyond those were cumulus clouds building for another storm sometime later that day. The scene was entirely too peaceful for Colleran, knowing what followed him on the highway in the flatbed truck. Traffic on this highway through the city was moderate, but Colleran continually worried about the creature within the canister and the damage it would do if it should get out in the city itself. This time they had taken the precaution of putting a timer on the canister to give them a sense of how far along the creature had developed. The Authority chopper followed overhead, and Colleran's clasher was up to full power. He was ready at a moment's notice to stop his car and clash the creature should anything unexpected happen.

Still, it was like driving down the road with a time bomb. Indeed, if their calculations were correct, it was just possible that they could locate Rex Wahlander before the creature got out. They had already made plans to remove the canister to a special site where they could watch the creature burst out. Then, presumably, they would kill it. That, at least, was the plan.

But for now Colleran wanted to deliver it into the hands of Rex Wahlander so that he could place him under protective custody.

The administration buildings of the Klasa-Eisner Reach complex was a tasteful gathering of mirrored high rises set in a kind of park with tall trees and fountains. Colleran wheeled his car off the highway and into the park, following the directions he was given to a rear entrance of the complex. The flatbed truck was right behind him.

As per Colleran's instructions, there were only a few—but heavily armed—guards waiting at the loading dock in the shadows of the immense buildings of the complex. They were unable to determine what the caliban in the canister was going to look like, but they believed that it was not like any of the others. So far, each caliban seemed to be a made-to-order commando.

As Colleran drove up, several workers hustled off the loading dock and began maneuvering the flatbed around to where it could be removed in case something happened. Colleran didn't expect to be gone long and he was dead set on escorting the canister to the special examination facility when it was time for it to hatch.

A foreman came out and ran over to Colleran. All of the other personnel stayed away from the ominous figure that Colleran cast among them in his black-and-silver.

The foreman said, "We'll take over from here. Mrs. Eisner is waiting for you right now." He pointed to the top floor of the twenty-storey building above them.

Colleran moved close to the man. "I take it that you've been informed that—" He motioned toward the canister, now draped with a tarpaulin on the flatbed.

The foreman nodded quickly. "I know, but my men don't. They've only been told to watch over it."

"Good," Colleran said.

He made one last check on the timer attached to the side of the canister to make sure that he had enough time. No sound came from inside it, but that didn't please him as much as it should have. This was the largest canister of all the caliban crates in storage back on Asarhaddon Four.

However, it wasn't as large as the one Jay Heger and his team hauled up from the gloomy waters of Lake Frederick back on Oakstaadt. That one had been the size of a MUD unit.

The top floor of the spired office building was the main executive suite of the Klasa-Eisner Reach, and like so many executive suites he'd seen in his many years, this one seemingly oozed wealth and comfort. Tall plants of familiar Lost Earth origins lined the carpeted hallways, and secretaries with squared shoulders and breast implants moved among the offices of the powerful people who ran the Reach. Colleran stepped from the elevator and checked his watch and his clasher.

With the exception of the armed security team down below watching the flatbed truck, the building was otherwise operating on a normal business-as-usual schedule. Computer speed-printers buzzed, phones rang, typewriters snicked, and above all this was an aviary of secretarial voices.

Several of the secretaries, however, became mute when Colleran stepped among them. One woman picked up a phone and called her boss as the others nearby whispered to each other.

A man in a conservative business suit came to meet him. This was Ford Klasa, one of the relatives of the founders. He was a nervous man who had gone bald and slack in the service of so powerful an organization. He didn't belong here and the presence of the Authority only caused him more worry. He escorted

Colleran as quickly as he could to his spacious office, where the
interested secretaries could not overhear them.

"We've done everything the Authority requested, Mr. Regulator," he said, a fretful look on his face.

"Lou Colleran," Colleran told him, trying to make him feel at
ease.

Ford Klasa's secretary placed a thick printout on the desk by the
large windows. Klasa pointed to it. "We've ran check after check
and we can't find anybody named Rex Wahlander."

Colleran had suspected as much. He pulled out the bill-of-
lading and unfolded it. "This is what went in over the Abou-
Farhaat invoice network. It's a standard request. We happened to
intercept it—and its cargo."

"I understand that," the nervous man said looking at the
request. "And we ran a cross-check of all of our employees. All
of them, everywhere. There's no one named Rex Wahlander in our
employ."

Colleran then gave him the names of the other men and women
who were due to receive caliban canisters from the Abou-
Farhaats, and Ford Klasa said that none of them were familiar to
him. However, he did order his secretary to begin a search in their
computers for the names in case they might at one time have
worked for the firm. They had freed up several hours of time from
their mainframe—computers built especially for them by the Cray
Reach of the Alpha Spoke—and they might be able to come up
with something.

Colleran noticed that Klasa's secretary, a pretty woman with
rich, auburn hair, had the moon-faced look of a lovely. She was,
as it turned out.

When the lovely left with the names for the computer Ford
Klasa closed the doors and went directly over to Colleran, who
was standing by the windows looking down at the loading docks
below—just to make sure.

Klasa said, "There's a rumor about a war. A Reach war. Is that
true?"

The man was one of those individuals who thrived on gossip
and let it eat him from within as he tried to figure out what impact
it would have on his life personally. Self-absorbed, Ford Klasa
was what used to be called a wimp.

Colleran kept mum. "We're looking into some illegal trafficking. That's all."

He was thankful that Ford Klasa was not the one the Authority had briefed. The person who was now entered the room, flanked by her own secretaries—three males who were not lovelies.

This woman had *power*. She had short brown hair with no streaks of gray, although she seemed to be in her mid-forties. She wore a neatly tailored business suit and smoked a legal cigarette.

Aside from her coterie of secretaries, she was followed rather insistently by a very tall, very athletically constructed man who was talking and waving his hands about animatedly. This person was not a secretary; Colleran didn't know what he was.

"But Sheila! There's an important golf tournament coming up. It's the Whetstone Classic and that's the best place to do business! They're expecting me—"

Sheila Eisner, kingpin in the Klasa-Eisner Reach, walked around Ford Klasa's desk, ignoring Colleran. Behind her trailed a visible cape of cigarette smoke, which, as it ghosted by him, nauseated Colleran. Cigarettes was a vice beyond comprehension to him. To Colleran, their smell made a woman repugnant and unapproachable. Sheila Eisner, however, cared very little what Colleran—or anyone else—thought on the matter.

The garish and gregarious blonde man who dogged her, and dwarfed her, turned to Colleran and grabbed his hand as if it was his most natural reflex to smile and shake hands.

"Hi, officer. Clay Desmond, glad to meet you!"

Desmond was a few inches taller than Colleran, and where Colleran's blonde hair was straight and combed back on his head, Desmond's was piled high in a pompadour. He also wore an open shirt and a cascade of gold necklaces. Each hand displayed at least three jeweled rings.

Sheila Eisner turned her steel-gray eyes on Colleran as Desmond came to a standstill in front of everyone, now that he could no longer lobby for his precious causes privately.

She said, "I see that you've met Mr. Klasa, and this is Mr. Clay Desmond."

Desmond threw out his chest proudly. "PR. Just call me Clay." The man's teeth, when he smiled, seemed incredibly huge.

Sheila Eisner sat down in Ford's chair, but not without a grimace from the chair's usual occupant over in the corner next to the wide window. She steepled her fingers, her elbows on the desk. Her cigarette burned in an ashtray that one of the secretaries brought along. She seemed more than just a trifle annoyed that she had run into Desmond out in the corridor.

She apologized to Colleran. "Clay here keeps our customers happy with golf tournaments, sales meetings, conventions. And occasional pimping. It's called public relations."

Desmond and Sheila Eisner seemed to have a "fighting" sister and brother relationship.

"Aw, Sheila—" The teddy bear-huge Desmond held out his arms, begging, pleading, loving his embarrassing show. "Don't call them whores. I'm not a pimp. Honest."

Ford Klasa—by the window like a palm tree placed in the sun so it could thrive but otherwise be ignored—cleared his throat, getting at least Sheila Eisner's attention.

"Sheila, Regulator Colleran is here with the shipment mentioned in yesterday's Authority drone."

She glowered at Ford Klasa. "I can see, Ford. Thank you." She rifled through the large printout on the desk, the search of employees for Rex Wahlander. Then she let the printout flap shut and looked at Colleran, leaning back in her chair. "So what's this about? You actually brought one of those monsters with you?"

Ford Klasa wobbled over in the corner. "Monsters? What monsters?"

Colleran stepped before the desk. "This one's under control, but it's important that we play the game of whoever is sending them around the Mandala worlds."

"This sounds exciting." Clay Desmond brightened. "What gives?"

Sheila Eisner lifted her cigarette and held it up in a sophisticated gesture. She scorned Desmond. "You're lucky I'm letting you in this meeting, Clay. Keep quiet about this." The woman had obviously run out of what little humor she had.

"Yes'm," Desmond said, saluting.

She turned her attention on Colleran and he suddenly felt as if he were sitting before a hanging judge back on the old Lost Earth. This woman was enormously unattractive to him. She said, "You've got six minutes of my time to explain to me why I had to use my computers to track down someone who obviously doesn't work for us, who never did, and who probably never even set foot on the planet. And then you've got to explain what right you have to bring one of those goddamn things here."

Colleran sucked in his breath and pulled out his clasher. The woman gasped. Everyone gasped. Colleran held it out before her.

"This and the badge on my chest give me the right to do anything I want regarding this matter," he snarled. "And I'll take one hour of your time if that's what it's going to take to help me get to the bottom of this. Your Reach, because of one specific employee named Rex Wahlander, is under attack by some unknown parties for unknown reasons." Colleran could smell the woman's breath as she tried to control her ire. Nobody had ever spoken this way to her before.

He went on. "I've dealt with these creatures and they are extremely dangerous. As I mentioned to Mr. Klasa—" The man by the window fidgetted. "As I told Mr. Klasa, we might be in the middle of a Reach war."

Score some points for Ford Klasa. But Colleran had Sheila Eisner where he needed her. He said, "If that's the case, then you and your party animal here—" He waved his clasher at the imposing Clay Desmond. "You are all going to suffer. That is, unless you cooperate fully."

He stood up, holstering his clasher. Everyone's eyes were on the live-leather holster as it gobbled the deadly weapon.

Sheila Eisner, not skipping a beat, crushed out her cigarette and drew another one from a tastefully decorated cigarette case. "Okay," she said as a secretary scurried over to light it for her. "You win. But we still don't know who Rex Wahlander is or what all this is about. Do we, Ford?" she asked the man by the window, who cowered out of range.

"Uh, no, Sheila," he said with fear and trembling. "That's what I told him. We did a mainframe scan of all our employees—"

"Ford."

"Sorry."

Colleran faced Clay Desmond, who was all bright eyes and eager. "Have *you* ever heard of Rex Wahlander?"

"Wish I had, officer. Honest! I'd love to help, but, hey. I meet all kinds of guys in my business."

"I wouldn't call it that," Sheila Eisner sneered, pulling hard on her cigarette.

Desmond loomed over her like a happy bear. "Right, and you just keep that thought the next time you look at our annual reports." He smiled triumphantly.

"Clown," she said without any true rancor.

"Love you, too." He smiled.

Colleran had once thought that the further human life spread from the Hub, the stranger it got. Here was proof. Maybe it was all the money. . . .

Clay Desmond slapped Colleran on the shoulder. "Sorry we can't help you, officer. Looks like this isn't your day."

Colleran gave him a disapproving look.

"Hey," Desmond said, backing off. "Just being friendly."

Sheila Eisner smiled at her PR associate. "He's called a *Regulator*. 'Officer' is an official term for civil authorities. Like the ones you keep running from."

"Great kidder," he said to Colleran, winking. Even his gold necklaces seemed to wink.

The door to the expansive office suite opened just then, and in walked an extremely beautiful lovely.

"Clay! I'm waiting, honey. We're supposed to be at the country club—"

Colleran almost fell over with shock.

It was another Heidi Beryl. However, this one was closer in skin color and hair style to his Heidi on Okeanos. His heart almost fluttered away. For a moment, he thought that it *was* the same Heidi.

She looked at him and smiled. "Oh, hello. I didn't know you were here."

But the *you* was more of a generic term, not meant for him specifically. Nevertheless, for an instant he felt as if it had been.

Clay Desmond, suddenly embarrassed by his pet lovely's awkward appearance, rushed around and escorted her to the door. "Darling, we're in the midst of real important stuff."

"You're goddamn right, we are," growled Sheila Eisner. "Get the hell out of here! Clay, I told you I didn't want any of your little twits around here!"

"Right, right," Desmond said, hustling the lovely to the door.

"Now, wait a minute!" Heidi protested. "I didn't know there was a meeting here, and I'm not an idiot!"

Good for you. Colleran's heart soared. *That's my Heidi.*

But Desmond hastily removed the lovely from the suite, to where the secretaries were waiting to see what developed in the room with the Regulator.

Sheila Eisner stubbed out her cigarette; she smoked the way a normal person would eat. The smoke was thick and sickening.

"Christ, I'm surrounded by weaklings," she said.

Colleran, however, had all of his attention taken away by the appearance of Heidi. A Heidi Beryl was the very *last* person he'd expected to run into this far in the Gamma Spoke. The feelings he still had for his first Heidi were strong enough to fight their way up through the effects of the metatryzine. The drug had the dubious virtue of suppressing any flights of romantic urges—the primary catalyst of a Lei experience—from occurring. It left him level-headed and calm.

Until this moment.

Desmond came back into the office suite and closed the doors behind him. He was now full of puppy-dog contrition.

"I'm sorry about that." He spoke in general terms, but always it was for Sheila Eisner. "She got loose. We've got a date with some people at the country club—"

"Clay."

"Yes, Sheila?"

"Drop it."

"Right." Still, he managed a conspiratorial smile at Colleran, which Colleran didn't return.

Sheila Eisner got out of her chair and placed the cigarette case in her coat pocket. "Time's up, Mr. Colleran. Thank you for coming here and wasting it for me. We've accomplished nothing, at least nothing that you and—" she indicated the hapless Ford Klasa by the window—"my colleague here could not have done on your own. The next time you drop by, don't let me know."

She began walking around Colleran when a secretary came in from the doors Clay Desmond had so recently closed.

When the secretary saw Colleran she touched her throat with her hand, but turned to Sheila Eisner, who was on her way out.

"Yes, what is it?" Sheila Eisner asked.

"Ma'am," the secretary began haltingly, looking once more at Colleran. "It's security. There's some trouble down at the loading dock."

"What kind of trouble?"

The secretary looked once at Sheila Eisner, then ran over to the window, standing beside her boss, Ford Klasa. She looked down the stainless steel side of the building. Ford Klasa did the same.

He suddenly cried out.

The secretary was terrified when she saw it as well. To Sheila Eisner, she said, "There's some sort of animal climbing up the side of the building. It's put our security team to sleep!"

20

Colleran lunged through the crowd gathering at the window, pushing aside the stunned male secretaries. Sunlight from above made the viewing difficult, but what Colleran saw he didn't like.

Far, far below in the grassy parklike area near the loading dock, he could see tiny figures sprawled on the concourse like dollops of color splashed by a painter's brush. Other personnel, recently summoned, were squinting upward and taking aim with their pistols at a caterpillar-like creature that was snaking slowly up the silver side of the building.

The caterpillar exuded wisps of gas from its sides—probably some kind of nerve gas or anesthetic, Colleran guessed. And like the caterpillars of the Lost Earth, this one looked as if it were going to metamorphose into something else.

"Everyone out," Colleran ordered. "Now!"

He turned to Sheila Eisner, who stood disbelieving and inconvenienced. "Where's the back way? Do you have any kind of fire exit or emergency elevator system?"

A bullet could be heard ricocheting up the side of the building, followed by the chatter of automatic rifle fire.

Sheila Eisner, however, wasn't budging. She gave Colleran a withering look. "What was in the box you brought us? What exactly?"

The secretary by the window, Ford Klasa's loyal lovely, gasped once more and pointed. "Oh, look what it's doing! *Look!*"

Colleran glanced down and saw that the caliban—perhaps thirty feet long—had cupped its many legs to the slick surface of the high-rise. It used its suctioned feet to pull out whole panes of window glass, which it tossed down at the men and women trying to shoot it.

The creature mounted a ledge or overhang in the natural design of the building and began bunching up. Its skin shuddered in a gastrointestinal fit as a few bullets managed to pierce it. However, it was now out of accurate range of the ordinary rifles—and far below Colleran's clasher range.

Sheila Eisner was behind Colleran, breathing hotly. "I was told that you had it watched!"

Colleran checked his own watch. "It wasn't supposed to reach its mature gestation for another hour and a half."

Ford Klasa turned a mushroom color by the window. "You mean that—"

Clay Desmond and his lovely stood uneasily in the doorway. "Listen, people. We're outta here. We got things to do."

With that, he yanked Heidi out into the lobby where other office personnel were making for the elevators. A low alarm was sounding and a security guard was directing traffic to the elevator bank.

Sheila Eisner spun around and shouted after them. "Oh, no you don't! Clay, you just wait right where you are!"

Colleran ran around to Ford Klasa's large desk and pressed a com botton to the security team below.

"What happened?" he demanded into the speaker. "How did the thing get loose?"

An unidentified guard came on, and over the connection he could hear the chaos and gunfire in the background.

The guard said, "Our men were positioning the truck so another vehicle could pass by and the damn thing broke out. There's this gas—" Gunshots buried the transmission.

The red-headed lovely by the window suddenly jumped up gleefully. "Look, look! They got it! *They got it!*"

When Colleran returned to the window, he saw the creature, or what remained of it, fall from the side of the multi-storied building. Its skin fluttered like a flag riddled in combat, a Chinese dragon-kite cut loose from its tether. Several of the segmented legs were left behind on the building wall, suctioned there by the remaining feet, all askew. Blood and body fluids drooled down the ledge.

But the ledge itself was near a window, most of which was effectively chewed out. Colleran didn't like the looks of that.

Sheila Eisner grabbed him. "You brought that thing with you! This is your fault!"

He whirled around. "And just maybe Rex Wahlander is here. Maybe he was one of the team on the loading dock. Maybe he's an accountant on the tenth or eleventh floor. Maybe he's one of your secretaries. But that creature knows that he's here somewhere!"

"Knows?" she countered. "The thing's dead!"

"I don't think so."

"What?"

The lights went out.

Sheila Eisner glanced around in the shadows. Enough light came in from the windows so that they could see, but all other electricity was down.

"Now what's *that* all about?"

Ford Klasa, at his desk, toggled switches and buttons on the side console. "The whole building's lost power!"

"That's *im*possible," Sheila Eisner said with indignity.

Colleran pulled his clasher out. "Everyone. *Now!* I want all of you to leave by the exit opposite where the creature came in."

Clay Desmond, perhaps because of his size and humor, couldn't fathom the depth of the occasion's seriousness. "Hey, Regulator. The thing's dead. Security's just shut down the building in case—"

Colleran ran up to him as Heidi stared at them both with wide, frightened eyes. He said, "The thing's inside the building, and *it* shut down the power. My guess is that the creature has divided itself into two or three smaller creatures. They're commandos and they know what they're doing."

Colleran whirled around and shouted at them. Their stupidity and arrogance were truly beyond belief. "*You idiots! Do as I say! Get to the elevators and get out now!*"

Ford Klasa was already moving around them all, tugging along his lovely secretary. "Come along, Ms. Wasson."

"Yes, Mr. Klasa," she said, making for the outer lobby.

As they all piled into the secretarial area of the large office, Colleran's attention was diverted by the sound of a distant rumbling. At first he thought it might have been an explosion from the lower reaches of the Klasa-Eisner building, but a bluish glow from beyond the window told him otherwise.

It was coming from the south of the city. A large spindle freighter's gravity lifts were accelerating tremendously. He didn't need to look. At the spaceport there had been only one freighter of that size, and that was the *Khadija*. Zir Abou-Farhaat had greased his way out of another bind.

Sheila Eisner showed no interest in spaceships and instead began walking down the opposite end of the hallway. Clay Desmond and his lovely followed, with Heidi staying quite near to him.

Sheila Eisner said to Colleran. "This way, Regulator. There's an executive elevator that we all use." She spoke like a practiced machine and walked on her high heels like a woman who was in control of her life.

Colleran ran after her. "Does the elevator have its own power source?"

The woman was surrounded by a halo of tobacco smoke. "Of course it does. You think we're that stupid?"

Colleran merely stared at her and tried to listen.

The rest of the building personnel, especially those on their floor, had made for the other elevators—and those, too, had independent power supplies. Several secretaries were crowding into the stairwells. It would be a long climb down, but at least they'd probably make it.

Colleran gathered with them at the executive elevator, which was, thankfully, at the opposite end of the building from where the creature had made its surprising entrance.

The elevator was recessed into a wall panel and when the doors opened, Colleran could see that it was large enough for all of them to make one trip. Colleran stood back for Sheila Eisner.

But the boss turned around and pulled Clay Desmond inside while blocking Heidi from entering. "I told you before. No lovelies."

"But—" Desmond began, blubbering suddenly. "She's mine, Sheila!"

Colleran suddenly felt an explosion rock the building. Plants in the outer hallway next to the elevator shook their green leaves as if a strong breeze had passed by.

"Move!" Colleran told them all. "They're on their way!"

But Sheila Eisner was holding firm. "No lovelies! I told you that a long time ago. I won't be near them and I won't have my life compromised because of them!" With that, she shoved the lovely out into the hallway, and Heidi fell backward onto the carpet with a cry.

"Clay!" she cried out as Sheila Eisner pulled Colleran inside. "Clay, don't go without me! *Please!*"

The door closed and Colleran turned to her as she pressed the down button. "You didn't have to do that. There's more than enough room in here."

She glared at him. "What's it to you? He's rich enough to buy or lease a hundred lovelies. They're expendable. You ought to know."

Colleran had to fight the urge to rip the woman's throat out. She stared him down as the elevator began descending.

"I thought so," she sneered. "I've seen your type before. You're one of the old ones. They all like lovelies, like Desmond here. You're afraid of a *real* woman."

For a moment Colleran thought he was experiencing his Lei, but the beauty and kindness of Beatrice was nowhere nearby. He thought instead of his last wife, the Plunderer. This woman before him acted on her own self-interests just as the Plunderer had. And no one could stop them. Their vision of the way things should be done made them *right*. And they did whatever they pleased.

He wanted to clash her.

Then, as she stared at him, she did an unexpected thing. She punched the *stop* button and the elevator halted its downward passage.

"What are you doing?" Desmond broke out. "Sheila!"

But the woman blocked the control panel and put her hands on her hips. To Colleran, she said, "Now, mister, you start talking. I want some answers!"

Could such a woman be human?

He looked around him, trying to visualize what might be transpiring on the floors where they were halted. How many men and women worked in the building? How many office suites were occupied? *How many people could those creatures kill before the security team finished them off?*

She caught his ruminations. "Don't worry. This elevator shaft goes all the way down. There aren't any other entrances until we get to the basement. We're safe. Now, I want to know what business you had bringing that creature onto our property. Tell me."

More explosions tremored throughout the building, but they

seemed far away and different from the first blasts. The security team *was* fighting back.

He said slowly, trying to control his vast anger, "There is a Reach war in progress and someone is using an army of specially constructed commandos to get at the people they want dead. One of those people works for you and they'll stop at nothing to get at him."

"Bullshit."

"*What?*" He was incredulous. His clasher in his hand suddenly felt like a wet sponge, utterly useless—as if *he* were suddenly useless. "We sent you the confidential memo! How can you say that?"

A strange, almost paranoid look filled her eyes as she scrutinized him. "What does the Authority want with the Klasa-Eisners? We've paid our taxes. We've done nothing wrong. This is just an excuse to get back at us, isn't it?"

"Sheila," Clay Desmond said, putting a cautious hand on her arm. "I think the man's right about this. He wouldn't be here unless—"

"Are you kidding me?" she shouted at the PR executive. "The last time we had the Authority here was years ago. They hardly ever come this far out in the Gamma Spoke." But her real challenge was Colleran himself. She flared at him. "A Reach war's impossible now. The Mandala worlds are too far apart and there's more than enough money for each corporation to make on its own. Whatever is going on is the Authority's fault!"

She fisted her knuckles and punched the elevator controls to resume their downward passage.

But the elevator didn't move.

"Hey," Desmond said, glancing around, suddenly feeling trapped. "What gives?"

Disgusted that the world didn't jump when she said *jump*, Sheila Eisner slammed her fist once more at the button panel. Nothing.

She looked up at Colleran, more perplexed than anything else. "Why aren't we moving? What did you tell my security team?"

"I didn't tell them anything," Colleran retorted.

Desmond sniffed. "Hey, what's that smell? You guys smell that?" He looked down to the carpeted floor at his feet and jumped back against the wall. "It's dissolving! Look at the floor!"

Colleran pushed Sheila Eisner against the other wall of the

elevator as they stared down. A mist seeped up as the floor and carpet started to crackle and fracture.

"Something's underneath us in the shaft!" she shouted.

The acid beneath them had only made it easier for the caliban. With one strong thrust, the floor forced itself upward and the entire car shook. Metal screamed—as did Sheila Eisner.

What came up was an *arm*. As long as a man, it had only three grasping fingers, but the power behind it was incalculable.

The arm flew up at Colleran as he yanked Sheila Eisner out of its reach. It then swept, just as quickly, for Clay Desmond, who was standing up against the wall with a horrified look on his face.

But the thing below couldn't see, and the thick-fingered hand struck the wall next to Desmond.

Desmond screamed and Sheila Eisner fainted dead away.

But that was long enough for Colleran to clash the creature without getting Desmond into the shot. The beast screamed once as it became a swirl of incendiary ash. Then it drifted on down the shaft into the bleak and hollow darkness.

21

The burnished, amber orb that was the sun around which the homeworld of the Klasa-Eisner Reach orbited now hung low on the western horizon. Colleran stood at the armored window of the makeshift Authority council room in police headquarters, three miles east of the Klasa-Eisner high rise. Plumes of nearly exhausted fires slanted vaguely into the twilight from the upper storeys of the complex as fire personnel finished extinguishing the incendiaries that the other two calibans had released. A police chopper, keeping the faxblabbers away, buzzed the skies like mean insects.

Inside the police council chamber, the Authority had assembled to assess the damages to the Klasa-Eisners and to convince Sheila Eisner that this was not some kind of mad plot to harass them. She wasn't buying.

Sheila Eisner, in the five hours since the attack, looked as if she'd aged fifty real-time years. Her makeup had faded, revealing hard lines around her mouth and eyes, but she still smoked incessantly. "This goes against all Mandala law. You just can't arbitrarily involve citizens in your petty squabbles, especially us."

Brianne Sagar sat comfortably in a chair, almost leaning back, so calm did she appear. Her eyes as she watched this woman were steeled and unwavering. Colleran was convinced now that for some time the Admin was on a constant dosage of metatryzine. There would be no flights of emotions for her. He could see why: Sheila Eisner, though she was a short-lived human, was extremely dangerous in her own right.

"When this gets to trial—which I'm sure you'll see to—we will know if Mr. Colleran's actions were prudent," the Admin told her. "But we did not know that the creatures had the ability to accelerate their own growth processes. Otherwise, we would not have brought the caliban down here."

"Swell." The other woman huffed. Her cigarette glowed in the encroaching shadows of the approaching night.

Sitting next to Brianne Sagar, with his secretary-lovely behind him and a Regulator guard behind her, was Ford Klasa, who had somehow managed to clean himself up, change clothes, and look his best—exactly the way one might for a public display. Sheila Eisner's riveting glances kept him silent.

The Admin continued from her chair. "But regardless of what has happened, we must find some connection between those Reaches that are receiving the caliban shipments. And your company is part of it. That's indisputable."

Sheila Eisner, her neatly sculpted hairdo frazzled and matted from a day's worth of fear and sweat, leaned over the table as if she were the chairperson of the board and the Admin some backplanet flunky. "And how are you going to convince my attorneys that this Rex Wahlander isn't some joke of yours? This is harassment, plain and simple!"

Brianne shrugged.

The other person involved in all of this was a considerably deflated Clay Desmond. Sheila Eisner had insisted that his lovely,

Heidi, remain outside with the other police personnel while they had this "chat" inside the conference room. Desmond looked like a man who had just had the fear of God put into him. He mopped his brow, his wrist bracelets clanking in the quiet of the conference hall.

"Sheila," he said slowly. "I think all this is for real—"

"What do you know?" she sniped.

He bent over in his chair and looked up at her—but not fearfully. "What I know is a goddamn big, black arm trying to kill me. When someone tries to kill me, I take it seriously."

Ford Klasa, in his own mousey way, smiled. Sheila Eisner caught this and froze him with an icy stare.

She paraded in front of the window beside Colleran, who wouldn't budge. He stood with his arms crossed over his chest, his badge gleaming in the sun's last light.

The woman pointed several miles to the west at her office complex, silent in the sunset. "Look out there! It's all over the fax channels that *something* got loose in our building. The people who fought those remaining two calibans, or whatever you call them, all have families who, by later tonight, will know what's happened. Com-drones go out every hour on the hour and they're going to be full of the news!"

Brianne Sagar said, "Let them gossip. It'll take months for all the important worlds of the Mandala to hear of your catastrophe. By then, you'll have recovered your business standings."

"And by then we'll have filed our briefs in the Mandala courts."

"We've got lawyers, too, you know," Colleran argued. "You might consider the possibility of helping us instead of working against us. After all, we did this to protect you."

"You call that *thing* protection?"

"It was actually an accident," he confessed. "You now know how advanced they are. There's no known organism in any of the explored Spokes like them and we have to fight them with everything we've got."

Ford Klasa seemed nearly invisible at the table. But he did look up at them. "Unless we're up against the Makers. Are they the Makers, Mr. Colleran?"

Brianne sat forward. "We don't know. That's a possibility, but we just don't know. It doesn't seem likely, after four-hundred and some years, that they'd strike out now at specific people, but it is a possibility that we're not overlooking." She held her stare on Sheila Eisner, silhouetted against the long bruise of sunset by the window. "But if they *are* the Makers, or their minions, then no Reach is safe. Even this far out in Gamma Spoke."

Sheila Eisner was undaunted by the Admin's presence. She said, "We'd be safe if you stopped bringing *them*!"

"We have to find Rex Wahlander," Brianne told her firmly. "Every designee of the calibans, so far, does exist. We're still tracking down a few of them, but at least those individuals do exist. There's no reason for us to assume that Rex Wahlander is *not* here."

"Well, he's not. Trust me," Sheila Eisner gruffed.

In the cloak of night settling about their world, Colleran could now make out the glittering star of the *Parvardigar* suspended in high orbit above the planet. *So much beauty in the midst of chaos.* He suddenly yearned for a Lei experience and the bliss that Beatrice's presence brought.

"Let's talk about something else," the Admin said, changing the subject.

"With or without my attorneys?"

"This is being recorded, so it doesn't matter," Colleran interjected.

Sheila Eisner paraded back and forth in front of the darkening window. She seemed at a loss for words, scowling at them. Brianne, however, filled in the vacancy in the conversation.

She began, "We're recording all of our dealings with the Reaches now because we're at war. It's official."

Sheila Eisner, arms held tight around her, stopped at the window. Ford Klasa at the table began, ever so slightly, to tremble. His lovely, Ms. Wasson, looked at her boss. Clay Desmond, the largest human in the room, choked.

"What?" Desmond blurted.

Brianne Sagar spoke quite precisely, her voice sounding like winds across the Lost Earth Arctic ice. She said, "Hence, all litigation will be based on established Mandala wartime policies. When you find out in court—the only place you're going to know—just what we've been through with these creatures, you'll change your minds about suing the Authority. Do what *you* want; *we* are at war."

"Oh, my God," Ford Klasa groaned. His lovely secretary got

up and stood close beside him, a move Sheila Eisner didn't like. However, she made no immediate complaint.

Brianne Sagar had brought with her a new computer analysis done while the *Parvardigar* was in flight toward the Klasa-Eisners. She said, "We've gone through your own personnel files and we can't find Rex Wahlander officially in your employ."

"That's what we've been telling your man here." She hooked a thumb in Colleran's direction.

"However, since Mr. Wahlander's been hounded by his wife for four years in a divorce battle, he's probably incognito, working somewhere on the planet where he'd be safe from subpoenas and the Meurers."

"The Meurers?" Sheila Eisner said, genuinely puzzled.

Colleran took over. "The designees of the calibans seem to be former employees of the Meurer Reach. That's the only lead we've got at the moment. Rex Wahlander evidently was one of the higher-ups in the corporation, at least before it collapsed."

Ford Klasa suddenly brightened. "The Meurers? Are you sure?" He glanced down the table at the ponderous, blonde PR man. "Clay, didn't you say that you worked for the Meurers at one time."

"Sure," Desmond said, looking at Colleran. "Long time ago. I cut my PR teeth there as an account executive. But I never heard of Rex Wahlander."

Sheila frowned in Desmond's direction. "This is the first I've heard of this."

Desmond laughed companionably. "Like hell. You hired me two weeks after I left them. It was on the golf course at Taija Downs where you finally broke par. I still won, though."

"And you've never heard of Rex Wahlander?" Colleran quizzed him.

"The Meurers employed hundreds of thousands of people," Desmond said, sitting up. He was quite animated now and much of what he had to say seemed to take the form of a sales pitch. "They owned a whole world that was solely devoted to raising their cattle and other farm animals. They were the best, in their time. Mostly because of the planet. Each continent, more than any other world in the Spoke, seemed perfect for raising farm animals, and the Meurers knew how to raise them. But, god, the smell—"

Colleran stared down at him. He then looked over at Brianne.

"Is it possible that the calibans might have been after Mr. Desmond here as well?"

Brianne now considered Clay Desmond in a new light. "It's possible."

"No, it's not," Desmond said. "The Klasa-Eisners employ hundreds of former Meurer Reach personnel all over the planet. When the Meurers fell, they had to look for work elsewhere, and since we're in much of the same business, a lot of them came here."

"You didn't tell me about this," Sheila Eisner said.

"That's because it happened six or seven years ago and because you aren't head of personnel and it's also because we hire all sorts of people from the other Reaches, especially those that operate near us."

"What else don't I know?"

"That there are at least ten former Meurer employees working in our building," Desmond said, pointing out the window to the smoky west. "And they're damn good employees." Desmond looked around to be sure his own lovely, Heidi, wasn't there. He then said confidentially. "And one of them is a close personal friend of mine, if you know what I mean." He winked at Sheila, who did not wink back.

Instead, she said to him, "You are in a load of trouble right now, Clay. Don't press your luck."

The Admin interrupted the tiff. "People, we need your cooperation in this. Desmond, can you tell us anything about the Meurer relationship with the Abou-Farhaats?"

Sheila Eisner laughed bitterly. "I can tell you about *our* relationship with those buccaneers."

Desmond, however, shrugged innocently. "I don't know. They used the Abou-Farhaats like we do. They took the shipments to wherever the Meurers had orders to deliver them. Why?"

"I don't know why," Brianne said, seemingly to herself. "But at least we know *why* those calibans wanted to destroy your whole building. If there are ten or more former employees of the Meurers working there, then everyone was at risk. Even Mr. Desmond."

Clay Desmond didn't like that at all.

"But the creature," Colleran persisted, "was after Rex Wahlander specifically. We need to know why."

Sheila Eisner walked up to Colleran, followed by a nimbus of smoke. "What *we* need to know is why *you* couldn't just come here and talk to us without bringing that horrible thing along."

Colleran defended himself. "It's important for us that they don't know we're onto them."

"It's a little late for that now, isn't it?"

"*Now* it is," Colleran admitted dryly. "It wasn't a few hours ago when the faxblabbers sent out their com-drones. Now most of Gamma Spoke will be hearing of it."

Sheila Eisner turned into the sunset's last rays and thought. She had cooled considerably. She said, "Six years is a long time to carry a grudge."

Ford Klasa peeped. "What if they are the Makers?"

Brianne Sagar quieted him. "Why would the Makers suddenly rise out of nowhere to pick on the Meurers? There are over one-hundred and forty-one official Reaches registered with the Mandala Authority. You must remember that the human population in the three inhabited Spokes is over two trillion now. There are another five Spokes left for colonization. We're talking about a widespread human population. The Makers would attack every-one everywhere. Not just the Meurers."

Ford Klasa withdrew into himself.

"So why the Meurers?" Sheila Eisner asked. "What did they do that was so wrong, other than make a bunch of catastrophic business decisions that put them out of operation?" She turned to her public relations liaison, who rose to the occasion by clearing his throat and jumping to his feet.

"They were in business for a long, long time," Desmond said. "They were masters at animal husbandry, developing bioen-gineered animals for domestic consumption. They fed most of the Gamma Spoke and the Beta Spoke. You should've seen the size of some of their cattle. In those last years I was there, some of the *urizen* got as tall as twelve feet at the shoulders."

"*Urizen*," Colleran said, listening. "That's from Blake."

Desmond asked, "Blake who?"

"Forget it," Colleran stated. "The cattle are called *urizen*?"

"All of the altered animals are *urizen*, or ur-cows, ur-pigs, and so on. They never did patent their process for altering their animals because they didn't want it duplicated or stolen. But their beef was the best, absolutely top grade. It went all throughout the Gamma and Beta Spokes. No other agribusiness anywhere could match them."

"Until they collapsed," Brianne said.

"I guess," Desmond said.

Colleran then asked the PR executive, "So why did you leave?"

Again, the scowl from Sheila Eisner. Desmond seemed embarrassed. "I got fired, actually."

Sheila Eisner said, "It's those goddamn lovelies of yours. They'll get you fired here, too, if you aren't careful."

Desmond spoke to both the Admin and the Regulator quite openly. "Hey, lovelies are legal. I can't help it if I like them better. The Meurers didn't like me bringing them around, and they asked me to quit. I tried to sue them, but, hey, what can you do when you walk into court with an attorney who has to face one of the largest law firms in the Spoke? I didn't stand a chance. I cut and ran."

Brianne Sagar faced Sheila Eisner. "What was the level of competition between your corporation and the Meurers? Our records show that they filed for Chapter Eleven in regular bankruptcy court and stopped doing business. What do you know about their collapse?"

Sheila Eisner didn't seem reluctant to part with company secrets. "We fly by the numbers here, Administrator. We were in the same business, expanding in dribs and drabs, as they say. The Meurers got greedy, from what I hear, and tried to grow too fast. They stayed away from us and eventually we started picking up some of their market shares."

"Would you say that *you* have a grudge against *them?*" the Admin asked.

She laughed as she drew out another cigarette. "Are you kidding? I'd like to thank them. We got most of their business."

The Admin drummed her slender fingers on the ebony top of the conference table. "What is your opinion—seriously—of the capacity of the Abou-Farhaats to wage a Reach war?"

"They've got a fleet of ships big enough to be battlecruisers, but as far as I know they don't have the guns or the clashers to do anyone any harm. Other than just being the cretins and cutthroats they are. Why? Are they behind this?"

Brianne said, "The man who delivered the last several caliban canisters is headed back to the system where the Meurers dwelled."

This surprised Colleran. "When did this happen?"

"Right before the *Parvardigar* spindled into orbit. We sent out a watch patrol drone to observe who spindled away from the Hub toward the Meurer's home planet. The *Khadaji* spindled away from the Hub exactly toward Courtenay Three where the Meurers lived. The coordinates that our drone picked up are unmistakable. The Abou-Farhaats are part of this; we just don't know what their part is."

The Admin folded up the printout with an almost surgical motion, clear and precise. "We can no longer afford to track down each and every recipient of the canisters even though we have several of them left. Our plan is this." She stood up and everyone watched her. "Mr. Colleran will escort Mr. Desmond to Courtenay Three so that the Authority can determine what is going on."

Desmond almost flew out of his chair. "*What?*"

"That sounds like an *excellent* plan," Sheila Eisner said, blowing smoke around her and leering at her PR executive. "I like it. I like it a lot."

"You can't do this! I don't want to go back, not if those caliban things are running loose!"

Colleran also managed a smile. "Our records show that their headquarters are probably deserted now. You're the only one who's got any idea of where to look for clues."

"But I was rarely there," the executive insisted. "I was always on junkets, going to the outer worlds, the other worlds of the Spoke—"

"Yes," Sheila Eisner said. "With your lovelies, probably wasting as much of their time as you've wasted ours."

"That's my job! It's the way business is done!"

"And that's the way *we* do business," the Admin responded. "But don't worry. Mr. Colleran is perfectly capable of seeing that you won't come to any harm. He's already done so. You can trust him."

At the table, only Ford Klasa smiled.

22

There was a long-standing notion, cultivated in a certain kind of genre writing in the twentieth century back on the Lost Earth, that when humanity reached the stars, their colonies would instantly devolve into medieval kingdoms, where myth and magic would replace the science that got them there and horses with pearlescent wings would ply the starry skies instead of spaceships. None of that had ever quite happened, if only that medieval kingdoms weren't nearly as lucrative as multiplanet-based corporations, or Reaches. The Meurers were just one of the many examples of what science and industriousness could accomplish.

However, when a Reach collapsed, it often did so with a suddenness that frequently threw its employees and the support personnel around it into utterly uncontrollable chaos. What followed could be termed "medieval," but it rarely had anything to do with juvenile wishful thinking or a harking back to Keatsian "realms of gold," when life was simpler and, by extension, better. That was all hogwash.

When a Reach collapsed—and one usually did every ten to thirteen years in the Mandala worlds—they did so for all sorts of reasons. Mismanagement was the most common malaise, but shifts in the market or outdated technology quite often contributed. Only those corporations that ruled whole asteroids or planets ran the risk of becoming barbaric kingdoms if the sole source of the population's livelihood was taken from them. This was what happened to the Meurer Reach.

Colleran had been a Regulator licensed to patrol the Gamma Spoke for only eighty or so years, and in that time—as long as it was—he had little contact with the Meurers. Their star was located close to the end of the Spoke about fifty-one light-years from the Hub. It was an isolated system that had only one huge habitable planet, Courtenay Three. But the planet was enough for the Meurers to farm and ranch effectively, enough to become a Reach, and enough to feed literally hundreds of worlds nearby. Their meat products were famous and Colleran had heard of them before. And because the Authority had received no complaints against the Meurers, or any requests for assistance in any regional disputes, they had all assumed that it was business-as-usual—until ex-employees began arriving on the worlds nearby and the Meurers themselves filed for bankruptcy and disappeared into an untraceable tax limbo. But that was six years ago.

Colleran's spindle contained three passengers when it left the homeworld of the Klasa-Eisners. One of the passengers he didn't much like, the other he did. Clay Desmond could have been a child kicking and screaming on his way to the doctor's office, for the man continually griped and complained as they spindled back into the event horizon of the Hub and spindled out toward the G5-type star called Courtenay. Desmond had, however, brought along his lovely, Heidi, who seemed nervous being in Colleran's presence, but not for any reason other than that. The Reach that operated the lovely industry never told the lovelies what their sister-clones were doing—or, specifically, how they perished. Rumors did circulate, however, that the lovelies were themselves mildly telepathic. His own Heidi had never confirmed this and he never pushed the issue. Clay Desmond's beautiful companion was simply uneasy at being dragged along by her owner.

Once they spindled into the Courtenay system, Desmond cheered up, biting the bullet as it were, and began filling Colleran in on the various—now abandoned—planets of the sprawling system. The Meurers, aside from ranching, had varied mining interests on some of the outer gas giants and their moons. The planet Courtenay Three was one of the best earth-normal worlds in the entire Spoke, but it was the *only* one suitable for *urizen* grazing. It seemed that the surface was composed of a tough topsoil on most of the mid-latitude continents, which was able to hold up the huge beasts. Moreover, the Meurers had developed a particular kind of grain for feed, and it could only be grown on Courtenay Three. Thus, they were able to corner a number of markets in their pursuit of better beef and pork and chicken.

However, as Desmond rattled on like an oldtime circus pitchman, Colleran could not rid himself of the vision of the man's meaty hands pawing Heidi's delicate breasts. Desmond was of a ruddy complexion and definitely a carnivore: his appetites were immense. He was also sexually aggressive and Heidi was always within his reach. Colleran wondered if all this had been a good idea. At least he could have insisted that Heidi stay behind. He needed Desmond happy, however, and that meant bringing this particular Heidi Beryl along.

There were no docking facilities in high orbit above the earth-normal planet. Colleran could discern a few fossilized communications satellites, but beyond those, the whole planet seemed to have lost itself in radio silence.

The *Khadaji* was also nowhere nearby. The Authority, however, was confident that Zir Abou-Farhaat was in the system. When the *Parvardigar* finished its visit to the Abou-Farhaat homeworld, it would enter the Courtenay system to scour it for the elusive Zir Abou-Farhaat if Colleran couldn't locate him on the planet.

Colleran passed several orbits about three hundred miles above the quiet planet, noting a few illuminated cities of modest dimension when they flew into the night side of their orbit. Those cities were along the western shores of the largest continent where, as Desmond informed him, the Meurers once had their main cattle depots and abattoirs. The ur-cattle, as Desmond told the story, were raised by various ranchers on a consignment basis. The Meurers owned the planet, virtually. The farmers and ranchers raised the cattle—also owned by the Meurers—but above a certain percent of the herd, the ranchers could keep the remaining profits. All of the cattle were then driven to port cities where they were slaughtered and prepared to be lifted into orbit. The cities they now saw from orbit were what was left of those processing centers. There weren't very many of them.

North along the coastline from one such city was supposed to be the headquarters of the Meurers, called Shuraat. However, on their last night pass, they could see no lights coming from where the city ought to be. When they came around again, allowing for dawn to rise over Shuraat itself, they found out why.

It was a thorough ruin.

Colleran alighted from his spindle, followed by an awestruck Clay Desmond.

"I . . . I don't believe it," he gaped, looking around at the city square. "This happened in just six *years*?"

Heidi kept quite close to Desmond, a fact that did not escape Colleran's notice—although he did not know why.

Colleran had set his black spindle down in the city square, dead center of Shuraat. The ruin of the former corporate headquarters was staggering and unlike anything Colleran had ever seen before. It looked as if someone had long ago fought a pitched battle here, and the city lost. That meant the Meurers.

The avenues and streets were broken slabs of asphalt and concrete, dotted with sharp-toothed craters. The buildings were burned-out husks. The freeways surrounding the area were like the skeletons of reptiles. High tension wire towers were steel scarecrows, their wires dangling forlornly toward the wretched earth.

The most important feature, as Colleran saw it, was the vast plant growth. Since the city was close to a river estuary, he could understand some of the lushness. There just seemed to be too much of it. But clearly these streets had not seen human beings in many, many years.

Colleran put on his sunglasses and scanned the area. He was wearing his standard Regulator's black-and-white tunic, but he also wore a thin, but efficient, armored vest. His clasher was in its waiting holster.

"It's hard to believe that you used to work here," Colleran commented as he stepped out onto the broken stones of the square.

Desmond lost most of his salesman's manners once they had gotten away from the granite-carved Sheila Eisner. Now he seemed more his true self. The rings on his fingers glittered in the bright morning light that fell about them. A bird shrilled invisibly in the dense cover of the green woods surrounding the city square.

Desmond pointed out a large assembly of buildings that undoubtedly were the apex of the city's former life. "I worked there," he said, standing beside Colleran with Heidi right behind him. "I worked in that far one, the one that's been blown out. I don't believe this."

The buildings were of an architectural style that Colleran found gothic and eccentric, clearly out of step with the Alpha Spoke. Even in ruin the buildings suggested a people whose interests had turned inward, a kind of internecinity that could only lead to self-destruction. Vines clutched at most of their lower reaches; other growth sprouted at the top. Birds wheeled in the sky like vultures coming home to roost.

Colleran pointed to the building next to Desmond's former office. "That one was hit by a tank-killer missile. Bazooka, perhaps. It's a wonder they didn't use atomics."

"Atomics?" Desmond asked, startled.

"A bit antiquated, but they would've done the job faster."

Desmond squinted in the bright morning light. "Who are we talking about, exactly?"

"You tell me. You worked here just about the time they started collapsing. This"— Colleran indicated the devastated office complex ahead of them—"wasn't done by insolvency. This was done by honest-to-goodness enemies. Enemies who were armed and highly dangerous. Any ideas?"

Colleran watched as Desmond surveyed the warscape around him. A small, lazy creek flowed down the street to their left and a kind of moss covered much of the stone benches and carved ornamentals around the square. "Hell, Regulator, every Reach has enemies. Ours does. You've seen Sheila. She gets a wild hair up her ass and even *I* go on vacation. The Meurers had enemies, all right, but who did them in is a puzzle. I was long gone." Then, as if for support, or to merely acknowledge that she was there, he turned to Heidi. "Isn't that right, sweet?"

"That's right," she said directly to Colleran. "We've been together for a long, long time. And—"

"That's enough, baby," Desmond said quickly, somewhat embarrassed. He pushed her gently aside. She didn't mind, or at least didn't seem to, and smiled sweetly at Colleran, a smile that dug deep within him and found something there to stir up.

"But there was a lot of in-fighting, back-stabbing, you know. The usual. Happens all the time," Desmond continued. "That's why I left."

"That's not what Sheila Eisner said."

"She tends to see the darker side of things," Desmond remarked, smiling widely. "That's why she hired me. She's night to my day. You'd be surprised the jams I've gotten her out of."

That's funny, Colleran mused to himself, *I'd have thought it the other way around. . . .*

Colleran began feeling that fist in his gut twisting. In the hidden reaches of his consciousness he could almost sense the whisperings of Beatrice. Perhaps it was only the wind through the strange trees nearby, trees that seemed more natural to this landscape than the city itself. He felt out of place, all wrong about this. He felt all wrong about Desmond, particularly in the way he treated his lovely. But maybe it was the stress.

Colleran faced him. "Look, Desmond. Let's get clear on a few matters. I know you're holding out on me. I know your kind. What goes on between you and Sheila Eisner doesn't concern me at the moment, but *this* does." He waved his hand around him to the ruin.

Then he upped the ante. He removed his glasses and stepped quite close to Desmond. "I also don't like the way you treat your lovely. But this is just between you and me. I'm not speaking on behalf of the Authority."

Desmond was taken aback, clearly. "What's Heidi have to do with this?"

"Plenty," Colleran said. "I've been informed that you have a significant share of stock in the Bayright Reach, which manufactures lovelies. Suppose you tell me what that means."

Desmond went through some sort of interior battle over deciding how to respond, but clearly Colleran had the upper hand.

Desmond's rings on his fingers clacked nervously. "I kept all my stocks and investments when I left the Meurers. Nothing wrong with that. Some wise guy in the Meurers thought it would be a nice idea to buy out the folks who run the Bayrights. It didn't work, but in the process I got to keep my shares. It's all legal and my accountants pay all my dividend taxes."

Colleran put his silver sunglasses back on and considered the ruins once more. He also wanted to avoid Heidi's probing stare. *Jesus*, he thought, *she's so much like . . . the other one*.

Colleran then said, "So maybe the Bayrights are behind this?"

"Maybe," Desmond was quick to reply. "They use a lot of the same technology in cloning."

"The Bayrights are among the cleanest corporations operating in the Mandala," Colleran stated. He began walking toward the ruins. "They've been audited every year and watched every year since they came into existence. They provide a useful service that no one wants interrupted."

Desmond became his chummy self once again. "Oh, *ho!* So that's why you've been giving my Heidi the eyeball. Bet that's not the only ball you'd like to give her." He laughed loudly.

Colleran's fist against his jaw was even louder.

Desmond fell over onto the mossy cement of the square with a crash, and Heidi ran over to him. She looked up at him accusingly.

"You didn't have to do that!" she cried.

But Desmond answered for him. "Sure he did. The older a man gets, the harder it is to endure the truth." For a PR man, he suddenly seemed articulate.

"So what are you running from, Desmond? What do the calibans want with you?" Colleran asked, his hand hovering above his clasher. "Are you so innocent? Sheila Eisner said you traffic in lovelies. I believe her. And I don't like pimps."

"Why? Because we get your money?"

"Clay—" Heidi cautioned, helping the big man to his feet.

But Desmond knew his rights, apparently. He got up and faced Colleran. "There's no law in making money through investments. So what if I've got a lion's share in the Bayrights? So what if lovelies are used by immortals more than the average man—or woman? So what? When the Mandala commonwealth decides for a change in the law, then I'll clean up my ways. Until then my ways will remain as they are. And right now, they *are* clean!"

Colleran stared at the man. What had he to do with the *other* kinds of lovelies, the Volner children or the Hofmeister Williams . . . the lovelies for lonely couples, the lovelies for companionship? The Bayrights had several dozen models. But which ones interested Clay Desmond the most?

He knew the answer: the whores. Those were the lovelies used most and came with the highest ticket. He turned away from Desmond.

"Looks like we're peas of a pod, Regulator," Desmond said, brushing himself off.

"You and I have nothing in common," Colleran insisted.

Desmond returned his gaze to the distant buildings. "Perhaps not," he concluded. However, he held Heidi to his side in such a way that his left hand covered her breast. He gave it a gentle squeeze and Heidi glowed with affection.

They entered a small forest that had invaded the city square. They threaded their way over a soft carpet of natural grasses, which somehow used the underlying asphalt and concrete in their biological processes. Trees sprouted right up through the concourse and Colleran was astounded at how tall they had grown in such a short time. Growth was everywhere, and it almost looked as if the forest wanted to do away with the works that humans left behind.

Desmond, fresh from his victory over Colleran despite the Sunday punch from him, looked around with absolute fascination. "Boy, there used to be all sorts of traffic here. Cars and trucks, you name it."

An overturned bus lay beneath a blanket of moss and ferns which seemed to thrive on so much metal. Some kind of colorful insect, followed by its noisesome brood, flew out a bus window. They flashed off into the trees, leaving behind a trail of shimmering dust particles.

"They're cute!" Heidi cried out excitedly. "Look!"

"Watch out for animals," Colleran warned. "I don't trust this place."

But Heidi was having fun now. "Really? Clay said it was earth-normal, didn't you, Clay?"

"That's right, sweet."

"That doesn't mean that it's a playground."

Desmond huffed. "There ain't no big animals around here. Look at the ground. No tracks."

Colleran had a sudden revelation: the Wahlander estate will look like this soon. A gutted ruin swallowed by surrounding forest. It happens all the time.

It happened here.

Desmond bounded up to a rise in the thick forest and seemed entranced by what he saw on the other side. His big legs thrust him through the knee-high underbrush, up out of sight.

Heidi started after him, but Colleran suddenly grabbed her. "We have to talk," he said.

This close to her, in the cathedral-like sunlight of the alien forest, she seemed exactly like his other Heidi. But this one was a stranger.

"What about?" she asked innocently.

"I don't like the way he treats you, for one."

They heard Desmond thrashing through the forest like a Lost Earth pachyderm nosing through Nigerian jungles.

"He doesn't treat me that badly," she said, pulling away. "If he did, I'd leave. I'm not a slave, you know."

Looking into her mesmerizing eyes, he could appreciate Desmond's possessiveness and lust for this model. He often wished he had known the real Heidi Beryl in her own lifetime. However, that would not have mattered. They all were bioprogrammed to think and act the same way as the original.

He took a different approach. "My Heidi Beryl told me once that there might be traces of telepathy in lovelies. Is that true?"

She seemed uneasy, but only in that she didn't want to betray her master. "Some," she allowed. "Just impressions, really. And those don't go far."

"My lovely was killed in a space accident above a world called Okeanos."

She shook her head. "I didn't know. I'm sorry to hear that."

Lovelies had the remarkable property of staying in their arrested form for their entire natural lives. Then they died; they just stopped functioning. This Heidi could expect to live for another sixty years. *His* Heidi, however, was dead.

Shadows tinged with a soft green fell across her wide-eyed face. All at once this Heidi became his Heidi and it was nearly impossible to imagine how a man named Peter Bayright had mastered the lovely process so many years ago. Bayright himself had disappeared several years back, but his legacy persisted in the dozens of made-to-order models. Colleran wondered just then if Bayright was somewhere on the Tally. He had achieved immortality status for his advanced understanding of human chemistry and cloning, but he had vanished. His Reach was now in the hands of its board of directors and its thousands of stockholders, Clay Desmond among them.

"How long have you been . . . his?" Colleran asked. "I mean, how long has Desmond been interested in the Heidi Beryls?"

Heidi looked into the forest where Desmond had gone on ahead of them. She took out a small case of pills and the canteen she had brought.

She said, "I've been with Clay for seven years. A long time." She swallowed the pills.

Colleran pointed to them. "What are those for. I thought lovelies were biologically perfect. Are you sick?"

"Sometimes I get nightmares. Clay gave the pills to me. He gets nightmares, too. Real scary ones." She handed the pill case to Colleran. "You want some? They'll calm you down."

"No, thanks," he said. He was a little relieved, however, to know that the man did appear to have a conscience.

Just then a covey of birds rose up into the canopy of the forest with startled cries. A bestial roar shook the forest, and it seemed to be coming from over the rise ahead of them.

"Stay here!" Colleran said to Heidi. "If anything happens, run back to the ship!"

Colleran scrambled up through the brush at the top of the rise, pushing aside the low-lying limbs of the strange trees. When he got there, he slapped his holster awake, and out came his clasher.

Down below him Clay Desmond stood next to the remains of a plaza fountain. The main office building he had been heading for was only a few yards in front of him. But crouched in the shattered doorway was a boar. A very *large* boar.

The creature had tusks almost six feet long and hooves the size of saucers. It snorted and the brown hairs above its massively muscled shoulders went rigid with hostility and fear. It was easily the size of an automobile.

"Desmond!" Colleran shouted. "Back off! *Now!*"

But the big pig, surprised by the bumbling public relations executive, was angry. Its territory had been invaded.

With surprising speed it charged Desmond, clattering its rock-hard hooves across the crumbling concrete and marble of what remained of the plaza.

Desmond, taut with fear, screamed and tried to climb back up the rise in the forest behind him. The trees were close, but not close enough. He slipped in the overlapping fronds of the embedded ferns and vines, and slid back into view.

The boar was very fast, faster than Colleran thought possible for an animal of that size. The plaza concrete cracked under its fury. *This*, he realized, *is a* urizen.

Colleran dashed out of the forest, lashing out to his left in order to get a better shot at the beast.

"Out of the way!" he shouted to Desmond, and the startled executive rolled into the mulch as quickly as he could.

Colleran brought up his Langstrom and fired a narrow-gauge beam directly at the screaming, grunting horror. It tripped, then tumbled into the fire of its own disintegration. One of its tusks survived the destructive power of the clasher, having snapped free when the creature fell. The rest of it became instant nuclear ash.

Colleran walked over to where Desmond lay, slopped with mud and covered with vines, and helped him to his feet. The man was thoroughly soaked in his own fear-sweat, the kind of sweat any dangerous animal might sense.

"I didn't think anything was living there," Desmond said, indicating the desolate building. "Honest. I just wanted to see."

The pig had taken up residence in the wide but devastated lobby. Colleran gazed closer and saw movement there, and after a moment or two of quiet listening, he could hear other noises.

Three piglets, each about five feet at the shoulder, stared out at them. One of the pigs had new, two-foot-long tusks, which probably wouldn't break on impact. Colleran also noted the look of intelligence in their eyes as the three of them watched and waited, choosing not to attack as their parent had.

"Let's get out of here," Colleran told Desmond. "We're not going to find what we're looking for here. This place died a long, long time ago."

They pushed their way back down the rise to the open area of the city square. To Colleran's dismay, Heidi was not there. The spindle stood alone at the south end of the concourse, but Heidi was nowhere to be seen.

"Now what," he said, disgusted with himself.

Desmond saw that Heidi wasn't at the ship and started calling out. "Heidi!" he shouted. He turned to Colleran. "She's always doing stuff like this. *Heidi!*"

"Probably because she's human," Colleran returned.

"Well," Desmond began, looking around. "In a place like this humans can get killed."

With his right hand, Colleran held Desmond back. "What else did the Meurers make? They leave anything else behind?"

Desmond, still shaken, looked at him disbelievingly. "I was gone long before they collapsed. I told you, I—"

Colleran wasn't listening. He had seen something move in the woods on the opposite side of the spindle. It was the same something that must have attracted Heidi away from the desecrated square. Colleran bolted after it. Whatever it was, it was moving rather slowly, cumbersomely through the forest beyond the spindle.

Desmond shouted after him, "Hey, *wait!*"

Colleran raced into the forest, flinging the vines out of his way. He came to a grassy opening in the forest quite suddenly, and found her.

He also found a man, dressed like a cowboy from the Lost Earth, astride a horse so big and so white that it might as well have had pearlescent wings.

The cowboy on top—complete in his riding chaps, spurs, and cowboy hat—waved to them as they broke cover into the clearing.

He was sitting so high up that his boots in their stirrups were six feet off the ground.

"Howdy," he said. "Thanks for getting the pig."

His smile was amplified by the upturned edges of his strawberry blonde mustache.

Heidi herself was holding on to the reins and bridle of the horse, which gave all the appearances of being quite docile and friendly. It, too, was a *urizen*.

"Look what *I* found!" she shouted with a child's sense of discovery.

23

The cowboy astride the fantastic steed leaned on the ornately carved pommel of his saddle and smiled down at them. He pushed his hat back on his head with an easy gesture.

"Saw you folks come down 'bout half an hour ago. Wondered what the hell anybody'd want with our little village here. Sightseers, I guess."

Clay Desmond came up close behind Colleran, and his breathing was ragged and harsh from the excitement. His pile of sculpted blonde hair was a mess and his gorgeous tunic was soiled. At least he still had his gold jewelry, Colleran thought wryly.

The cowboy did not appear in the slightest to be intimidated by the presence of a Regulator. Colleran wondered—to judge by the man's age—if he even knew what a Regulator was. If anything, the cowboy on his mountain of a horse seemed casual and confident. Perhaps it was the waxed mustache upturned at its ends that made it seem as if he were always smiling, always cheerful.

The young cowboy caught sight of Desmond as he stepped in

behind Colleran. "You look like a man who's seen the devil himself."

Desmond made a brief, feeble motion of brushing himself off as Heidi hung on to the bridle of the ur-horse, happy with her find. With the slightest nod of its head, the animal could easily have lifted her off her petite feet.

"You knew about the pig?" Colleran asked, sheathing his clasher. The cowboy's intense blue eyes watched the holster swallow it.

He said, "Yep." Then he laughed. "I don't know who you folks are, but you got a lot of guts coming here. This whole place is full of renegade *urizen*. You got one of the normal ones. Go back in there about half a mile and you'll really find something to shoot at."

The cowboy, who looked to be in his mid-twenties, about Heidi's age, waved a gloved hand toward the ruined towers of the city. The glove was fringed in buckskin in a style Colleran hadn't seen outside of Lost Earth histories.

"Hell, man," the cowboy started. "Even some of them *trees* are *urizen*. I knew you was from out of town when you landed right in the goddamn middle of them."

He laughed and his humor was genuine, earthy. But the cowboy also knew *exactly* how dangerous the forested city had become.

Colleran gazed up at him. "We saw at least three other pigs, young ones, in the building just beyond those trees there."

"That's where they've been nesting for some months now that the rainy season's passed," he said, tweaking his mustache. "Old Pop sometimes comes out and raids one of our beefsteaks."

"Beefsteaks?"

The cowboy chuckled. He bent over with an air of condescension, making an exaggeration of the pronunciation. "Cows," he said. "You've heard of them? Meat hangs on their bones. People eat them." He leaned back in the saddle. "Some people, anyway."

Clay Desmond pulled a reluctant Heidi away from the reins of the huge white horse.

"I've heard of them," Colleran said, unamused. "You called the pig Old Pop. Where's Old Mom?"

Heidi giggled. Desmond quickly pushed her around behind him in a motion that Colleran caught out of the corner of his eye.

The cowboy scanned the forest in a rather stagey fashion.

"Around here somewhere. She'll be back." He didn't appear to be overly concerned.

"So who are you?" Colleran asked him. "Do you live around here?"

"The name's Leroux. Jean-Jacques Leroux," he said, smiling broadly. "I live about ten miles east of here as the ur-crow flies. Your turn."

Colleran made the round of introductions, leaving out the part that would explain the wide, innocent expression on Heidi's face and her overt friendliness. Jean-Jacques Leroux, for his part, was quite pleased to make her acquaintance.

He smiled down at her. "Do you like my horse?"

"She's beautiful," Heidi smiled girlishly.

"It's a he. His name is Piccolo," Jean-Jacques announced, patting the beast on its powerfully muscled neck. Piccolo snorted at the attention.

Colleran noticed that the young cowhand sported a sidearm in an ordinary leather holster. "So what is it you're doing here, Mr. Leroux?"

"Funny," Jean-Jacques said with a rueful grin. "That's what I was going to ask you."

Colleran held his ground. Clay Desmond, meanwhile, fumbled for some pills in a pillbox he had been carrying in his belt. They evidently were the same pills Heidi had and Colleran noticed just how jumpy Desmond had become. He could understand. Being attacked by two different kinds of ferocious animals in as many days was rather unnerving. The executive crunched the pills noisily without water, and dry-swallowed them.

Jean-Jacques Leroux was obviously an easygoing soul and he seemed happy at discovering someone new to talk to out here where there shouldn't have been anyone at all.

"I come into the city about once a month or so when I make my rounds. We've been losing beefsteaks—I mean *urizen*—to the renegades here in the city. Sometimes we have to fight back."

"You said there were other beasts here."

"That's right," he said, tugging the horse's reins gently. "There are ur-cats, panthers, we think, and some beasties we haven't seen that are quite hostile." The cowboy's right hand rested on the butt of a gun Colleran couldn't recognize. It was definitely not a Langstrom weapon. The young man would have to have been an immortal for it to be registered in his possession.

"You were after the pig, then?"

"Just checking on it. They're very hostile when they drop a litter. But your friend there surprised Old Pop and that's why he attacked you. This is their territory, more or less. Your turn."

Colleran nodded. "We are trying to track down a couple of parties. Someone named Zir Abou-Farhaat and anyone who can provide us with information about the Meurers, the people who built this place."

A somber cloud passed across Jean-Jacques' face. "Ain't heard of the first. I know lots of folks who can tell about the second."

"Can you take us to them?"

"You're talking to one," he said, then went silent. The young cowboy had quiet blue eyes, but now they became wary as he surveyed the strange trio before him.

He nodded toward Clay Desmond, whose breathing had calmed somewhat but who was nonetheless troubled.

"You'd better see to your friend there. This isn't a place to be sick. This isn't a place to be, *period*." He tugged the reins of the white horse and the creature nimbly pulled around—it was like a house turning. "My people back at the ranch can tell you more than I can, or care to. I'd get out of these woods before mid-afternoon. That's the first thing you ought to know."

"Why?"

"There's a creature that tunnels and it gets hungry about that time. And see that tree over there?"

Colleran and Heidi turned to a stately, sentinel-like plant that resembled a Lost Earth conifer. Desmond stared at the cowboy and his horse.

"Yes, what about the tree?"

"Near sunset it gets up, walks around, and eats just about anything that moves. We call it a *vacq*."

Heidi gasped and hid like a little girl behind Clay Desmond.

The needle-tipped branches of the *vacq* seemed to ooze a noxious substance that might have been a tranquilizing poison. Many of the lower branches seemed folded around its trunk, and they could have easily been arms. The base of the *vacq* itself also had the appearance of being thick with legs that could move the creature around. But they noticed these things only because Jean-Jacques had pointed them out.

"It's the Meurers," Desmond said to Colleran. "They did all this."

Jean-Jacques agreed. "That's right. You fool with Mother Nature long enough and this is what you get." He waved a frilled glove around them, indicating the encompassing forest and the overgrown city square.

Colleran looked closer at Desmond. "Are you all right?"

The PR executive nodded weakly, gritting his teeth slightly and tensing his jaw muscles. Colleran had stronger stress medicine on his spindle, but the best remedy would be to get the man away from this place and onto a golf course. Still, he needed Desmond's help in finding his way around.

The cowboy said, "Lunchtime's approaching around here, so I'd be moving along if I were you. My cousin's ranch is on a mesa you can't miss from the air. Go ten miles east northeast. Try not to scare the *urizen* along the way. Anna won't like it."

"Anna is your cousin?"

"Anna Lockrow. It's her daddy's ranch, but he's dead. Killed by the people who did this—" Only the sweep of his blue, blue eyes told them what they needed to know about his uncle's demise. This place, Colleran concluded, was built for death. It was alive with it.

"I'll radio ahead that you're coming," Jean-Jacques told him, patting his saddlehorn, which was itself a small radio unit. He became suddenly serious and in his manner Colleran could discern the young man's rugged life on this degenerated world, now that the civilizing touch of the Meurers was gone. He said, "We don't get visitors from the Spoke any more and we don't like trouble. If you belong to the Meurers and have come back to reclaim Buck Lockrow's spread, you'll have to fight for it. But unlike ten years ago . . ."

Jean-Jacques Leroux pulled out his strange weapon and aimed at the *vacq* sleeping close by.

"Unlike ten years ago, we will not sit back and let you take it all away from us."

He pulled the trigger of the gun and an explosive snake of blue-white lightning snapped out thunderously and blew apart the *vacq*. The dark green creature blasted apart in a shower of poisonous needles and cream-white sap.

Heidi screamed and Clay Desmond flinched. Colleran merely watched with his hand poised above the waiting lip of his organic holster. The remains of the deadly *vacq* crashed into itself, away from them.

Piccolo calmly pranced in place, snuffling disapprovingly at the sudden presence of ozone in the air.

The display jarred Colleran's memory. The pistol was called a jumpgun. It was often used for crowd control. Leroux adjusted the gun's firepower, lowering the setting. He then calmly slid the McGuane jumpgun into its holster.

"We've just come for information, Mr. Leroux," Colleran told him. "As far as we know, the Meurers are dead and gone. The Authority will back any claim you have to this land."

Jean-Jacques Leroux was the sort who acknowledged no one's authority but his own and that of his family. "We had this land before the Meurers. We don't need your help. It's ours. That's a fact."

He swung his enormous horse around and pointed to the east. "Fly on. I'll let them know you're coming."

With that he dug his starred spurs into the horse's flanks, and Piccolo trotted off into the forest, its mighty hooves gouging up deep holes in the turf beneath it.

Watching the big animal, Heidi clapped her hands delightedly and squealed.

Clay Desmond , however, had gone pale and sick. "Let's get away from this place," he said. "Anywhere but here."

24

From the air they could see just how much the invading forest had consumed the city that the Meurers had built. Even the outlying estates the Meurers had lived in like royalty were bomb craters filled in with pond water and life. The entire area had quickly fallen prey to the roots and vines and dense growth of the bizarre lifeforms that the Meurers themselves had apparently unleashed in their final hours. It was a biology experiment gone bad. Even the river to the north seemed befouled with green slime and pustulent yellow muck. All bridges were down.

Beyond the city, though, eastward for what seemed to be thousands of square miles, was a different scene entirely. The continent was lawned with a grasslike growth that made the plains seem like a huge, endless park. Islands of woods grouped themselves in small oases, but otherwise the plains remained free of any sign of civilization. There were no roads, no high tension wires, no indications that men and women moved across this pleasant landscape.

And there were dozens of individual herds of grazing *urizen*. The herds seemed to be families of twenty or so very large beasts—and Colleran respecting the cowhand's advice kept his spindle away from them.

The Lockrow Ranch was easy to make out. It sat atop a lone mesa, the geological remnants of a volcano chimney, and seemed to be the perfect spot to survey all the various herds around them.

As Colleran approached, he noted several modern housing units scattered around, many topped with various communications towers or weather instruments. He radioed ahead to the communications personnel.

Colleran was impressed with the sophistication of the Lockrow operation. This was a thriving business, not a slapdash operation thrown together by a few shitkickers in the wake of the Meurer collapse.

Colleran eased the spindle down. Ranch hands, curious, walked from their work stations to greet them. Several trees grew at one lip of the mesa—none of them *vacqs*—and a strong wind blew up from the steep sides.

Anna Lockrow was not the kind of "boss" he had expected to run a ranch. She had no grease or grime in the creases of her jeans and there was no crusted *urizen* dung around the edges of her boots. She was mid-thirtyish with short, dark-brown hair and blue eyes. While she might have been prettier, she nonetheless had a rugged kind of beauty about her that was born of an inner strength and confidence, and perhaps a past history of rough living, even tragedy.

"Jean-Jacques said you might have a sick man on board," Anna began even before Colleran had a chance to introduce them.

Colleran helped Heidi out of the spindle as three men came over and assisted Desmond onto the soft grass of the mesa.

"I don't know what happened," Desmond said weakly.

Anna considered him closely. "Jean-Jacques said you had an encounter with our big pig."

"It attacked him," Colleran informed her.

She noticed that he was a Regulator, but was just as unimpressed as Jean-Jacques Leroux. "We'll take care of him."

Desmond draped himself around two strong ranch hands and was taken away to the main building.

She went on. "We've got proper facilities here. I just hope we can do something for him."

"We won't be here long," Colleran said as they started for the large ranch house.

Although he assumed that Jean-Jacques, back in the ruin of Shuraat, had told Anna who they were, and what they were, Colleran introduced himself and Heidi to the proprietress of the mesa. Anna seemed happy to meet them. She gave Heidi a bemused look, perhaps not used to seeing the pronounced wide-eyed expression of a lovely. Nonetheless, she was courteous as they took Desmond inside the house.

One of many homes atop the mesa, the ranch house was the largest. It was of modest, utilitarian design, built from the trees and quarries natural to the area below them. With its wind-generated electricity, solar panels, and high tech communications gear, the ranch as a whole seemed to be an assortment of technologies, ancient and modern, that worked symbiotically. Clearly, they had survived here where the Meurers had failed.

As Clay Desmond was assisted to a comfortable bed in a room off to the side of the main room, Anna took Heidi and Colleran to a very large living area of wide windows, *urizen*-skin throw rugs on the floor, and stuffed ur-deer heads mounted on the walls. Several maids went into Desmond's room with trays of medicine.

As Anna Lockrow seated herself on a large chair, he could feel the medicinal qualities of the place. This was her *home* and just by being here—somewhere normal—he could feel its powerful healing qualities.

Anna remained friendly and cordial throughout, but she rarely smiled. Her life did not allow for the mistakes that unbridled openness and naivete could create. She'd seen enough trouble.

"So what brings you to our peaceful world?" she said to them with obvious sarcasm.

Colleran did not see any reason to hold back what he knew of the problem and so he informed the rancher of the reason for their visit.

Through it all, Anna nodded with recognition as he told her of their suspicions of the Meurers. The name made her go cold, but her sullenness was not directed at them.

As he spoke, he noticed that Anna kept glancing at the row of framed pictures of family members on the mantel of the great fireplace across the room. There was one of Buck Lockrow, and another of Anna's pretty mother, and Colleran could see where this woman got her rugged features and good looks. The grim smile—when it shone through—came from her father.

"It suits me fine that someone is on to the Meurers," she said when he finished. A servant brought drinks for them, none alcoholic or soporific. Heidi sipped hers in silence next to Anna, fascinated with the woman.

"You saw the city," Anna went on. "You should have seen the war."

"War? What war?" He looked through the window, which faced the abandoned city on the horizon.

Anna held her drink in her two capable hands. "The Meurers collapsed in one long bad night. We've got it on videotape, which we filmed with telescopic lenses from the mesa here."

She spoke joylessly about the rumors her family had heard six years ago of the Meurer infighting, the currying of favor that some executives let get out of hand. The Meurers had been known for their ruthlessness in cornering the meat-packing market throughout the nearby systems, but for many years it simply grew, rising to power and strength the way magma would underneath the earth, waiting to erupt.

The various ranching families who did the actual husbandry of the *urizen* somehow were left out and ignored in the fight. Anna was quite open concerning the fates of her father and mother in the Meurer collapse. Her father, on that last night when fires dotted the city and spaceships lifted into orbit, had gone into Shuraat to confront his immediate Meurer supervisor.

As Anna told it—and as Colleran had been briefed by Clay Desmond—their lives were indentured to the ruthless Meurers, who got richer and richer off their labors. No one else in the Spoke was aware of the Meurer ways; they only relished their incredible meats. Such were the ways of a free market.

"Did the Meurers work with the Abou-Farhaat shipping Reach?" Colleran asked.

Anna grimaced but managed to laugh. Evidently, the Abou-Farhaats had a reputation. She said, "They had some dealings with the Abou-Farhaats, but there are rumors that someone double-crossed them. We don't know. But the Meurers went with another outfit and the Abou-Farhaats didn't like it much."

Companies lost contracts all of the time and for all sorts of reasons. After all, human beings ran businesses, and their decisions were often made for the silliest of reasons—or the deadliest of transgressions.

"I take it that you don't like the Meurers," Colleran commented.

"Hell, no," she said quickly. "They turned my Daddy gray and that night when he went into Shuraat, he was killed. He never came back."

Colleran went silent for a minute. Heidi remarked, "That's awful. Why were they so bad?"

Anna looked at the lovely. "Why is anyone bad? Maybe they got so rich that they figured they could do whatever they wanted."

Heidi looked as if she truly understood. If she had been hanging around Clay Desmond for six or seven years, then she would have considerable experience with the way business is done in an open, capitalistic market. *This* Heidi, Colleran realized, was just as intelligent and sensitive as *his* Heidi had been.

Anna became distant. "The Meurers even had a way of disappearing their rivals."

"Disappearing? What do you mean? Assassination?"

"Or whatever," Anna reported. "They even disappeared their own kind when things weren't going their way. Until that last night when Shuraat was attacked, Daddy and our hands never went into town. We just stayed here, where it was safe, biding our time."

Colleran asked, "Who attacked the Meurers? You have any idea?"

She shrugged her sturdy shoulders. "Enemies. Whoever. No one knows. But they struck the Meurers all across the planet. They came down in old-style shuttles and used old-style guns and weapons. But they did the job."

Colleran couldn't imagine who could have succeeded so

thoroughly. Only the Authority, with its seven roaming preservers like the *Parvardigar*, had the real guns in the Mandala worlds. Not even the Soviets in their distant colony had weapons so large.

"And they didn't attack you here?"

A servant brought in a tray of sandwiches and pasta salad. Heidi began to eat quickly, as did Anna. It all looked and smelled delectable, especially the meat, which Colleran nonetheless declined.

"No," Anna said, munching on a small wedge of sandwich. "That's the strange part. All of us ranchers belonged to the Meurer Reach. We paid taxes into the Meurers and they protected their investment by helping Daddy keep up the ranch. But whoever took the Meurers out only wanted them, not us. They blasted the two fusion stations that gave us continent-wide electricity, and they shot down the Meurer docking stations from orbit. One of them's piled up in a big crater about fifty miles north of here. I'll take you to it if you want."

Colleran declined for the moment. "What happened to your mother? You said your parents—"

"Jean-Jacques said that he killed a *vacq* for you," Anna said, gone sad for a moment in her mind.

Heidi paused over her pasta salad. "One of those trees killed your mother? Oh, Anna, how horrible!"

Anna bent over her tray of food, playing with the triangles of neatly prepared sandwiches. "The Meurers were wild on experiments in those last years. They made awful creatures and just turned them loose. We found out all about *vacqs* when one attacked my mom three years ago."

Heidi couldn't eat any longer.

"So they left you here," Colleran said. "What about the other ranchers on the continent?"

"There are still a lot of us here, but in the last five years or so most have migrated off-planet. It's a lot of work to herd the *urizen*. But this is a good spot for them and we've got a new spaceport being built south of here. Those of us who have remained are going to pick up where the Meurers left off. We're going to be a Reach someday."

Colleran looked at her and smiled. "I don't doubt it."

Anna Lockrow seemed to be a woman who had postponed the pleasures of having a family until she could establish herself independently. There were no pictures of children on the mantel, although he did recall seeing a small schoolhouse and playground close to the communications building outside next to the spindle. The other men and women of the ranch had families. Anna seemed to be on her own.

Colleran then said, "Well, you might be interested to know that the war is apparently still going on."

Anna Lockrow only nodded.

"Although," he added, "who's doing it and why are still a mystery to us. That's why I'm here with Heidi and Mr. Desmond. He used to work for them."

"He did?" Anna's eyes were suddenly fiercely alive.

Heidi jumped to Desmond's defense. "Oh, but he left a long time ago! He got fired! He wasn't part of them at all."

That seemed to mollify Anna for the moment.

Heidi then added, "But they're trying to find someone named Rex Wahlander and—"

"Wahlander?" Anna interrupted.

"You've heard of him?" Colleran asked.

"You're goddamn right, I have. He was one of their heads. Daddy said that he was a murderer and a thief. Wahlander was the one responsible for disappearing people. Is he still alive?"

Colleran saw a glimmer of both hope and anger in Anna Lockrow's eyes. Her father had disappeared, and Rex Wahlander had been part of the vanishings.

"We think so," he confirmed. "But no one's seen him in over four years."

"I hope they catch him and put him on trial," Anna said grimly.

"Well, they think he's working for a Reach run by the Klasa-Eisners about thirty light-years down-Spoke from here. The Authority is running a full-scale search operation there. We'll find him."

At that point, Heidi walked over to the wide window, which faced the distant horizon. Its view was spectacular since the mesa dropped off suddenly just a few feet beyond.

"Oh, look! It's Mr. Leroux!" Heidi exclaimed.

Anna consulted the watch on her wrist, then looked at the clock on the wall as if to double-check. Then she got up and stood next to the lovely.

"He's due in about now."

"Look how fast he's going! What a wonderful horse!" Heidi said happily at the window.

Colleran walked over beside her. Out on the smooth, green plain between the mesa and the desolate city, a small white dot was approaching the Lockrow ranch at an incredible rate of speed, leaving behind a speckled trail of hoofprints as sod flew up behind the highballing ur-horse.

"Is that your cousin?" Colleran asked.

Anna Lockrow smiled. "Sure is. Crazy son-of-a-bitch. He does this all the time. I keep telling him to go slow so it won't rouse the *urizen*, but he likes to push them to the limit."

Off in the green distance, the cowboy prodded Piccolo over the plain. Anna cranked open the window where they stood and they could just barely make out the thunderclaps of Piccolo's hooves.

"Now watch," Anna told them. "He does this on purpose."

Jean-Jacques turned Piccolo quite close to a gathering of *urizen*, two big bulls and about sixteen or so cows, all twice as tall as an average man or woman.

Piccolo's passage must have awakened them from their bovine slumber, for one of the ur-bulls raised its very *large* horned head and snorted with enormous indignation.

Leroux whistled and hooted in the distance as the white horse presented itself as an obvious target. The cowboy waved his white Stetson-type hat, and, sure enough, the bull took off after him.

Anna stared out the window. She said, "The bulls can get up to speeds of thirty-eight miles an hour. Young ones slightly faster if the ground's good." She pointed down to where the little drama was being staged. "The ground's particularly good here."

Leroux galloped his steed as fast as Piccolo could go, but the bull was gaining. Moreover, the other bull and one cow had now separated themselves from the grazing pack and had joined the chase.

"That happens, too," Anna added. "We think they can communicate to each other somehow. Either that or it's in their genetic code. They're quite smart for beefsteaks."

Heidi gasped. Leroux was losing ground fast. Piccolo had been running all the way and the bull closest to the rider and horse had only just begun. The cowboy wasn't going to make it.

Then just when it didn't make sense to do so, Leroux pulled Piccolo to a quick, grinding halt and whipped the white giant of a horse around, facing them.

"Oh!" Heidi cried out.

The *urizen* bull bore down on Leroux, towering over them by several feet.

However, Leroux didn't seem worried. He merely drew out his jumpgun and suddenly there appeared between them a softer bolt of lightning, of much less intensity than the one that struck down the *vacq*. The bolt cracked the air apart and punched the ur-bull directly in the face.

The bull, like all of the other *urizen*, was wearing a brass ring in its nose, a perfect conductor for electricity. The ur-bull stumbled over the grass of the plains, churning up dirt and debris.

Leroux fired off several more cautionary blasts at the *urizen* that were following their leader, and they were halted where they stood by less effective bolts. They merely blinked, shook their massive heads, and went back to the business of being cattle grazing on the plain.

The first ur-bull got to his feet and wandered off dizzily as Piccolo escorted his rider proudly to the base of the mesa where ranch hands waited at a hidden elevator apparatus.

"He does this for fun," Anna said. "It sometimes gets boring here."

She showed Colleran a gun case full of shiny new jumpguns, both handheld pistols and rifles. "But that's all right with us. Nobody's going to take our ranch away from us this time. Especially the Meurers. If they do, then we'll provide them plenty of excitement."

Colleran believed her.

25

Morning on Courtenay Three broke fresh and clean over the eastern edge of the continent, and Colleran was up early to see it.

Desmond had been too indisposed for them to do much more than wait out his malaise. Colleran found out that his pills were for high blood pressure and stress, and Desmond had taken a turn for the worse after Jean-Jacques Leroux had arrived from his wild ride.

Colleran took the rest of the day off, as it were, and allowed Anna Lockrow to show him around their outfit atop the mesa. As she informed him, theirs was a unique operation, having been located so close to the city of Shuraat. There were a few other large ranches elsewhere on the continent, but mostly they had folded over time when there were few off-world Reaches available—outside the Abou-Farhaats—to ferry their goods into orbit, and from there into the Hub.

Colleran told her that they had sighted other cities on a few of the continents and she admitted surprise to this. But she wasn't surprised when he told her that the planet was mostly empty, at least in so far as they were able to discern on their few orbits in the Authority spindle.

But Colleran also got her in touch with diplomatic corps on board the *Parvardigar*—through the use of a com-drone—so that Anna and her people could get back in contact with the rest of Gamma Spoke. Colleran also found out that the *Khadaji* had been tracked near them and that the *Parvardigar* was looking into its erratic flight. The Admin also added—in the com-drone shipment—some information concerning two calibans that had broken loose. One creature was killed instantly, but another had fought its way into a civilian zone on a planet where it had been delivered.

The fight had been unpleasant, but the caliban had eventually been clashed.

Colleran also asked Brianne to inform Sheila Eisner of Clay Desmond's ill health—and he left it at that. He was determined to learn more about the Meurers from the ranchers who had known them the most, but he also didn't want to jeopardize Desmond's condition. No word returned from Sheila Eisner. Colleran took the hint.

The dew on the rough grass of the mesa compound still beaded delicately from the night. Colleran, as the day before when Anna had shown him around, was struck by the simple beauty of the fortress. The air was alive with the faintest of smells, which drifted from the plains several hundred feet below. A kind of late-winter flower, an incarnadine pink, bloomed at the basalt ridges of the mesa, its eight-petaled heads catching the fragrant winds from the plains. He understood why Anna would fight for this place. If he was anywhere nearby, he would fight for it, too.

A breeze always blew here, and as Colleran stepped out onto the grass of the compound, it tugged lightly at a flag atop a pole before the main ranch house. The flag bore a design that Jean-Jacques had created for the upcoming Lockrow Reach. They had plans, these people, and Colleran envied their industry and hope. The cattle below, the wind above, it was all part of a peaceful yet arduous life. In its way, it reminded him of that world where Beatrice lived. It seemed equally as real, equally beautiful.

Anna Lockrow came out on the porch, fresh from a morning shower. She rolled up the long sleeves of her print blouse, snapping back the pearl studs.

"It's not a bad life," she told him. "Especially on mornings like this. But you should be here in the winters."

"Why? Is the weather rough?"

She nodded, looking distantly at the rising sun. "The planet is tilted thirteen degrees away from our sun. Winters we get here are cold and tough. But I wouldn't live anywhere else."

"I don't blame you."

Other ranch hands were moving about in their homes on the mesa top. Lights came on, breakfast dishes clattered in kitchens, children ran to eat.

Heidi came out on the porch, buttoning up a cowgirl shirt she had borrowed from Anna the night before. They were nearly the same size, although Heidi had more of a bosom and she had trouble buttoning the shirt all the way up.

"They're made special for me," Anna said to her, almost embarrassed.

Heidi had left the top two buttons unsnapped, and her cleavage was quite pronounced. "That's okay. I like it."

Colleran turned away from her, hoping that neither woman noticed his discomfort. For an instant as he gazed at the curves of those breasts, he felt a surge of jealousy. Even though Desmond had been out for most of the night, Colleran had to fight his feelings knowing that Heidi had been lying next to him. Clothed or unclothed, it didn't matter.

"How is your friend?" Anna asked Heidi. Colleran was convinced that Anna did not know what Heidi truly was.

"He's better today," Heidi said with a smile. "It took much of the night for his medicine to work, but he was able to sleep through most of it."

The floorboards of the main living room behind them groaned as Clay Desmond came out, buckling up his tunic. He seemed much better and moved with more energy than the day before.

"I thought you all deserted me!" he said loudly, smiling.

Heidi went over to him and wrapped her arms around his girth. "No, we didn't."

"I'm glad to see that you're feeling better, Mr. Desmond."

"Thank you, Ms. Lockrow, thank you." The big man bowed. "So when's food? I could eat a bear!"

Anna checked her watch. "Breakfast will be in about fifteen minutes. We've got an airbus coming in early and—" She scanned the horizon with her sharp blue eyes. "They like to keep to a tight schedule. If we're going into Jasper today, we've got to be on it."

Desmond had lost whatever it was that bothered him the day before. He now was excited over the day's prospects for adventure. "A bus? You got bus service out here?"

In the southeast, along the pinkish wash of clouds veiling the sunrise, a small "cloud," a gray nonentity seemed to float toward them at an easy pace.

"There it is," she said, pointing. "It's how we've voted to do our traveling, now that the Meurers are gone. We do it so that the *urizen* don't get riled. Jets and helicopters make all sorts of noise."

About thirty miles to the southeast, rolling along at a casual pace, was an airbus using ancient but effective visual screening shields as it hovered over the ground.

"I don't see it," Heidi said to her.

"If you look close enough you can see it. It's not totally invisible, but the *urizen* can't see them and that's what counts. It's that little tiny cloud right . . . there."

"I see it!" Heidi said, turning to Desmond, who held her tightly. "I see it!"

Colleran stood alone with his emotions, trying to keep his eyes from Heidi's exposed breasts. He needed more metatryzine. All sorts of feelings were starting to simmer in him now, and he didn't like it.

"So where is this Jasper town?" Desmond asked Anna.

"It's a ways south of here," she told him. "Mr. Colleran wanted to see what we've done now that the Meurers have gone out of business."

"Oh," Desmond muttered noncommittally. "Well, that should be fun."

"I don't know if it'll be fun," Colleran said to him. "But it's something I want to look into."

Desmond looked once at the horizon and seemed to change his mind about something. "I'm going to need some more of my pills soon. I didn't expect to be gone this long."

"We'll get you more medicine," Colleran said. "I just wish you had told me earlier that you had this problem."

Desmond smiled down at Heidi. "Well, for the time being I've got all the medicine I need. Right, little flower?"

"Right," Heidi returned.

Colleran merely stood quietly. He felt suddenly vulnerable in the winds lifting off the plains.

Anna turned and opened the door to the ranch house for them all. Breakfast smells moved around them like a seductive *jinn*. She looked up at Desmond. "If you've got the prescription for it, we might be able to synthesize your medicine in Jasper. We've got an excellent facility there."

"Oh, no," Desmond said quickly. "It's a brand new drug, experimental, from what I hear. There's some kind of patent law attached to it forbidding duplication." He smiled at Colleran, who, to all of them, represented the law. Desmond smiled down at the mistress of Lockrow ranch. He said, "We'll get back in time. It was just a relapse."

Colleran crossed his arms. "We'll be gone as long as it takes for me to track down the source of these killers. It might be wise to take Ms. Lockrow's advice."

Anna shrugged; she wasn't about to involve herself in disputes among strangers, despite her hospitality. "Just let me know."

They went in for a big breakfast.

Their slow flight in the shielded airbus toward the city of Jasper gave them a view of the environs around the Lockrow mesa that their flight down from space had not. For hundreds of miles to the north and east stretched anvil-flat plains, which were flecked by occasional wooded areas. Jean-Jacques, their enthusiastic tour guide, informed them that the trees usually clustered around artesian wells and that they were vital geological features necessary in the upkeep of the roaming *urizen*. The *urizen* themselves were hardly distinguishable from so high up. But they were down there, thousands upon thousands of them, quietly grazing in family bunches of about forty or fifty.

Colleran watched everything closely—not only the landscape, but the passengers on board the airbus as well. He even kept an eye on his own feelings. This isolated world, although riven with its own violent history, did have a rugged peacefulness that he admired. Anna Lockrow's eyes rarely stopped watching the terrain pass beneath them. Colleran could sense her pride. This was her home and she herself would probably never leave it. He envied her for her grounding, her centeredness here.

He thought of Regina Wahlander just then. He could now better understand her unhappiness and outrage when her home had been destroyed on Oakstaadt. It had been her *home*, not some ornately decorated toy to play with or real estate to sell at a bigger profit. It had been her home in the same way that all the land beneath him now was Anna Lockrow's home.

But when Colleran considered Clay Desmond and his lovely, he could feel the *angst* engendered by Mandala living. There, everyone was always going someplace; MUD units always looking for better places to be. Desmond, in his function as a public relations account executive for the Klasa-Eisners, was always spindling hither and yon, looking for new clients or keeping current clients happy. And that meant the use of the Heidi Beryl. How many clients had she kept happy on Clay Desmond's behalf?

He turned away and watched the forests and plains unfold

beneath him. He could have been a cloud passing through all of their lives, unseen, uninvolved.

But he *was* involved. Their status, their luxuries, their endless striving did not come without a price. And Colleran's job was to see that the wheels of the Mandala Authority kept turning, kept the money coming in, kept the Law alive with some kind of clout.

And why did he do this? He knew. So that people like Clay Desmond could wear his gold and jewels, so people such as Anna Lockrow and her funny cousin could keep their lives from falling apart.

He also knew which of the two he preferred.

As they approached Jasper, the land began to rise to a seawall plateau. The coastal city was at the base of a series of protective cliffs, and Colleran could see the advantage they provided for Jasper. Long ago, engineers had managed to cut a narrow canyon through the cliffs to allow the *urizen* to funnel into the city in nice, neat, and very manageable columns.

The city itself was divided exactly in half in order to facilitate the *urizen* traffic down the central avenue. Elevated streets and walkways forded the *urizen* avenue, which itself led to areas of slaughterhouses and gravity-lift pads and gantries. The whole city was virtually brand new, constructed after the collapse of the Meurer Reach. Laputas that had been abandoned by the Meurers had been reworked for the use of the cattle herders, and Colleran could see just how far they had come. Anna Lockrow had not been bragging. They would achieve Reach status soon and Jasper would be the center of their commerce.

The airbus switched off its shield and drifted over the cliff wall. Beneath them, a long line of *urizen* were making their thunderous way through the canyon toward the main street in Jasper.

Jean-Jacques pointed for Colleran to see. "Those are long-horns. The Anglins raise them specifically."

"Who are the Anglins?"

Jean-Jacques smiled knowingly at Anna, winking. She actually blushed. He laughed. "It's hard to say. All depends on Anna here."

"You stop."

Colleran wondered what *that* was all about.

Jean-Jacques provided the answer. "Grant Anglin runs his daddy's spread and one of these days, when Anna gets around to it, she and Grant are supposed to get married."

Anna leaned back in her seat and scowled at her cousin. To Colleran, she said, "Grant's father vanished the same night my Daddy did. We've got a lot in common."

Heidi got excited over the prospect of Anna's marriage. "Are you and Grant getting married?" she said brightly, moving near her.

Anna gave Heidi a mysterious smile, one that the lovely probably understood, but Colleran did not.

Jean-Jacques whispered aside to Colleran. "We got a bigger spread than the Anglins. Anna's making *real* sure Grant's going to toe the line, if you know what I mean."

Colleran nodded. He'd toed that line many times himself.

The airbus gracefully set down in an area designed for incoming air travel. To the south of them were the waiting small-scale laputas at the gantries, but to the north of them, just beyond the buildings that lined the main avenue, were the unhappy sounds of lowing *urizen* sorting themselves through the city.

"Wow," Heidi said excitedly to Clay Desmond. "I can feel their hooves!"

Desmond glanced around the terminal area, constantly holding Heidi by the arm.

She went on. "Listen to them. It's like they're talking to each other!"

Leroux stepped out after them and put on his tall Stetson. He said, "They're very smart animals. It's in the genes."

Heidi frowned as they walked through the terminal past the other workers in the area. "And they're going to be killed?"

"'Fraid so, sweet," Leroux said, walking beside her.

Desmond carefully pulled Heidi away from Leroux. The young rake had been making eyes at the lovely, not much caring who saw or who minded. Desmond commented, "I bet they're talking about roast beef sandwiches."

"Clay!" Heidi chided.

Colleran walked behind them as Anna led them all through the terminal, on toward a larger row of buildings, clearly the rear entrance to the structures that faced the *urizen* avenue beyond.

Colleran stepped close to Desmond. "Were you ever here in Jasper when you worked with the Meurers?"

Desmond glowed slightly. The man was always waiting for his cue to orate on stage it seemed. He said, "When I was working *for* the Meurers, I flew here once. There used to be a golf course back that way." His thumb vaguely considered a northern part of the city.

Leroux laughed. "Hey, dude. We ain't got *no* more uses for a golf course."

"I saw," Desmond stated. To Colleran, he said, "Back then, this place was a small seaside resort. Now look at it." He was truly amazed at what the surviving ranchers had done to the former resort.

As they entered the large building, they began to run into more cowhands, both men and women, rushing about, trying to maintain some kind of order as the *urizen* began their parade through the city. Colleran wondered what else the small community did when there wasn't an approaching herd, but at the moment they had arrived to witness Jasper doing what it did best.

Anna escorted them down a confining hall to the increased rumblings of *urizen* hooves. Heidi clutched close to her owner. The smell of *urizen* dung was stultifying inside the building and Desmond complained loudly.

Anna turned to Colleran. "I think you'll find this rather interesting."

Through a rear corridor of hustling cowhands, packed with the odor of dust and sweat, Anna took them into a larger room where several men and women were standing before a very large, floor-to-ceiling glass wall. Beyond the wall was the *urizen* avenue. And the *urizen* themselves.

Heidi gasped as they watched the cattle march by. Even Desmond was without words. Leroux laughed and wandered off to talk with his friends there.

The *urizen* were much taller than Colleran had originally surmised. Most of them were over twelve feet at the shoulders and their long horns seemed prehistoric and deadly. Their hooves flung great gobs of earth from the street behind them as they paraded by.

Anna turned to Clay Desmond. "That's a big roast beef sandwich, wouldn't you say?"

"Yes," Desmond swallowed, his eyes wide. "I'd say so."

Strings of spittle dangled from the mouths of the *urizen*, and their basso cries rattled the glass window as they passed.

Colleran could make out through the dust the other side of the avenue. There stood other buildings with glass walls, and a different bunch of cowhands were also watching the *urizen* funnel through.

The men and women in this particular viewing room were all associated with the Lockrow operation. Some held clipboards, scribbling numbers; others spoke in low voices in headsets to distant, aerial observers.

Behind them suddenly came a call and Anna turned around. "Hey, kiddo!"

A strapping young man, all windblown, mouse-colored hair and sun-riched freckles, stepped into the room, cocky in his riding chaps and dung-covered boots. He walked right up to Anna and wrestled her into a kissing position.

"Grant!" Anna struggled shyly.

"Hi, sweetie! Did you miss me?" Grant's gray cowboy hat was banded by sweat and dirt. He was close to Anna's age, perhaps younger by a year or two, but it was clear that he worked hard for a living. *Very* hard. He waved a gloved hand at the window. "It took us a couple of weeks, but we did it. Finally brought them in!"

Anna flinched at Grant's aroma. "Christ, Grant. You're filthy!"

Grant Anglin glanced down at his roughened Levis and boots. He smiled proudly as if cowshit was his element. "Can you believe it? Fell off my horse in the canyon right after the first herd got through. We had a spook run on us, crapping all over the place. Scared to death. I sorta fell in some of it."

"Sorta isn't the word," Anna said, standing back. However, she was definitely happy to see him. This was her element, too.

Grant turned to the glass window. "This is our second herd right now. A third one is on its way in half an hour, if everything goes okay."

He kissed her once again, quite brazenly. "I've missed you tons, sweetie. Tons and tons."

Anna wiped the kiss away and introduced Grant to Colleran, Desmond, and the lovely. Grant didn't seem to take a shine to Heidi or recognize her as anything other than possibly Desmond's consort. Maybe he, too, had never seen a lovely before.

He also didn't seem to mind Colleran's Regulator uniform. He was either fearless or naive. Probably both.

Outside in the walled avenue one of the *urizen* bolted and scuffled with a ur-steer nearby. There was so much dust that it looked like angry clouds colliding. A huge body slammed against the glass wall, leaving a streak of sweat and dirt. The *urizen*, however, continued on down the avenue toward the stockyards and slaughterhouse.

Anna turned a professional eye toward the *urizen* boulevard. "You said you got a spook. Was it that one?" She indicated the ur-steer that had just bolted.

"Naw," Grant said, shaking his head. Jean-Jacques was at the window, watching the steer in question continue down the street.

Grant said, "Started yesterday, actually. We got a couple of wild ones. Had to jolt both with my gun. That didn't calm them, though. Maybe they knew where they were headed."

"And another one spooked in the canyon?" Anna asked.

"Yeah. A different one."

"It wouldn't go through, or what?" Colleran asked.

Grant laughed. "Damn funny thing. It just ran on through the canyon like it wanted to get there ahead of all the rest. One of my men snapped it good before it got to the city limits. The gates were up, but, hell, there's no telling what kind of damage it would've done."

This dynamo of the plains, exuding a pungent smell, scratched his rear unconcernedly, having been too long in the saddle. Then he looked at Colleran, finally recognizing his uniform. "Hey, are we in trouble, or what? Regulators don't come around here much any more."

"We're not in trouble," Anna said to her boyfriend. Then she reconsidered, glancing sideways at Colleran. "Maybe," she conceded. "There's been some trouble with the Meurers."

Grant Anglin had gray eyes that could look mean. They did so now. "The Meurers? Are they back?"

"No," Colleran assured him quickly. "At least we don't think so. But somebody's trying to kill all the people who used to work for them. It's possible that they may be coming here."

Grant patted his deadly jumpgun at his side. "Let them come. We can take care of ourselves."

"I'm sure you can."

Jean-Jacques Leroux touched Colleran on the arm. "We've got a viewing platform just above us, if you want to get a better look at the cattle from the outside."

Colleran approved, but Clay Desmond clearly was in an alien landscape. Too much sweat here, too many signs of *work*. To Colleran, he said, "Just how long are we going to be here? Don't you think we ought to get on with it so we can get out of here?"

Anna said, "If you go down that hallway to your left, you'll find a lounge area. It's much cleaner than it is here and you can wait there until Mr. Colleran is through with his visit."

"Let's go, babe," he said to Heidi, taking Anna Lockrow's considerate advice.

Heidi gave Colleran a pleading look; she very much wanted to stay with them. It was exciting to her, all of this. However, she went with Desmond.

Grant Anglin removed his gloves with an impatient gesture, snorting at the departure of Clay Desmond. "Some folks don't like to see where their meat comes from."

Leroux signaled Colleran and he followed the cowhand, leaving Grant and Anna to be alone with one another.

The area above the main building was a viewing platform, and several cowhands were already surveying the progress of the herd. The whole city, seen from this angle, seemed designed entirely for the movement of cattle. The street itself had been carved below the ground level, which made it easier for the *urizen* to be moved.

The cowhands gave Colleran's black-and-silver tunic a wary look, but when Leroux walked up beside him they seemed to relax. By the hostility in their stares, Colleran assumed that they'd seen much in the way of trouble from the people who used to run their lives. They clearly didn't want any from him.

Leroux took Colleran to a protective rail and leaned over. He twisted his blonde mustache. "Your friend down there doesn't much like the way we live in these parts."

"He didn't like being enlisted," Colleran said. "He'd rather be on a golf course somewhere."

The last of the *urizen* were making their way through the sunken, dust-clouded avenue. Right behind, two women on the huge ur-horses prodded them along with whistles and hoots. Leroux waved at one of them.

Leroux then said, "We'll get our pharmacist to replicate Mr. Desmond's medicine. That should keep him calm. Unless you think you can live with him until you get back."

Colleran watched the cowgirls beneath them. "I won't have to live with him much longer. There's nothing here for us that I can see. The Meurers have been gone a long time."

"Not long enough for me," Leroux stated.

The two of them watched the girls herd the strays around a bend in the avenue. Months and years of *urizen* traffic had made the boulevard into a veritable canyon.

Leroux stared out across the rooftops. "Well, I don't know what you're looking for, but if what you say is all true, then it does make sense. Sort of."

"What do you mean?"

Leroux sighed heavily and removed his jaunty cowboy hat. He also checked to see if Anna had come up the stairs behind them. She hadn't.

"We've always known that something's been wrong," he told Colleran confidentially.

"Like what?"

"There was a rumor going around for many, many years that Meurer meat was tainted. Not our meat, you understand." For a moment it looked as if Leroux forgot to whom he was speaking. But he didn't seem to let it bother him.

He went on. "The Meurers, from what my father used to tell us, had begun losing their hold on the market because of it. Anna's father—my uncle Buck—swore that some of the *urizen* were spooks. The Meurers were always experimenting with livestock, then turning them loose when they were done. Remember that *vacq* I shot?"

"Yes."

"That was one of their experiments gone bad. They were trying to develop a kind of mobile plant that could ferret out its own water source. They wanted a plant that could take care of itself but wouldn't mind being harvested when the time came. Didn't turn out that way."

"What happened?"

Colleran recalled the poisonous leaves of the *vacq* and its innocent demeanor.

"It got loose and multiplied. You know those oases of forests scattered across the plain? Each one's got a *vacq* lording over it. Sometimes whole families. We don't go near them, but the cattle aren't afraid of them. They're too big for a *vacq* to capture and kill."

"What about that big boar I shot? You said that was a renegade."

"Right. Some ranches got caught up in the fight. There were some folks north of Shuraat who raised pigs bigger than the one you killed. Those folks were caught up in the siege of Shuraat and were destroyed. Their animals all got loose. Plus, there are some real beauties just offshore in the ocean that the Meurers tried dumping years ago. That's the reason why no one sails our seas."

Colleran listened, and listened closely. That fist in his gut was beginning to tighten again. He could almost hear *reggae* music in the background and Regina Wahlander's ill-fated party. . . .

Leroux continued. "You see, we can't ship our meat products until the Meurer reputation is forgotten. Our meat is fine and those of us here on Courtenay Three have been eating it for years. But Anna and Grant, assuming that they get hitched before they get old and die, are going to have a hell of a time becoming a Reach. That's why we've chosen to stay quiet these last few years. A few more years won't hurt us none, though. If that's what it takes. Besides," he concluded, "that time will be good to build up the herd."

Colleran wiped sweat from his brow; the dust of the animals' passage had begun adhering to him. He said, "Shuraat didn't look like an industrial city to me. Did they do their experimenting there?"

"Not that we know of," Leroux told him. Only his mustaches made it look as if he were smiling. He wasn't. "There doesn't seem to be a place in Shuraat where they could've done it. If there is, I haven't found it, and I've been all through those ruins."

Leroux turned and faced the empty *urizen* avenue. Some of the dust was beginning to settle. He said, "The Meurers had spindles, though, and they worked most of the planets of our solar system. I know they once had an incredible research facility on Courtenay Seven, but they closed it ten years ago when it was no longer economically feasible to maintain it." He looked squarely at Colleran. "It's all business, you know?"

The third herd of cattle were being shuttled through the northern part of the city. Evidently, the *urizen* were moved in small bunches in order to keep them under control. It made sense to Colleran.

"I'm glad they're gone," Leroux said. "They were ruthless. That's why I don't trust your friend with the pills. If he's one of them—*truly* one of them—then you'd best keep an eye out."

Colleran watched as the first of the third company of *urizen* slowly walked around the bend in the avenue, plodding along with a look of weariness and defeat in its large, sad eyes.

He found himself fingering the pouch in his tunic that held the caliban crystal from the beast that killed Kit Brodie. He took it out and showed it to Leroux.

"You ever see anything like this?"

Leroux took it and was impressed. "That's a nice jiva-stone. I haven't seen one that good for a long time. Where'd you get it? Anna give it to you?"

Colleran looked at him. "No. I've had it for a while. You've seen these things?"

Leroux gave Colleran a peculiar stare. "Of course. We've got dozens of them back at the ranch. Or at least Anna does. They're called jiva-stones, but they're worthless." He handed Brodie's stone back to Colleran, who stood dumbfounded. "Nice asterisms, though. Pretty."

"And she's got *dozens* of them?"

"Hundreds, probably," Leroux said, surprised at Colleran's amazement "They're from *urizen*. We get them when we slaughter them. They grow just between the horns. We used to find a lot of them, but lately there have been fewer and fewer. But yours is a beauty."

Colleran grabbed Leroux firmly. "You say they come from your *cattle?*"

Colleran felt that his heart was going to fly up out of his throat.

Leroux almost laughed, not knowing what to think. "Sure. And the pigs and everything else engineered in *urizen* form. Even the *vacqs* have them. Hell, when we tranked Mr. Desmond last night and put him to bed, we found three of them in his pockets."

Suddenly, from down the street, far within the crowd of approaching *urizen*, several of the cattle began getting nervous. One of them jumped up and seemingly bellowed with pain.

Leroux stood back and unholstered his jumpgun. "Watch it," he said to Colleran, guarding him with an extended arm. "We've got us a spook down there."

Leroux stuck two fingers in his mouth and whistled across the wide sunken avenue to the other cowhands on the opposite viewing platform. "*Spook on the way!*" he shouted to them.

Colleran backed off with the crystal in his hand, the jiva-stone. It almost throbbed. Thunder and heat rose up from the avenue beneath him.

"*Here they come!*" Leroux shouted above the ruckus.

An alarm went out overhead and the whole avenue filled with the horrified cries and moanings of the panicked cattle. All because of one lone bull. The herd came at the buildings—several hundred tons of angry meat, hooves, and horns.

It was a full-fledged stampede, and it was being led by one particular *urizen*, which to Colleran had the look of a caliban.

26

The fortified main street of Jasper shuddered with such an unearthly spasm of *urizen*-inspired fear that Colleran thought the buildings lining the sunken boulevard would actually fall apart.

The bull out in front of the herd, which had leapt in its frenzy, had gotten a glimpse of Colleran and Jean-Jacques Leroux, and deep within it something dark and troubled was triggered. Its eyes, no longer glazed from its idyllic, lethargic life on the plains, sparked with recognition. It leapt and kicked and bellowed, furiously bashing its head and horns about.

And the others behind it panicked, sending ripples even farther back into the oncoming herd.

"This way!" Jean-Jacques shouted, yanking out his gun. The two men, along with several other cowhands, ran back into the building even as plaster lathing cracked around them and beams splintered.

They made for the stairs—just in time for them to collapse. Jean-Jacques fell onto Colleran, and Colleran fell onto a female cowhand who was shouting into a radio headset. They dropped into the lower reaches of the sheltering building unharmed, and Colleran helped the woman to her feet. She ran off into the darkness of the lower hallway. The electricity had been knocked out.

In the lower rooms cowhands shouted to each other, running down the corridor that paralleled the avenue beyond the windows.

Colleran followed Leroux into the large viewing area. "Desmond and Heidi are in the other room," he shouted to Leroux.

The wall before them was almost like a movie screen, with bodies the size of ten-ton boulders jumping over each other and colliding with the wall itself.

"Don't worry about this," Leroux said, worried nonetheless. "It sometimes happens. But they'll never breach the walls. If they make it to the freight yards in this state, though, there might be trouble."

Leroux followed another female tech into the dark corridor with Colleran right behind him. More metal groaned, more thunder shook them. Emergency lights flashed on.

Into another viewing room they ran, and in the almost aquarial light he could see more of the *urizen* stampeding beyond the translucent wall. Blood and spittle splashed the wall, caked with dung and dust.

But the ur-bull that had spied the two of them on the balcony above was now way out ahead of the pack.

"*Heidi!*" he yelled above the din and the cowboys' shouts. "*Desmond!*"

The dust clouds were thick now and he could taste them even as they raced through the inner corridors with the other men and women. Somewhere, one of the *urizen* had torn a gap in the walls and the gusts from the sunken street had reached its ectoplasmic fingers into the building's air ducts.

His clasher was suddenly in his hands, his heart in his throat. Beatrice seemed to loom dead ahead of him in the foul air of the corridor. *Heidi*, he called out in his mind. *Where are you?* Or was he calling to Beatrice?

The corridor emptied out into a larger viewing station and the whole arena was filled with a sudden *clack!* of lightning from someone's jumpgun. Thunder punched Colleran's ears and a fierce wind followed the concussion.

One whole wall crumpled around Colleran, but he managed to fight his way through. Jean-Jacques kicked aside a man-sized piece of sheet rock, which had dropped down around him. They were all coughing and gagging as the stampede outside got worse and worse and worse . . .

Heidi screamed.

It pierced the cacaphonous clamor around him, but he knew it for what it was. *Heidi!* A scream that might have gone up in fire

above Okeanos or down into the depths of Lake Frederick. It was
Heidi.

Leroux suddenly batted Colleran's clasher down. "No!" he
shouted. "We don't want them dead!"

"But—"

Leroux pulled them into the last viewing chamber where the
glass wall was a spider's web of several bloodied impacts, and one
bull in particular was actually trying to make its way inside.

Desmond and Heidi both were at the rear of the room, having
been surprised by the bull's onslaught. Grant Anglin, who had lost
his hat, came in from the other corridor brandishing a jumprifle.

Desmond held Heidi so tightly—so frightened was he—that he
threatened to strangle her.

Heidi cried out, *"Lou!"*

"Desmond!"

The bull roared as others behind it pushed it partway into the
glass. Its malevolent eyes stared at them and Leroux shouted,
"Here it comes!"

The wall came down in a crystalline collar around the giant bull
as its forelegs reared up for its leap into the room.

Jean-Jacques Leroux and Grant Anglin raised their guns
simultaneously and fired.

Colleran bounded for Heidi and ripped her from Desmond's
desperate grip. Clay Desmond fell back against the wall as
thunder and bright white light slapped them all. Heidi screamed
again, falling into Colleran's arms.

The ur-bull, punched twice in the face via the brass conductor
ring in its huge snout, dove face first onto the floor, completely
knocked unconscious. Its rear legs, however, were halfway
outside the window. They twitched uncontrollably.

Beyond the window in the avenue the other *urizen*, still driven
by their blood fear, continued on. The strange lightning guns that
the cowhands carried meant something to the beasts, and they ran
even harder to get away from them. Leroux and Grant Anglin
plunged into the corridor, dashing out ahead of the stampede,
trying to head it off.

Heidi sobbed hysterically as Colleran held her. *"It tried to get
us! It came just for us! I saw it!"*

In her watery blue eyes, Colleran could see the mouth of the
caliban haunting the waters of Lake Frederick as it had swallowed
the second Heidi. *How that lovely must have been scared. . . .*

What *this* Heidi saw before her was just as frightening, and for that she seemed all that more human to him.

Clay Desmond rose shakily from where he had fallen into a brake of chairs and tables. His face was flushed and crimson with sweat. The gold necklaces around his neck glittered dully, even obscenely, in the midst of so much destruction. In the distance and throughout the city, they could hear the tremendous roaring of the jumpguns as the herd was selectively halted.

Colleran gently settled Heidi down into a leather couch, pushing aside a chunk of ceiling that was already there.

He then turned to Desmond. "You're under arrest, pal," he said angrily. He reached out and grabbed the bulging pocket of Desmond's tunic. It came away with a powerful rip.

"Hey, wait," Desmond protested, staggering back.

Colleran held it up and, true to Jean-Jacques' words, Desmond was carrying three of the jiva-stones.

"Where did you get these?" he demanded, shaking them in Desmond's face.

Desmond looked around the room. Other cowhands and Jasper personnel had gathered to inspect the fallen beast and the damage it had done. They watched the Regulator.

Desmond could hardly reply. He seemed to be sinking into a state of shock. "I . . . I've had them for a long time. Years," he choked.

Colleran pushed him down into a chair and Desmond didn't struggle. His breathing was ragged.

Behind Colleran, the ur-bull groaned, still unconscious. One leg still twitched. Its head was at an awkward angle because of its huge horns, each one twice as long as a man is tall.

However, as the cowhands bent over it, the beast opened one eye and seemed to hold Heidi's image within it. It stirred slightly and Heidi rose up from the couch carefully.

Colleran watched, hand on his clasher, as Heidi stared into the brown, filmy eye. She held out the flat of her hand to it, almost as if it were a receiver of sorts. With her other hand she covered her mouth.

"Get away from there!" Desmond grated at the lovely. "You stupid whore! It tried to kill you!"

Colleran pulled out his clasher and those cowhands—male and female alike—who recognized what his gun was, backed off, aware of its unquestionable power.

To Desmond, he said, "You shut the fuck up. You're the cause of this in some way and you're going to answer a hell of a lot of questions now or I'll kill you."

Desmond trembled—laughing, fighting for some kind of control, over both himself and the situation. "Have you lost your mind?" He pointed to the jewels in Colleran's other hand. "I'm in trouble for carrying jiva-stones? I've had them for years, Colleran. They're worthless! Just good luck pieces—"

"Some luck," Colleran growled.

At that point, three of the Anglin crew came into the demolished room with long cattle prods in their hands. Similar to the jumpguns, the prods were used for closer work with the cattle.

One man spoke to Colleran, pushing his cowboy hat back on his head in a kind salute to Heidi. "You folks better scoot on out back. We gotta get this boy back on his feet."

Heidi was beside herself, crying as Colleran holstered his clasher, fighting down his own sudden emotions. "Come on," he said carefully to her. "Let's get out of here. You, too, Desmond. You can move."

Desmond was a study in emotional conflict as he kept staring back and forth between the monstrous longhorn and Colleran. He rose painfully to his feet, coughing in the dust of the place.

The cowhands, meantime, set upon the task of getting the stunned creature back on its flinty hooves and back out into the street where it could join the others.

The stampede at that point had gone on through the town and the mooning cries and thunderous tramping had died down, along with the snap and pop of jumpguns. Cowhands moved through the buildings with bandannas tied around their mouths and some wore filter masks. *Soldiers in a war*, Colleran thought, *with casualties lying all around*. . . .

With the help of a local pharmacist, Colleran found something to sedate Heidi, who had become hysterical. Her sobbings had left her incoherent and helpless. He handcuffed Desmond and put him on board the waiting airbus—out behind the buildings where it was safe—and waited for Leroux and his cousin to return.

Anna herself looked a little worse for wear. She had lost her expensive cowboy hat and her clothing was soiled with dirt and sweat. Her boyfriend, Grant, seemed a bit more shaken as he dropped Anna off at the airbus. He had been instrumental in stopping the stampede, doing so by jumping out into the path of the *urizen* and snapping their brass nose rings as they approached. They were, after all, his herd and he wasn't about to let any of them do any more damage, either to themselves or to the town. He had almost been killed as a consequence.

In the stampede, they had lost four of the creatures, who had gotten trampled. The bull that had caused it all was now safely in its pen at the waterside stockyards. Stampedes, as Anna informed Colleran, were common; that was why Jasper had been built the way it was. But she wasn't of the opinion—as Colleran was—that someone specific was to blame. The jiva-stones, she insisted, were quite common and quite worthless. However, she said that Colleran could take some of her jewels back to the Authority for analysis if he liked.

Colleran allowed Desmond his one perfunctory call to his lawyers in the Klasa-Eisner Reach by way of an orbiting com-drone. Desmond was shaking as he made it and pleaded for Sheila Eisner to get him out of this mess. Colleran also sent a message by com-drone for Brianne and her team on the *Parvardigar* to track down what they could of *urizen* technology. Inwardly Colleran smiled. The com-drone would spindle toward the *Parvardigar* before it spindled to the Klasa-Eisner system light-years down the tunnel of the Spoke. Brianne would get an earful before Sheila Eisner would get Desmond's message. The Admin would know what to do.

As the airbus prepared to lift, Colleran watched everyone climb aboard. Jean-Jacques Leroux lingered in the arms of a grease-dolloped sweetheart who had been working elsewhere in the city when the stampede occurred. Grant, tired and weary from the strain of the stampede, walked with Anna, speaking to her in low tones as only a lover or a dear friend might. Her blue eyes were alive and she kissed him lightly before getting on board.

It struck Colleran then and there that these people had what so few people had elsewhere in the Mandala. This was real life here—and real love. *We're so often sidetracked in our lives*, Colleran thought, *that true happiness can be right under our feet and we can't see it or feel it*. What was all this running back and forth in the Spokes about? he wondered.

He knew. It was in the form of the lovely in the rear of the airbus sleeping in her drugged condition. She was worth more to him than a hundred Clay Desmonds, even though he knew that he could not afford the luxury any longer of real love. Not after the Plunderer, not after Marji Ciani.

He also needed more metatryzine. As the airbus lifted and the cloaking shield aurora surrounded them, he could feel Beatrice watching him patiently. Those calm fields of Meru, those beautiful nights . . . he felt as if he were about to break through the mystery of the calibans and he just could not afford another disruptive Lei experience.

The sun had lofted below the horizon long before the airbus neared the Lockrow mesa. Food had been provided by the airbus service back in Jasper, but to Colleran's concern, Heidi wouldn't eat. She was delirious, and he wondered if there might be something wrong internally with her. She kept refusing food or conversation.

As they drifted slowly into the night, with the plains and *urizen* families dozing below them, the pilot came back to them. He handed Colleran a sheet of faxpaper. Leroux sat up and leaned in over Colleran's shoulder.

"This just came in," the pilot said. "But just barely. We might be in for some kind of trouble."

Colleran sat up. Anna, beside him, looked at the message. It read: BAYRIGHT REACH HEADQUARTERS DESTROYED. CHAIRMAN KILLED. NEW CALIBAN STORAGE FACILITY FOUND IN BETA SPOKE. NOTHING NEW ON DESMOND. CLEAN AS A BABY'S BUTT. WATCH YOUR OWN. ADMIN SAGAR.

"What's that mean?" Anna asked.

"It means that this fight is getting worse and we still don't have any answers." Colleran looked back to see Desmond asleep, still cuffed to the passenger seat. He had eaten hugely and the remains of his supper lay in a jumble on the seat beside' him.

Colleran looked up at the waiting pilot. "You said that we might be in for some trouble."

The young Jasper citizen pointed to the faxsheet. "This came in from the Lockrow ranch by an incoming com-drone. I got some static right at the end of the transmission, then it was cut off. I tried raising the ranch, but nothing happened."

Colleran didn't like the sound of that. Nor did Anna. "What kind of militia do you have here?" he asked her.

"It's just us," Anna said, worried.

Jean-Jacques Leroux wasn't worried, though. He smiled and

slapped his jumpgun in its ordinary holster. "It's just us and our guns. Why?"

"I think you might find yourselves enlisted."

"Enlisted?" Anna breathed.

"In a Reach war. A full-scale Reach war." To the pilot, Colleran said, "Send a relay message to your people in Jasper. Have them forward a Priority Summons to the *Parvardigar*. They can spindle it on the same com-drone that brought in this message." He held the faxsheet.

"Right," the young pilot said. "A Priority Summons. Anything else?"

"That'll be enough," Colleran said dryly.

Anna turned to Colleran. "What's this about a Reach war now?"

Colleran said, "You might be in the midst of a Reach war and not even have known it."

"What are you talking about?" Leroux asked, his mustache still smiling even though he wasn't.

Colleran pulled out Desmond's three jiva-stones and the jewel from the beast that killed his best friend. "You said that these things were found inside of your *urizen* as well as some of the *vacqs*."

Anna looked at her cousin, then back at Colleran. "Well, yes. There used to be some *vacqs* growing within a few miles of the mesa. But they—"

Leroux interrupted. "You trying to tell us that we might be under attack by our own cattle and pigs?"

"As well as a few other nasties left behind when the Meurers abandoned Shuraat." Colleran indicated the faxsheet. "The Bayright Reach is now caught up in this and what they do is quite similar to what the Meurers did, except they do it with cloned human beings."

"That's disgusting," Anna said.

Colleran did not look behind him to the sleeping lovely. He continued, "These artificial creatures, including your *urizen*, are being used in a war against the Meurers and their former employees. That means you and all of the other ranchers."

"*What?*" they both exclaimed.

"You said that there are *urizen* birds and *urizen* wild cats and even *urizen* swimming in the oceans. It's possible that you could have a whole planet turning against you."

Leroux laughed. Anna sat upright and rigid. "That's ridiculous. We haven't had any trouble for years."

"Except that a *vacq* killed your mother," Colleran stated. When Anna's face went cold, Colleran's heart sank. "I'm sorry," he told the rancher. "But it's true. You saw what the stampede did." Colleran looked out the window at the dark landscape beyond where nothing could be seen. It was a virginal terrain, unblemished by city lights or any sign of humanity. "The only problem is, we don't know who's doing it."

"The Meurers were all killed during that last battle," Anna informed him.

"Yes," Colleran countered, "but who did the fighting? Who attacked the Meurers six years ago? The city was totally destroyed and not a single trace of the attackers remained. *You* people didn't do it."

Anna agreed to that.

Colleran walked up to the pilot's compartment. There, he and the copilot were busy bringing the airbus into its approach pattern. The mesa was somewhere out ahead of them.

Colleran said, "Turn off the shield and the interior lights. Can you do that?"

"Sure," the pilot said, looking up. "Why?"

"I want to come in as quietly and as invisibly as possible. I don't like it."

The pilot had a sheen of perspiration across his forehead. He apparently didn't like it either. The copilot was a fourteen-year-old boy, and he was scared to death.

The pilot switched everything off but the gravity-lift engines and drifted toward the mesa. Jean-Jacques Leroux looked in over Colleran's shoulder.

"It's dark," he muttered. "The whole mesa's dark."

There was no moon in the sky above Courtenay Three, but thanks to the crystalline wash of the Milky Way, there was enough illumination to make out the silhouette of the Lockrow mesa.

Colleran looked at Leroux. "What kind of guns do we have on board?"

Leroux looked down at Anna, who had no weapons at all. "Just your Langstrom and my McGuane jumper. But between us—"

"That'll have to do," Colleran said, stepping back among the passenger seats. Anna was now very alarmed. Leroux followed.

"Colleran!" Desmond shouted from the back of the bus. He had come awake and rattled his handcuffs. "Uncuff me! If there's something wrong—"

Colleran walked up to him and unlocked the cuffs. He said, "You're still under arrest and if you interfere in any way I will not hesitate to clash you." Desmond rubbed his wrists. Colleran nodded to the lovely in the seat across from his. "And if you so much as lay a finger on Heidi, I'll pull you apart with my bare hands."

"Eat shit, Regulator," Desmond said, standing in the darkness that filled the hovering bus. "I've done nothing wrong, and you know it. My lawyers will chew you and your Administrators alive, and these people are witnesses."

"Leave them out of this. They've suffered enough."

"They've only just begun to suffer," Desmond vowed.

Heidi stirred and opened her sleepy eyes. Everyone watched her as the lovely's movements seemed to fill in the empty space that the tenseness of the moment had left. She looked up at Colleran as she sat forward. She seemed entirely different now, not the gay bedwarmer she was designed to be. She said to Desmond, "You're all wrong about this."

Then she got up and walked around them, down the aisle, to the door, waiting for the airbus to land. She ignored them all.

Desmond shouted to the rebellious lovely, "You're finished! Back you go."

Heidi said nothing.

The bus began to rock back and forth as it bucked the winds lifting up from the sides of the basalt tower of the mesa. In the dark, Colleran heard Leroux check the charge in his jumpgun. Anna stood by the forward windows, silent in the darkness. Nothing moved on the mesa below. Somebody seemed to have covered it with a shroud of calm.

"Coming in," the pilot said in a loud whisper. All engines were down now; only the guiding gravity vanes aimed them in.

The bus ground itself easily onto the tough turf of the landing zone and Anna flung open the door, easing down the metal stepladder.

"Oh, my God," she gasped, stepping out into the utterly black night.

Colleran was right behind her and Leroux behind him. The pilot had his eye on Desmond, as per Colleran's command.

The landing zone was surrounded by tall, spectral sentinels. Every one of them was a *vacq*. And in the darkness, other things were moving as well.

27

Mist licked at their ankles as they stepped from the airbus. Everything about the wide mesa was rooted in utter dark. The *vacqs* stood at the southern edge of the ranch top, massed by the dozens. Within that darkness, with the bright leopard spots of the Milky Way above, Colleran could make out a bulbous form. *A ship? A spindle of some kind?* The mesa was more than three-quarters of a mile long at its most extreme point. It was hard to tell.

Anna shouted back to the pilot, "Alan, lights! We've got to see! And radio for help!"

The lights before the airbus flared on, casting them all in plain view.

Jean-Jacques Leroux began running toward the main bunkhouse dormitory and communications buildings. Anna started for her own large house. All lights were off. Quiet flowed everywhere about them.

"Anna!" Colleran shouted, not knowing what to expect. "Be careful!"

Heidi stepped out of the airbus with Desmond as the young pilot, awash in the greens and yellows of his console, began radioing Jasper and all points in between.

But there was no waiting army that Colleran could see, and as Anna ran into her house—her boots thumping loudly on the oakwood floor—calling out to her servants, the entire mesa seemed deserted.

Except for the *vacqs*, who seemed grouped for an attack. How fast *could* they move? Colleran asked himself. How had they made the climb so quickly?

More than forty people worked the upper part of the mesa and another twelve down below at its forested base. Where were they?

He felt those questions rise up in him, starting down around his ankles, reaching up to his thighs and waist as if traveling up his arteries and veins, then prying open a trapdoor in his brain and entering. He watched his own hesitant shadow angle sideways, cast in amber from the landing lights of the hovering airbus. The bus itself suddenly leaned ever so slightly to one side, as if pushed by a breath of air.

The headlights of the bus turned. Were those bodies lying out ahead? The stars above him, so unfamiliar at this edge of the Spoke, threw their light down about them. Yes, they were bodies. Men and women stricken, perhaps asleep, caught in the midst of fleeing or fighting whatever it was that attacked the mesa and cut its power source.

Colleran heard Anna calling her friends and servants. Her voice was strong, alarmed, and bounded about the empty ranch house as if it were a living thing.

Heidi fell on the ground. Clay Desmond crumbled beside her, falling onto the misty grass without so much as a sound.

Colleran looked up at the rising airbus. The pilot was fighting for consciousness as the younger copilot had already donned an airmask of some sort. The pilot, unconscious, fell forward on the console as the copilot swung the airbus off the edge of the mesa. Its shield went up and it disappeared.

Gas, Colleran realized. He wasn't prepared for this, for anything like this. He tried running toward the silent ranch house, but Anna could no longer be heard. Leroux had succumbed as well.

Darkness ghosted up around him as he spun around, holding out his clasher. The *vacqs* only stood where he had first seen them, unmoving.

And the night said: *No, not this time . . . this is the time for sleep . . . this is the hour for peace and redemptive slumber . . . the sleep and peace of death . . .*

Colleran fell to his knees. Out ahead of him, as if risen from the soil itself, was a somber presence. It moved about the grounds, stalking its prey. Colleran lifted his clasher, but his fingers unfolded themselves from the gun's grip.

Now close to the ground-hugging sleep-mist, Colleran felt himself fade. Up in the sky, receding, was a fuzzy cloud eclipsing the strange constellations of this part of the universe. The airbus? Had the young boy made it?

He didn't care. For standing where the airbus had lifted away in the misty night was the figure of Beatrice. She was neither approving nor disapproving. She merely smiled at him as the arms of *something* took him deeper and deeper into the realm of sleep.

He awakes again from the recurring dream of distant worlds to find Beatrice, this time, gone from their bed. Colleran sits up, pushing aside the covers as the light of the predawn begins to illuminate the windows of his small home.

He tries to blink away the dream. Creatures shaped like trees . . . new-found friends, the strong rugged cowboys . . . invisible sky-buses piloted by children. It is all so inventive and peculiar that he just has to share it with Beatrice, his wife. His companion.

He feels suddenly empty, both from the frenzy of the dream and from not knowing where Beatrice has gone at such an early hour.

The city on the plains before Mount Meru is still asleep as he steps out onto the marble walkway, the stones beneath his feet still cool from the gentle night.

A carnelian rose-color floods the eastern horizon even though there are yet a hundred constellations visible above him. He knows all their myriad names, as he has known them all of his life. This is the real world. This is his true center.

But where is Beatrice?

There are chitterings from the far distant fields of animals stirring, and some birds can be heard. For most of the world, though, it is much too early.

He finds the city's central aqueduct and there he bends to cup some water, tasting its sweetness. He stands and looks to the north where Mount Meru seems to hover like an airborne island of mysterious rock. The cities of the Suras burn there still, their lives like fine jewels.

The dream had been too real and he shivers in the predawn dark as if held between two different climes, not knowing what to feel. Was it true that dreams were memories of former lives? Or were they fictions?

He glances down at his hands, a maneuver he learned long ago. These hands, he suddenly thinks, had once killed, pulled the trigger of a gun only immortals could wield. But he is an immortal now. When had all this been? Whose Law had he been defending?

He turns away from the culvert and walks back toward his small white-bricked house. The unimaginably distant lights sprinkling the ridges of the mountains to the north twinkle in their constant activity. Their lives counted, too. But they were gods and gods do not comport with men. . . .

Colleran heard weeping, and it awakened him by touching something buried deep within his heart. A *human* crying. Real and sad.

"Heidi," he managed to call out. It was Heidi, he knew. Not his Heidi, but Clay Desmond's Heidi.

He called out her name once more, but his throat was parched and he was nauseous. Moreover, he could not move his hands or his legs. And his eyes could barely open.

A kind of brownish-green growth surrounded him and he had the sensation of swaying in place. *A cocoon*, his mind told him through its haze. *A cocoon from a living being.* Only his face protruded from the encrustation that engulfed him, and at the moment some of it was beginning to slip down over his face.

There was also another familiar sensation coming to him, the whine of spindles. He was in a spindle ship and they were in flight somewhere.

"Heidi," he tried calling out again as the sobbing continued. His voice cracked. The gas that had knocked them all out had also done something to his entire system. It seemed to coat every organ and nerve with a torpor that pulled him down and down and down. . . .

He swung back and forth in the vibrating passageway and the dreams were brought back to him. He almost thought he had heard Beatrice speaking to him in Heidi's weeping.

"Is that you, Heidi?" he called out above the spindle's energetic trembling. "Are you all right?"

"Lou," she called. Her sobbing broke off. "Are you awake? Oh, Lou—"

Another sound invaded. To his left came a *slithering* sound and he jerked around to see what it was. Something reptilian walked down the corridor with a long pole in its grip. It moved on six, perhaps, eight short legs, but with its forearms it gave Colleran a prod with the stick.

It was just a stick, not a McGuane jumper.

"*Quiet!*" it hissed. "*Quiet, quiet!*"

It was a master of the stick, and it aimed right where it would do the most damage. Colleran's ribs flared painfully.

Colleran screamed and the creature backed off, back to where it came from.

However, the force of the jabbing was enough to twirl Colleran's cocoon around. They were clearly in a short-haul transfer spindle and were probably still within the Courtenay solar system. A kind of vile yellow bioluminescence on the wall gave them light, but it also gave off a wretched smell, as did the cocoon substance. The place was alive.

Beside his cocoon was another cocoon, this one much larger. Within it was Clay Desmond. A hand without its rings stuck out where the cocoon had weakened. But no movement came from Desmond's cocoon.

Beyond Desmond was a smaller cocoon, containing Heidi. He could see her face clearly; she evidently had been awake and crying for a long time. Colleran's heart almost broke. *Three Heidis he couldn't save* . . .

"Where are the others?" Colleran whispered when her eyes caught his as his cocoon turned.

"It's just us, I think," she whimpered. "They just wanted us. Left everybody else sleeping. Oh, Lou."

Colleran's right arm had been woven into the cocoon where his right hand was above the organic holster. But his clasher was gone.

The lizard-creature, surely one of the calibans, returned to their perch and Heidi closed her eyes, feigning sleep. Colleran did the same. The caliban did something to Clay Desmond's cocoon, perhaps moving it in a better position, but Colleran did not even attempt to look. When it had gone, the cocoon looked no different to him.

However, as the creature crawled out of view, Colleran did see its tail end. It looked like a smaller version of the monstrosity that attacked the *Judy Holliday*, even down to the ruddy skin color.

Heidi whispered, "I think they beat him badly. Look."

Underneath Desmond's cocoon lay a small pool of congealed blood. No more blood dripped, but clearly it had come from an open wound somewhere.

"Jesus," Colleran whispered, now feeling the fear.

"It's Clay," Heidi said quietly. "It's Clay they want."

Colleran listened for the beast-pilot to return. Only the spindles hummed around them. "What are you talking about? Of course they want him. He was a Meurer—"

"They want to take him where it all started." Heidi spoke now with great confidence—and great guilt. "Courtenay Seven. That's where we're headed. There's been radio communication coming down the corridor."

"I don't—"

"This is Rex Wahlander," Heidi confessed. "I didn't get as much gas as you and Clay, I mean Rex, did. They're after him."

The spindle engines shifted their energies into a descent mode and all three of the cocoons swung like pendulums. Colleran could now see how much of a beating Desmond had taken. He also found out where the blood came from.

Clay Desmond's face was partially missing. But what had been torn off had been plastiderm molding. There was a different face beneath.

"I couldn't tell you anything," Heidi began. "I was sworn not to. I'm his lovely. All these years we thought it would come to this."

And now it had.

28

Colleran fogged in and out of consciousness, fighting the nausea that clutched him. Only the knowledge of Desmond's identity kept him trying—and the fact that throughout the ship, coming from its many recesses, droned the chants of several unseen calibans. "*Wahlander, Wahlander,*" was their litany, their mantra of hate.

Colleran shifted into wakefulness when the spindle's energies began to diminish and the effects of a large planet's gravity began to take hold. Bodies with grotesque hands and arms unlatched their cocoons, and carts were placed underneath them so they could be towed to their destination.

During that process, Colleran glimpsed their home.

The cocoons, led fore and aft by eager caliban monstrosities, were taken from the spindle jitney down a long clear glass corridor, a connecting or docking tunnel between the spindle and the caliban fortress.

Through the thick glass Colleran caught a view of orange-pink methane clouds, swirling continents of ammonia, and much higher up, an incredible universe of ocherous yellow hydrogen. It was the sky, turbulent and murky, of a Jovian planet—Courtenay Seven, far away from the pleasant plains of the third planet where Colleran hoped that Anna Lockrow was safe.

Apparently, they were now in some kind of floating station very high up in the methane clouds of Courtenay Seven. However, it was not a station bouyed by gravity-lifts like a laputa. The station seemed to rest on some kind of hydrogen-filled balloon. The "ground" upon which the station sat was bubbled with encrustations and pustules, and the whole construct swayed in the high altitude winds. The sky seemed to stretch beyond forever, the horizon almost impossible to imagine.

As they rolled down the corridor to the shufflings and slitherings of the calibans who escorted them, Colleran also caught sight of an insignia on the side of one of the outside buildings. It was a stylish "M" for the Meurer Reach, the original people who had constructed this secluded aerie so far from the probing eyes of the Authority.

The landing area, as seen through the glass enclosure, held many small spindle jitneys, some quite odd in shape, as if the calibans had made them in their own grotesque but streamlined image. And in the sky, like the specks of ordinary birds, were *things* that Colleran had never known to exist before.

They were calibans. This was their world. They bunched in flocks or sailed the hurricane winds alone. Some resembled actual balloons with long tentacles dangling for what seemed to be miles. Others were sleek, arrowshaped. A solitary caliban, V-shaped like a wing, knifed its way into and out of ugly brown clouds—clouds that seemed to congeal as if alive, as if they contained food of some kind. Still another creature was saucer-shaped with spokes radiating from a lenticular center. It rotated and dipped and weaved, doing so with all indications of enjoying itself.

Some of the creatures, spinning close to the floating platform, showed interest in the arrival of the spindle jitney. Others, particularly the slow-witted, blimplike beasts, did not.

But mostly—and this was the horror of it—the skies of Courtenay Seven extended for thousands and thousands of miles and seemed empty. The creatures had this empty world for themselves.

Right before they left the connecting tunnel, Colleran managed to crane around and see something else. Standing at one end of the landing zone, huddled alongside the odd-looking vehicles, was an Abou-Farhaat short-haul spindle freighter. It was a standard ground-to-orbit transfer vehicle, one probably used in getting the calibans from this awful place into orbit where the Abou-Farhaats could pick them up.

And the place *smelled*.

The air was old, somehow, as if the environmental recirculation system barely worked. Whatever it was, the area had a stench about it that came from a wild variety of organisms, creatures that secreted and oozed and snorted all sorts of gasses and flatulence. The smells were almost placental, the residue of organic processes, vats of them. This, he realized, was where calibans were made, nurtured, and turned into fighting machines.

They were immediately wheeled into a room with high windows and peculiar equipment. It was filthy. Muck and slime soiled the floor and a kind of algal growth clung to the moist insides of the windows. But Colleran could see through them with no problem. The cocoons were rehung to the ceiling as soon as they arrived.

Through the window Colleran saw and felt the sheer *power* of Courtenay Seven. He could detect no surface at all—so high up were they. More creatures, like herds of *urizen*, moved in the distance. They seemed to be chasing after a very large brown cloud, a cloud that said *food* to their primitive survival urges.

The cocooned captives were left alone for a brief time, guarded by an obsidian-skinned creature, quite like the one that marauded Surane Four. That same beast was responsible for keeping out the other calibans who wanted in. *Wahlander, Wahlander* . . . was their chant. They knew who had just arrived.

From another part of the room Colleran heard a door open, and in walked a man. Sort of, Colleran thought.

He looked as if he had been part of an experiment gone haywire. His legs and lower torso looked like those of a normal man. But above that was a horrible mass of bubbled skin and swollen limbs. He had no neck and his head was larger than normal, as if to accommodate more brain matter, or more hate.

For hate filled the man's eyes, a hate Colleran had never seen before in his long life. And although this wretched man wore an ancient clasher at his side, in a long-dead live-leather holster, he seemed to restrain himself as he pondered the three captives.

Colleran struggled with an uneasy sense of recognition. The man-creature looked very familiar.

The altered man before them walked right up to the three cocoons. Evidently, he had been interrupted in the midst of his labors elsewhere in the station. But *this* was important.

"Wahlander," it whispered close to the shredded face of the former Clay Desmond. The whisper was edged with excitement. The creature prodded Wahlander's cocoon with a bony finger. "Wahlander, wake up and die. You can do it, boy."

The creature reached up to Wahlander's torn face and delicately—and intentionally—peeled back the rest of it. It roused

Wahlander, and the huge cocoon shook as the man within groaned back to consciousness.

Heidi, fully awake and scared, watched and cried out as the plastiskin disguise came away, ripping the dermal layers underneath.

The man-creature tossed the facial skin to the slippery floor as if it were obscene, and something that Colleran could not quite see scurried forward quickly to snatch it away, then skittered out of sight.

The horrible man faced Heidi and, for an instant, wore a look of pity, *human* pity, on his face. "My lovely," he said in a strained voice. "My young lovely, so innocent."

Colleran now recognized the man. Perhaps it had been the voice. It certainly was the sensitivity.

"Bayright," Colleran said, trying to find his own voice. He was incredibly thirsty. "Peter Bayright."

The man—Peter Bayright—turned and stepped closer to Colleran's cocoon.

"You know me," he said. It was not a question. And he was not happy with the recognition.

Bayright waved his hand around behind him, indicating the wide window and the methane storms beyond. "You know me, but do you know *this*?" he mocked. His eyes were red and his voice trembled. His fists had balled up with a dangerous rage.

"No," Colleran said.

"Of course not, *Mister* Regulator," Bayright grated. "There are some places the Authority will not go, some Reaches the Authority will not police. Am I right?"

Another reptilian creature came in, bearing a weapon Colleran couldn't recognize. It didn't matter; he was helpless without his clasher.

But Bayright, with his clasher and his anger, was more than in control of the situation. The man, immortal in his grotesquerie, was clearly going to do away with them, once he was through playing with them. He seemed to have a great deal on his mind.

"The Authority knew nothing of the Meurers until this started happening," Colleran said hoarsely. The smells of the place, plus the traces of anesthetic in his blood, were still tugging at his mind.

Bayright crossed his gnarled powerful arms. "This? What do you mean, *this*?"

"The caliban attacks," Colleran told him. "The murders."

Something close to a smile cracked the surface of Bayright's contorted face. "Ah, I see. You are calling us calibans now. I would have called us something else."

"Such as?"

Bayright jumped at him and shouted, "*Human beings! Men and women! Innocent men and women!*"

Wahlander's huge cocoon stirred as the man within came around. Bayright leaped over to it and shoved it violently against the back wall behind them.

"Wait," Colleran pleaded. He thought he was going to vomit. Other creatures had begun gathering in the room, letting in a fetid cloud from the outer hallways of the station.

Heidi choked back a sob.

Bayright snapped his fingers and a creature—one of the more human ones—came over and began spraying down the cocoons with a foam, which began dissolving them.

Wahlander fell to the floor with a loud slap and did not move. The cocoon had done much to destroy his clothing.

Heidi ripped out of her cocoon and sank to her knees. Her nakedness was made worse to Colleran when he saw the abrasions and welts she had incurred at the hands of their captives.

Colleran came loose, and although most of his Regulator's tunic had not dissolved, he wasn't in any better condition than the others to get up and do anything significant about their captivity.

Wait, his body seemed to tell him. *Just wait and see where this leads to. . . .*

Bayright's clasher was out and aimed at Colleran. He seemed imminently confident that no one was going anywhere.

Colleran sat up, shaking the foam from his arms. As an immortal, he might be able to use Bayright's clasher—if he could only get his hands on it.

Heidi, however, was in an almost worshipful position, crouched on her knees. But the look on her face was one of terror, not reverence.

"So you recognize me, Heidi," Bayright said. "Look upon your creator."

Heidi, without taking her eyes off the distorted man, quickly edged over to Colleran. Colleran reached out and held her.

Bayright shook as if the machines of the caliban factory all around them were supplying him directly with energy. He shouted at Heidi, "I created you, yet you turn away from me!"

"What's this all about, Bayright? What are you doing here?" Colleran demanded.

Guns clicked and were elevated all around them as the guards— not one resembling another—surrounded them.

Bayright relaxed, but just barely. "I guess you wouldn't know, now would you?"

"Hardly," Colleran admitted. "What happened to you?"

"What happened to me?" Bayright laughed bitterly and holstered his ancient Langstrom. "What happened? Let's just say that a certain corporation, on its way to Reach status, a corporation in *this* solar system, stole my autolife process. Let's say that certain men and women of this unnamed corporation bought out *my* company's stocks and marketing rights to *my* patents. Let's just say that these people conspired to corner the market in genetic engineering and expand their own Reach in order to make money and *more* money and *more* money!" Bayright bent close to Colleran and the fearful Heidi. "Let's just also say that what happened to me had to do with certain payoffs within the Mandala Authority, which allowed the Authority to turn a deaf ear to what was going on."

"That's not true, Bayright," Colleran countered. "And you know it. We had no idea of the Meurers' dealings. We only knew that they went out of business."

"And you also knew that Peter Bayright vanished. But did you do anything about it? I don't think so."

Bayright walked—painfully it seemed—to a wall and slid back a hinged casing. From it, he pulled a glittering assortment of jewels. Jiva-stones. They were all identical and were like the ones Colleran had run across before.

"You've seen these, I take it?" he asked Colleran.

Colleran nodded. Heidi held him desperately. Wahlander groaned and then fell back into unconsciousness. Blood pooled at his ravaged face.

Bayright held two of the jiva-stones in his fingers. "You've seen them, but have you compared them closely?"

Colleran said nothing.

"Ah," Bayright said dramatically. He showed them to Heidi, who backed away. "Well, Heidi recognizes them for what they are."

"What are you talking about?"

"I invented these two hundred and eighty-one years ago."

There was pride in his voice, and also anger. He went on. "I achieved immortal status for my contributions to Mandala life, as did you, I believe. I made it possible for great men and great women to endure by sharing their brain patterns with humankind by encoding their personalities on these crystals. Jiva-stones. My lovelies."

Colleran looked at the moon-faced lovely. He understood that there was a small crystal submerged in her medulla oblongata, and in it was the charm and kindness of the original Heidi Beryl, now long dead.

Bayright said, "And the Meurers robbed me of them!"

Colleran shifted his position on the floor, fighting for control over his body. He said, "Bayright, the Authority's on this whole case now. We can get back your patent rights. The Meurers are defunct, out of business."

A barking laughter rose from one of the guards. Bayright exploded at Colleran's apparent naivete. "You don't know the first thing about this." He held the crystals before them. "They took my autolife process and did something horrible—and Rex Wahlander was responsible. The Meurers took their enemies and encoded more than just their personalities on the jiva-stones. Yes! Can you imagine the deviousness of it? Lovelies are alive with memories and desires and hopes, just like you and me. But this is different!"

Bayright kneeled down close to Colleran. He almost whispered. "Have you ever tasted Meurer beef? Beef from their altered cattle?"

"I don't eat red meat," Colleran confessed. "I don't like it."

Bayright threw back his head and laughed. "I love it!" He stood up and walked around, laughing. "I love it!"

Colleran also stood up, if a bit raggedly. Heidi rose with him. Colleran urged him to continue. "So what happened? How did you end up this way?"

Bayright faced him. "Okay. I'll tell you what happened, not that it's going to do you any good. You see, I worked for the Meurers. Oh, they were clever. Here, on this station, I made advances on their own processes, improving my own as well. All the while, *they* siphoned off royalty profits from *my* process. But they kept me happy with my work and my lovelies to keep me company."

He paused and in a gentle fashion fingered one of the lavender jiva-stones. "The Meurers had enemies, even among their own corporate kind. So one by one they began to disappear. Do you know where they went?" he asked, holding up the jiva-stone.

Colleran was grimly silent. Heidi stood horrified.

"These stones are not crystalline computers put in embryonic brainstems. These are real people! This one—" He showed them the crystal. "This one right here has a woman trapped in it. The Meurers placed the stones in their cattle and their pigs and other farmyard animals, turning them loose to graze and eventually be slaughtered. And eaten!"

Bayright shook. It was a speech he had held deep within him for dozens of years. He said, "And when there were so many enemies encoded onto jiva-stones, they began wearing them as jewelry."

Colleran looked throughout the large room at the beasts gathered there. "And these . . . people—"

"Yes, these *calibans*, as you call them. They are the barbarisms the Meurers left alive. I found them and have been taking care of them, but their human bodies have long since been destroyed."

Heidi moved closer to Colleran. He could feel her tremble.

"But what about putting the crystals into human bodies, like the lovelies?" Colleran countered.

One of the blimplike creatures loomed in the distance beyond the wide window. In its eyes was a trace of intelligence. Colleran realized that all the creatures in the incredible sky beyond were artificial—calibans made to order, turned loose to wander the methane and ammonia storms of Courtenay Seven.

Bayright laughed at Colleran's suggestion. "But we thought of something better than that. Not only do we want out lives back, we want revenge. I can live in this body, this cell I'm trapped in, much longer than I can live with the Meurer crime. I decided to manufacture the perfect killing machines and place my friends in them. Every being you see here and out there—" He pointed an indignant arm at the huge window before them. "Every one was an enemy of the Meurers. But now we're tracking down all those who remained *and* the jiva-stones. They call out, they sing, they yearn for the release only real revenge would bring! If you don't believe me, ask the lovely here. She is part of the same technology."

But Heidi was too frightened to speak.

Colleran looked down at Wahlander, who lay drugged and beaten.

He pointed at him. "What's he got to do with this?"

Bayright controlled his breathing. "*He* was the one who authorized the transformations. It had been his idea. The cattle ranching had been so lucrative for the Meurers that he got the idea of imprisoning his enemies in the poor *urizen*. And some are still on Courtenay Three. The ones in the oceans we will probably never find, but we've got time." Bayright grinned—or tried to. "You see, I've also cracked the Kotlicky-Powell gene-splicing technique, and I've shared it with the new bodies my friends now inhabit. Our war will last forever if it has to."

Colleran recalled the ur-boar that had attacked Desmond—or Wahlander—back in Shuraat. Who had that pig once been? It had recognized Desmond in some way—or perhaps it had been the slight telepathic resonances coming from the three jiva-stones the executive carried.

Alarmed, Colleran realized just how far-flung the crystals must have been. The escaping Meurer executives were everywhere in the Alpha, Beta, and Gamma Spokes. Even in the black tunnels of Surane Four.

This was a Reach war of unprecedented scope.

And yet there was a kind of logic to the righteousness Bayright felt. Colleran could not recall when he stopped eating red meat, but others—*billions*—continued to do so. The Meurers had willfully perpetuated cannibalism throughout the Mandala worlds.

The gnarled, warped man who had once been human stood his full height before them. His fists clenched against the hatred he was feeling. He said loudly for all to hear, "And when this is over and every one of the Meurers is dead, we will clone human forms around every jiva-stone we can locate and return life as it should be lived to them."

"But what about us?" Heidi spoke up, her musical voice filling the room so incongruously. "We didn't do anything."

Bayright leaned toward her. "But *you* knew. Didn't you hear the tiny voices? The calls for help? The pleas whispered in the back of your brain whenever you came near his jiva-stones?"

Heidi was pale and shivering from her nakedness, her nipples gone hard. "But I didn't know what they were. They were just . . . voices . . . voices, that's all."

"I don't believe that," Bayright said.

"She's an innocent," Colleran told the grotesque man.

"Only saints are innocent," Bayright sneered. "And even they must wash their hands sometime."

Suddenly, one of the lizard calibans behind Colleran fell sideways against him as the prone form of Rex Wahlander jerked. An arm shot out and the creature fell over, dropping its rifle. It was a pulse-gun and Wahlander himself was fully conscious—and had been for some time.

With half of his face missing, torn away and bleeding, he came up with the pulse-gun in his hands, firing.

29

Colleran's response was pure reaction. His mind, dazed by drugs his body couldn't fight and dreams his conscience couldn't ignore, told him to get Heidi out. *Heidi!*

In this nightmare place of twisted realities, the only true innocent among them was Heidi. Colleran swept his arm around her and rolled to one side as the crazed Rex Wahlander fired white-hot gouts from the deadly pulse-gun in every conceivable direction.

The caliban guards were completely taken by surprise, and they were the first to go, their bodies pulped as fist-sized pulses of supercharged electricity caught them where they stood, their rifles and ancient guns still clutched in their leathery hands.

"*No!*" Heidi screamed as bullets and laser light scissored the air. But Colleran pushed and rolled through an open door, slipping on the organic floor as the creatures behind him fought it out.

It was the clasher in the hands of the demented Peter Bayright that troubled him the most. Bayright, despite his physical prison, had maintained his Kotlicky-Powell transformation. His clasher would still work, geared to his own special touch.

"Run!" Colleran shouted to Heidi.

Despite her partial nakedness, Heidi stumbled ahead with Colleran right behind.

The hallway in which they had found themselves was dimly lit, but as soon as an alarm went off, the lights began throbbing. The gunfire and the sirens crashed tremendously around them, echoing from everywhere at once.

Heidi rounded a corner and suddenly collided with a reptile-like creature who carried a rifle. She screamed as the two of them slammed into each other.

But Colleran was right there. The rifle skittered out of the creature's grasp, and Colleran scooped it up. The reptile rose, balanced on its long, slender tail, and turned away from the surprised lovely.

Colleran fired once and the creature broke in half with a thunderous roar from the gun.

Heidi flinched as blood rained about her, and she screamed as Colleran grabbed her and helped her to her feet.

With the rifle in one hand and Heidi in the other, Colleran hustled her into the strange factory as the gunfire behind them ceased.

He pushed Heidi into the blinking shadows and watched in the distance as two calibans—both hulking furred beasts—ran to the main event, running right past their nook.

"Oh, please—" Heidi whispered.

Colleran held her as he waited, and waited. The two heavy calibans ran into the large room only to be met by angry bolts of ball lightning.

"*Colleran!*" came a shout as Wahlander stood in the doorway caressing the pulse-gun. Rags of dissolving clothing hung about his battered body.

Colleran didn't think; he acted.

He shouldered the pulse-gun—a weapon structured for a different shoulder from his—and stepped out into view, pulling the trigger.

The gun kicked him with a burst of light, but he held his ground. Wahlander, at the far end of the corridor, fell back as pieces of the wall and ceiling spattered at him. Molten metal sizzled overhead and several fluorescent lights went out.

Heidi screamed behind him. "Lou! Look out!"

Colleran spun around, facing several surprised calibans, who evidently were merely checking up on the commotion at this part of the station. Only one had its gun out, but Colleran had to fire at them all.

He was almost deaf from the concussive thunder.

"*Colleran!*" Wahlander again shouted. "You can't get away from this place alive. I know it like the back of my hand. Let me have Heidi or I'll leave you for the *urizen*. There are dozens of them living here. You can't fight them all."

Colleran, peering around the corner, saw the man hesitate. Bayright clearly was dead, along with his caliban guards. Wahlander crouched just inside the fiery ring of the doorway as if there was nothing behind him to fear any longer.

Heidi cowered behind Colleran like a child. He said to her, "He can't use Bayright's clasher, and the pulse-gun he's got is no more powerful than this one. It's just a question of aim."

Heidi quivered powerfully. "I'm scared. He's always been this way. I knew this would happen. Those jewels—"

Colleran suddenly lifted Heidi by the elbow. They moved down a flanking corridor. He said, "He can't fight them all by himself any more than we can. We've got to find the communications center before he does."

They plunged down another corridor as gunfire picked up behind them. Other calibans were now investigating, keeping Wahlander occupied.

They found themselves running down a corridor where some of the metal of the walls had rusted into great cancerous welts. Some of the large ventilation ducts had fallen loose and Colleran could see just how much disrepair the station had suffered. The floor itself was cracked and there was a constant rotten-egg smell of methane, but he couldn't tell if it was leakage from the outside coming in—which seemed possible given the condition of the ancient floating station—or if the caliban engineering process allowed for the pungency that engulfed them. Probably a little of both.

Heidi stopped, breathing with great difficulty and gasping. "Lou, he'll find us. It's like he said."

But Colleran also knew the place.

"This is a standard off-world manufacturing construct. They put them on asteroids, comets, and any other inhospitable surface. The Meurers did this long ago, back before they started chewing

each other up." Colleran pointed down an adjoining corridor.
"There's a lifeboat station down this tunnel and a communications
section down that one." He pointed the other way.

"If it's still there," Heidi said, worried. "They've changed this
place. They're crazy! They aren't even human anymore!"

In Heidi's blue eyes he saw the blue skies and dark blue waters
of peaceful Okeanos. And he saw the beautiful soul with whom he
had spent so much time. She was much more than a personality
programmed onto a crystal chip, placed inside a growing human
embryo, then grown to her full size. This was Heidi. His Heidi.

The image of Beatrice transposed itself across the face of Heidi
just then and what he felt tugged at him plaintively. Could a man
love a lovely for the *person* she was? He knew the answer. He had
always known the answer. And Beatrice had always been there to
guide him.

The alarms continued to resound throughout the station as he
and Heidi ran. Nor did the gunfire behind them cease. Wahlander
Colleran thought, must be having one hell of a good time. It
sounded as if he were chasing them, hunting them down, picking
them off one by one.

And that gave them time to reach the lifeboat dock.

The corridor ended where Colleran believed they would find a
lifeboat, a vehicle that would take them into low orbit. If the radio
within hadn't rotted with age, they might have a chance.

Colleran gripped the decayed metal of the door hatch and threw
all of his might behind it.

The lights overhead stopped their incessant blinking. Then they
went out entirely.

"Lou?" Heidi cried. "What's happening?"

"I don't know," Colleran said, groaning above the hatch.

Then the environmentals ceased. The movement of air halted.

Colleran looked up and around in the eerie darkness. "He's shut
down most of the environmentals. He *does* know this place."

The wheel suddenly gave way and a hiss of desiccated air, old
and unused, rushed at them—but it was breathable air nonethe
less.

They rushed into the lifeboat bay, and before them waited a
lifeboat, as new as the day it had been built.

Except that it was a pod, a single-seater.

Heidi looked fearfully at Colleran as he considered what was before them. As he did so, he unlocked the hatch and bent in, inspecting it. When he punched in the power source, the gravity-lift engines began humming smoothly, the whole ship coming alive. All the lights on the console sparked go-ready green.

Colleran backed out.

"Get as high as you can as fast as you can. You may have trouble with the magnetic field, but you should be able to get a radio message out."

"Lou," Heidi started.

"Just do it," he told her. "The *Parvardigar* will have sense enough to home in on it. I'll do what I can from down here. But if Wahlander takes out the communications center, or if the calibans crash their beacon, then it'll take the Authority a thousand years to find this place."

He said this grinning. He *had* the thousand years, if he wanted them.

"But, Lou," she said softly. "I'm a lovely—"

He held her tightly to him. "You sure are," he said. He then kissed her long and lovingly, feeling more in his heart at that moment than he had in hundreds of years.

He placed her gently into the waiting bubble of the lifeboat pod as its lift engines came up to power. She gave him one last, frightened look, but he smiled at her and stepped back. The capsule sealed itself.

Grabbing the pulse-gun, he jumped from the airlock and pulled the hatch shut behind him. The bubble on the other side came up to full flight power and blew itself out into the deadly skies of Courtenay Seven.

Colleran didn't waste any time.

He ran back toward the central chamber of the floating station, listening to the sporadic gunshots and the howling of an occasional dying caliban. Darkness flooded the station, but the red phantoms of fires here and there gave the place enough light to move by. It also provided plenty of shadows in which an adversary might be waiting.

But now the smells were getting worse and worse, especially with the air filtration system turned off. Carbon monoxide would be one of the gases—the one he'd be unable to detect until it killed him.

He was going to have to find an oxygen supply or some kind of environment suit. But he doubted that any suit would be discovered easily in this place. There was no need for a man-shaped suit in a place full of non-men.

Colleran struck out for that part of the factory where he thought the communications center might be. Not knowing how many calibans might be lurking about, he had to summon help. A surviving com-drone in its launcher would do.

He also wanted to make sure that Heidi would be picked up, not intercepted. So he ran and avoided the moving shadows of the nightmare calibans as they themselves hunted down the man who was responsible for their condition.

Feeling his way through the station, fighting the thickness that seemed to be invading his skull from the virtually unbreathable air, he came across a large laboratory and processing area. It had its own power source and thrummed like a beating heart.

This was where the calibans were made.

In the center of the room, as if in the very center of their lives, was a row of floor-to-ceiling pillars made of glass. Inside of them, in various stages of growth, swam calibans. The place smelled abysmally of amniotic fluids. Several of the smallest calibans were still transparent, and Colleran could see pulsing veins and a single jiva-stone each through the thin membranes.

In an adjoining room, unguarded and unlocked, Colleran found a treasure trove of the peculiar crystals, all the same pale vermillion color, all the same size. And each one felt almost alive.

Why hadn't Bayright given his calibans human bodies, like his lovelies? Colleran would never know. The man's hatred of the Meurers ran unfathomably deep.

But it was over now. Colleran dropped the crystal he was holding. A kind of fog had moved in around him, making the air more difficult to breathe. The jiva-stones glittered in the subaqueous light, the jewels of a ransom paid to a renegade king.

Colleran stumbled against a shelf containing perhaps several hundred of them, and they came crashing down around his feet, a bejeweled waterfall.

He heard a hiss somewhere above him.

He fled the treasure trove room, into the pulsating darkness of the larger laboratory, lit only by the pillars. Gas was everywhere. Silence was everywhere.

All gunfire had ceased throughout the floating city.

"Colleran!" echoed a call from an outer hallway. Water dripped. Someone was coming.

Wahlander's alive, still alive, Colleran thought to himself as he staggered. And that meant a fair amount of calibans had been killed, caught by surprise, done in by their own arrogance.

Colleran lifted the pulse-gun and considered shooting away at the growing calibans, but thought against it. The calibans, despite their mandate, despite their *contents*, were victims only. Wahlander was the source of all evil in this universe.

Colleran lurched out into the dark corridor, seeing his death. He raised his pulse-gun and fired. The figure at the infinitely stretching end of the corridor dodged out of sight.

Colleran slumped against the wall, his uniform in tatters, water and fluids soaking through to his legs as he slid down, sitting.

He thought of Heidi and lifeboat acceleration vectors and standard megahertz radio beacons and spindle drones. Heidi . . .

"Colleran," the voice mocked, the dark voice. It was calm now, as it spoke, calm and confident.

Down the hallway stood Rex Wahlander. The eyes of his breathing apparatus wide and blank, a visage of demonic might.

The last thing Colleran remembered was the sound of Wahlander's feet slapping rhythmically as they slowly approached him. Rhythmically, like a beacon, like a heart's lonely beat.

The caliban war was over.

30

The children call him Dream Man and when they laugh, it is not *at* him but *with* him, for he finds it amusing, too. He is the only one among all the adults in this beautiful place who has dreams he can recall with such vividness. To the others who live here, they are illusions.

Even tonight, as the stars show themselves in their pristine clarity above the plains of Meru, the children ask that the story be told once again, the Dream.

Colleran, snared by them at the city's fountain, now that twilight has descended about them all, is facing a giggly bunch. There might be a Volner here or a Hofmeister Williams. They are all adorable. He looks once at the far mountains and the lights of the Suras glowing there. He breathes deeply, feeling the bliss he has always felt in this place.

He rubs the back of his head, feeling the joyful tingling there. It's as if there is truly a jiva-stone implanted in the base of his skull—as the Dream says—sending out its programmed ecstasy.

But he believes none of it, for he has always lived in Meru, the center of the universe, the Hub. Even so, he still enjoys telling the young, giggly ones, the squirmy ones who climb in his lap, of his Dream. In their bright little eyes is the joy of the stars above.

The Dream ends, as it ends every time he dreams it, in the same way. Only this last time did it seem more real to him. But he doesn't tell the children this.

The creature known as Rex Wahlander—for creature he was— had destroyed every last caliban dwelling in the floating Meurer factory high in the skies of the massive Jovian planet. This man had found all its defenses and turned loose all the sleep gas he could find, and in that flood of gas, he got one last prisoner, whom he did not kill.

He had plans for Lou Colleran. Colleran knew this.

There was nothing he could do but drift in ur-dreams, phase into and out of ur-reality as he felt himself transformed. He had no voice to cry out, no legs to move him, no arms to help him fight his way free. Everything conspired against him.

Instead, dreaming or not, he awakes to a feeling of transcendental happiness as he floats and spins, flying through clouds the size of continents, storm systems and cyclones that could swallow asteroid colonies.

He laughs, in this Dream, as he dives in the currents of the sky, feeling absolutely no need for his feet to be on earth—for *this* is true happiness.

Around him appear others of his kind, themselves saucer-shaped, hundreds of yards wide, turning, spinning. Each is a bright yellow color, each with eight strong spokes filled with buoyant gases, and each with a single autonomous crystal in its center—jiva-stones that somehow, in their own peculiar way, electrify him with the joy of flight, the joy of *being*. He spins and spins and spins, at times diving for hundreds of joyful miles, never seeing the surface below, only more clouds.

The children like this part best.

But the scary part of the Dream is when Colleran tells them how he rises to where the big blimps are. They are people, too, and they have gathered in a formation around the floating factory, which sits on one mountain-sized bioblast filled with lifting hydrogen sacs. He knows he must go there for the voices of the others tell him it is important.

It is the place where they were born—and he himself just released—but it is dead now. He knows this from the whisperings deep within his mind, from his new friends in the clouds floating sadly around him.

But this is a sadness—so he tells the little ones at the fountain every time they ask—blooming with joy for the sky creatures know what Wahlander does not. The jiva-stones, a Bayright legacy, are eternally progammed to transmit euphoria within the physical body. It is joy and sadness at once. The sadness comes only as they watch the lights of the floating station wink out, close down. The massive fusion reactor that runs the place is quieted as Wahlander prepares to leave once and for all.

But there is balance in the universe, and this is the joy.

As Colleran twists and slices through the clouds around the station, he fights the fierce but pleasurable winds near the floating platform. There is nothing he or any of the others can do about this but watch, for they are beasts of the sky with no feet or claws or any way of fighting back. But they do have eyes with which to see and hearts with which to feel.

The short, squat escape ships of the station lay at the far end of the docking port, and they huddle there almost like creatures themselves, all finned and ready to fly away.

Through the clear glass docking corridor they see Rex Wahlander, in a new flight suit, looking injured yet vindicated. He knows he has won.

He sees them up in the clouds looking down and he waves, the victor. He proceeds down the docking tube and enters one of the smaller ships.

Colleran is honest with the little children at the fountain, telling them how he genuinely wants to stop the man. But a little doe-eyed girl dangling her feet in the cool waters tells him that it is all right because Heidi did get away. This makes Colleran smile and he continues with the Dream.

What happens next always makes the children go quiet. This is the scariest part.

Wahlander takes a long time preparing his quick ship for flight, but the ship does not rise. And Wahlander does not exit into the glass corridor to search for another. The winds surrounding the factory are hard to negotiate and, indeed, some of the other strange watchers drift off to pursue their own private interests.

Then Colleran, through one diligent eye, observes with horror as the small, finned escape ship begins to collapse, change shape, fall in on itself—alter.

The ship, indeed, all the others crowded next to it, was *itself* a caliban. Wahlander had walked into it and is now being digested by it.

Some of the children gasp with fright, others bravely laugh.

The tiny ship folds up its leathery wings, adjusts its true shape, then leaps right off the bulbous mountain, spinning into the skies of the big planet. Soon, six or seven others like it jump away as well.

And there, as it always does, the Dream ends.

When it is time for bed, Colleran shoos away the children, and he stays by the fountain for a time, feeling the light of the stars fall about his shoulders pleasantly. Beatrice, as she has always done at this time of night, walks up to him and kisses him. But not before kissing and hugging some of the little ones who are on their way home.

Colleran laughs. In his other dreams it had always been Beatrice who disappeared. But now he is with her forever, and she with him.

Together, they stay at the fountain well into the night, absorbed with the pleasure of each other's company. They watch the busy Suras in their jeweled cities on Mount Meru and talk about their lives together.

Colleran is happy as he holds her close to him. Somewhere he knows that there is a lovely riding a horse named Piccolo and this makes him even happier. Heidi rides, Beatrice smiles; it is all the same everywhere—all their beautiful and foolish souls.